NEW YORK STATION

NEW YORK STATION

LAWRENCE DUDLEY

BLACK
STONE
PUBLISHING

Copyright © 2018 by Lawrence Dudley
Published in 2018 by Blackstone Publishing
Cover and book design by Kathryn Galloway English

Printed in the United States of America

First edition: 2018
ISBN 978-1-5384-6919-4
Fiction / Thrillers / Espionage

1 3 5 7 9 10 8 6 4 2

CIP data for this book is available
from the Library of Congress

Blackstone Publishing
31 Mistletoe Rd.
Ashland, OR 97520

www.BlackstonePublishing.com

"They're coming after America…and they will be back."
—James Comey, former FBI Director,
Senate Intelligence Committee, June 8, 2017

-1-

Eighteen Months before the Bombing of Pearl Harbor

That morning ten thousand men arrived at one of France's biggest arsenals, the Renault works in Billancourt, and punched in their time cards. Not one punched out. Abandoned tools littered the floor at odd angles, saluting the tricolor banners hanging down, POUR LA DÉFENSE DE LA PATRIE.

A lone man in a black business suit and fedora came racing around a corner inside the huge plant. He kicked a forgotten lunch pail. It bounced down the long aisle, rattling and clanging. The man chased after it, jogging past rows of unfinished Char B1 tanks. Despite it all, despite his haste, he was cool, professional, in the tunnel vision of a job to be done. The horror of it all hadn't quite had time to sink in.

Ninety minutes earlier he'd gotten a long-distance trunk call from MI6 headquarters in London with a frantic question: What was the status of the French defense plants? Now he was here.

Some fool left the radio on. A broadcast echoed through the building. The announcer's measured, overcontrolled tone, punctuated by a couple of short tense breaths, underscored the urgent gravity of the news flash,

"… in an extraordinary statement earlier today, Marshal Pétain, the new head of the government, declared that all fighting is to cease …"

That did it. The man stopped, swung back, darted over and hurled the radio against the wall, hard—not just to smash the radio, but to knock down the wall itself, if he could.

"Go to hell!" The set started to buzz, burn and smoke.

Appalling. All of it, the man thought, rage now in his face. Not even time to turn off the bloody radio. The French army should've blown the damn place over the top of an Alp. The SS would have the arsenal running in weeks. They now had six million hostages to man it, in just the Paris area alone.

The French-sector people back at headquarters aren't going to believe this. Army and air intelligence, too. Need proof. Get the Minox out. He pivoted in a circle, carefully but quickly snapping overlapping shots of the abandoned assembly lines with the slim silver camera, winding the film as fast as he could.

Then he stood for a long moment in the center of the plant, tapping the camera on his palm. *Can't walk off and leave all this*, the man thought. *But what? How?* His eyes swept the factory floor. A large cart of gleaming new shells sat behind the machines. He ran over. Even better—a long row of the carts stretched the length of the outside wall. Hundreds of shells, enough to vaporize the entire center of the building.

He slipped a shell off the closest cart, cradling it in his arms as he ran over to a nearly finished tank. With a couple of leaps he climbed up on back, flipped down the hatch, then sat the shell inside and stepped in, sliding into the gunner's seat. With a spinning whirl he cranked the turret around, sighting on the carts through the open breech. There, dead on the carts. He tipped the shell against the breech, then realized. No fuse. He sat it back down and climbed out the back, running around to the carts.

Empty holes gaped in all the noses. Where were the fuses? The cabinets? Racks? Vaults? Throwing doors, boxes, canvases aside—where were they? *One fuse, if I can find just one*, the man thought. *Load it in a finished tank. Fire it. Set those carts off.* But there were no fuses, anywhere.

Must make them someplace else.

From a distance came an unearthly groaning, a metal on metal noise over a low throbbing beat—panzers. *Of course,* he thought. *They're encircling the city first. Damn. Running out of time. What else?* Against the far wall, a large pair of black tanks on heavy steel legs.

He ran over, twirling open a pair of spigots. Oil gushed onto the floor. He grabbed a grease-soaked rag from a lathe and held it above his Dunhill lighter. It took a second to catch. He lobbed it into the spreading pool of lubricant. Leapt back. But no roar of flames. Instead the thick oil slowly started burning, more smoke than flame.

The sound of the panzers again, getting really loud now, coming up the quai. *Enough,* he thought. *Time to go.*

He vaulted out a window. Sprinted along a narrow embankment by the Seine. Jumped on his bicycle at the north bridge. Pedaled furiously past the big white factory and across the river onto the quai.

A small Wehrmacht armored column stretched over the bridge up to the main entrance. It half-filled the road, blocking the only way out. He glanced down the street to the east, orienting himself. There! The Eiffel Tower, rising over a low warehouse, maybe six or eight kilometers out. No choice but to risk running for it. *Slow down,* he thought. *Just carefully pedal on by, unhurried, normal, nonchalant.*

A panzer drove up the front steps, crushing and breaking them, popping out flying bits and chunks of cement from under its treads. The tank commander climbed up the turret. He pulled down the tricolor over the door, carefully folding the flag. *So respectful … but oh, no, not really. A souvenir of the big day. Of course.*

The soldiers began smiling and waving. *They're certainly in a merry mood, aren't they,* the man thought. *Pretty pleased with themselves. Not on the ball at all. Smile and wave back. Going to slip by. Only another minute.* Then an Oberstleutnant, turning around. Probably the commander. He waved curtly.

"Sie! Kommen sie her!"

That's it, the man thought, *time to stop. Not giving anyone an excuse for shooting today.*

-2-

The Oberstleutnant was young for a colonel, his smooth, sunburned face still freckled. He held out his hand for the expected papers, businesslike, polite, even saying please. "Papiere, bitte."

The man reached into his coat pocket and handed over what was the most precious object on the European continent—a bona fide American passport. *Careful*, the man thought. *Smile slightly. Not too ingratiating, though. Don't let on how uneasy you feel.*

The Oberstleutnant demanded his name. "Wie heissen Sie?"

"Roy Hawkins. Ich bin Bürger der Vereinigten Staaten von Amerika."

The Oberstleutnant's all-business face relaxed into a broad, easy smile, his blue eyes now dancing, barely glancing at the passport.

"Amerikaner? Sehr gut! He!" The officer quickly handed it back, thrusting his other hand out for a hearty handshake. "Der Krieg ist beendet! Von jetzt an ..." He smiled and caught himself, switching to terrible English, to prove his friendliness beyond any doubt. "Fram now ahn"—he jovially waved in the direction of the Eiffel Tower—"Germany und Amerika kan be truer friends. Ja?" He eagerly awaited an answer.

"Ja." *How oddly you sometimes hear your own voice*, Hawkins thought. *Like it's echoing through a tunnel overhead.* "America und Deutschland können treue Freunde sein." The watching soldiers began politely clapping their hands, smiling and nodding in affirmation. *As if this, or anything else equally unimaginable and madly insane, could ever be good or normal again.*

The Oberstleutnant smiled and switched back to German. "How are people there feeling?"

"To be honest, I haven't been home in a long time," Hawkins replied truthfully.

"Ah, naturally. Are you returning soon?" the Oberstleutnant said.

"No. I'm a businessman. I'll be staying." *Damn right I'll be staying,* Hawkins thought.

The sky was darkening, getting on toward dusk. The Oberstleutnant glanced up, checking the light. He reached into his pocket for a new Leica.

"Please!" He handed Hawkins the camera and turned his back to the Eiffel Tower. Holding his arms straight out, the Oberstleutnant gently gestured with his fingers for his men to gather in, to pose with la Tour, cooing, "Schnell."

Make a nice show of it, Hawkins thought, *check the frame and all that.* He conscientiously motioned to a pair of grenadiers to kneel in front, then snapped a couple of pictures.

Hawkins handed the camera back. One of the gunners turned and spotted a huge swastika flag unfurling from the Eiffel Tower's radio mast. The first scouts had already penetrated into the city center. The light from the setting sun caught it with a flash. Hawkins expected the soldiers to burst into cheers. But there was no singing, no stirring anthems. Instead a hush settled over them. The soldiers all stood transfixed at the sight. Tears welled up in their eyes.

Hawkins got back on the bike and quietly pedaled off. He glanced back. No one watching.

He looked downtown again. At the sight of the flag on the Eiffel Tower his professional demeanor burst like a bubble. He almost choked and nearly spilled, wobbling hard. He glanced back. The column wasn't paying any mind. They didn't even notice a small plume of smoke starting to seep from the arsenal. Out of danger, Hawkins relaxed slightly.

Now released, rage started building. Three years it'd been, three long years since he'd gone into a chemical plant in East Prussia to sell some valves and realized they were making chemical weapons, violating all the treaties and promises going back to the last war. Every warning had been ignored. Now this. He began pedaling faster and faster and harder and harder as he went down the street.

-3-

Madame Delage. Waiting with a large tote bag over her shoulder. White hair immaculately coiffed as always. The statuesque aristocrat owned an antiques shop in the Faubourg Saint-Germain, the toniest neighborhood in Paris. It was the kind of shop where the front door was always locked and they gave you the third degree before opening it—as if it were a private club for the very rich. An American passport pressed to the glass usually did the trick. Visiting Madame Delage was like paying a visit to court. Same cool demeanor. Only now the art-world royal was calmly standing on the sidewalk outside Hawkins' flat, head and eyes raised in defiance.

"Monsieur Hawkins." She opened the tote slightly, pulling a chamois back. An extraordinary sight flashed into view. Hawkins instantly recognized it—as an auction catalog would unctuously parse it, it was a "historically important" and possibly unique vermeil *Louis XVI* tea, coffee and chocolate set, stamped with the royal cipher of the Château de Saint-Cloud. Somehow it had survived being melted down in the Révolution. Ordinarily you'd need a special permit to remove an object like *that* from the country. But the French customs service had no doubt vanished, along with the rest of the government. Hawkins and Madame Delage had done business in the past—antiques trading as he traveled was a small sideline of his. But nothing like this.

"Madame Delage ... I—"

"Non! You will take this," spoken as authoritatively as a grammar lesson.

"Madame, I know this. I saw it in your gallery. This isn't just any art object. It's a national treasure. To take this from France ... it's not just against the law, it's wrong. This belonged to le Roi himself—"

"Les Boches," her voice a low hiss, "are going to steal everything."

"They wouldn't dare."

"Non! Are you not aware the top Nazis have already looted all the great Jewish collections abroad? It will not stop with the Jews now that they've gotten used to it. Mark my words, they will take everything of value."

"All the same, I can't afford this."

"It does not matter. Pay what you can. American dollars." She hesitated a moment, leaning in confidentially. "Who knows what may come." She shrugged, swinging the tote at him. "Whatever happens, they'll be safer in your—"

"Madame Delage, no—"

She grit her teeth, again hissing in fierce determination, visibly vibrating with anger, her voice rising to a soft shriek. "I will throw it in the Seine before I let them have it!"

"Very well."

No arguing, Hawkins thought. *How much do I need? The next couple of months: Rent. Money to live on. Travel. Hide out. I'll have to do that.* He took out his wallet, put aside what he needed and gave her everything that was left.

"That's all I can spare. There's some Swiss francs there, too."

"Suisse aussi? Très bien."

She glanced around to see who was looking before stepping into the alcove. With a quick tug she pulled up the skirt on her Chanel suit and stuffed the wad into the top of her girdle. She winked and gave him an air kiss on both cheeks.

"Au revoir, mon jeune ami, et bonne chance."

"Bonne chance à vous aussi, Madame Delage."

Yes, Hawkins thought, watching her stride down the street. *Getting American dollars is probably a very smart idea under the circumstances.* He hefted the tote. Surprisingly heavy. He headed inside.

-4-

Have to hurry, Hawkins thought. *Get to another location temporarily. After what happened in Holland, the Gestapo could be here at any moment. A few weeks will tell.*

He looked up. Marie Chevalier was waiting at the top of the stairs.

Marie, his Paris, his personal incarnation of the city he loved. That was how she affected him. Its style: effortlessly chic, her hair tied in an elegant swirl with the ribbon from a Hermès box. Its seductive beauty: her tan legs rising from satin mules to a short silver chemise trimmed with black lace. Its welcome: her smile brushing aside the curl hanging down her face, greeting him with a slightly warm bottle of champagne. And at the top of the stairs, its relief: raining hungry, drunken kisses on her American boyfriend, her pillar, her anchor in the Nazi storm. The Gestapo, forgotten. For a long couple of hours, they transcended the worst day of their lives.

She'd gotten quite tipsy. In fact, the city seemed to be full of people getting hammered as fast as possible. As if the Germans would be going house to house confiscating all the decent wine. An alcoholic haze would hardly make the sight of gray uniforms any better. Marie usually opened up enough without any booze. Her earnest fingers would warmly clasp his hand, caressing his palm as they walked along the Boul'Mich, eagerly telegraphing their desire, each letter hotly written in the palm of the hand. She walked holding her head high, eyes straight, taking in the shop windows.

Hawkins watched her nestled in his armpit. *What does she really see?* he wondered. *Me? Or un Américain? Not to imply that she's using me, or anything like that. Or I her. Not that kind of person, either one of us. In fairness, she knows nothing of my occupation, nor my British half. Just an ordinary Yank salesman.*

Got to go, Hawkins thought again. *Could wait until she's sound asleep before packing.* But no. Detestable, leaving her to find a note on the dresser. "Sorry, ma chérie. I have to leave." She'd done nothing to deserve that.

At his movement she drunkenly sat up in the sheets, watching him pack, a tad bewildered. Simmering resentful glances followed, growing in vitriol. She got up for her robe, psychological armor, tightly tying the knot, like a soldier fastening his kit.

Abruptly, for all she'd drunk, she became remarkably and hostilely voluble, in both languages.

"Ainsi, tu pars."

"Yes. I have to leave for a few days."

"Tu nous abandonnes!"

Abandoning—us?

"No—I have to go. It's temporary." *Could I call and give her my address?* No. There would be too many questions, and that knowledge might actually endanger her. "It's business. Je dois partir! I'll be back soon."

"Bientôt? Quand?"

"I … I'm not sure. Maybe a couple of weeks. Pas plus de deux semaines."

"Non! I know what you are doing. You are all leaving us, abandoning us, the French. We who relied on you! We who gave up moving the Germans across the Rhine because you said so and then le double jeu!"

The Treaty of Guarantee again. *Of course,* he thought. *The last of her incarnations of Paris: the intellectual. Had to chat up a poli-sci major at Les Deux Magots, didn't I? First time I ever heard of that sorry episode was from Marie.*

After the WWI victory the French had initially insisted on annexing the few German provinces on their side of the Rhine. All things considered that now seemed a damnably good idea. But President Wilson talked them out of it with the promise of an American guarantee of France's borders. When he got home the Republicans in the Senate rejected the treaty. The French were left holding the bag against a Germany that now had twice their population.

His bags were packed. By now she was trailing him around the room, an irate shadow a few steps behind. He tried embracing her at the door.

"Je suis désolé. Je reviendrai. Really. I'll be back."

She angrily pushed him away. He turned and headed down the stairs. She tried to spit, couldn't find any saliva in her wine-dry mouth, then really let loose. "Va-t'en, cochon! Go off by yourselves, bâtard égoïste! Be like Garbo, go it alone!" Of course the legendary actress had to be brought into it. A cinéaste as well as a poli-sci major, yet another incarnation. "Ignorez nous! Abandonnez-nous! Retournez en Amérique! Laissez la France au Nazis!"

"Non! Attendez Roosevelt. Trust him. Les Américains finiront par revenir—"

Hearing the shouting, the landlady militantly flew out into the hall, her white head bobbing atop her rounded black-clad form. She froze at the sight of the bags.

"Monsieur Hawkins! Vous partez?"

"Oui, Madame Aubry—"

Incredulous, Madame Aubry gaped as he counted out two months' future rent. Then the dam broke. Who knew tears could burst out in such a flood through so shattered an expression?

"Les Américains? Vous partez tous?" repeating it in growing tones of surprise, anger, resignation and despair, "Vous partez tous?"

"Non!" He said, "Ne vous inquiétez pas." Don't worry. "Je serai de retour." I'll be back. "Dans deux semaines." A couple of weeks. He pressed the rent money in her hands, a hundred dollars, all in American greenbacks. "Voici le loyer pour deux mois—"

She kept softly repeating, "Les Boches, les Boches …"

Marie arrived back at the top of the stairs, champagne bottle in hand. She flung it overhand by the neck, fast and hard. Hawkins barely caught the glint of it from the corner of his eye and ducked. It glanced over the crown of his hat and slammed into the wall, half smashing a blue robed figurine of the Madonna, gouging out a spray of flying plaster. Then it bounced off the bags and crashed onto the tile floor, shattering into a dozen pieces. Madame Aubry began shrieking, "Mademoiselle! Mademoiselle!"

Marie shouted, "Quelle merde!" and slapped a hand on her biceps as she pumped a fist to the ceiling.

-5-

"You've orders from London. Get out now." Gordon, the Paris station chief, was on the other end of the line. Hawkins was calling from an MI6 safe house near Place de l'Étoile. Another half-track rattled by in the distance.

"What?" Hawkins said. "But we need to start organizing, resist behind—"

"No! Leave. Now!"

"Where?"

"Through Spain to Lisbon."

"Lisbon? Why? That'll take weeks."

"Don't know. That's the order. Any way you can. Just get out. Then go to Lisbon. Remember, this comes straight from the top."

"But our French counterparts—"

"No time. We're shutting down here now. We'll be gone within the hour."

"We can't leave them behind! Besides, we're going to need them."

"We're on our own now. Don't trust anyone. Don't talk to anyone. You don't know, some of them might go with this new government. Could hand everything over to Hitler, including you. Just get out now."

"What about the papers here?"

"Damn. I forgot that. Burn everything. Then get out. Oh, and don't use the phone. They'll be in the exchanges shortly."

A click. The line went dead. Hawkins rushed to a small steel cabinet, clicking in the combination, throwing the lid back. A rattling noise on the street outside. He slipped to the window, looking down at a careful angle, out of sight, one finger on the blinds. The usually bustling market was empty. Blowing papers floated through the air, darting over bits of rotting castoff produce, flattened boxes and upended stands. A lone Wehrmacht half-track turned the corner and vanished. *Another scouting party. The Gestapo can't be far behind.*

Back to the cabinet. Hawkins pulled out a green binder, set it aside. He swept everything else up in his arms, throwing the wad in the old fireplace, fluffing it up, mixing in some newspapers, flicking out his Dunhill lighter. A quick hot fire blazed up. Hawkins kept one eye out for large floating pieces while he went through the binder. Several British and Commonwealth passports—Canadian, New Zealand—all useless now, into the flames. He paused at a South African one. *No, probably useless, too.* In it went. Also the forged Italian and Swiss ones. Dead ends, no getting out through those places. They hit the fire, too. That left the neutrals. He pocketed the Swedish, the Brazilian, the Mexican and the two Turkish ones. Gordon could go to hell.

Hawkins hit the avenue half running, then slowed to a walk like everyone else. *Be careful*, he thought. *Don't draw attention.* The people seemed to be moving in the same direction, a tide against him. A gray-haired man in his fifties bumped into his shoulder. His cheeks were wet with tears, eyes red. There were several service ribbons on his chest—a veteran of the last war.

He gestured up the street. "Quatre ans! Nous avons survécu au front! Mes deux frères … mes deux frères."

God, hard to imagine the agony, Hawkins thought. *Going through that for four years, then this.* Weeping, the man started to collapse. Hawkins helped him to a café chair, then ran up and turned the corner.

A gray German column was parked at the curb. Acting like they'd driven into town on a shopping trip, calmly sitting and waiting—for what, wasn't clear. A few of the soldiers were idly walking around. Completely relaxed, like there'd never been a war at all, gawking at the buildings, taking in the sights. The line of vehicles, hundreds of them and several thousand men, stretched up the boulevard, vanishing in the distance.

The government had declared Paris an open city and the French and British armies withdrew. The usually busy street was otherwise empty of people. A private turned, saw Hawkins, nodded and smiled slightly, then a sergeant spotted him, gestured him over, patted him down and gently tapped his shoulder to get going. Hawkins walked past them, barely glancing sideways, turning into an arcade, up a street eerily devoid of traffic and pedestrians at midday.

Twenty minutes later he reached the apartment.

-6-

The safe house once lodged people the Deuxième Bureau, France's intelligence service, brought in and needed to hide. First dissidents from Germany. Then refugees from Czechoslovakia, Poland and the Baltics. Finally, Norway and Denmark—wherever Hitler reached. Now the old apartment was hiding the men and women of French intelligence itself from the enemy rushing in. People were milling around, rapidly pacing from one antique-filled room to another. Restless. Anxious. Agitated, as if unable to stop, unable to focus, bumping into each other, the mood shifting in seconds from consternation. To anger. Blame. Then to guilt. And back to blame again. All wrapped in a thick blanket of confusion and indecision. Everyone talking and shouting over one another in a crazed jumble. Words like blows.

"They're traitors I tell you!" one shouted, unclear if he expected anyone to listen, aimlessly walking through into the other room.

"That's not true. The marshal, he's trying to salvage something," another said.

A thick pall of smoke filled the room from a mix of too many cigarettes and a messy mass of records burning in the old fireplace. One man was standing over it, coughing, stirring the burning embers with a poker. He turned and shouted through the haze.

"The government should go to Algiers and the empire, take the fleet and the air force, all the troops they can round up."

"Will someone shut that damn window? They'll see the smoke."

"They're in the street outside?"

"Only makes sense to go to North Africa if the Americans are coming—"

"The Americans! And where the hell were they?"

They finally seemed to notice Hawkins standing there. They all turned and stared, Benoît, Dodier, LaDue, Marcellin, Champigny, Blanchard, Archambault and Godette. Good men and women, colleagues, friends, all of them, the last three years. The hollow expressions on their faces. That was the worst.

"Hawkins, what now for you?" Benoît said.

"I have to go," Hawkins said, "I have orders."

"You're leaving the country?" Benoît said. Hawkins nodded. The sad expression in Benoît's gray eyes was heartbreaking. But there was no anger or judgment. "How long?"

"I don't know. I just got them an hour ago."

"From Gordon?"

"Yes. Straight from London."

"You're staying with the British Secret Service? You're not returning to America?"

"I'm sticking it out."

"You could go."

"I know."

"Hawkins, President Roosevelt, the Americans, what will they do? Surely they cannot abandon France, their sister in liberty …" Blanchard said. Hawkins and Stéphanie had crossed the Rhine together several times, posing as a married couple.

"I can't say," Hawkins said. "You know I haven't been home in a long time."

"Of course." She looked down, fighting tears.

Hawkins handed the four blank passports to Benoît. He seemed to be the highest-ranking officer present.

"I'm sure you'll know how to use them."

"Oh, yes. Thank you, Roy." Benoît scanned the tense, expectant faces. He sighed heavily. "We'll draw lots."

"I'm going to get my car now."

"Roy, you must not attempt that. The Germans have given orders to confiscate all private autos. Haven't you heard? It's part of the settlement."

"But I'm not French—"

A slight note of exasperation crept into Benoît's voice. He slowly shook his head. "What kind of car is it? Did you bring it from America? Does it have American papers?"

"No. It's a Traction Avant. I bought it here."

"I thought so. Then to the Germans it is an enemy car. British, French, it doesn't matter. If you try to drive it out they'll stop you and take it. Then comes the interrogation and search. You must not risk this. At the very least you'll be stranded on the road, many kilometers out in the country. But it will likely be far worse. You don't want to draw their attention, make contact, have them start checking. You'll have to take your bicycle."

Marie. Oh dear God. Marie may be right after all, Hawkins thought. *This is going to take time. By bike? Certainly far more than two weeks. She'll think I lied to her, that I've abandoned her. Fuck all.* For a moment he felt sick and queasy, his face flushing prickly cold and clammy, then the rest of him.

"Hawkins, are you all right? Perhaps you should sit down."

"No. I'll be fine. I have to hurry, then. I'm sorry. I am so sorry. I'm sorry I don't have more—" his voice started to break.

"Hawkins, you don't have to apologize. We all did all we could."

"London's taking me out to put me back in. I'm certain of it. Since the US is neutral I'll be able to go in and work undercover on my American passport. There'll be plenty of Americans staying on in the city. All kinds of possibilities. We can organize, keep fighting."

Benoît looked dubious, then worried. "Roy, mon ami, you were certainly blown by the mess in Holland, too. They may not have a new name, but they will find your photo in the files. You may be more at risk than any of us—"

"No. I'll be back. I know I will."

"Listen to me. You have been operating undercover as an American. The US government cannot help you if you are caught spying for Britain without violating its neutrality. And you are breaking American law, non? The government in Washington cannot help you and will not because to them you are a criminal, and London cannot either without admitting that it is violating the sanctity of an American passport, which would damage relations with America. Even a British agent could be exchanged, in theory. But you are naked. It's suicide."

"I'll be back. I'll just go to ground if I have to."

"Eh bien, we'll see. Bonne chance, Roy."

"Bonne chance, all of you." Hawkins shook hands all around.

Benoît began tearing up strips of paper, four long, three short.

"Stéphanie, you should take one first," Benoît said, "you went over there with Hawkins. You are most at risk." They all mumbled "oui, oui" in agreement. She nodded, half sobbing, then ducked her chin down, took the blank passport and left for the lab to fill it in and attach a new photo. The faces of the others actually went white as they watched. They stood frozen, knowing they were likely drawing lots for who would live and who would die. Hawkins turned to leave. LaDue finally reached out, his hand shaking slightly.

-7-

The top of the hill, finally. Hawkins climbed off the wobbly bike, parking it, legs aching. Time to rest a minute, check the ropes on the suitcases stacked on the fenders, hanging off the sides. He turned, looking back. The suburb of Meudon lay below, dark and asleep. Farther out, the city. After the Armistice the power had been turned back on. All of Paris was lit up, glowing before him—for him. The dome of Montmartre. The Eiffel Tower. The Arc de Triomphe. Notre-Dame. All still there.

From up here, on the hilltop, it seems so peaceful, so normal, so inviting, Hawkins thought. *It can't be true what happened. It's impossible. Go back— it's too much to lose, too much to bear.*

Why am I leaving?

Then, remarkably, starting in the northeast, one arrondissement after another went dark. The Wehrmacht was shutting off the power, enforcing a new blackout on the city. As the quarters of the city went dark, one after another, the quarters of his heart seemed to tumble into a dark abyss, too.

The streetlights around him went out, plunging him into total darkness. *Is this what it's like to die? The switch is thrown, the lights go out? Maybe it's just as well. Maybe the dark is where I belong.*

Hawkins staggered around, almost tripped over the bike, angrily grabbed it and tried to throw it, then kick it, heavily flipping it over instead. He paced up and down a moment, holding his head in his hands. With the image of the city gone, all that was left in the dark vacuum was the pull of his orders. Everything else was gone. After a few minutes he groped around, found the bike, got on and rode down the hill and out of the city and into the empty countryside, following the bike's dim flickering yellow light.

-8-

LISBON
1 AUGUST 1940

Hawkins felt the suitcase with his heel and sat on it, rocking back.

Somewhere out there, an alleyway, rising up a small hill. Two or three shops. A crossroads farther up by a fountain. Probably two dozen houses with lots of overflowing flower boxes. A pleasant lane outside Lisbon—in the daytime. At night, utterly black. Like being swallowed like Jonah. No electricity here in this ancient, poor neighborhood. It could still be the eighteenth century. Not even a candle, not even stars.

Also at least fifty windows where anyone could stand and shoot. All invisible in the dark. Like staring into oblivion.

He rummaged in his jacket pocket, pulled out pouch and pipe, filled the bowl and clicked his Dunhill, lighting up his face. He waited.

Nothing. No shots. *Still here.* He reflexively brushed his American passport again. *Still there, too. Be good to quit this place.*

The entire European continent had turned into a giant overpressurized boiler with Lisbon the split in the seam firing out human steam. Desperate refugees were lurking everywhere. The bolder ones sized you up eye-to-eye, like prizefighters probing for a vulnerable moment of opportunity. The women were harder to stare through, their desperation, their need for protection—*your* protection—revealed so willingly, so startlingly apparent.

A hint of brightening down at the end, toward the crossroads. He checked his watch's radium green glow: three-forty.

The lights turned and flashed around the corner. In the predawn silence the narrow lane magnified the approaching Daimler's low purr, its tires ripping over the cobblestones became a roaring, rhythmical clatter.

The sound instantly triggered an image—standing at the window in Paris listening to the growing beat of treads from the Wehrmacht scout car.

A familiar, slightly sick feeling welled up. And rage. *Can't indulge that,* he thought. But the longer he chewed it over, the harder he fought it, the duller his mind felt. Eventually his brain seemed to close like the iris on a camera, nothing but darkness.

In the weeks on the road the same questions kept coming up with an accelerating frequency, advanced by that final image of the long gray column stretching up the avenue. *How could it have happened? How will we ever get them out?*

Isn't it all really hopeless now?

Hawkins mentally flicked the image away. *Thank God this one's punctual.*

The driver tapped the high beams, signaling. Hawkins darted across the courtyard in a low crouch. Threw his bags through the back door. Jumped in front, so quick only an expert would've seen. As they pulled up the lane he carefully rechecked the street again. No one watching. Strictly routine. The old Daimler wound its way through the dark outskirts of Lisbon. The driver looked over, his face illuminated by the dash lights.

"You lit a pipe? You always break protocol like that? Suppose someone saw you, took a shot."

"Probably do me a favor. Who the hell are you?" The driver was a much older man, a sedentary, bureaucratic type, around sixty and close to retirement, with a strong Scottish accent. He kept glancing at Hawkins, his alarm tinged with uncertainty. Hawkins still had a young face but the dark circles ringing his eyes gave him an almost dissipated quality, making him look older than his twenty-four years.

"Wilkinson. Deputy station chief here in Lisbon. We've been expecting you for over a month!"

"I know. Couldn't be helped. Forty kilometers south of Paris the back tire on my bicycle blew out. Had to push it 260 kilometers, all the way to Châteauroux."

Wilkinson glared back, almost accusatory. *He's wondering about the accent*, Hawkins thought. *Any second now.*

"Say, you a Yank?" Always the same squinting question. *What are you?* No easy answer there.

"My father was."

"I see." He gestured at the seat between them. "You've new orders there."

Hawkins stared at the envelope. *New orders?* He tore one end off. A thin strip of tissue designed to melt in water drifted down. He bent over to read as it settled on his knee.

tks waiting lisbon—he knew that already. Then came the unexpected part, the punch in the gut. *paa. report w new york station. inspect bermuda station en route.* Signed C, the chief of MI6. Right from the top, indeed. As he reflexively popped it in his dry mouth and swallowed Hawkins could feel the flush of anger rising on his face.

Now there's a hell of a greeting. Good show, old sport, you walked halfway across France. Crossed one fascist dictatorship—Franco's Spain—to another fascist dictatorship—Salazar's Portugal. Only got taken in and interrogated by the Guardia Civil three times. Don't let the door hit you on the way out.

"What?" Hawkins said. "Bermuda! Then New York? And who the bloody hell is W? In Forty-Eight Land?" lapsing into British Secret Service slang for the US and its forty-eight states.

"W? Can't say."

"I need to go straight to London. Check in. Get new papers. Get back to Paris. We've got to get going, rebuild our networks."

"Perhaps they're putting you back in from there." Wilkinson indifferently shrugged. "Forty-Eight Land's a neutral country, too. Just farther away."

"So that's it, huh? New York. Then back in. And how long will that take? You know, it's fine by me. Maybe I'll just stay in New York if they want to run me all over the goddamn map. Hear a little music. Go dancing. Tell 'em to sod off."

Wilkinson glanced over with a real tinge of alarm. "You don't mean that."

"Oh, I don't know that I don't."

As he chewed the paper he chewed over the orders. New York. It had been a long time. *After all this, maybe I do have a break coming. Is that the idea? Well, no. Wilkinson's probably right. Merely another neutral transit point. Just happens to be my other country.*

Then another thought. *Madame Delage. The silver. New York. Maybe something will come of this hellish mess after all. Figured to sell the set in London. Now I can sell it in New York at peacetime prices. Even better, get American dollars free of wartime currency restrictions. Probably going to make a killing, actually. The dealers in New York are crazy about Louis-the-whatever anything, as long it's gold and glitters. Amazing luck.*

Still—doesn't feel right. And yet ... well ...

With a bump Wilkinson changed onto the coast road west of town. Ahead lay the international flying boat base at Cabio Ruvio and the Pan American Airways terminal. They passed a car by the side of the road. Its lights flicked on, catching the rearview mirror, flashing back into Hawkins' eyes.

-9-

A Citroën. Pulling out behind at a suspicious distance. Not too close. Not too far. Hawkins kept his voice low and calm. "We're being followed. Don't do anything sudden. Just start slowly speeding up." Hawkins began digging into his bag for his Browning Hi-Power.

"They tailing us again? Only a curious foreign colleague, checking up on their British counterpart."

"Uh-huh." Hawkins could feel the weight of a full clip: thirteen 9-millimeter rounds plus one in the chamber, the longest load of any pistol in the world. He reflexively snapped the clip out. Checked it. Clicked it back in.

"Nothing to be alarmed about," Wilkinson said. He glanced over in a rather fatherly manner. "It's the way the game's played here." As if they needed nothing more than a stiff upper lip to ward off danger.

"Game. Right. Just pick it up slowly."

The genteel ways of the peacetime spy business had obviously persisted here in the relative obscurity of Portugal. Probably been rather enjoyable, too, slyly nodding at each other across a good travessa with a velvety glass of Colares in hand.

Hawkins kept levelly watching the car close the distance, muscles tensing, Browning on his thigh—*Any second now*, he thought. *An olive grove—no, not here.* Pasty trees twirled by in the darkness like gray ghosts. A rocky cliff overlooking the shore. *That's it, here*, he thought. The Citroën's driver floored the accelerator, leaping forward, now only a yard or two from their bumper. A gunner with a submachine gun pivoted out the passenger door, one foot on the running board, aiming down for their tires. Muzzle flashes flickered in the darkness.

One lucky hit and we'll be off the cliff, Hawkins thought. *Or do they only want to stop us?* Wilkinson sharply swerved around a blind turn. The bullets bounded harmlessly off the cobblestones.

"Stop the car!" Hawkins said.

"They're shooting at us! How dare they!"

"I said stop the goddamn car!"

Wilkinson stomped on the accelerator. "They'll catch us," his voice crackling and warbling on the edge of panic, tightly gripping the wheel with all his might, jerkily twisting it, as if squeezing it would force more speed from the old Daimler.

Hawkins butted into him, struck his foot over and jammed down on the brakes. The car stalled, skidding, spinning about, screaming to a halt sideways across the road. The Citroën slammed into the Daimler's side, pushing it down the road. The sudden stop threw the driver and shooter hard into the dash. Hawkins aimed through the side window past Wilkinson's face. The two men bounced back from the impact. Point-blank range. Impossible to miss. Hawkins shot each man once in the head.

They were easy targets, mouths open wide like hungry baby crows from the shock of being flung forward and back. It was all over in a split second. Each bullet's entry into the mouth flipped its victim's head back over the seat. Their eyes now stared straight up, mouths still open with surprise, filling and overrunning with blood.

Hawkins started getting out, then leaned back with a tired sigh, gesturing with the Hi-Power. "Wilkinson—Christ almighty. Never try and shoot it out in a moving car. You can't hit a goddamned thing. This isn't some bloody Hollywood flick." Wilkinson wheezed and shuddered, still panicked.

Hawkins darted around to the Citroën and yanked a handkerchief from the driver's pocket, trying to keep the rapidly spilling blood off his hands. The dead man's jacket yielded a Finnish passport. Mikael Tuomomen. Helsinki. *Maybe*, Hawkins thought.

He ran around and began rifling the other man's pockets. Now some Turkish papers. Göker Celik. Istanbul.

Oh, now this is disgusting, Hawkins thought. That came from a professional's decent sense of respect for his craft. Individually, maybe plausible. If it was Istanbul and Izmir, or Helsinki and Espoo, possible, too. But taken together, Finland and Turkey—my, my, what a coincidence. That almost screamed fake. *What were they thinking? Not thinking, is what it is. But I'll get nothing off these two.*

"Hey! Wilkinson! Over here!"

Wilkinson slowly slid out, holding on to the door and then the fender, steadying himself, panting heavily. Hawkins grabbed the dead driver's hair, lifting the face for Wilkinson to see, spilling blood down the man's chin. Wilkinson stared like he'd seen an apparition, an expression of horror in his eyes as they wandered from Hawkins to the dead man and back.

"What the hell's with you?" Hawkins said.

"How can you be so bloody casual?"

"What—"

"We almost got killed. And those men—"

Hawkins glanced at the driver, puzzled. *Yes, we could've been killed*, Hawkins thought. *They're dead instead.* Hawkins looked back at Wilkinson. He really did seem stunned and rattled.

"So what?" He shook the dead man's head again, splashing more blood. "Come on, know him? Gestapo? Abwehr? SD? Maybe the Italians?"

Wilkinson finally responded, "No. Not the Italians, I shouldn't think."

"Ah, God dammit—"

So, who were they? Hawkins thought. *Thieves trying to steal papers? No—had to be foreign intel men. Not very professional, though, especially for Gestapo or Abwehr.* And yet … every intelligence service was rushing to expand. Inexperienced men were bound to start filtering into everyone's organizations. *Green as hell to get so close behind, in either case. Always shoot from the side. What a mess.*

Hawkins whipped a good gold Swiss pocket watch from the shooter's vest by the chain, popping it open, checking for engraving. Nothing. A quick search of the pants yielded up a fat money clip—always handy. But the man's jacket brought the real prize: a Pan Am Clipper ticket and a matchbook.

Hawkins held the ticket under the headlights to inspect it. "This bastard was booked on my flight."

Wilkinson finally found his voice. "Might be black marketeers in papers. That neutral American passport of yours—"

"These weren't freelancers. They had forged papers. And where'd he get the new Schmeisser?"

The ticket was blank. No one had filled it out yet. Maybe they weren't intel men. Had they stolen it? Planned to sell it? Or pass it to someone else? That would explain why every line was empty. *Did they need two? Maybe they were agents, had two important people they needed to move out. Or were they planning to scalp this if they couldn't get mine? No way of knowing.*

Hawkins held the ticket in hand a second, studying it. *Disgusting, the number of people dying every day for lack of an incredibly expensive Clipper ticket. But no one's going to use it now. What's so important the Service is digging into its threadbare pocket to buy one for me?*

He angrily crumpled it up, started pocketing the matchbook, remembered it wasn't his, and checked it, too. Gitanes. Nothing special. But inside he discovered writing: *ludwig hotel, lisboa.*

"Wilkinson, is there a Ludwig Hotel here?"

"Not that I know of."

Hawkins threw it all in the car, kicked the door shut and started pushing the vehicle off the road, down the hill and off a low cliff. After a moment of hesitation Wilkinson pitched in to help. In the distance the huge four-engine flying boat bobbed at its mooring in the estuary at Cabo Ruivo. Floodlights lit the plane like a silver mirage floating in the darkness. The car picked up speed, flipped end over end and landed upside down in the tide. As it floated out, it slowly sank. They soberly watched until it was gone, then ran back to the Daimler.

"Are you armed?" Hawkins said.

"No, I never—"

"You are now. Take this." Hawkins handed Wilkinson the Browning. "I won't need it where I'm going. You're going to have to be more careful. They've changed the rules. Get that? They've changed the rules. Nothing's going to be the same. With France gone, this place is now the front trench. Remember to pull the slide to chamber it."

Hawkins watched the Clipper grow larger as Wilkinson drove around the bend in the Tagus. *It's a great day when blithering idiots try to kill you and you've got no idea who they are or why. A fitting farewell to Europe.*

-10-

The Yankee Clipper hummed across the mid-Atlantic toward Bermuda. It hit some turbulence. Hawkins fitfully rolled in his sleep. Faces, he could see them. Benoît … Marcellin … and Stéphanie. Running into an orchard, pulling a wire overhead, grabbing an apple off a tree on the way. Takes a bite. *No! Don't! Snow White's apple!* She slowly melted to the ground. The Eiffel Tower. Marie. An angry face. *You promised!* The Oberstleutnant. Smiling. *Germany und Amerika can be truer friends, Ja?* Benoît. Tearing strips of stationery. LaDue nervously plucking one from the closed fist. A look of horror on his face. It's short! His skin starts to shrivel, mummify, turning to dust, his bones falling to the ground with a rattle.

The droning plane plunged into another patch of turbulence. Hawkins woke with a gasping start, flinching, blinking. He grabbed a drink from the tray and took a big gulp. He snapped the curtain back. Nothing yet. Just endless ocean. Even with sunglasses the intense light hurt his eyes. He snapped it shut again, half stood, stretching his spine, then forced himself back down into his seat. He leaned out into the aisle. The tall Danish woman at the front was still asleep. No chance for conversation there. Must have had a rough trip to Portugal. It was lights out the moment she hit the seat.

Lucky at that, he thought. Several whiskey sours and the monotonous flight via the Azores had outwardly quieted him, but a fitful sleep came hesitantly. It wasn't the seats or the comforting drone of the engines. Always, the faces—Benoît … Marcellin … Blanchard, all of them, especially Stéphanie. So many weeks working together, might as well have deserted her on the other side of the Rhine. Instead of rest sleep left an agitation, an itch to get moving. *To what end, though?*

When they were boarding there'd been rumors the Duke and Duchess of Windsor were about to join them—the disgraced former king and his American spouse had been in Lisbon. The man who'd resigned the Crown to marry his mistress. And then—as if that wasn't enough—doubly disgraced himself by making friends with the Nazis. Seeing them board would have been something different. But apparently they'd gone out by ship.

Hawkins jumped up and paced back into the next cabin. Another passenger sitting at a table held up a deck of cards. "Wanna play?"

"Sure." Anything.

The man dealt. With a popping squeal, the overhead speaker abruptly clicked on. A little cheer echoed through the cabins—they were finally coming within radio range of the continental US.

Hawkins threw a chip down. "Hope it's music. Think the Dane'd be interested in a little spin around the cabin?"

"No," the dealer said. "She's a refugee. She's not in a very good mood."

"Well, she's not alone."

A tall, thin, fiftysomething man with a wiry dark goatee ambled over from the opposite side of the cabin. "Mind if I watch?"

"Don't play poker, Doctor?"

"No. Frankly, I've always found studying games, creating them, writing the rules, more interesting than playing myself."

"What kind of games? Card games?"

"Oh, all kinds of games. Didn't you make up games when you were a child?"

"Yeah, I guess I did. You're right, it was fun."

The doctor, who had a slight German accent, sat down facing Hawkins, resting his arms on the edge of the table.

"Oh, Dr. Ludwig, this is …" The dealer looked at him expectantly.

Hawkins had put on his poker face when they'd started playing. Even so, he caught himself in a very slight double take. The name in the matchbook? *Careful*, he thought. *Maybe Ludwig at Hotel Lisboa? A coincidence? Or is he connected to those gunmen? Or could he be a target, too? Given the circumstances, that ticket was more likely stolen than not. Still …*

"Roy Hawkins."

"Hawkins, this is Professor Hans Ludwig. Fred Farrell, here." They all shook hands, Hawkins carefully glancing at Dr. Ludwig.

"Hello. You're—"

"Swiss," Ludwig said. "I'm actually not at university anymore, I'm now in the reinsurance business."

In fact, quite possible. Who else but neutrals were free to travel these days? It was awfully risky or arrogant if he was a German agent. It might be an American flag plane, but there was no guarantee the authorities in Bermuda wouldn't lose their heads, say sod off to the Yanks and grab him.

"Ah." Hawkins gestured lightly at Ludwig. "You're sitting in a very scarce empty seat, there, Doctor!"

"Yes. Seems someone missed their flight." Blasé, unconcerned.

No, slim chance of it, Hawkins thought. *He probably is what he says he is.*

A loud buzz of radio static drew everyone's attention, then a broadcast finally came in over the speakers.

-11-

"So mentholated means fine tobacco, personally preferred by three out of four surgeons surveyed!" A lone musician began playing a traditional version of "When Johnny Comes Marching Home Again" on a fife. The band leapt in on the third stanza, exploding into an upbeat, jazzy swing version of the old Civil War ditty, soon joined by a baritone soloist.

> *The men will cheer*
> *the boys will shout*

Followed by a boogie-wooging trio of women.

> *the ladies they will all turn out*
> *and we'll feel gay when*

Then the man reaching for his lowest note.

> *Johnny comes marchin' home!*

Ending with a long, low trombone blast. By now Hawkins was tapping his toe under the table as he sorted his cards.

The MC intoned, "Ladies and gentlemen, Walter Ventnor!"

The live studio audience burst into a frenzy of applause. *No aces,* Hawkins thought, not paying much attention.

"He's going to come home in pieces, that's wha—Hey! Walter Ventnor here, folks." A big burst of applause interrupted him. "Thank you, everyone," Ventnor said. "You know, folks, if Roosevelt gets his way, every fourth American boy's gonna get plowed under—and it's already over, over there! The British haven't figured out they're licked, that's all." That got Hawkins' attention. More applause from the radio. "Folks, you know what I did last night? I took a pair of scissors to an old copy of the *Geographic.* I cut Britain out and slid it around the map of Europe. It rolls and rolls all over Europe, like watching a pea rattle around inside a can." The audience *oohed.* "You could put dozens of Britains inside the new Europe Hitler's created. And the British government thinks they've got a chance against all that?"

"NOOOO ..." the crowd echoed. Hawkins' hand started lowering, then he caught himself before he tipped his cards.

"We need to build a new Fortress America, stick to ourselves and—"

The crowd joined in a thunderous spoken chorus, "Go! It! Alone!"

"That's right! America first, America last, America always!"

"What the hell?" Hawkins said.

Fred glanced back, shrugging indulgently. "You been out of the country awhile?" Hawkins nodded. "Walter Ventnor's the hottest thing on radio. Overnight sensation. Came out of nowhere. Set up his own network last winter to broadcast his programs. Bigger than Father Coughlin or Gerald L. K. Smith ever were."

"He thinks the war's over?"

Fred tipped his head slightly to the side, as if to say, *Well, don't look at me.* "A lot of folks—" He caught and quietly corrected himself. "Probably most people back home think it's all over."

Ludwig smiled very slightly. "With Herr Hitler in Paris one would reasonably draw that conclusion, wouldn't one?"

On the radio, Ventnor continued, "The Roosevelts want to adopt loser countries the way batty old ladies take in stray cats. Folks, don't let them pull the wool over your eyes with their so-called facts. I'll give you a fact: we're mad and we don't care. Nobody can touch us. Remember what happened when he tried to fill the Supreme Court full of crackbrained party-line socialists like himself? We let the Senate know what we thought. We had 'em shaking in their boots, they were afraid we were gonna come down there after 'em. With us fillin' their sails, they began knocking down one crazy scheme after another." People started cheering again. "That, ladies and gentlemen, was the end of his so-called big deal New Deal, and there aren't gonna be any more of his crazy big government—"

To hear the American president talked about this way. *Astonishing*, Hawkins thought. In Britain. On the continent, even inside Germany, oftentimes, for men and women Hawkins' age, Franklin Roosevelt's name brought a glow to faces, hushed tones to voices, things that came with hope. All abruptly seemed dark again, the brilliant sunshine notwithstanding.

"We don't need anybody for anything. The biggest break we ever had was when that old wooly headed, wooden head Woodrow, you know who I mean"—even over the little speaker you could hear the audience giggling and cackling along—"that old schoolmarm President Wooden-head Woodrow Wilson thought the best thing America could do was run to a so-called League of Nations and negotiate forever on bended knee with a bunch of foreigners for permission to exercise our sovereign rights as Americans. Why, he wanted us to agree to negotiate before we even knew what we were gonna negotiate about! Now how does that make any sense?"

That stirred Fred. "I sure hope we don't. I've been over there to Berlin and they're locking everything up in big cartels hooked into the top Nazi leaders. You wouldn't believe the bribe one of Göring's aides demanded, just to get in and make a pitch. Not to the big guy either," he said unironically, "but to the next flunky up the ladder. I walked out. Crooked bunch of bastards."

That roused Ludwig. "Sir, I ..." then he seemed to change his mind.

More applause. The radio boomed on. "And you know what? The average Jacques and Jacqueline don't care jolly squat either because they know their government wasn't doing them any damn good at all. What the French had there in June is a sort of little election where they let the Germans come in and help clear out the politicians for 'em. They got a new government going on down in Vichy now, and when they canned the old one people in the galleries stood up and cheered. That's how the French feel about it."

How the French feel about it? Hawkins thought. For a moment he saw Paris. Marie. That old soldier crying in the street. People fleeing. The men and women back at the safe house drawing lots …

Then a woman's cry, piercing enough to shatter a plate-glass porthole. The Dane, her eyes red with tears, was shouting up the spiral staircase to the flight deck, bracing her hands on the doorframe.

"Tuvrn dat hoff! Tuvrn dat hoff! Hvow can he say dat! Dey stole my chountry! Dey stole my chountry! Dey lied and said dey'd leave us ahlone then dey came wit thanks in de mittle av da night—they took my vather to a kamp! A journalist! Oh, he vas so dangerous, little Danmark so dangerous to big, helpless Germany!"

She started sagging into the doorway, crying uncontrollably. Hawkins and Fred caught her short of the deck. The captain spun down the stairs, an appalled expression on his face.

"Shut the bloody thing off!" Hawkins said.

Two stewards rushed to carry her into the forward sleeping compartment. Hawkins and Fred returned to the lounge. Ludwig had collected the cards. He sat playing solitaire as if nothing had happened. Fred slammed down next to him.

"Jesus!"

"Is the young lady all right?" Ludwig said.

"I don't know," Hawkins said. "She may never be all right."

Ludwig kept playing solitaire, almost musing as he spoke, "She'll get used to it."

The intercom clicked in.

"This is the captain," the voice clipped and short, "we'll be landing in Bermuda shortly."

"Thank God!" Fred said.

Ludwig shuffled the cards and began arranging them on the small table again. He didn't invite anyone else to play.

-12-

The pitch of the motors shifted down. Bermuda, finally. A few banks and a circle over Great Sound. The mossy green islands in Hamilton Harbor began rushing up. A bob up, then a dip down. The Clipper's long keel snagged the waves with a heavy thud. Everyone shook from side to side and forward in their seats.

The plane taxied to the terminal on Darrell's Island. Hawkins cautiously tarried until the other passengers deplaned. Jamming his hat as close to his eyes as possible, he stepped out onto the floating pier and into the blazing sun.

A Royal Navy ensign was waiting, face creased with worry. It wasn't every day they had orders to rush a Clipper passenger—and a civilian, no less—into the colony outside of customs and passport control.

Hawkins followed the ensign along the pier and up and over the crest of the small island to a dock on the north side. There, out of sight of the big flying boat and the prying eyes of its passengers, waited a triple-cockpit Hacker launch: thirty-eight feet of gleaming mahogany, chrome, green leather and brass with the hotel's name still in gold leaf on the stern. An overweight Royal Army officer in khaki shorts over tanned hairy knees and an immaculately dressed female RAF officer were facing each other in the back cockpit. The woman nervously fussed with her aide's shoulder rope.

She quickly stopped when they saw him coming. They looked surprised.

But Hawkins presented an at-odds sight in the tropics in August. He was wearing a black double-breasted suit topped by a dark charcoal fedora tossed on his head as casually as a beret. His hair was cut in such a longish Continental style that there was something rather bohemian about him, in a polished Parisian way. His blue eyes were relentlessly in motion, soaking in everything around him. Pacing rapidly ahead, he almost overran the ensign, impatiently swinging his arms and shoulders as if he wanted to pick the man up and set him aside. He'd nearly step on the ensign's heels, then pause, checking himself, barely letting the ensign stay ahead, lending a tinge of syncopated agitation to his movements. He kept blinking in the bright light—the startled impression given by a large, powerful owl caught in the daylight and not liking it.

Hawkins almost flew over the rail, only lightly touching it with his hand, landing easily and gracefully in the back of the boat.

"Mr. Hawkins? I'm Brigadier James Houghton, Chief of the Imperial Posts and Telegraph Censorship Station here in Bermuda." Hawkins shook Houghton's hand. The woman stood too, greeting Hawkins military style, a snappy white-gloved salute. "And this is Flight-Lieutenant Stroud, my aide-de-camp."

"My pleasure! And to be out here," Hawkins said, shaking her hand. He smiled. "A breath of fresh air."

"Yes, miserable things, those planes, rather go by liner anytime," Houghton said.

"Not me. Haven't the patience." Hawkins turned back to her and winked. "Couldn't be a sailor. Too slow."

"Then I have just the thing for you." Stroud laughed, reaching down, drawing a blue Royal Air Force officer's jacket and folding service cap from under the seat.

"A little camouflage," Houghton said.

"I think I heard once we're all supposed to have reserve commissions of some sort," Hawkins said. "I'll have to ask for RAF now. Exactly what am I?"

"A squadron leader," Stroud said. "And you have the cap on backward."

The launch cast off. They began quietly motoring out onto Great Sound and into the main channel to Hamilton Harbor. Both Stroud and Houghton were looking at him with the same quizzical expression: *What is that accent?*

"Are you a Canadian, Mr. Hawkins?" she said.

"No. I've dual nationality. My mother's English, father's an American. Obviously, I travel exclusively under a US passport."

"Oh! I see. Your accent sounded a bit ... off. Sorry. I took you for one of those irritating men who like to affect Americanisms. But you are a Yank!"

"Halfway there, anyway—come to think, that's why I can't take that commission. My doing this is *very* illegal back home—uh ..." Stroud's right eyebrow rose a tick. "I mean, here—there. In the States. You're supposed to lose your citizenship automatically."

"Aren't you worried?" she said.

"No. They could never find out. They don't have an intelligence service."

"You're not career Service, then?" the general said.

"No, they recruited me in '38 when all the trouble started."

"How extraordinary! I mean, you could go off to America, avoid all this fuss and bother."

-13-

"Don't think I don't ..." Hawkins was leaning toward the lieutenant, only half paying attention to Houghton, one arm up on the seat back. He caught himself and stopped, frowning. General Houghton nodded slightly, almost knowingly. Flight-Lieutenant Stroud surveyed his expression intently, if blankly. In a second Hawkins picked up again, "... know. I"—struggling over his answer—"sort of grew up in England, mostly. My father was based in London, although we lived for a year or two in Paris and Zurich. England's my mother's country. It's where I mainly went to school. Then two years of college in New York. When the tensions rose the valve business went down ..."

"That's what you were in?" Houghton said.

"Yes, industrial valves, Bolley Manufacturing, I was their European representative. I couldn't help seeing things for myself. And then there was my father. He died shortly before I went to Europe. Had to drop out of school. He got gassed in the last one. At first he was fine. But he got hydrochloric acid in his lungs from the chlorine, like all the others, and it rotted them out. It took a long time."

In his mind's eye Hawkins could see his father in the oxygen tent, spine heaving, trying to force a breath into wasted lungs. A long time.

"So. The Secret Service?" the general said.

"Oh. Right. Not long after I went over I started getting calls from Germany. They were very interested in Bolley's line of high temperature, high pressure industrial valves. Rather odd, special-purpose things, mostly for the oil and chemical industries. Valves are a surprisingly difficult engineering problem. If they don't seat right under a wide range of heat and pressure conditions, a minuscule trickle you can hardly measure gets through, your factory blows up. They're at the center of everything."

"Oh! Of course. And so were you," the general said.

"Exactly. You couldn't miss that the Germans were going full tilt into munitions, synthetic fuels, these new plastics, all that lot. The last straw was a plant in East Prussia. Actually gave me a tour. Didn't think I could figure out what they were making. Or else they didn't care."

"Which was?"

"Gas." Stroud actually gasped. "Phosgene, to be exact. Went to the American embassy—couldn't even get an appointment. The US was neutral and out of the spying business, the secretary told me. Very huffy about it, actually. So one day an offer came to join MI6."

"I see ... huffy, you say?"

"Oh yes, quite. Snooty, actually."

"Remarkable. By the way," the general said, "you'll be amused to know that island to starboard is named Hawkins Island."

Hawkins had no sooner turned to check the semieponymous spit of rock and palm when a flash came dead ahead, outside the opening of the sound. A dull thud, not quite a boom, followed an instant later.

The general shouted at the ensign. He opened up the throttle full on. In seconds the boat was slicing through the waves, the roar drowning out any conversation. A mixture of anger, fear and worry roiled the general's face. Within a few minutes they reached the entrance of Great Sound and what amounted to front-row seats.

A dense black column of smoke was rapidly billowing up from an island of dark orange fire just outside the bay, past the Royal Naval Dockyard, perhaps a mile or two away. Another explosion followed. The black silhouette of a ship's bow lifted out of the flames and water for a second, rolled slightly and disappeared back into the smoke.

Hawkins had to lean in to the general's ear. "What is it?"

"A tanker, down from New York with a load of oil for the colony," the general said.

Skipping and hydroplaning, the boat approached the ship, turning slightly, all four passengers holding their hands up to shield their faces from the heat. They were a few hundred yards from the edge of the burning slick when a wide bubbling roiled the waves between them and the tanker. A black U-boat abruptly breached, bow first, leveling off in a second, diesels blasting to life, cruising in a circle around the burning tanker, throwing a huge wake sending the speedboat up and down hard into a trough. Two officers popped out of the conning tower, watching the tanker, scanning the sky, backs to the speedboat. Then a third man, a seaman swinging an ammo box, rushed out to man the rear AA mount. The speedboat mounted the wake's crest. He spotted them, turning to call his skipper, gesticulating back, slapping the box into the gun.

Houghton shouted, "Hats! Get down!"

The general and Stroud ripped off their service caps, throwing themselves to the deck. The ensign turned the helm hard, gunning the motor. Hawkins sat erect, staring at the sub. Stroud reached up and grabbed his cap off, "Get down!" then ducked again, crouching below the seat. The wind caught Hawkins' hair. He kept gazing at the U-boat, an idle, almost expectant expression on his face.

"Hawkins, in the name of God get down!" Houghton shouted.

The U-boat's officers glanced over their shoulders and shrugged. The sailor charged the machine gun and let go a few rounds, sending small plumes of water zipping alongside the speedboat. The ensign swerved. One of the officers on top of the conning tower waved and whistled at the gunner. He instantly stopped and began stowing his gun, pulling the ammo box off, darting up and back down into the submarine. The U-boat turned toward open water. The two officers took one more nervous glance around at the sky, then slipped down the hatch. Within seconds the U-boat slid into the water like a letter into an envelope and vanished.

"They're leaving," Hawkins said. "You can get up now."

The general and the flight-lieutenant shakily climbed up, tugging their hats back on. Stroud picked up Hawkins' cap and held it out, a horrified and quizzical expression on her face. He glanced down, took the hat and put it back on as if nothing had happened.

She turned to Houghton. "Should we go pick up survivors?"

"No. We have to get back. We've risked him enough already!"

Hawkins said nothing, calmly watching the black smoke rising. *U-boats blockading Bermuda? Well, that figures, he thought. They weren't content with running me out of France or chasing me from the shores of Europe. They're following me to the beaches of the New World, right to Hawkins Island, no less.*

-14-

Hawkins followed Houghton and Stroud up the path to the Princess Hotel, staring at the pink building and its green lawns, palm trees and flower beds—a merry, sensual riot of color. *Pink. Incredible*, he thought. In London or Paris everything came in tasteful shades of gray. There was something quite obscene about the hotel's celebratory quality, simply not right at all. Not after what he'd just seen, after everything since the beginning of June.

"This cockamamie place is your HQ?"

"That's right," the general said. "Actually, it's one of British Intelligence's biggest centers." They settled into wicker chairs on a terrace. In the distance a siren slowly wound up a tardy warning, followed by some imbecile frantically blowing a ship's whistle. The general ordered iced teas.

"Think there are many survivors?" Stroud said.

"What, from that?" the general said. "No one got off alive. When those tankers go up like that they boil the water around them. Nothing escapes."

"Are U-boats out there all the time?" Hawkins said.

"No. We know they're not. The navy sweeps constantly. Must have slipped in after dark and sat on the bottom to wait. They knew in advance to be there, then. There's got to be a spy in that damn town," jabbing a finger toward Hamilton.

"Nowhere else on the island you can go?" Hawkins said.

"No. Facilities are scarce. Water, housing, big problem. At least we lucked out on one thing. For a moment we thought they were sending the Duke and Duchess of Windsor here, but we got them to make him the governor of the Bahamas instead. That's the last thing I need, two high-ranking Nazi sympathizers on the island."

"On?"

"Yes. On. We've been getting intel the Germans are thinking of installing them as king and queen in an occupied Britain. Those two would play along. Especially her, very pro-Nazi. We can't take a chance of anything like that happening."

"Too bad no one told me in Lisbon, I could've settled it."

"What do you mean?" Houghton said.

"Bullet in the head. Simple matter. I'd have gotten in."

"You're talking about the man who was our king!" Stroud said.

Hawkins shrugged. "Just two more Fifth Columnists as far as I'm concerned. I don't know what the big deal is. I don't give a damn about his choice of women or him quitting as king, but he didn't have to go to Berlin and make friends with Hitler and Göring."

"That's true, but there'd be a scandal if we shot them. The whole world would know we did it," Houghton said.

"Put them on the plane, then, I'd have taken it down," Hawkins said. "It'd look like an accident."

"But you'd die! And what about the passengers?" Stroud said.

"My chances of living through this war are piss poor anyway. And innocent people are dying left and right, by the tens of thousands. At least I volunteered for it."

"Oh, come now," Stroud said. Her expression had initially been slightly amused at his presumed bravado. But Hawkins was utterly matter-of-fact about it, hardly celebratory. Rather he was quietly resigned, like a man who'd long accepted a terminal diagnosis. Her tone shifted to open-mouthed alarm. "You can't mean that."

"I do. There's no chance in hell I'm going to survive this. That's the way it is." He turned to the general. "Want me to go to the Bahamas now? I'll take care of it."

"No. They can't get in trouble there," Houghton said. "Water's too shallow for a U-boat to get in. That's why we picked it."

"Good. Tell me," Hawkins said, "what's the real picture? All this miracle-of-Dunkirk talk. You know how one only gets bits and pieces."

"Oh yes." The general thought a second. "Well, what we put out about the army escaping at Dunkirk—now that's true. What we're not saying is the troops had to throw off their packs and sidearms to swim out to the ships. Obviously, nothing like artillery or armor made it back."

"What about the fleet?"

"There's no room in the Channel for ships to maneuver around to avoid Luftwaffe bombs. It all hangs on Lieutenant Stroud's colleagues. If the Luftwaffe can get the best of them, get air control over southern England, there'll be an invasion. Probably an air drop. Seize a field. Fly in a division or two a day. Break out to the coast. It'd be over in a fortnight. Who knows"—he fatalistically shrugged—"the flyboys may hold."

"They will," Stroud said, a touch of irritation in her voice. "I know these men."

Houghton blandly continued as if he hadn't heard her.

"They may not have to invade. If we keep losing ships like that the U-boats will eventually starve us out anyway."

"But the Royal Navy's blockade? Won't they run out their oil stores?"

"No. Stalin's replaced every drop they lost because of the blockade. It's a queer business, the invasion of France, fueled with Soviet petrol. Thank the pact between Molotov and Ribbentrop for that." The general slammed his glass down and began lightly tapping his knuckles together. He motioned to a nearby waiter and ordered a double scotch.

"What about the States?" Hawkins said. "What about President Roosevelt?"

"It's not encouraging," Houghton said. "His hands are tied. He's in a tough election. The idea of a third term, it's very unpopular."

They all sat in complete silence for at least a full minute, the only sound the ocean rustling in the distance.

"How could he lose?" Hawkins finally said. "So many hopes hang on him—not just the war—everything, a new deal for everyone—"

"Ah, the Americans! I don't know. We watch them pretty closely from here, with their damned Neutrality Acts, all this Fortress America rot, building a wall around their country—I simply can't understand them. We get their radio all over the band here. You should have heard that new commentator last night—"

"Ventnor?" Stroud said.

"Yes, that one. Walter Ventnor, he's the really big fish now—"

"Caught him coming in. Caused quite a row in the plane," Hawkins said.

"I heard him, too. Wants the Yanks to turn their backs. Thinks it's too late, that it's all over," Stroud said.

Hawkins took out his pipe, started fidgeting with it, half filling it, then stopping.

"A lot of people like to turn their backs on it. Maybe it is too late."

"I'm not sure I follow," Stroud said.

"None of this should've happened," Hawkins said. "None of it! It's senseless—totally senseless!"

Houghton and Stroud sat back and said nothing, just waited and watched.

"They sent me over to the other side of the Rhine a year ago when Hitler invaded Poland. The Wehrmacht had vanished. It wasn't big enough, yet, for a two-front war. There weren't even sentries in some places. When you walked into the bunkers you could hear your footsteps echoing. We could've occupied Germany up to the Rhine and the Nazi regime would've collapsed. I filed report after report. Drive off in an orchard. Get the radio set out. Start signaling. Get in! Get moving! Bugger 'em good! But what happened? Nothing. The biggest military force in Europe sat in their camps polishing boots. So tell me, exactly how much are we supposed to risk our necks because of other people's stupidity? Or because they won't listen? Who the hell wants to die for stupid people?"

Hawkins slumped back in his chair. For a long moment there only came the distant sound of surf and seagulls.

"Because you know they will care," Houghton said.

"Maybe. But half the time I feel I'm fighting to save people from themselves."

"You can't condemn people to slavery forever because they made a mistake," Stroud said.

Hawkins sighed heavily, grudgingly. "I suppose."

"Perhaps the Axis will provoke the US like the last time," Stroud said.

"They'd certainly be provoked if they had any idea of the scale of Nazi operations in their country," the general said. "Hitler regards the Americans as an enemy, even if the Americans don't."

"Getting a lot of that?" Hawkins said.

"Oh, yes. Come along, Hawkins, let me show you my baby while I can."

-15-

After the brilliant sunshine outside the lobby was dark as a coal mine. Stroud snapped off another quick salute and vanished into the office. The general bolted down a side staircase. Hawkins groped down after him. Heat and humidity menacingly rose. An armed sergeant passed them through a checkpoint. They stopped on a landing. A long, dark, cavernous basement loomed in front of them. Dingy ceiling lamps caged in dusty wire baskets cast a dim light on the nightmarish scene.

Down the room stretched row upon row of worktables studded with teakettles. Several hundred female clerks, most barely out of their teens, were laboriously steaming open mounds of letters. Each girl's work had a methodical, frantic rhythm. First, snatch a letter from the pile. Hold it up for scrutiny in front of a gooseneck lamp. Check the paper for unusual watermarks or patterns. Then peer across the letter sideways, then all over with a magnifier. Occasionally, a girl rushed a suspicious one aside to smear stripes of chemicals across it in search of invisible ink. Finally, each letter was cleaned, ironed flat and meticulously resealed without a trace of surreptitious entry. All done at a furious, sprinting speed.

The atmosphere was as close and dense as a steam room's, only without benches or masseuse. Heat from the lights and vapor from the kettles continually roiled up. The clerks constantly wiped their hands dry on towels slung over their shoulders lest their fingers mark the letters. Every face glistened with sweat. Perspiration matted their clothes to their bodies. Most had their hair wrapped up around their heads in braids. A fetid, slightly rancid stench of glue, sweat, wet paper and mildew pervaded the air. A hollow-sounding pair of metal horns weakly piped in the Bermuda radio.

With a reflexive jerk Hawkins loosened his collar, sweat already running down his face. "My God, how long can anybody stand working in this place?"

"Oh, they get used to it after a while," the general said. "Of course, we only do this in short bursts. The Clipper flies in. We unload the mail, rush it here. Then the lassies go take a dip in the pools or surf to cool off."

Hawkins intently scanned the scene, leaning on the banister. *Appalling*, he thought. *These poor girls are probably stuck here in this sweatshop—literally—until the end of the war, rummaging through other people's private papers.*

General Houghton straightened up, slapping his hand on the balustrade for emphasis. "This whole Bermuda operation is a godsend. The Clippers are the only transatlantic civil airliners operating right now. That means virtually all the mail between the Western Hemisphere and Europe passes right through this choke point."

"Righto. So how do we pick out the German letters?"

"We don't."

"What'ja you mean—don't."

"We don't pick them out."

"Then how do you know which ones to check?"

"We don't."

"I don't understand—"

"We inspect them all."

"All?"

The general waved his hand over the rows of clerks. "That's why we need so many."

"Every stinking piece of mail between the entire Western Hemisphere and the European continent?"

"Why, yes. Every bit. From all of North and South America. Well, except Canada. They do that there. But, really, there's no way of guessing or knowing. We open and inspect it all. Have to. When we add the submarine telegraph and telephone cables, plus any ships we can intercept, to this, we have a formidable intelligence resource, for all over the world. We can't replace it."

Hawkins' perspiration now felt like cold sweat. *All the mail is opened?* he thought. *That means all my mail, too. What about my luggage, the Louis XVI tea set? Are they ransacking the plane, right now?*

-16-

The job with Bolley Manufacturing had come with an interesting perk. Hawkins got paid to travel. And he always had a few spare hours. That meant he could slip into antiques stores, flea markets, curio shops and auction halls. Turned out he had a good eye. Picked up small, easily shippable treasures and mailed them back to New York. It'd grown into a very lucrative sideline, one that became almost a necessity once he went on the MI6's payroll.

Unless one had family money there was almost no way to credibly keep up the appearances needed to do the job, given what the Crown paid. It seemed to be more or less assumed agents would cover certain expenses out of their own pockets as a form of national service. Unfair. Foolish in terms of how it limited who could be recruited. But no less real.

Hawkins mentally raced over the trail he'd left. The packages went by ship. *Probably safe, there*, he thought. But the letters, invoices and statements all went by air mail. *Could they be reading my bank statements? Never told anyone about my little sideline. None of their damn business. Especially that I needed money.* Not a good thing to admit in this business. It could be interpreted as meaning he had an exploitable vulnerability.

The alarm dug in deeper. Suppose they only intercepted part of the correspondence—the checks and bank statements coming back from

New York? Someone might suspect the money might be coming from the Abwehr or the SD. It could look like a payoff.

He did a quick inventory of the environment. *Any coppers around? No … no visible reason for alarm. If I was in trouble, would the general be showing me this incredibly sensitive facility? Maybe they'd missed it. Still—*

"And they actually read them all?" Hawkins said.

"Yes. Of course." Houghton caught something in Hawkins' tone or expression and eyed him carefully. "Our networks on the Continent?"

"Swept away. At least all the ones I was privy to. It's going to be very risky, but when I get back in we'll have to rebuild everything inside Europe from scratch."

"And what happened to the people?" The question more a statement.

"God only knows. I tried to help some Deuxième Bureau people I worked with in Paris. Had some blank passports. Nowhere near enough. Most of the rest went to ground. At least I hope so." He paused a moment. *Not true*, he thought, or knew, *not true at all.* "Well, no. Actually, the odds are the ones that didn't make it out are all dead. Or captured. Which is as good as dead. I … I …" His voice started to choke, breaking slightly. The faces, he could see the faces again. "I couldn't save them. I had to leave them behind."

"It's not your fault."

"I know. But I still see them every night."

"Friends?"

"Yes. Good friends."

"I'm sorry. Truly. But the disaster you saw in Paris is what's behind all this. The Continent's become a dark void. We've no idea what's going on. As you say, our networks were swept away. What you see here is the only alternative we have left."

"There's nothing else?"

"No. Hawkins, don't miss this for what it is. This"—he waved his hand out again—"is an act of utter desperation. It's a measure of how weak we really are. It's the kind of thing people do when the odds are against them and the last chip's down, the act of people who have absolutely nothing to lose."

"We've nothing to lose?"

"No. Nothing. We're going down. Like that ship. Face it, Hawkins, our world is ending. You can count the number of democracies left on your fingers. So, righto, we've not a damn thing to lose now."

"You could ask what the point is. Maybe they've already won."

"I know. Makes us like the Nazis. But it's nothing to what's coming. If the Nazis win, this is the future of the human race, only worse. There'll be no going back."

Yes, Hawkins thought. *That's exactly what it's like inside Europe now.*

"US government have any idea we're doing this?" he said.

"Hardly! I'm sure they'd be huffy, as you say."

"But you are tracking actual Nazi agents?"

"Absolutely."

"How do they code their messages?"

"They're using a sort of open code, first letter of every sentence in words of three or more letters in length. Makes for long, windy, contorted messages. That's how you spot them. You have to read it for sense."

Flight Lieutenant Stroud rushed down the stairs waving a transcript. "Another one—on the New York source! They just finished translating it."

"Come!"

-17-

The general, with Hawkins and Stroud chasing his heels, ran back up through the lobby to a spacious office that apparently had been expropriated intact from the former management, tourist promotional pictures and all. Here and there military charts had been tacked up over sunny posters of beaches and tennis players.

The general sat, hooking a pair of half glasses methodically around his ears. They stood waiting in anticipation.

"Let's see—'need funds soon Orator'—um, something, something, 'typ convoy times excel wants money house rented.' Also a note here, those words after 'Orator' they couldn't figure out, 'Stahl Wadenetz.' Must be a person."

"I doubt that," Hawkins said. "'Stahl' means steel, of course, but a 'Wadenetz' is a seine net."

"Interesting. Given the American military's predilection for alliteration it's probably one of their code names, Steel Seine. Who knows what that could be."

"So, spy seeks to steal secret of Steel Seine," Hawkins said.

Houghton looked up in openmouthed surprise before exploding in laughter.

"Oh my God! You'll do just fine!" Leaning back, sheepishly pushing at the papers, "Haven't had much to laugh about lately."

"I know the feeling."

The general handed the intercept to Hawkins. He silently read it again. "Convoy—typ—typist? A clerk perhaps? Like a shipping clerk? Has the schedule?"

"Convoy times!"

"Yes. That tanker—you said you've been hunting for someone here in Hamilton …"

Houghton took the letter, studied it a moment, started to hand it back, looked again, then started waving it in fury.

"Righto. Not here at all. Ah dammit! God dammit to hell!" He threw it down.

"Why, what? I thought you were worried about that?" Hawkins said.

"No. Very limited population here, only a matter of time before we caught someone sending sailing times out. Now we're talking about the entire United States instead. Millions of people. Wholly different picture. Trust me, I'd rather have an agent here, by far. Since you're flying out, you better take this straightaway to our new HQ in New York. This is a job for them."

"Headquarters? You mean the New York station—"

"No. There's been a change. There's a big new headquarters being set up in New York. Very hush-hush. Going to coordinate activities, so on. They're over us, that's all I know."

"What? Am I being sent to some damned desk job? I've got to get back into France, for Christ's sakes—"

"I doubt that," the general said. "You've been inside Europe. That's why you probably haven't heard."

"It's all been very chaotic," Stroud said.

"I suppose," Hawkins allowed.

Houghton slipped the paper into an envelope and handed it to Hawkins.

"We better get you back."

A quick walk brought them around to the dock and the speedboat. The ensign had returned several minutes earlier with a grisly cargo. General Houghton had been right. Not a single sailor survived the U-boat attack.

The ensign and a pair of Hamilton ambulance drivers lifted a body onto a tarp. It was burnt a brownish black above the chest, like overcooked bacon, marking where the sailor had jumped into the flaming oil floating on the water. His hands were seared to his face. Below the chest, under the protective water, the legs and feet were intact, the skin still pink. As they set the half-charred corpse down one arm broke off and fell away with a soft crunch. Houghton and Stroud put their hands over their mouths and quickly walked away.

The ensign stumbled to the side and threw up, holding on to a piling with a shaky hand, his face seasick green. Hawkins blankly stared at him. Then he looked down at the burned body at his feet. Then back at the ensign. When the ensign recovered Hawkins indifferently stepped over the body and tarp and into the boat.

-18-

The powerboat sped off. The flight lieutenant began unknotting the aide's rope off her shoulder, then replaced the medical service caducei on her lapels.

"Well, Doctor, what's your psychiatric prognosis?" the general said.

"Been under tremendous stress for quite a long time."

"Stress? We can scarcely credit he survived—"

"He's a remarkable man. Quite exhausted, close to burnout. Obviously, he's upset about the Nazi victory, deeply angry, wants to know why, who's responsible, who to blame."

"Aren't we all," almost growling, leaning over her.

"Ye-s-s, that's true. But I see no evidence of undue paranoia—given his job—or any incipient psychosis or dissociative thought patterns. There's a cynicism I suspect wasn't there before. The extreme isolation of the kind of life he's been leading is beginning to grind on him. That's a vulnerability. But it's the sense of fatalism that I find most worrisome, and a complete lack of affect when he was talking about killing the duke and duchess, or not surviving the war."

"Affect? Affect what?"

"Affect is the total sum of your feelings—mood, which is the way you feel in general, it's not specific to any event, and emotions, which are reactive to things that happen. When he said he had no chance of surviving, or offered to kill the duke and duchess by taking the plane down, that wasn't bravado. The dead flat way he talked about it, I'm certain he really meant it."

"Good. That's what we want."

"Excuse me?"

"It's an interesting option, a plane crash. We'll need to do something like that if Britain falls. It may well be necessary for him to sacrifice everything, even his own life."

"You can't be serious. Hawkins—"

The general's reaction was instructional, but firm. "Flight Lieutenant. Remember, you're a Royal Air Force officer first, then a psychologist. We're here to win the war, not make people feel better. The mission comes first."

"Yessir."

"Anything else?"

"He's latently suicidal, he needs a good vacation and some counseling—"

"He's not getting it, dammit. Can he keep it up and maintain his grip?"

"Yes. He hasn't cracked. Yet."

"He damn well better not. A lot's riding on him—he's the only bona fide we've got. Big risk we're taking. What about the accent?"

"Rather transatlantic, but only to us. He'll easily pass as a top-class Yank from an elite private school."

"Good. Did that goddamn Swiss bugger even peek out the porthole?"

"No."

"Bloody hell of a thing. Neutral rights. Neutral rights my arse." He angrily searched down and around for something to kick, found nothing. "Fuck that! Fuck them! Why the bloody hell aren't we interrogating him? What are they thinking? Who knows who he could be!" Stroud had a slightly shocked expression on her face. He sighed and glanced down. "Oh. Damn. Sorry. Shouldn't have—maybe we're all a bit burned out."

"Yes. I know. It's quite all right."

The general started back inside. "I'll let New York know. U-boat in sight of the dockyard. Damn, anyway." As they turned the Clipper began climbing over the harbor. They stopped and grimly watched it circle and fly overhead, heading north. "An awful lot riding on him," he said, his voice hushed.

-19-

"You sure you don't want to go to Parke-Bernet?"

Hawkins plucked the sugar bowl from the counter and pointed to the marks on the bottom.

"Bruno, when's the last time you saw one of those? That's Louis XVI's signet. From the royal chateau at St. Cloud."

Gravity claimed him. Bruno slid down from his stool. Try as he might, he couldn't hide his fascination. "To be honest, I'm glad my wife's not here, it'd be going back to Queens. Either that or I'd be sleeping on the sofa until New Year's."

Hawkins well knew Parke-Bernet. Sent them things before. *Don't want to say so*, he thought, *but there are problems with that.* For one, you have to wait for the right sale. Then you have to wait nine or ten months to get paid. But that wasn't the really bad part. No, the real problem was that no big auction hall paid in cash. Some asinine tax regulation. After the visit to that basement in Bermuda, it was going to be cash only from here on out. That meant small dealers like Bruno in the downtown antiques district between Greenwich Village and Union Square.

"Two thousand? That's cash?"

Bruno spread his hands out as if to say, *Are we all fools here?*

"And fifty for the watch?" Bruno nodded. "I'll take it."

Bruno hung a CLOSED sign in the window. They made a quick trip down Broadway to the bank. It was as packed with people as a small train station, nearly ten minutes in line merely to reach a teller. Hawkins had been in this bank before. He'd spent his two and a half years of college at nearby NYU. There'd never been more than a handful of people in it before. The torrent of cash flowing in and out required a bit of an adjustment after the austerity of Europe.

Hitler created an artificial prosperity in Germany with his military buildup. But in broad terms Europe had never recovered from the Depression. In Britain every penny was still pinched. You could see it in people's faces as they entered stores, an expression of worry and tension at the prospect of having to spend money. And when was the last time anyone put up a new building? London might have been the seat of the world's greatest empire, but it was basically a Victorian construction. Paris, nearly untouched from before the Great War.

And at that moment a small downtown New York antiques dealer left the counter and handed over a little green and white envelope filled with a wad of cash that, just a few years ago, only the biggest galleries uptown could've come up with. And Bruno had done it quickly. Hawkins pocketed the cash, shook hands with the dealer and left.

Out on the corner the smell of money being made and spent was in the air everywhere. The men in threadbare coats selling apples from boxes—gone. Empty shop windows—now full. Every other person crossing the street carried a bag or a package. Happy smiles all over, delivery men pushing pipe racks of bright new clothes over from the garment district as grocers restocked fresh produce. Half the flooding river of cars coming down the street looked sparkling new, gleaming with bright chrome.

Standing and watching on the street—incredibly enough, he could do it that easily—told Hawkins he was in a different country from the one he'd left more than three years before. Shared hardships then brought people together. Now people clutched their bags and packages and smiled to themselves. *Mine.*

The country had pulled itself out of the ditch of the Depression, a

New Deal done. Now it was roaring down the highway in unspoken celebration. That was the sense it gave. For a moment Hawkins felt a bit melancholy, as if he'd just learned he'd missed a great party.

At least an hour before the pickup, he thought. *Got to kill some time. Might as well walk down Broadway to the hotel.* He slowed and gazed at the menu in a deli window. Pastrami on rye. *Always partial to that. Always reminds me of New York. But, then, here I am. The people inside seem so very distant, almost in another world*, he thought. Talking and smiling. *Smiling about what? Behind the glass in more ways than one. Another party I didn't hear about.*

Simply don't feel like eating, somehow. Repelled by the idea of food? No, he thought. *Not a sick feeling. More like there's no room inside for anything. Well, why? The money can't have triggered it. Made a good profit. Ought to be happy, even thrilled.* But the money hadn't brought happiness. *Guilt at taking advantage of Madame Delage? No, not that, either.*

Bringing out the vermeil set brought up Paris. That was the problem. It was the mental camera iris closing in again. Try as hard as he could, the same dialogue he'd had on the road all the way from France through Spain, from Portugal to Bermuda, on the plane last night, still kept coming up. It kept churning over and over in the mind. *So stupid. So senseless. And Marie, gone, too. How could it all have happened?*

He flowed with the busy crowd down to the corner of Tenth Street by his hotel, the Brittany House. Grace Episcopal church, the best Gothic building in the Western Hemisphere, towered right across the street. A comforting little piece of old England.

Hawkins was the kind of ordinary low church man who never went, maybe Lessons and Carols on Christmas Eve. He stood on the corner a second, watching the cars.

Without any actual conscious decision, he ducked across Broadway and passed through the familiar red doors. A choir was rehearsing out of sight, back in the nave. He dropped a mess of coins in the box out of habit. Then he lit a candle, then a couple more. He sat down and numbly watched them burn like a late-night campfire, oblivious to the choir and

Gothic splendor. The door opened. A bus roared by, shattering the illusion of a country church in Devon or Kent. The choir stopped, then restarted the passage, with the choirmaster nosily singing a note for a boy with a breaking voice who couldn't get the pitch right.

Hawkins shifted in the straight pew, legs in the aisle. *What will the Germans do once they get across the Channel?* he thought. *No horses. Won't need churches like this for stables. Maybe use them for jails.*

He closed his eyes, listening to the singers. Then he saw the faces, Dodier, LaDue, Champigny … and Stéphanie, always Stéphanie. He startled up, looking around, not at the faces.

Why do I want to go back in? Do I want to get killed? Maybe I don't really care anymore. Maybe that's why I'm willing to go back in. Escape the pointlessness of it all, one way or the other. Or is it that I just can't let go? Maybe there's no difference.

Someone came in and left the door wide open. The sound of horns and truck engines blared. A deacon or vicar came up the aisle, watching Hawkins as he passed by, closed the door, and came back. He paused.

"You should take your hat off."

"Yeah." Hawkins didn't move.

"Can I help with anything?"

"Got any burning bushes?"

"I'm afraid not. Are you trying to be funny?"

"No. Nothing is funny these days."

"I suppose not."

"Do you always feel God in here? Because I'm not feeling a thing."

"No. That's too much to expect."

"Thanks."

The man hesitated, unsure whether to leave or not.

"I'll be out back," he finally said and went up the aisle.

Going back. It's the only thing that makes any sense. Got to get out of here and go back in.

-20-

The frosted glass door already bore simple new black characters: BRITISH SECURITY CO-ORDINATION. Hawkins pulled the knob. Two burly movers were blocking the door, bellowing at each other nose to nose. "Oh—all—right! Jeez ..." the first man shouted. With an irritated, self-conscious flourish he carelessly slapped a bookcase flat on top of a desk and stepped aside. The other man grunted in irritation, either at him or at the idea of the performance—it was impossible to tell which. Then he hoisted a file cabinet on a dolly and propelled it down the aisle with a rumble. A padlocked chain running through the drawer handles rattled loudly as he went.

Up and down the long airy room several competing furniture rental companies manhandled more desks, chairs, file cabinets, shelves and typewriters in a manic game of musical chairs. Staff members in suits or dresses rushed after them, pointing and gesticulating, here, there. Then they resumed the main business: arguing with each other over the seating arrangements.

The usual unruly drill of bureaucracy in a crisis, Hawkins thought. Everyone trying to do everything simultaneously and getting in each other's way. *All the scene lacks is the Marx Brothers swinging on a tippy ladder.*

Was it only late winter I was going up the creaking stairs to C's office in Queen Anne's Gate? Now this show. Incredible balls, Hawkins thought. *Or something.*

A short man, midforties, with a full crop of graying blond hair and a hard but sharp look emerged from the crowd. He waved, a big grin. For a split second Hawkins started to call his name. But the man held a finger up to his lips, softly whispering, "W!" He seized Hawkins' hand, gripping it in a delighted shake.

William Stephenson, now officially known as W—the same as the chief of the Service was known as C—was the last man Hawkins expected to see in New York.

There were certain givens in their closed world. One was that the real name of a top intelligence executive was only used in a secure office or conference room. Even then, you only used it if you enjoyed a privileged status yourself. Clearly, Bill had now acquired such a doubtful but undeniably elite distinction.

His friend had been, to a considerable degree, erased from the world. For security reasons the Service had been scrubbing the public records of traces of Stephenson's life for several years. Now, with this designation, the process was complete. William Stephenson was once one of the most powerful and successful industrialists in Britain. He'd invented the telephoto machine used by newspapers all over the world. Parlayed that into an industrial empire that included Pressed Steel Company, the largest manufacturer of auto bodies in Britain. Now he had vanished into a parallel shadow world. It was a scary and weighty moment. In a way, a man had ceased to exist, very much the way Hawkins had.

The large corner office enveloped them in calm. Stephenson strode to a refrigerator humming in an alcove. He began pulling bottles of gin and vermouth from the icebox.

"So. It's W now."

"Yes. Also 48100."

"I should have known you were behind this. Little obvious, isn't it? The International Building?"

"Would it make more sense to hole up in the Bowery? At least here people are used to crowds coming and going. Hide in plain sight. That's the plan."

"Well, I'll grant that. Still, to actually do it, Bill, some balls, there."

"Thanks."

"Bit of a step down, isn't it? The New York station?"

"Not anymore. We're now formally responsible for the entire Western Hemisphere and all of Asia. And more." He handed Hawkins the fresh martini and half sat on the front of his desk. Hawkins took a sip. Perfect icy vapor going down. "Here. Have a seat."

Hawkins ignored the offered chair, slowly pacing back and forth, back and forth, a nervous hitch in his movements, a tic perhaps. "More?"

"Yes. A contingency plan's being set up." W began speaking almost as if he were musing aloud, fiddling with his glass. "If the Nazis cross the Channel we're to control and direct resistance in occupied Britain and British territories worldwide." A level late afternoon light filled the room, piercing the steel blue blinds. It couldn't relieve the now somber mood. Hawkins' pacing sped up a bit.

"How?"

"The fleet—or what's left of it—will go to Canada with the royal family and a government in exile. Churchill's made it as clear as words can we'll never surrender."

"Very good. About time."

"Yes. Since the US is a neutral country, we'll have access to home through here. If Britain doesn't fall we get other jobs." His tone cheered a bit. "It's a good location to get agents in and out of Europe, direct activities. There are people here you won't find anywhere else. We're also hoping to coordinate intelligence and technology-sharing with Washington. Their good stuff for ours. And hopefully, we can persuade them to get in, like the last time."

"Quite a list."

"That's not all. We've also got a big job here in the US. Like a damn cowboy movie. Dodge City with Nazi agents." He began rubbing his neck.

"Or maybe Chicago with gangsters. Spying on our shipping, slipping saboteurs into Canada, routing agents into Latin America and the Caribbean, spying on the Americans—"

"What's C think about all this?"

"I'm getting my marching orders straight from the PM, so not much. I'm Churchill's personal liaison with President Roosevelt."

"Roosevelt? You've actually met him? That's …" For a moment Hawkins' face began to light up. He stopped for a second, then resumed his agitated pacing with a new energy. "That's tremendous. What's he like? What's he going to do?"

"Very hard to read his mind. He's in a dicey position with the coming election. The America Firsters, the conservative isolationists, in both parties, are on a tear. Incredible, what they're willing to say, absolutely ruthless. He's vulnerable. That's the problem now." W paused, watching. "Hawkins, sit down and relax." Hawkins kept pacing. "Like a bloody tennis match."

"An awful lot of people's hopes hang on him."

"I know. In the long run, ours, too."

Hawkins wandered over to the windows, curiously peering down at St. Patrick's Cathedral.

"So. You're putting me back into Europe from here."

Hawkins' back was turned. He missed the rapidly shifting expression on W's face. Regretful. Sad. Sympathetic. But determined. And then hard.

"Hawkins, I'm sorry. I know you'd prefer the Continent. But I desperately need you here. You know the business. What's more, you're half American. You can fit in in a way others can't. That's why I paid your airfare myself."

"Ah—ah, what? You paid for a Clipper fare? Have you lost your mind?"

"Remember when we first met?"

-21-

Never forget that day, Hawkins thought. Started in the morning at Shepperton Studios, going to Bill's office across a studio lot teaming with actors, extras and men pushing lights and gear around. Learned that night it was Stephenson who had built Shepperton, the biggest film studio in Europe, along with Alexander Korda, Britain's leading filmmaker.

Sold a hundred thousand dollars' worth of Bolley's specialty valves. In a stroke Hawkins went from being a junior hire to Bolley's top man for the British Empire and the Continent.

"You know what impressed me most?" Stephenson said. "Remember what we spent the rest of the day talking about? Your contacts in key German industries."

Never forget that night, either, Hawkins thought. It had been getting on, late afternoon. Stephenson had offhandedly said, "Come and have a bite at my club." He'd driven them into town in his new Bentley 4¼-liter coupe, pulling up in front of a palatial 1770s Georgian building on St. James Street. Turned out to be nothing less than Boodles, one of those astonishingly exclusive upper-crust men's clubs. Inside Stephenson began casually chatting with someone he knew. So happened it was the Duke of Devonshire, the new Undersecretary of State for the Dominions. It seemed the duke wanted to pump Winnipeg-born Stephenson about Canada.

They served thick ham and cheese sandwiches with too much mustard over the butter, although the drinks were good. One hardly noticed for the awe-inspiring procession of rooms that had once housed Hume and Gibbon and the Duke of Wellington. All in all, a heady day. Like having the stars fall out of the sky and crash on your head.

"Oh God, yes, the Krauts were always fascinated by those damn Yank specialty valves of mine."

"Did you know I passed everything you told me to Churchill? You helped set all this in motion. Roy, why do you think you got into my office in the first place? We needed some parts, yes. But I wanted the information more than I needed those valves."

The thought that Hawkins might have naively assumed Bill had no ulterior motive was more than he wanted to deal with at the moment.

"Bill, I can best serve in Europe. That's where I belong."

"No, you're needed here. I've got to have experienced staff I can rely on, people who have a feel for the Yanks, fit in. You wouldn't believe some of the toffs they send over here. Listen, Roy, it's not like we're spying on the US government."

"No, Bill. I have to go back."

"You'll die. What's the point?"

"I have to go back."

"Why?"

"I have to."

"Roy." W stepped forward, grabbing him by the shoulders. "Without this country civilization is—" but Hawkins brushed one hand away, putting his right hand on W's chest, pushing back. For a split second the two men were on the edge of a tussle. W let go, holding out his hands, dropping them loosely at his sides, "—finished. Everything hangs on the United States. Everything. We can't hold on forever without her. You know that. That's why the Nazi agents here are every bit as dangerous as the ones anywhere else."

"What about the FBI? It's their Nazi problem. Let them deal with it."

W walked back around his desk, sitting down heavily. He contemplated Hawkins for a long moment.

"You haven't dealt with them. They think counterespionage is merely another form of law enforcement. To them, spies are criminals to be arrested, hauled into court and jailed. Preferably with news cameras running."

"They don't try and turn them?"

"No—NO! That's totally alien to their thinking. They can't see the opportunities. That if people can go one way, they can go the other. If they do find a suspicious suspect, they arrest him right off. Like that." He snapped his fingers. "Oh, very indignant. Get tough. Crack down. Knock 'em around. That's the mentality. Then they try to build a case. Of course, by then everyone's bolted, changed IDs, addresses, contacts, the works. So they're perpetually starting all over from scratch."

Hawkins stopped pacing. They faced each other in silence for a long moment. Hawkins remembered Houghton's intercepted message and handed it to W.

"I was asked to give you this."

-22-

W studied it for a long moment. "You see this?"

"Yes. Might be a shipping clerk."

"You're right. I know exactly who this is. Damn! Can't believe it—"

"Why?"

"Only possible candidate. What's more, I happen to know he recently bought a new car."

"One of our people? Working for the Nazis?" Hawkins began making his way back to the front of the desk, his pace smoother and quicker, his expression once again alive, his tone sharp. "Who?"

"Man named Bailey. A Canadian, works for Cunard. Has access to everything because they're constantly calling back and forth between the shipping firms trying to line up convoys."

"I saw a tanker get hit yesterday."

"We were thinking it was someone in Bermuda. But it's Bailey who gave the sailing schedule to the Nazis." W tossed the intercept on his desk. He tapped a pencil on the desk twice, jumped up, grabbed his coat and hat and rushed to a file cabinet. He pulled out a snub-nosed .38 Colt Detective Special and began loading it.

"What are you doing?"

"Going to go bring him in."

"You? The chief of station? Bill—"

"I know." He repeated it like a litany, "I'm the top man. Strictly against regulations. If there's a foul-up and we get involved with the local authorities all our operations will be compromised."

"So?"

"Somebody's got to do it."

"You? That's crazy. There's no one else?"

"No. We've got to act fast before he beams out today's schedule. He's at work. He can't send anything out right now."

"You really mean to do this, don't you?"

"Yes."

Hawkins plucked the intercepted message from the desk. W watched attentively as Hawkins began studying it again, his conflicting expressions of interest and anger and God knew what else. "Hawkins. I really do need you. A couple of weeks. Just give me enough time to bring someone else over. Then if you want to go hand yourself over to the Gestapo, if you want it that badly, fine, go get yourself killed." The paper wavered in the air. Another nudge. "A Nazi agent is ... a Nazi agent." That did it. There was a sudden burst of energy. Hawkins angrily threw the paper down.

"A couple of weeks. But that's it! A couple of weeks!"

Stephenson hooked the loaded gun into the back of his pants, started for the door. Then he stopped. He stood up on his toes, stepping right into Hawkins' face, their noses practically touching.

"But remember—"

"Right, what—"

"We're forbidden to attack, abduct or harm any Americans, even if they're Nazis."

"Believe me, that's fine here."

"Good. The US has got to come into the war against Hitler. Harming Americans won't help. This man Bailey, he's one of ours. We've a right to bring him home. But we have to operate within US law. We're not vigilantes."

"Check. Let's go."

-23-

Hawkins held up his hand, blocking the sun slanting in across the Hudson, squinting, waiting. *Where's Bill—or rather, W? After five now.* Long shadows were darkening the forest of columns under the West Side Highway, shading the truck entrance of a pier facing Fifty-Second Street. W emerged, barely glancing over, his gaze directed back inside. Then a flick with his fingers. Hawkins geared up, swinging directly in front of him. W lightly stepped into the car.

"He's parked inside the pier. Be coming out those big doors any second."

"What's he driving?"

"Black Cord convertible."

"A Cord? Expensive. Interesting."

A minute later a black Cord rolled out and drove south under the elevated highway. Hawkins followed at a respectable distance, weaving back and forth through the columns so that they couldn't be spotted. Bailey turned up the ramp and onto the busy elevated highway. A few minutes later he took the exit for the Battery and the Staten Island Ferry.

"Bloody hell," W said.

"No. It's fine. He can't outrun us if he's taking the ferry. That car's got a supercharger on top of a big Lycoming airplane engine. We'll never catch him if he gets a chance to run." Hawkins stomped on the accelerator, racing around an old Plymouth and onto the loading dock one car behind him. "I'm checking him out."

Hawkins slowly walked forward, past the line of waiting cars. He kept his eyes fixed on the old ferry crawling across the darkening harbor like a brightly lit snail. Paused, made a quick glance sideways at Bailey. *Good*, he thought. *Not looking up.* Pudgy man, balding, dark blond hair. Not too old. *What the hell's he fidgeting with under the seat?*

Bailey pulled out a nondescript package the size of a shoe box and plugged it into the car's cigarette lighter. Very businesslike. Then reached under the dash and snapped a wire to the car's radio antenna with an alligator clip. With a finger Bailey gently tipped the box sideways. Vacuum tubes lit up through a row of slots. He quietly began tapping Morse code on a small telegraph key bolted to the top. As blasé as one could get. Not giving a fig who saw. Just another radio bug.

Hawkins visually swept the scene, fists clenched in his coat pockets. *What have we got?* he thought. *A hundred, no, probably more like three hundred people are in line waiting. Make that three hundred witnesses.* Back at the car he deliberately stretched up on the running board, peering forward again, watching, then slouched in the driver's seat.

"He's transmitting."

"What? Now? God—"

"We can't—"

"I know. The crowd."

"It's amazingly small"—Hawkins gestured with his hands—"like this."

"We want that, too. Never dreamed they had anything like that."

Several minutes later the ferryboat finally clanged against the pier. Hawkins motored down into the ferry's dark maw, cutting across and pulling up on Bailey's left side. The radio sat on the seat, unplugged. The transmission had gone out.

The last car lumbered aboard. The car passengers boiled out of their hot vehicles, mixing with the pedestrians on the fantail. Bailey absent-mindedly stowed his radio under the seat, then joined the crowd for the spectacular view of the glowing Manhattan skyline. W and Hawkins followed. As they passed each car they methodically checked for passengers. No one remained in the dark tunnel through the center of the ship.

A jolt. The ferry started moving away from the pier. A cool harbor breeze began sweeping through the ship. Several women clutched the ballooning skirts of their light summer dresses, holding their straw hats with one white-gloved hand. Several pairs of eyes found Hawkins. His eyes stayed locked on Bailey, an increasingly dark, tense expression on his face. The women drifted away.

A quarter mile out Hawkins motioned to W. "I'm going to tell him I scratched his car. Draw him back."

"I'll wait here."

"Right. But give me the gun." W hesitated. "We can't risk you." He nodded, palming off the .38 into Hawkins' coat pocket. Hawkins walked up behind Bailey, tapping him on the shoulder. He carefully flattened his accent. "Excuse me. You own a black Cord convertible? I think I scratched your door."

"Oh Christ! I've barely had it three months!"

"Hey, I'm sorry! Let's go back and take a look. Maybe we can settle it up."

Bailey stamped down the dark tunnel glowering at Hawkins. When they reached the Cord Bailey bent over, peering at his door.

"Where?"

"Here." Hawkins pointed the snub-nosed Colt straight at Bailey's chest. W kicked his door open, blocking Bailey's path. "Just be a good sport and get in the car." Hawkins flipped open the Cord's door, the pistol low against his hip where it couldn't be seen.

Bailey froze, hovering in indecision. Then glimpsed the people at the end of the tunnel. A hopeful expression telegraphed it all: It's a bluff. He won't shoot. Or so Bailey thought. He pivoted, ducked his head and tried ramming his way back to the safety of the crowd on the stern. But the second he turned Hawkins caught him in the stomach with a quick left uppercut. Bailey doubled over, every ounce of air knocked out of what felt like a crushed chest. He desperately tried shouting for help. Nothing came but a strained wheeze. Hawkins hit him twice more as hard as he could. Bailey collapsed on the deck. Hawkins picked him up by the belt and flung him in the Cord's trunk. W stood up on the running board, checking for witnesses. Then he jumped down to snap a pair of handcuffs on Bailey's wrists. Hawkins slammed the trunk shut.

"Not too hard. What now?" Hawkins said.

"I wish I knew what was in that transmission." The lights of Staten Island were growing large through the end of the tunnel.

"Remember the intercept? He wants more money. That's our in. He's not a true believer."

"I hate the idea of bargaining with him."

"Maybe we won't need to."

-24-

Twenty miles off Sandy Hook the dirty greenish-brown waters of the New York Bight rolled steadily over a black form resting silently on the ocean floor. A barge from the New York City Department of Sanitation cruised by in the distance, ready to dump its cargo. The ocean actually fizzed slightly, like seltzer, from all the rotting garbage on the sea floor, rendering the water as opaque as pea soup, the perfect hiding place. A wispy radio mast quivered above the waves, a seeming piece of flotsam.

Kapitänleutnant Fritz Eberling, commander of Kriegsmarine Unterseebooten 56, waited in his cabin, listening on a pair of headphones to a live broadcast of the Metropolitan Opera's performance of *Il Barbiere di Siviglia*. He kept a careful eye on the clock in his diminutive cabin—would there be a transmission today? The orchestral thunderstorm had ended and Count Almaviva and Figaro were climbing a ladder to Rosina's balcony. He closed his eyes, trying to imagine the staging. *Could there be any way to get the schedules in advance?* he wondered. *I could bring some librettos from home.*

Radioman Niesen came padding down the passageway. The porky sailor stood outside, filling the hatch, and handed in Bailey's radio message. Enough opera for the day.

Eberling handed him the headphones back, grabbing the paper, poking Niesen in the belly with it. "Too much sitting, hey, Willy?"

"Aye, Aye, sir," laughing, "too much sitting." He saluted and took off for his station. Eberling walked out to the chart table, leaning into the light, mulling their position.

So. Six freighters plus escorts. Busy night, tonight, he thought.

The small convoy didn't match the glamour of a big fish like an ocean liner or a battleship that most skippers were always keen for. But to Eberling it didn't matter. After all, whether large or small, when he'd fired their last nine torpedoes—he'd already fired one off Bermuda—he was free to sail home.

Studying the chart and the sailing times, he marked out a general area where he planned to lurk and wait, about seven kilometers off Rockaway Point, a bit outside the United States' three-mile territorial limit. The convoy was heading northeast to the British Isles. It'd exit the harbor and bear hard to port, hugging the coast, close to US waters but still necessarily outside.

He waved to the exec. "Time to wake the crew." No more than a minute later the chiefs started quickly moving down the boat, gently shaking awake the sleepy crewmen in their claustrophobic berths over the torpedoes. Within five minutes they had the entire crew milling about in their felt boots, either lining up for breakfast or checking the long banks of batteries that powered the boat across the ocean floor like a silent shadow.

-25-

Hawkins drove the Cord off first, gunning it, speeding past the little houses of St. George. In the middle of a dingy commercial strip he swerved over in front of a small deli. W drove in behind and waited. A minute later Hawkins jumped back in the Cord carrying a small brown bag. He sped off again. A couple of fast turns, a long street up a hill. He veered into a cemetery and slowly drove down into a wooded section behind a large mausoleum.

No haste now, the brisk, businesslike manner gone. Hawkins got out slowly, almost leisurely walking around the car, taking his time. He stopped, eyes searching a point off by the side of the road. As he stared his shoulders noticeably sagged, his expressionless, mute face followed, a numb look. Looking down at the ground, slightly shaking his head, chin almost on his chest. Then he abruptly turned, snapping up the trunk lip, jabbing Bailey with the barrel of the .38.

"Get out," in a flat voice. "Get out of there," an emotionless monotone. Then something happened. A switch thrown. Or the lightning from a hidden storm front found its rod, firing all its pent-up energy down to earth. His face blank, Hawkins' voice began rising, "Get—out. Out! Fucking bastards. All of you! Sons of bitches. Now. Get! Out! Now you bloody fucker!"

Hawkins didn't merely drag Bailey from the trunk. He ripped him out, banging Bailey's head into the latch. Hawkins ran him hard a few paces and flung him face-first into the gravel in front of the other car's headlights. W moved a step forward, an uncertain look on his face.

"Roy …?"

A split-second delay. Hawkins picked Bailey halfway up. Threw him as hard as he could face-first into gravel again. Stood over him a second. Stepped away. Swung back. Kicked Bailey as hard as he could.

W ran forward, shouting, "Roy! No! Christ almighty! Stop it! That's enough—" He reached them just as Hawkins lifted Bailey by the jacket collar, hurling him back toward the lip of the Cord's trunk. W crashed into them, knocking them forward, uneasily half tackling Hawkins. He tightly grasped his arm and elbow, holding on, unsure whether to pull him away or not.

Disoriented, blinking from the headlights, Bailey's face shone white with fear. The bluster shown on the ferry had vanished. Now the clerk's voice quavered when he spoke, like a child's.

"Please—please don't kill me—you want money? I've got money—in my wallet—you can have it! There's a lot there, please! For gawd's sakes, whatta you want?"

The hand on the elbow checked something in Hawkins. He took a deep breath. Took a step back. A second passed. He loosely shook off W's hand, his face completely expressionless. Stared down at Bailey. Then gazed at W.

Hawkins nodded at W, reassuring him. Hawkins stepped back to Bailey, ready for what came next.

-26-

"We're not interested in money. We know who you are, Bailey. What you're doing. Who you're doing it for."

Harold Bailey had carelessness at the center of his character. In all the time he'd spent practicing the business of selling secrets he'd never once paused to consider the risks his chosen profession posed. His only concern, easy money. Now he knew better. Not the sure thing he'd anticipated. Overwhelmed by this sudden reality, his chin began quivering.

"Oh gawd, oh gawd!"

"Shut up! We're not killing you."

"Please!"

W slowly eased back into the shadows, watching carefully, but letting Hawkins carry the interrogation.

"Now, we're going to give you a choice," Hawkins said. "It's a real choice. Cooperate with us. You won't be harmed. I promise you. Or, we lock you in the trunk and call the FBI. They're going to be very interested in that little radio set of yours. What'll it be? It's up to you."

"Who are you?" Bailey turned his head, desperately, imploringly, looking for W to pull Hawkins away and save him. Hawkins poked him with the gun.

"You know who we are, don't you?" Bailey finally caught the accent.

He quickly ducked his face down. "Do you know what you're chancing here, Bailey? Right now the US is still neutral. So that's what? Five to ten in Alcatraz? Do you know what five years on the Rock would be like? The sea damp creeps up the walls and the foghorns blow all night long. You're never dry and you never sleep.

"And you're taking your chances there. If the US is still neutral when you're sentenced, you'll get ten, but suppose the US gets in the war first? Remember the *Lusitania*? One big liner goes down like the last time. Bang, the US gets in the war. And here *you* are sending signals to enemy submarines. You know what that means?" Hawkins poked him with the gun again.

Bailey barely shook his head, his eyes focused on a distant tombstone. Hawkins angled in, pushing into his face.

"Once the US starts fighting, that little box with the wires coming out isn't a trifling violation of the Neutrality Act. It's espionage." Another poke. Bailey's mouth hung wide open, panting more from stress than pain or the effort of the fight. "That's the death penalty. You know how they do it in this country, in the federal prisons?" Bailey tried an indifferent shrug but only managed to hike up a single shoulder. "Electrocution. After they give you your last meal a trustee barber comes in and shaves your head. You have to pay him a quarter for that. Then they take you out to the chair and strap you down with thick leather belts. A guard brings in a heavy braided copper cable with a clamp on the end. He bolts it to your ankle with a lug wrench. It cuts right in. After that they come in with the helmet."

Hawkins reached through the car window into the paper bag he'd bought at the deli. He pulled out a jar of kosher gherkins. "Before they put it on you they pour brine over your shaved head so the metal plate in the top of the helmet makes a good contact with your scalp." With that Hawkins cracked the lid with a soft pop. He began slowly dribbling the pickle juice over Bailey's crown. The liquid ran down over his face. A pickle skipped off Bailey's forehead and bounced off his nose without his noticing. "It runs in your eyes and burns."

Bailey furiously blinked, twitching his head. It did!

"And on goes the helmet," Hawkins said. "It goes right over your eyes and ears so you can't hear or see a thing." Hawkins dropped the paper deli bag over Bailey's eyes. "The last thing you sense in this world is the smell of brine dripping off the end of your nose." Hawkins held the trigger down, pulled back the .38's hammer, waited a second. Then he let it go an inch behind Bailey's head. The shot resounded like a thunderclap in the deserted cemetery.

With a convulsive *YELP* Bailey sprang off the trunk. He landed facedown in the gravel, chest and legs furiously swimming. Hawkins grabbed his jacket collar with both hands, dragged him back up onto the trunk, handed W the Colt, snapped the bag off and walked away.

W put one foot up on the bumper, tilted his hat back and leaned into Bailey's face. He spoke in a low, smooth, confidential tone, gently waving the pistol. "Don't be stupid. The man's making a very generous offer. What do you do this for? For money, right? You're not a believer, are you? For Hitler? For *him?* If you go to jail, what good's the money?" Bailey barely shook his head. The vein in his neck pulsed more. "Can you cancel that signal?"

Bailey finally spoke. "No. Too late. I signed off." He began slowly calming down.

"Good. That's better. Where'd it go?"

"Submarine off the coast."

"Which one?"

"Don't know. They change all the time."

"They signal back?"

"No. It's only a transmitter."

W glanced at Hawkins and nodded. Almost everything he wanted. One more push.

"How much they pay you, Bailey? What's a car like that cost, eleven, twelve hundred?" Bailey nodded. "And who brings the money?"

Bailey hesitated. "A German businessman. Name's Hans Ludwig. Don't see him that often."

"Ludwig!" Hawkins swung around and over, leaning into Bailey's face next to W. "Hans Ludwig? A doctor?"

86

"Not a medical one. I don't think—"

"Has a small beard, rather like a goatee?"

"Uh-huh."

"Maybe fifty?"

"Right."

"Straight black hair?"

"That's him."

"I'll be damned!" Hawkins stepped away, turning his back to Bailey, facing W, raising his eyebrows, then mouthed "*wow.*" In seconds his whole expression, voice, demeanor, even his posture had changed slightly. The dead look vanished, an intrigued, questioning gaze replacing it, voice quickening as he straightened up.

"When do you meet him again?" W said.

"Seven weeks."

"Very good." W nodded back to Hawkins. He shoved Bailey back into the Cord's trunk. "That's enough for now. If you make so much as a peep, I'll drive this damn thing off a bridge."

Hawkins pulled Bailey's belt off and buckled his feet to a strut in the trunk. Bailey seemed comically relieved, obligingly squirming into position. It was proof somehow they weren't going to hand him over to the Bureau, or worse. Hawkins, the inquisitive smile still on his face, lightly closed the trunk without a word, as if it contained nothing more important than old laundry, then stood in front of it, hands on his hips, whistling softly.

-27-

Hawkins picked up the pickles, munching on one, offering another to W. They began walking across and down the gravel lane.

"What's that doctor business about?" W said.

"I found the name Ludwig in a matchbook on one of the men who jumped me in Lisbon. Then a Hans Ludwig showed up on the plane. Claimed he was a Swiss insurance executive. Former professor."

"Huh! He's not Swiss."

"Not a chance."

"You didn't give anything up. That was good," W said.

Hawkins offered W another pickle. "I'm glad he didn't call our bluff."

"We were bluffing?"

"What do you mean, Bill?"

"Some rather rough stuff there—"

"No. For show."

"That was an act?"

"I had to rattle him."

"All of it was an act?"

"Yes. You have to convince them you mean it."

"Maybe you've been watching too many gangster movies—'You're never dry and you never sleep'?"

"No. You have to find a shortcut, go for the senses, hit the gut. Can't try and reason with him. No time. The senses are a more direct path to the mind. Sensation distracts him from what he's thinking, breaks his train of thought. Sea damp and brine. Not really hurt him."

"Throwing him around?"

Hawkins drifted to a stop, a pickle hovering in midflight, his hand shaking ever so slightly. "That, too."

W stared at him skeptically. "I hope so. Remember—"

"Yeah, I know. No ticking the Yanks off. What'll we do with him?" He popped the pickle in his mouth.

"Think I'll have that new fellow who picked you up—Ian Fleming's his name, he's a naval officer, just came over—have him drive Bailey to Canada. He needs some experience."

"We're there, too?"

"Yes. The RCMP will hold him. He'll be working for us before that seven-week payday comes around."

"Mounties!" Hawkins laughed. "Oh, brilliant! There's a lot of boot to lick."

"Indeed. We'll give you cover as a civilian employee of the commercial section of the consulate here in NY."

"Good. Thanks."

"I have a contact at the FBI. See if you can bluff out of him how Ludwig entered the country. What's your take on him?"

"Very high-level type. That lout in the trunk's the tip of a good-sized iceberg, whatever the hell it is. Ludwig probably sent that letter Bermuda found."

W wrote a note on a card and tore it off. "I agree. Here's the name of that Bureau contact."

Hawkins studied it. "Is this safe?"

"I think so. I know, it's a bit unusual, contacting the locals. You do have to be careful. Obviously, it's quite the sham. He'll suspect everything and know he can't prove anything. It'll be an interesting little dance."

"Only going to be here a couple of weeks. By the time—"

"Think about that. Meanwhile, remember, while you're here, you're undercover. Don't draw attention to yourself. Whoever knew you in the past. They're all off-limits. They all could ask dangerous questions."

"I figured I'd be back in Europe now anyway. Nothing new."

"No, it's completely new. The real danger here is feeling at home in your father's country. You don't have the cues of a foreign society to keep you on edge, keep you alert. You've got to act like a stranger to keep your guard up. It's the only way to stay safe."

"I can handle it. It's temporary anyway." They stopped walking. "You said the Americans don't turn people. It doesn't occur to them—well, to be cynical—that Bailey merely took the initiative in penetrating Ludwig's ring?"

"No. They don't reflect on what a huge investment a mole represents. How hard it is. The time. The money. The energy. With us, if Bailey agreed to con his former employers and kept it up, he might get a medal for all the lives and ships he saved. The very idea'd probably give the Bureau hives."

"That's what I call irony. We have to be the ones to keep Ludwig from being arrested."

"That's it. The last thing we want is to start from scratch finding Ludwig's replacement. This FBI man can save you hours of tedious legwork, but you've got to be careful not to let on too much. We'll tip off Ludwig ourselves, if we have to, to keep him from being arrested. He'll recontact Germany eventually. Bermuda will pick it up and we'll get back on his trail."

"Right."

"So. We're done. Why don't you relax tonight. Have a drink, go see a picture. Remember, no calling friends, relatives, girls."

"Right."

"By the way. How'd you know about this place?"

Hawkins gestured with a pickle down at a Veterans Benefits Administration headstone in front of him.

WILBUR EMERSON HAWKINS
COMPANY A, 14TH NEW YORK INFANTRY
1891–1937

Under the name was engraved a small Purple Heart.

"Ah. I see," W said.

"Didn't bring any flowers." Hawkins put the jar down in front of the stone. "Maybe this will do."

"I'm sure your father won't mind."

"No. He won't."

"A pickle jar. How'd you ever think to interrogate a man with a pickle jar?"

Hawkins shrugged, took the Cord and drove off back to the ferry. W watched him go, unloaded the .38 and started laughing, a relieved, happy laugh.

-28-

With nightfall the heat of the day broke. People began pouring onto the avenues to catch a cool breeze off the harbor. Hawkins strolled down Broadway through the nightclub district. *A movie*, he thought. *Maybe a cold beer. Been a hot day.* Enthusiasm was lacking, though. The cemetery, that's what had done it. That was always a sobering trip.

He reached Times Square and the explosion of lights and neon overhead. The Planters Peanuts man, glasses of Coca-Cola, a Gulliver-sized cancan dancer flipping her neon skirt all riotously fought for attention. Not a sight like it in the world. Impossible to resist. He finally started to grin. Amazing. But then—

New York had no blackout, unlike London or Paris. Seeing the lights on was normal. But normal now felt deeply strange. And that was strange itself.

A man his age pushed by. A girl with red hair brushing her shoulders in time with her hips curled her arm through her date's. Their eyes danced together as they walked. They disappeared in the crowd. That was New York at night. Times Square, life, exuberance, the sense of possibility. Only not tonight, not for him. Or any night here, for him.

The news ticker wrapping around the Times building posted a news flash: LONDON BOMBED. The sense of strangeness wound up some more. *East End must be catching hell*, Hawkins thought. Another news flash rounded the ticker. WILKIE TIES ROOSEVELT. The election. It was close. *Houghton, W,* *they were right.* The chilling sense of strangeness rose again.

Past Forty-Fifth Street he hurried by the front of the Hotel Astor. Inside the lobby loitered the usual gathering of young men and women waiting to meet their dates. Dainty hats with wispy veils crowned neat summer hair and dresses bursting with flowers.

Hawkins thought of the man with the redhead again. *Probably came from here. Could I hustle someone else's date?* W's little brief popped back to mind. No fraternization.

He slipped into the plush lobby, idly wandering around, scanning the crowd. The feeling he had that morning, watching people through the deli window, returned full force. The glass was still there. Impenetrable, all around him. Who were these people? They still felt impossible to touch or reach, as far away as a movie star on a screen. He circled around and left.

A blue and silver satin banner fluttered down the high window of the Paramount Theatre. AIR-CONDITIONING. The marquee proclaimed, THE GREAT MCGINTY, PLUS CAB CALLOWAY AND HIS COTTON CLUB ORCHESTRA. *That's it. A midnight show.* He hurried into line. A nearby store selling radios had speakers blaring onto the sidewalk. As he moved along Hawkins heard a familiar voice.

"Thank God, the polls have Wilkie ahead, folks. But I'm not surprised." Ventnor again. "After all, Wilkie's not accusing Roosevelt of anything. A third term is gonna mean 'dictatorship and war.' We've got to stick to Americans and Americanism. The only threat we face is from Washington. They're our biggest problem. They actually want a war so they have an excuse to take us all over and run everybody else's lives. All their gab about the so-called clear and present danger is a ploy to make us shut up and go along with their big government schemes."

The people in line seemed to be oblivious of Ventnor. Or were they merrily distracted, seized by the indifference of a night on the town? Occasionally a couple would whoop and flip out of line and back with a quick snappy dance step. They seemed happy, not angry like Ventnor. No escaping the broadcast, though.

"You know, folks, a day or two after President Rosenfeld and his pointy-headed friends, all those so-called in-tee-lectuals, the big Jewish bankers, they're all in cahoots with the British royal family—they own half the world, along with the Masons—they proposed repealing the Neutrality Act. We let you know and you did the right thing. Yessir. Tons of angry letters swamped Congress. Why, Senator Wagner alone got twenty thousand letters in a single day. That really stunned them down there, I'll tell ya."

By now the line had finally snaked through the cavernous lobby into the huge theater. The multistoried chandeliers dimmed and winked out, hushing the crowd. The curtains rolled back with a fanfare. In recognition of the growing patriotic mood the projectionist put up a rippling picture of the Stars and Stripes accompanied by a medley of patriotic music.

The crowd stood, singing. Hawkins heard a familiar tune and rotely followed along. "God save our gracious King, long live …"

People around him began turning and staring. He flinched and nearly dropped his popcorn—*My God*, Hawkins thought. *I've been singing "God Save the King," not "My Country 'Tis of Thee."* He chimed in at the last stanza, extra loud, "From every mountaintop, let … uh … freedom ring."

The music segued to "America the Beautiful." The man in front of him stiffly spun around, fists clenched. "Wise guy!" He stood a second. Then, as if not knowing what to do or say, repeated it, louder, shouting over the music, "Wise guy!" The rebuke retribution itself. Hawkins froze, waiting in horror. What next? *Oh no. They're going to call the usher.* But the music segued to a rousing rendition of the "Star-Spangled Banner." The man instantly spun back to join in.

When it was over Hawkins squeezed down into his seat, mind racing. *My God. How could I have done that? Quite the secret agent I am. This is the Paramount, not the Odeon. Times Square, not Leicester! A slipup like that at the wrong moment—could wind up dead. W was right. I don't have the cues of a foreign society to keep me sharp.*

The curtain rose on the stage show. An explosive cord. The band started up. A huge *whoop* rose through the audience. Dozens of young couples sprang into the aisles. *Watching other people dance—ugh*, Hawkins thought. *Should've gone back to the hotel.* He glanced down at his still feet for a moment, then up at the dancers. *Righto. Time to go.* But the aisles were packed. Another ruckus to get out. He grudgingly eyed the dancers, then began actually paying attention. *What?*

Swing hadn't really crossed the Atlantic yet, at least not to the Continent. In Europe the latest thing was still Dixieland. This was new. All new. The sound. The dance style. Wilder. More energetic. Startlingly more sexual.

A man in a white satin suit dripping with sequins leapt onstage and threw his arms up. Cab Calloway. A huge roar from the crowd. He began whirling and spinning, one leaping acrobatic dance step on another, waving his arms and baton, cranking up the tempo, grinning widely, long hair flopping over his forehead. The music, the beat, thunderous.

A white satin suit. Sequins. Outrageous. A defiant, outlaw quality to it, lewd and rebellious. The dancers in the aisles matching him step for step. Loose and free, boys spinning the girls out and around. A different move every time, chiming along *Hi-dee hi-dee hi-dee hi ho—*

If I'd stayed at NYU, I'd know all this, Hawkins thought. Painful realizations began dawning.

In school in England I was always the Yank. Saw myself that way, too. Well, because they all said so. The outsider. They made me feel that way. Something exotic. Always different. Different accent, whatever. The other boys picking on me, when I let them. The girls, standoffish, wary. Then there was Will Wanders, big kid, big knuckles. Used to wait outside of school, pick a fight all the time. Had to fight, had to get tough. Mother used to sigh so when I came home all dirty with torn clothes. At university, over here, it was better, but still. The girls all loved the way I talked, the accent. But in the end, it all said, "You are different. You don't fit in. You don't belong."

How much time have I actually spent here in the States? A bit out of touch. Well, more than a bit. That's why the music, the dancers and Ventnor caught me so off guard.

But he began happily clapping along with the music. Like the lights outside, the music was impossible to resist.

-29-

Kapitänleutnant Fritz Eberling rocked back and forth as the U-56 rolled gently on a swell. Fresh air roared through his head. Manhattan's reflected lights glowed like an aurora over the bow. *What glories lay behind them?* he wondered. *Girls. Champagne. Music. But we'll have an entertaining time tonight.*

Off to starboard the lights of the Rockaways glimmered, tantalizingly close, individual streetlights a white necklace lining the dark shore, the neon marquees of stores and yellow house lights barely visible. A passing car's headlights traced the shore road. To port the Sandy Hook light winked across the sky, followed by the West Bank light off the bow.

Rubbing his eyes, he squinted through the binoculars again. Out there, between him and the lights of the city, steamed six British and Canadian ships and a pair of escorts. If he didn't go blind from eyestrain first, and if his luck held, he'd see the ships silhouetted against the glowing horizon. They'd be running dark, without lights.

He called down to the soundman, "Any pings?" The exec shook his head. Eberling grunted. Too bad.

Convoy commanders had basically two tactics. They could run for it or take a defensive approach and use sonar. That meant stopping dead in the water periodically because the ship's engine noise and particularly cavitation, a singing sound caused by the propellers, drowned out the sonar pings. They'd travel a few miles, stop their props, ping, and when the coast looked clear, proceed.

But to Eberling the pings were as happy a beacon as an East Frisian lighthouse. A pinging convoy was practically crawling—fat hens squawking for a plucking.

No pings meant they were running for it. Some kapitäns preferred attacking submerged, relying on their quiet electric motors to intercept ships—much safer. But the electrics ran slow. Running on batteries meant sinking one ship but no more. Eberling wanted to maximize his chances and use his fast diesels. The U-56 had five torpedo tubes, four forward and one astern. Since it took a painful half hour per tube to restow the crew's gear, unbolt each new fish from the hull and slide it in the launcher, each torpedo had to count.

A shape flicked against the glowing horizon through the binoculars— ships or a tic? His eyes were watering now. No. Ships. Too soon to tell their direction. He paused a minute, waiting, resting his eyes. Opening them, he looked again. The ships were definitely there and moving fast. The lights at the tip of Rockaway Point winked out as a dark wave passed, obscuring them, thirty-five degrees off the starboard bow, about six kilometers away.

"Battle stations." The deck crew loitering below him in the darkness instantly began stowing the cannon and the two aft antiaircraft guns. Inside the boat others latched up and secured the berths and bunks. Eberling peered through the binoculars again. The convoy turned hard east once it cleared the harbor and the three-mile limit. Plotting their path on a mental map, he slid down the ladder.

"Periscope depth." The boat's deck tipped slightly down as it sliced beneath the waves, the crew standing at their positions bathed in red light, waiting and watching for the next order. Eberling took off his uniform blazer and cap, leaving him without any symbol of rank on his turtleneck sweater. They knew the familiar ritual well. U-boat crews became as close as families and he didn't need to assert rank. The boat leveled off.

"Up periscope." Eberling swung the 'scope around, relocating the convoy by the shadows passing the shore lights, exactly at its expected location. After several tense minutes they arrived in position directly in front of the convoy, turned ninety degrees, bearing east, and slowed to three knots, just keeping pace with the current.

They listened breathlessly to the growing rumble of the approaching ships. Eberling motioned to the helmsman to move slightly to starboard, adjusting their positions on the sound alone, centering them in the convoy's path, and stopped their motors. At the right moment Eberling nodded to a rating and the sailor gradually pulled a lever, slowly blowing the tanks as quietly as possible. The U-boat's diesel clanked to life when they broke the surface. He sprang up the reopened hatch. With her diesels running the U-56 easily matched the convoy's speed.

No reaction showed from the ships. They'd penetrated undetected, their engine noise masked in the rumble of the group. On each side steamed two freighters less than a thousand feet apart. Two more sailed in line ahead, two behind.

"Hard to port." The U-56 quickly swung to north, pointing its sharp bow at the black shape of a ship at almost point-blank range. Missing would be nearly impossible.

"Fire number one." The torpedo chugged out the number one tube. "Hard starboard." The boat swung sharply southward until it again pointed directly at a ship.

"Fire number two." Another torpedo shot out. Only seconds had passed. "Hard port again."

At that moment the first torpedo struck home. A brilliant flash lit the water with an eerie greenish glow all around and under the ships, fading out into the ocean, silhouetting the dark hulls, suspending them in air for a long moment. A tremendous concussion thundered through the water, the boat and into the soles of their feet. As they swung to port he fired the two fish remaining in the front tubes at the ships in line ahead. The starboard torpedo found its mark, lighting the ocean with another green circle, floating the dark ship in midair.

The escorts on the outside crashed into action, launching dazzling white star shells with a cracking pop, bathing the convoy and the U-56 in a harsh bluish light, reversing the light from under the water to over it. The escort's gun crews pivoted around and opened fire, quickly dropping a pair of shells perilously close to the U-56's hull, throwing up two huge white columns of phosphorescent spray.

Ears ringing from the explosions, the kapitän abandoned firing the rear tube and half-climbed, half-fell down the conning tower hatch into the control room.

"Crash dive!" *Those two shells were a bit close*, he thought. *The Brits are improving.* The diving planes rammed the U-56 under. The crew heard the distant thud of the third torpedo striking home. They counted, waiting, but no fourth hit resounded. A miss. The kapitän shrugged and began shaking hands all around. Three ships in six minutes? Not bad. Not bad at all. And they still had nine fish left.

-30-

The midday heat and humidity on the street steadily crawled up into the nineties. Roiling eddies of burning sausage and bacon fumes acridly mixed with billowing clouds of traffic exhaust. It all churned together, suffocating, weighty. Hawkins gingerly rested against the white enameled wall outside a Nedick's luncheonette on Herald Square, testing for a clean spot with his fingers. There weren't any. Filthy. Greasy. Impossible to ignore the revolting stench.

Several drivers crawling by in the traffic began angrily beating their fists on their horns, their mouths wide open like baby birds panting from the heat. Then the noise stopped dead. All the mouths gaped at a solitary yellow Packard gliding along the street. Its windows were rolled up, the only air-conditioned car on the market, drawing a wake of jealous awe behind it. Several of the men actually hung an elbow out their windows, angling their heads out to watch.

Hawkins missed it. He'd just spotted his contact, Special Agent in Charge Mike Kelly, striding up the street a half block away.

The FBI's director, J. Edgar Hoover, ran the Bureau like a personal fief and it mirrored all his well-known eccentricities, which were considerable. It might have been a sweltering Manhattan August but Kelly came tricked out in full FBI regalia: dark fedora, dark wool suit, a topcoat, and best of all, white socks. Rivulets of sweat ran down Kelly's face. A raw band of prickly heat erupted above his visibly damp shirt collar. From his expression Kelly was not in a good mood.

They both had a copy of the *Daily News* opened to the same page, Kelly's suggestion. *Needn't have bothered*, Hawkins thought. A ten-year-old could spot Kelly, his rig and demeanor that ludicrously obvious. Might as well wear a signboard proclaiming PLAINCLOTHES COPPER. An upward twitch started itching Hawkins' cheek. *No, no*, he thought. *Need that stiff upper lip now. Won't do to crack a smile, not even a little one.*

Kelly offered his sweaty hand and gestured inside. As they sat down Hawkins bent forward, carefully avoiding the sticky green linoleum tabletop to see if Kelly sported the usual suspenders. Yep. There they were, along with a bulging .45-caliber Colt revolver in a shoulder holster. A hogleg indeed. Big as brick.

Hawkins ordered a cup of tea, Kelley coffee. He got right to business.

"What can I do for you, Mr. Hawkins?"

"I've been hired by the British consulate here in New York to represent their commercial interests. I felt it'd be a good idea to check in with you. We may be crossing paths occasionally since I'll be handling shipping and the like."

Kelly leaned forward in the booth, hands clasped, manner short but correct. He watched Hawkins with a steady, expressionless gaze, his voice a featureless and unrevealing monotone.

"Yeah, I guess that's right. I'm really glad to know there's another foreign *representative* on my beat. I've got the Limeys, the Krauts, the Wops, the Japs, the Frogs—oh, wait, we lost them along the way—the Reds, and then there's the Irish mob, the Italian mob, the Jewish mob, our usual bank robbers, embezzlers, forgers, white slavers. It's a nice list. They keep me busy. Thank you for coming."

"Ah—Yes ... As you know, through our various operations overseas we may periodically come into the possession of information that might be of interest to the FBI."

"What do you have today?"

"Nothing at the moment." Kelly's eyes narrowed a fraction. "However, I want you to know if—when—I come across anything of interest to the Bureau, I will personally bring it to you first."

Kelly's whole manner and expression subtly changed, leaning back in the booth, easing slightly.

"All right, yeah. I'd appreciate that." A waitress brought the tea and coffee. Kelly smirked. "I must say, Mr. Hawkins, you seem a little savvier than the last one. He came around demanding all kinds of stuff without offering a damn thing."

"We really want to promote cooperation."

Hawkins saw that puzzled expression again. *Here it comes*, he thought. *The Question.*

"Who the hell are you? Where you from? England? Canada? You look more like a slick executive type, not a government man."

Hawkins told him. American father. English mother.

"Okay. Where's your residence then? You going back there, London, after the war, I mean?"

"I might stay here."

"You vote here?"

"No. I've never actually voted anywhere. Always been on the road."

"What are you then?"

"Well—I'm—" Hawkins stopped. "Anglo American."

"But what country are you loyal to? You're working for them, aren't you?"

"Yes. As a civilian employee. But I don't see my loyalties as necessarily mutually exclusive."

"But if you're a loyal, patriotic American, how can you work for a foreign power? How can you have it both ways?" *Not an unfair question*, Hawkins thought. Not even an unfamiliar one. *Asked myself exactly that more than once.*

Hawkins twisted his head slightly, silently straining for an answer. *He knows the score, and I can't possibly tell Kelly I only plan on staying for a couple of weeks. He won't be bothered.*

But Kelly finally seemed to sense he'd pushed far enough and backed off. He pulled out a pack of Lucky Strikes and offered Hawkins one. Hawkins said, "No, thanks," and took out his pipe and pouch instead.

"What you doing now?" Kelly said, waving his lit lighter so close Hawkins could feel the heat on his nose. "And don't you dare bullshit me, I know Stephenson sent you."

And so we dance, Hawkins thought.

-31-

"Research. We're making an inventory of German business interests," Hawkins said. "See who might become involved in efforts to infiltrate espionage agents and saboteurs into Canada and the UK using neutral countries like the US."

Kelly drained his cup, tilting his head back, raising his eyebrows slightly. A crooked smile crossed his face. "And you have no interest in the activities of these potential Nazi agents or saboteurs here?"

"Our mandate is the security of Britain and Canada. And British shipping worldwide, of course."

"Ah, yessir. Slipping agents through here would indeed violate the Neutrality Act. Okay, you've read the law. So who's attracting your interest? Right now." A polite order, but an order.

The tricky part. After a moment of feigned surprise, anxiety and indecision, Hawkins tried to *seemingly* make a leap of confidence.

"Very well. We have—allegations, only—against a certain Hans Ludwig. That he might be aware of certain types of activities. I think it's more likely he knows who does."

"Oh, yeah, we're aware of him!" Kelly's tone boastingly blasé. "The new commercial rep from the Reich Trade Ministry."

The dodge had worked. An official commercial representative. *That's a little more than we expected,* Hawkins thought. *Ludwig might have traveled on a Swiss passport but obviously didn't enter on one, then. One more little piece—*

"Yes, but he bears a routine check—even if he is traveling officially."

"Oh, well, that doesn't mean anything. Very busy fellow. There's a big meeting at the Waldorf Astoria tonight. He's one of the speakers. Regular star."

And there we are, Hawkins thought, *official cover.* It would be interesting to know exactly where in his luggage Ludwig hid his diplomatic passport. Maybe it never left his person.

"What kind of meeting?"

"It's a jumble of right-wing, pro-Nazi types and isolationists. The German-American Bund helped set it up for them. Officially it's a neutrality rally but the German government's using it to concentrate on businessmen here. Perfectly legal and up and up as far as we can tell."

"I'd still like to check him out."

"That'd be a good idea." Kelly glanced at his watch, then blandly announced, "I've gotta get going. Got an interstate stolen-car case to investigate in New Jersey." Kelly jotted on a napkin and pushed it to Hawkins. "Here's his address at the Waldorf."

"The Waldorf? *The Waldorf?* He's staying there?"

Kelly seemed intrigued at that little slip, smiling slightly. He grabbed a wad of napkins from the dispenser, wiping his face and hands. "I tell ya, they got dough to burn."

"They must. Thank you."

Kelly threw the napkins down, started to leave, then settled back down again and added, quite unthreateningly, "I'll try and see you there."

"Good."

Hawkins watched him go. *What to make of that?* he thought. Kelly's manner's maddeningly opaque. And yet this man, obviously a highly experienced officer, let drop a seemingly pointless story about chasing stolen cars. Hawkins remembered an old Service joke he'd once heard, "There are two things you tell your wife—when you get a transfer and when you get a cut in pay."

So I'm on notice. Kelly plans on following me. But he's letting me know that. Also the fact he has other claims on his time. Taking advantage of the situation, after a fashion. See what I come up with. That's fine with me. Out front's exactly where I want to be.

-32-

A double row of police black-and-whites stretched up Park Avenue. The cabbie's eyes disappeared behind a bushy, gray frown. With a loud cough he spat a stream of cigar juice at the corner of Forty-Eighth Street.

"That's it, pal. End of the line. No fare pays for trouble."

A tremendous, echoing mob swarmed around the Waldorf Astoria like an army of ants trying to carry away a stupendous bauble with spires.

Hawkins ran up, pushing to the front of the throng. He peeked through the crowd past a police line and across the street. A densely packed mass of neutrality supporters milled around behind another police line on the opposite curb, nervously trying to edge away from a small clutch of about fifty young uniformed "storm troopers." They had brown outfits similar to German Sturmabteilung uniforms, complete with caps and boots. Only no swastika armbands or insignia.

The would-be storm troopers were rapidly strutting up and down, leather belts striping their puffed-out chests. A loud taunt rang from across the street. They defiantly snapped their arms out in a sieg heil salute, arm arched, hand down. Then they cupped hands to mouth, shouting back.

A motley group of counterdemonstrators teemed behind the nearer police line, facing the empty street between them. A mix of anti-Nazi factions—labor unions, WWI veterans, Zionists, Hebrew fraternal associations, Trotskyites and several generic factions of socialists—all rudely contended for the crowd's allegiance. People fluidly surged up and down the line like gawkers at a circus midway. They'd briefly take in a speaker, who mainly seemed interested in attacking the other protesters, then excitedly drift on.

The police riot squads pushed backward, their arms linked into a human dam, braced against the emotional tide. Their feet scrabbled for a grip on the slippery pavement, sealing off the hotel. By now, both lines of blue were slowly shifting into squiggles from two angry crowds thudding against them in waves.

Behind the lines of cops demonstrators assaulted each other from the safety of the "barricades," lobbing eggs and rotting vegetables at the other side. Mounted patrolmen rode the empty street. Their broad, mostly Irish faces were red with anger as they ducked the slime from the flying produce dripping on their caps. A vastly larger group of spectators hovered farther up the block, passively gaping at the fuss. Enraged screams and insults pierced the crowd's deafening rumble.

It's all so very familiar, Hawkins thought, *that quality I've seen so often before.* Chaos. Fear. Anger. Hate. Crowds nearly out of control. The flamboyant, belligerent gestures of men who knew they were actually safe from harm. The new world was catching up to the old. Fascism was no longer something that happened somewhere else.

No getting into the hotel through there, though. Hawkins doubled back around and headed up Lexington Avenue. Two smaller rallies blocked the back entrance. Then he spotted his chance. A small group of patrolmen stationed on the corner were pushing the crowd back, keeping the street partially open for deliveries.

Hawkins positioned himself on the Forty-Ninth Street curb. A few minutes later a milk van slowly rounded the corner. He lightly stepped onto its back bumper. The police missed him in the turmoil, waving it through. But the crowd spotted him with a raw, angry howl—"Nazi shitface! You'll eat it when the workers take charge!"

A pair of eggs splattered against the side of the van. Hawkins ducked, flinching. He checked his trousers and relaxed. *Missed. Good.*

The milk van sharply veered right, tires screeching and dove into the service entrance. Hawkins jumped off the back at the last second, running up the street, pushing into the crowd. Ahead, the group of imitation storm troopers blocked the hotel entrance. They'd taken it upon themselves to check all the tickets.

Hawkins quickly scanned the crowd. Near the end of the line loitered a hatless, scruffily dressed man badly in need of a shave. A ticket stub showed in plain view in his shirt pocket.

Hawkins bumped him, plucking the ticket from his shirt. Then he pushed the man and cried to the brownshirts near the door, "Helfen Sie mir! Schnell!" *Time for a little theater*, Hawkins thought, *maybe a little mock German, too,* just for their benefit. *Play it up, look wide-eyed, astonished.* To think anything like this could happen on the streets of Manhattan!

The heads of six muscular late-teenage boys with whitewall haircuts and imitation SA caps swiveled toward him. Their narrow eyes locked onto the ruckus. The scruffy man pushed Hawkins back, grabbing for the ticket, shouting, "Hey, you prick!"

Hawkins waved at the storm troopers.

"Dieser Mann—" Hawkins stopped and gasped, twisting to keep the ticket out of the man's reach. "Dis Mans tryen mein Ticket zu stehlen." Hitler wasn't the only one who could use the Big Lie technique.

The would-be storm troopers saw exactly what Hawkins wanted—a respectable German businessman in an expensive suit being assaulted by a shabby prole. Probably a red. One American Nazi sympathizer with a five o'clock shadow was about to learn the importance of wearing a tie in Midtown.

Indignant, the man shouted, "Hey, buddy!" and took a swing at Hawkins. He ducked and reflexively swung back, his fist snapping the tip of the man's nose. The cartilage buckled under Hawkins' knuckles, breaking the veins. With a heaving gasp, the man blew blood out his nostrils. It covered his shirt, speckling the pavement with red. Enraged by the sight, he made the mistake of lunging at Hawkins the instant the brown-shirted bullyboys arrived.

Locked arms outstretched, the brownshirts rammed into the man like a pack of linebackers, blocking his blow, knocking him down. They must have smelled the blood. Punched him to the ground. Chased him with kicks. Sweaty excitement beaded their faces. He crawled in a circle on the sidewalk. Trying to protect himself with his hands, he recoiled from each blow, scrabbling on his side with his elbows and knees, desperately trying to escape. He began incoherently crying—"GAW! HAWL!"

Is he crying "God"? Hawkins wondered. *"Help"? Can't tell.* In seconds part of the man's shattered jaw dangled uselessly from one side of his bloody face. Pink bone protruded from crimson muck.

The man's spinning on the ground brought him in a circle back around. The storm troopers turned to Hawkins, laughing, giving him a gentle nudge. *Your turn!* He looked at their faces. Expectant. Eager. Filled with high spirits. Laughing. An overpowering urge overtook Hawkins. It was as if something or someone else were controlling his legs. Or he was viewing himself from afar. Stepped forward. Slammed in a hard kick. As it sank into the man's chest the pressure forced a low, gurgling scream from his throat. A pair of ribs gave and splintered like an old basket under the toe of his shoe.

Ear-piercing blasts of police whistles rent the air. The crowd was shoving and struggling around them, frantically trying to get clear. Two of the brown-shirted thugs grabbed Hawkins and shoved him forward, shouting, "Get in!" racing him for the safety of the crowd bunched by the door. The mounted officers galloped up, their horses' hooves protectively straddling the crumpled form quivering in the growing pool of blood. The cops furiously spun around over him, eyes white, shaking yard-long riot batons at Hawkins' "rescuers." Scattered teeth gleamed on the pavement like broken icicles.

At the door, for a split second, Hawkins glanced back at the man, then the brownshirts. They were snickering, the expression of men who knew they'd gotten away with it. Started to laugh, too, a little bit, because they were laughing. Then he caught himself and froze.

What? What am I doing?

Shouting, "Get out of here! Quick!" the brownshirts threw him into the front entrance.

-33-

Hawkins spun through the revolving doors into the lower lobby. His body shook in a silent cry of relief as the air-conditioning washed over him. The rancorous din outside fell to a muffled murmur as he sped past the gilded Corinthian columns. In the quiet he stopped.

What'd I do that for? I had his ticket.

But then—*No. No other way. Couldn't have simply taken the ticket. He'd have fought back. There'd have been a scene, questions.*

So why kick him? Hawkins queasily remembered W's injunction. "We're not to harm any Americans. Even if they're Nazis." *God. Three days in the country. Already breaking the rules. The risk. Could've killed that man for a stupid ticket.*

Shivering now, he ran up the stairs. In the main lobby, all gilt and green marble like a tabernacle, the high holies of hostelry, the noise disappeared altogether.

Hawkins rounded the corner to the Grand Ballroom and stopped dead. On the great room's stage, above a speaker's platform covered with red, white and blue bunting crossed a large pair of American flags. Between them hung a Nazi swastika banner covering half the wall.

Such a huge flag, like Nuremberg. The swastika seemed to vibrate and spin in place, dominating the room with savage energy. Under it, between the two American flags, stood a long portrait of George Washington in uniform, resting his hand on the hilt of his sword.

The victors had come to accept their tribute.

An official approached.

"Good evening. Your name?"

"Roy Hawkins."

The official gave him an overly broad, unctuous smile, like a church usher on a Sunday morning.

"And what firm are you with?"

With great effort Hawkins tore his attention away from the swastika. "United Specialty Valve Company." He handed the official his new business card. They'd decided to stick to a subject he knew.

The man walked a few paces with him, scribbling on a little piece of paper. Then he gently slapped it on Hawkins' lapel. Hawkins' eyes dropped down to the gummed label bearing his name and alleged company and then up, glaring at the man. He brightly smiled back.

"Just to get acquainted." Hawkins nodded, grinding his teeth. "I'll put your name on the guest list." The man dropped out of sight. Hawkins ripped off the name tag, crumpled it up and threw it on the floor as vehemently as if he were tearing down the swastika flag.

Up front the red-jacketed orchestra began segueing into "America the Beautiful." A small knot of men leapt to their feet, shouting, "Knock it off … knock it off … we don't wanna hear any of that!" Low, baying boos rang through the hall.

The bandleader stiffly pivoted as if mounted on a turntable, his mouth a round hole in a face almost as bright red as his jacket. The baton kept flicking up and down like a mechanical toy. The booing started afresh.

"Play something else … we don't wanna listen to Jew music."

By now the catcalls were getting really loud. The conductor protectively hunched his head down into his shoulders, trying to stare them down. All over the ballroom people began climbing on chairs to watch, alternately perplexed and horrified by the booing. Would the hecklers up the ante?

But they didn't have to. The conductor spun around and rapped his baton on the top of the music stand. The orchestra instantly stopped. A second later it jumped to a new tune. The hecklers shut up.

The noise brought another wave of people surging into the hall. Hawkins floated along on the tide, searching for a seat. Then he spotted a familiar face.

-34-

Special Agent in Charge Mike Kelly. Fifty feet away. Kelly must have had a long day. Crinkly blue-black bags ringed his eyes. He still sported the same badly rumpled, sodden suit he'd been wearing that morning.

Kelly coyly slipped up to a nearby knot of men who'd been booing. He studiously examined them, then darted away. By cupping a small pad of paper in the palm of one hand and a short stubby pencil in the other he could read each name tag and then surreptitiously record the information. There were obviously many names on his little pad. It seemed a rather indiscriminate if ominous form of police work.

Hawkins quietly walked up next to him. "I hope you're being paid by the hour, Kelly. It's a big hall."

The agent's head jerked around, face winding up in annoyance. "Jay-sus Christ, Hawkins! Not so loud!"

"Sorry. Do you want mine? I took it off." He bent over and read Kelly's name tag. "Mr. Jones? Laying pipe today, I see."

"No, I don't think so," dropping his hands, laughing, "but I'm gonna get every other bastard I can."

"What the hell was that a minute ago?"

"What? You mean the song? Oh, they claim it was written by a Jewess. Big conspiracy. You know the type."

"I see." Cautiously, "You think there's a conspiracy?"

"Who, me? Naw! Those guys are assholes. Great song, everybody loves it. Who gives a rat's ass who wrote it? That's the real spirit of America. Nobody gives a shit. No, I'll tell ya where the big conspiracy is. All these Reds out in Hollywood. They're wormin' in there, trying to take over show business. The movies are a powerful thing. Ya know what I mean?" He faced Hawkins, earnest, worried, lightly pressing his fist into Hawkins' sleeve, an apostle possessed by a great epiphany. "Real power, the movies. Get everybody thinking crazy. Stir up trouble. We gotta do something about that. The Reds we got back here? They're nothing. Bunch'a threadbare garlic eaters down in places like the Village, that's all. Folk dancing, ugly modern pictures—you know, the painted kind—and yak, yak, yak all night about socialism. That's all they do. And swill cheap red wine. What a fuckin' waste of time."

"Folk dancing?"

"Uh-huh. Like old-timey barn dances country rubes use'ta do. Only from Polack-type countries. They love that stuff down there. Hold hands, stamp around in a circle, drink cheap Dago wine."

"You've been down there."

"Oh yeah. Christ …"

"Take your wife?"

"She'd hate it. Her folks worked like hell to get out of there. And I'm bustin' my butt to get out of here."

"To Hollywood?"

"Hollywood. Then Washington. That's the way to get promoted. Catching Commies taking over movie studios. We got a big operation settin' up out there and I wanna get in on it. That's how ya make a name for yourself. Not tailing friggin' garlic breaths from one ugly paintin' show to the next."

"I know how you feel."

Kelly eyed Hawkins suspiciously, like a gold miner spotting an approaching claim jumper. "Yeah?"

"Know where I was before?" Kelly shook his head. "Paris. They pulled me out, transferred me here to follow him around," gesturing toward the stage. As Hawkins' confidence sunk in, Kelly's face relaxed in surprise at the resentful tone. "You ever been to Paris?"

"No. Ya only dream about going ta' places like that."

"Righto, you only dream. But I was there." Hawkins pulled out his pipe, fiddled with it a moment, lit it up. Kelly got his pack of Lucky Strikes and lit one off Hawkins' Dunhill lighter.

"Is it as nice as they say?"

"It's better. Cheap, too. Dollar goes a long way." He fished a photo out of his wallet. "That's Marie Chevalier and me on the Quai Voltaire. That's the Pont du Carrousel and the Louvre in the background." Kelly soaked the picture in, obviously impressed, then handed it back to Hawkins.

"She your wife? Girlfriend?"

"No. Neither. She tried to brain me with a champagne bottle when I told her I had to leave."

"I'm sorry. Damn."

Hawkins glanced at the photo, then crumpled it up and tossed it on the floor. "The hell with it."

"Was there a promotion in it? The transfer?"

"That's where the action is, over there. This chap?" Hawkins diffidently shook his head toward the stage. "You'll never find garlic on his breath but he's not exactly the main chance either."

"Yeah, I get it. No. Not the main chance at all." Kelly shrugged, then sighed sympathetically. "What can I say? That's government work for ya. Some wanker in an office decides to yank your balls and that's it."

"I'm sure Hollywood'll make a good impression on your wife."

"You bet'cha."

The music paused, then the orchestra swung into "When Johnny Comes Marching Home Again." The crowd noise abruptly rose. Cheers roared through the ballroom as the familiar voice filled the room.

-35-

"Hiya, folks, Walter Ventnor here! How ya all doin' tonight?"

Hawkins stood, carefully applauding, then rose on his toes trying to see with the rest. With a small wave, Ventnor began speaking in a soft, round voice crackling with continual amusement.

"Ladies and gentlemen, America's a land that admires winners so this is a real happy night tonight 'cause we're gonna celebrate some really big winners." An anticipatory wave of applause rose from the crowd. "Yessir, folks, Germany's turned the page of history's big book and a new era's emerging all over the world. The question is, is the United States going to be a part of this new world, or is it going to be left behind?"

He gripped the podium with his arms straight out in front of him, confidentially bending forward slightly. As he talked the expression on Ventnor's face began subtly shifting away from simple amusement to a smirk. It was a very jejune smirk, bursting with high-spirited adolescent contempt.

"You know, folks, those snobs up there in Hyde Park—you know the ones I mean—the president and our First Lady, yessir. They and their ilk came stomping into our nation's capital a few years ago acting like they owned the place. But they don't own the place. We do! Reg-u-lar Americans!

"And reg-u-lar Americans don't want any part of this New Deal government the Roosevelts and their culture-vulture friends are creating. Nope. What reg-u-lar Americans want is for government to leave them alone so they can take care of themselves."

Kelly snorted. "That's not what they say when they call my office."

But the crowd heartily applauded Ventnor's line, whooping and baying.

"Take this Social Security nonsense. Now most people aren't looking for the Roosevelts—excuse me—the Rosenfelds—and their big-deal New Deal government to stick their big noses into their family affairs. They'll take care of their parents themselves. They're saying ..."

The crowd loudly joined in with a mooing whoop, "Mind your own business!"

Hawkins leaned into Kelly, "Do you think Roosevelt will win or lose?"

"Not my job to think about that," Kelly said.

People were gathering impatiently on the dais. Ventnor tightly gripped the podium, hurrying on, eyes darting back, hogging more time. "And that's the same reason reg-u-lar Americans don't want the Rosenfelds sticking their long liberal noses into European affairs. Folks, we've got to get going on building Fortress America. That's what we really need, an impenetrable air and sea wall over the Atlantic. Why'd we come here in the first place? To get away from Europe's problems, that's what! No, folks, we need to mind our own business and think of America first ..." With an eager rush the crowd chimed in, "America last and America always!" followed by a huge wave of applause.

Ventnor wound up, glancing over his shoulder with an ingratiating smile. "And now it's my pleasure to introduce the man we've all been waiting for, a representative of the winners who took a beaten Germany, reorganized it with awe-inspiring efficiency and in seven years brought it from bankruptcy to total victory. Ladies and gentlemen, my friend, Dr. Hans Ludwig."

-36-

"Thank you, Mr. Ventnor. I am glad to confirm that we are indeed on the brink of a new era. Twenty years ago Germany lay shattered and defeated, its economy ruined, its people near rebellion. Today Germany is the greatest power on Earth. How could Germany have reversed such adversity and despair? We did it because of the will of a leader. America once had such a leader." Ludwig gestured at the portrait of Washington behind him. "Through his will he took a raw land and made a nation. So, too, in Germany today, Adolf Hitler has made a new nation and a new Europe."

The crowd interrupted Ludwig for a huge round of applause. Kelly quizzically leaned into Hawkins' ear. "I've never heard much of this stuff."

"It's a pretty standard fascist rationale for a dictatorship," Hawkins said. "If you want problems solved, you need a strongman, not a leader who gets people working together." Kelly nodded.

"What was the decisive point wherein Germany seized control of its destiny?" Ludwig demanded of the cheering crowd. "When a great man declared Germany would no longer be the victim! It was one man alone, one man with a sense of destiny, Adolf Hitler, who made that declaration, and in making it, altered the course of human history."

Kelly bent his chin to his chest, half laughing. Then he leaned over in Hawkins' ear. "Aw, shit, have I heard this before."

"You have?"

"Yep. Victims! Go into police work, you'll hear all about victims."

"Well, who else would people go—"

"Naw, naw, not them. The perps. Every mug in the lockup feels he's really the victim, too. Never fails."

"America has nothing to fear from the new Germany," Ludwig said. "Would we attack America? How? By walking on water?" The crowd roared with laughter.

"Director Hoover really likes Ventnor, though," Kelly said.

"He does?"

"Yep. They're big pals, actually."

"The question is, will America be drawn into a war that's not its fight?" Ludwig said.

"NO!" the crowd roared.

Hawkins nudged Kelly. He gestured at Ludwig. "You get an invitation to talk to him?"

"Naw. I think they made me. Don't know how."

"Might be the suit. You know, you're a bit out of season."

"Hey! I gotta. We get very specific memos from the SOG."

"The what?"

Kelly's tone was almost reverential. "The seat of government!"

"You mean the president?"

"No! Director Hoover's office! Director Hoover insists on appropriate attire at all times."

"You mean all FBI agents have to wear topcoats with dark suits in the summer?"

"Of course! It's a career ender."

"Do me a favor?"

"Yeah?"

"Stay off my tail."

"Aw, shit—go ahead. But I wanna hear what you get!"

Onstage Ludwig continued. "Seize control of your destiny as Germany did! The Führerprinzip, the leader principle, shows the way! You have such leaders of vision! Will Americans consent to be victims?"

"No!" By now the crowd was cheering almost continuously. Ludwig paused, waiting for it to quiet down. When they settled, he softly, almost gently concluded. "America is a lucky land, separated by vast oceans from foreign shores. How I envy your splendid isolation. Would it be so easy for us. But guard your nation. Keep it strong and pure, behind your Fortress America."

Ventnor leapt from his seat, seizing Ludwig's hand, pumping it enthusiastically. The crowd rose for an enormous standing ovation lasting several long minutes. Hawkins rose with them, trying to blend in. Kelly impassively sat with his arms folded across his chest, chewing gum with an easy, relaxed rhythm, his face once again maddeningly opaque.

-37-

Hawkins reached the front of the receiving line. Ludwig finished with the last supplicant. A brief expression of surprise and recognition flicked across his face. Hawkins broadly smiled.

"Dr. Ludwig! We meet again!"

"Mr. Hawkins—from the plane!"

Hawkins grabbed his hand, pumped it up and down. As he did he could feel Ludwig starting to relax.

"I really enjoyed that speech. I had no idea! And you slipped right by those British officials. That is hilarious!"

Ludwig finally smiled. "Thank you. It was amusing. I can't take much credit for the speech, though." Ludwig lowered his voice confidentially. "The Foreign Office wrote it."

"Oh hell, your secret's safe with me!"

"Good, good—thank you."

"I'd certainly be interested in opportunities for American companies. I'd loved to have talked on the plane—it's really too bad."

"What business are you in?"

"Industrial valves. High pressure, high temperature ones, exotic alloy specialty stuff." Hawkins handed him his new fake card. "Most people find it kinda boring—we turn things on and off, that's all."

Ludwig's eyes opened wide, just the way the Nazi officials' had back in the Reich a few years earlier.

"On the contrary, Mr. Hawkins, they're at the heart of many of the Reich's needs. Do you make many overseas sales?"

"No, not really. We've always wanted to become more export oriented. Tariff barriers, the political situation, all that prevented it."

"That's unfortunate. We'd welcome doing business with your company now."

"That's great news! Are you going to be in New York long? I sure could use your help."

"Actually—this week I'm inviting a select group of executives to the Saratoga meet."

"Ah, Saratoga."

"Please come. Day after tomorrow."

Ludwig handed Hawkins one of his closely guarded invitations. Hawkins shook his hand, patted him aside the shoulder and blended back into the crowd.

Kelly was watching a third of the way back, still trying to copy names on his little pad. "Hey! Hawkins, you got to that guy!"

"What's this Saratoga meet? He's staging a conference at it the day after tomorrow."

Kelly scowled. He nearly threw his pencil down. "Aw, shit!"

"What?"

"Shit! There's no way I can get up there—"

"Up where?"

"Don't you play the ponies?"

"I've been to Ascot."

"Saratoga Springs. Upstate New York. They race horses there in August. Richest horse-racing meet on earth!"

"Oh? Really. Richer than the Derby?"

"That's only one day—Saratoga lasts a month."

"Not the one in Kentucky. The original one. In England."

"Oh. I dunno … There's one in England?"

"Yes. Lo-o-ng time. Anyway, it explains why he's going there. Top executives. Millionaires. Big money."

"Really big money. And you don't know the half of it. That town is dirty as they come. The mob owns the place. They put the politicians, the cops on the payroll. Gambling. Bordellos. Loansharking. They got it all. Used to be a big bootlegging center. Everybody gets their little cut. So it figures. If you're up to no good, that's where you go."

"Why can't you go?"

"I'm tied up in court—look, you said if you had anything. You're going to keep me posted, right?"

"I'll give you a full written report if you like."

"Yeah?"

"Of course." Kelly's poker face broke, suffused with guileless appreciation.

"Great! I'll tell my office."

Hawkins left. Kelly happily resumed writing down names on his little pad. He began idly whistling "When Johnny Comes Marching Home Again."

-38-

Hawkins' shoes loudly creaked as he hurried through the hushed hallway. A lighted doorway glowed at the end. Inside, most of W's embryonic staff were still at their desks, busily filing and sorting. A secretary shook a thumb over her shoulder at W's door. He'd barely knocked before W snapped it open. A tense urgency filled his voice.

"Ludwig sent another airmail this morning. Bermuda found it two hours ago." W picked up a message and started reading. "Orator escrows, cutouts ready, all covered—"

"Escrows—so there's money being spent. Whatever it is."

"Well, perhaps there is a 'whatever it is.' It goes on, 'bullet people blind. Await go-ahead.'"

"Bullets. So there's a shooter. Or shooters?"

"Yes. I'd paraphrase it this way: Operation Orator is ready. Everyone involved is in place. All locations are covered. The source of the escrow accounts is hidden by a cutout so that the people with the bullets don't know where the money is coming from."

"They're hiring local muscle, then."

"Makes sense. You use what you have. They have money."

"Right. Anything else?"

"They also used that odd phrase again—the girl who spotted this one must've been sharp—Steel Seine."

"Saw that in Bermuda. Sounded like a code word."

"The general and his people thought that, too. We've been making discreet phone calls in Washington."

"What is it?"

"A top secret US Navy project, one of the items the PM specifically charged me to get the Yanks to sell. Standard Labs has come up with a new asdic system—what they call sonar. Familiar with it?"

"Can't say I am."

"Sonar uses reflected sound waves to help destroyers find submarines. The big problem with asdic—or sonar—is that the ship's propellers can drown out the echoes. Apparently they've found a way to filter out the prop noise."

"Is that part of Orator?"

"We don't know. Maybe."

"Is Orator a US code name?"

"No. They're telling us Orator's definitely not a US code name."

"Bullets—could they be planning to hijack a truck or a train, steal Steel Seine?"

"Anything's possible at this point."

"This sonar thing. They won't sell it to us?"

"No."

"Why not?"

"Submarine warfare is a sore spot with the Americans. Subs are central to the US strategy in the Pacific, if they get into a war with Japan. It's conceivable. Japan would like to add the Philippines to their empire. But the US is about to get out of the colony business and give the Philippines their independence. It's a dangerous situation. That's one reason why the US Navy has more submarines than Germany—"

"More?"

"Yes, and they're better ones. And bigger. Fleet class sub, 1500 tons—type Seven U-boat? Half that. The length of a football pitch. The Yanks never stopped developing them after the last war. The US has a superb navy, don't believe this talk about American weakness, that's only the army. They're a continental island. They don't need a big army to defend the country, their defensive perimeter is the middle of the ocean. That's why the US Navy has always gotten what it needs. They've built a true two-ocean navy. Nothing like it in history. You can sing 'Britannia rules the waves' all you want, but we could never do that, fight two completely separate sea wars simultaneously. Not now, not in Nelson's time."

"What's all this talk about Fortress America, then?"

"Complete lie. Fortress America? They already have that. Did you know Roosevelt was assistant secretary of the navy in the last war?"

"What? No—"

"The secretary was a political figurehead. Roosevelt actually ran the department. Trust me, he's taken care of the navy. If Hitler had the US sub fleet instead of his own Britain would be done for. Japan is an island nation, exactly like Britain, imports half their food. A submarine blockade is an obvious strategy to beat them, starve them out the way Hitler is trying to starve us out now. The US Navy is afraid we can't hold out and that when we go down, their submarine warfare technology—if they share it with us—will fall into the hands of the Germans. They'll then hand it over to the Japanese. That would wreck their whole Pacific strategy."

"Suppose we're too late?"

Stephenson mulled that a second. "They wouldn't have any excuse—"

"Let 'em steal it. It'll do us more good than them."

"No. The political consequences would be devastating if the Americans realized we were two-timing them. We can't risk alienating them. Nothing is worth that."

"That's a fine affair. We're to stop the Germans from stealing a system the Yanks won't sell us. Why bother. Why not give this to the FBI?"

"We still have to find out if Ludwig got his hands on it. If we warn the Bureau now, then they find out he's stolen it, well, the navy'll never admit it. We need proof beforehand. Then the US Navy'll have no excuse not to sell it to us."

"Where's it coming from?"

"That's a problem. There are several sites in the Department of the Navy and a number of contractors where it could leak."

"We have to follow Ludwig for Orator, Steel Seine, the whole show."

"Righto. He's our only lead. Stick close to Ludwig. If he's already stolen Steel Seine, get proof. Then we can convince the Yanks they've nothing to lose by pooling technology. We've got things we can trade. If he hasn't stolen it yet, keep him away from it. At all cost, don't get yourself into a position where it looks like we're pinching it. Any questions?"

"No."

"So! That's it! You're off."

"What about backup?"

"None to be had."

Fine with me, Hawkins thought. *On my own, that's the way I like it.*

"One other thing. Who do I see about my expenses?"

That provoked a vaguely pained expression. "Keep track of everything, get receipts. You'll be reimbursed later on."

"Later? How much later?"

"I don't know. Maybe much later. Maybe after the war. I'm not drawing any pay at all. In fact, I'm covering most of the overhead here out of my own pocket. One of the reasons we chose you was because we knew you have assets here in the US you can draw on. The Crown can't pay you right now, not here in America. Britain's entirely run out of foreign exchange. Not a shilling's left. Everyone will be reimbursed eventually."

"No money?" Hawkins glanced around the office. "How in hell do you pay for this place?"

"Nelson Rockefeller's forgiving the rent. He manages the center for his family."

Hawkins assented with a knowing shrug and left.

In the outer office, phoning his train reservation, it sank in. *No money. Incredible,* he thought. *Like a bloody tale out of Don Quixote. The Nazis have been invincible so far. And we're being asked to fight with no money against enemies with room service at the Waldorf.*

The fog lifted a bit more. *General Houghton. Of course. The Imperial*

Posts and Telegraph Censorship Station. They've been reading my bank state-
ments. Reporting back to London. They probably know what I have right to
the last nickel. Moonlighting in antiques trading. The checks from dealers
sent back and forth. Sales letters. Invoices.

Too late to be embarrassed. What a sucker. Damn fool to get involved in
this business. Had to volunteer, didn't I? Just had to. A bloody, buggered fool.
Britain damn well better win.

-39-

At the height of the summer season there were few runs anywhere with the quietly aristocratic overtones of the Delaware and Hudson Railroad's Laurentian. The line of people who'd queued at the gate in Grand Central represented a virtual who's who of what might be called track society: The wealthy descendants of the original New York Four Hundred, dressed for the country. Southern planters and horsemen in loud jackets. The haute couture remains of café society. And the new elite: industrial managers and financiers in expensive business suits. Flashy movie stars accompanied by producers in riding pants. Exotic European aristos fleeing the disruption of war. Liberally salted among them were the raffish human spectrum lovingly chronicled in the newspaper columns of Damon Runyon— bookies and handicappers tricked out in blanket plaid suits and straw boaters, seedy gamblers, overdressed gangsters and their ostentatiously underdressed dolls.

As the streamlined stainless steel solarium car disappeared north out of Grand Central, Hawkins leaned back and unlimbered his pipe. Ordinarily, the company and this kind of busman's holiday would put him in a splendid mood. But he'd been idly skimming the *Times*. Headlines leapt out: "Massive Air Battle Over Britain"; "Roosevelt Attacked Over Deal to Trade Fifty Surplus WWI Destroyers for Bases in British Possessions in Caribbean"; "Food and Fuel Shortages Predicted for Winter in Europe Due to Rail Shortages." Then the kicker: "FBI Investigates Reds in Hollywood." He threw the paper on the floor in disgust.

Jesus, one day's news, he thought. *And what a sense of priorities. Ludwig's running a spy network, God knows how large, while tapping into the US Navy's top secrets. And what are Kelly's colleagues doing? Chasing bohemians who stay up too late and talk too much.*

But the reports of fuel and food shortages prompted his darkest reflections. *That means my mother. Sister, Jill. Aunt Bernice and Uncle George. My cousins.* Faces would be thinner, belts shorter by spring. *No one would probably see another orange before the end of the war. Pop had such American expectations about things like oranges. But Mum certainly came around. She'll miss that.*

And here I am in the land of the second helping being conveyed in the epitome of rolling luxury to the summer pageantry and hilarity of an elite resort in season. Like taking advantage. Shameful. The whole world's out of kilter.

What's happening to them? Can W help get them out? But the answer would be no, of course. What if everyone did that? Besides, Mum's probably employed by now. Most likely an office, maybe a government ministry. She'd calmly refuse to leave. Easy to hear her voice: "Why, Roy, what an idea."

When was the last time we were together? In her London parlor. She was holding the new gas mask I got her in her lap. Kept smiling and nodding, trying to act appreciative, not succeeding. Gas. Never stopped to think it'd be a reminder of Pop dying. And no bloody coal burning in the grate. Thoughtless, utterly thoughtless.

Haven't written in months. Never thought of it. Always on the run. Could've easily mailed letters from Lisbon, or had Wilkinson, Houghton or W send word. Never mind. It'll only be a couple of weeks anyway. Then pass through on the way back to Europe.

The brakes squealed sending everyone in the car lurching forward. A sign whizzed past the window. Yonkers? His morose, guilty rumination and the entire privileged assembly unceremoniously ground to an unscheduled stop.

Hawkins looked out and ahead. Mike Kelly. On the platform, talking to a rattled-looking stationmaster. Kelly clipped a badge to his lapel and gestured for the conductor. Then he climbed onto the train. Doors began slamming open and shut between the cars.

A sense of alert tension spread over Hawkins, mounting with each angry-sounding slam.

Christ. The bugger made them stop the Laurentian? His office is in Manhattan. What's the show for? Only one reason, he thought. *An arrest. For spying. That's it. The only possible explanation. Director Hoover's decided to boot me out. So much for the big dance.*

Rage began building, heart accelerating, banging harder and harder against the front of his ribs. *Bastards. Bloody bastards! Why can't they simply* say *move along. No, have to ruin everything. Let Ludwig slip away. Blithering idiots.*

Maybe it won't be the big boot. Maybe it'll be "American Traitor Arrested as G-Men Guard US Neutrality." Does the Bureau know about MI6? Could they take my citizenship? How far could this go … Could they blow up W's entire operation?

He eyed the latches on the side window.

No, jumping's not the answer. He began rubbing his wrists, then caught himself. *Stop that,* he thought. *Anyone else on the platform? No. Kelly's alone. Said I looked like a slick executive type. Probably thinks I'm merely another businessman called to national service, that I'm an easy mark. Big mistake there, buddy. Oh, yes, fellow government man.* Hawkins' rage shifted to a ready, cold focus.

What will it take? Get him in a choke hold, just like training. He'll never see it coming. Pass out in seconds. Then throw him under the wheels. Wouldn't be hard. He's a pudge. Look like an accident. Without a witness, no pathologist could detect it. At least buy enough time to get to Canada. But what about W, the office? Warn them? But what would they do?

That thought brought back W's orders. "Not to harm any Americans, even if they're Nazis." *Could I get away with it, anyway? No. Never get away. Nothing sets the police off like a dead copper.*

Then another realization set in.

But … so what if they throw me out? All right, fine. I want to go back to Europe, anyway. W will not be happy, but I'll get to go back in. Just hope they don't blow my cover in the process.

-40-

Kelly entered the car, saw him, waved slightly. He exhaled with relief and extended his hand, self-consciously looking over his shoulder at the gaping crowd.

"Hawkins, I need to talk to you … Come on, between the cars." Hawkins tapped his pipe in the ashtray, deliberately following Kelly out, on edge, still tense and angry, waiting. On the platform between the carriages he looked down, checking the gap between the cars. Enough room for an unconscious man. He glanced across at the station. No. Too many people on the platform. Worse than the ferry. No choice but to ride this out.

Kelly banged the door shut behind them.

"What, no newsreel cameras?" Hawkins said.

"Huh?"

"Don't I rate cameras?"

"What are you talking about?"

"I thought that's how the Bureau likes to make big arrests."

"No—"

"What the hell, Kelly."

"I received special instructions directly from the seat of government this morning."

"You mean Director Hoover's office—"

"Uh, yeah. I've been sent on an important mission. Now we happen to know you're with British Intelligence, although we can't prove that. Either that or this new MI6—"

Hawkins couldn't stand it anymore, almost shouting, "What the bloody hell? Am I being arrested or not!"

"Why, no." Kelly seemed genuinely puzzled and put off. "The Bureau is very interested in the fact you're an American citizen. As you're aware, the US has no real intelligence or counterintelligence service. With the changing situation in Europe the director feels that's now his responsibility."

"What's that got to do with me?"

"This isn't a formal thing, mind you—obviously, the director needs to know in advance—but, if you're interested, the director would be willing to consider your appointment, as an American citizen, of course, to an executive level position in the new intelligence division he intends to organize."

"What?"

"I'm talking GS-16 or -18 most likely, assistant or deputy director. Senior civil service, sub-cabinet level. That'd probably only quadruple your present pay but additional considerations could be worked out."

"Additional considerations?"

"Oh, car—personal assistants, you know, at home. We know this places you in an awkward position. We don't expect an answer until your present assignment is over. But the director'd like to know your inclinations as soon as possible."

"You mean you stopped the Laurentian—*the* Laurentian—to make me a job offer?"

"They called at home. I live in the Bronx."

"Suppose someone sees us!"

"Aw, you can imagine all kinds of things."

"Imagining what can go wrong is what we do!"

"Oh, Jesus—"

"And did you see who's on this bloody thing?" Hawkins pointed back at the car. Kelly shrugged. "Millionaires, movie stars, rich, powerful people—"

That really annoyed Kelly. "Hey, they don't rate any—"

"No! Not the point! They're people who are used to getting their way and know how to complain. That's drawing attention. You don't do that. If you did this in Britain the minister'd have your guts for garters! You'd wind up colonial police in some mud-brick shit hole in the Sudan! This is the kind of thing they do in the Reich."

"Hey! Excuse me! I'm only making you an offer way over my head! You think I'll ever see a job like this? Fuck you, pal—"

"No, bugger you—"

Kelly pushed Hawkins, hard. Hawkins pushed back. They grabbed each other by the coat sleeves—not enough room to swing—and slammed around in a circle in the confined space between the cars. Hawkins pushed Kelly away. They stood apart, glaring at each other. Then they began to cool. Hats flown off, Hawkins realized. He reached down, picked both up and handed Kelly his. Kelly snapped it away and flipped it back on his balding head.

The proposal began sinking in. It was a struggle to mentally switch from the anticipation of being handcuffed to the broad vistas such an astounding offer presented. Or grasp that Hoover could act so swiftly and with such breezy but ruthless pragmatism: *Let's just hire him away.* It didn't help that Kelly hadn't chosen the best of all possible moments.

"It's not that I'm not appreciative. I'm sorry—I am—intrigued."

"Good. That's a relief."

"But—wait, the federal criminal police are taking this on themselves?"

"You've lost me here."

"In Britain we keep Scotland Yard, MI6 and the Security Service strictly separate."

"Why?"

"Too much power in one pot. That's how the Soviets do it! Besides, intelligence isn't law enforcement. What you and I do is completely different—"

"What? How?"

"You *react*, investigate *crimes*, not people, *after* they do something. We *act*, follow people, gather information—go on the offensive *before* they can. We *keep* secrets. Your job is to *expose* secrets—to judges, juries."

"Aw—well, shit, now that helps a lot, doesn't it?"

"And does Congress or the president get to say anything?"

"Hey, I never signed up for this kind of stuff. I wanted to be a G-man, fight crime. That's all any of us ever wanted to do. At least the director's trying to do sumpthin' here. Give 'im some credit!"

"But does he have any legal mandate?"

"I don't know—but let me tell ya, getting you on his team would go a l-o-o-ng ways to staking his claim."

"I'm not sure I want to be a pawn in his power play."

"He's going ahead whether you're along for the ride or not. Wouldn't you rather see it done right? Come on, you could make the difference—"

"How do I know he doesn't want to break off one of the Service's wheels?"

"I'll be really honest with you—Oh! Now you're admitting it, huh?"

"Don't bullshit—"

"Okay, okay, yeah, that did occur to me. But we don't know much about this stuff. You sort of just proved that. I'll bet my badge the offer is real. Hey, listen, Hawkins! I stuck my neck out on this. I told them I thought it was a good idea. You don't know what that means at the Bureau. At least give it a decent chance. I mean, come on! We're the Yankees! It's like you're with some crap team like the Phillies."

"Jesus—I—right. I'm sure you did. Thanks, Mike. I appreciate that. I'll think about it. Really."

"Great. Say, I gotta get off, somebody's holding up the train." Kelly jumped off and waved to the trainmen. "Which one is it, by the way?"

"What—"

"The Secret Intelligence Service or this new MI6?"

"They're the same."

"They are? No shit. That's news."

"Code names. Military Intelligence Bureau Six. The Security Service is MI5. They handle domestic internal security inside Britain. Scotland

Yard is still Scotland Yard. Strictly criminal police. Like you are. Or were."

With an impatient surge, the train pulled out of the station, throwing Hawkins. He grabbed a handle, catching himself, his head vibrating like a string on a guitar that'd been plucked too hard. Kelly waved, smiling a bit.

"That'll make a nice report. Oh, by the way—he's on board."

-41-

The smooth blue locomotive thundered into Saratoga trailing smoke and steam. A swarm of children darted out of the station and tore along the platform, racing it to a halt.

Inside, Roy Hawkins edgily perched on his seat, waiting to spring. Kelly's offer, all the reflections, gone for now.

Ludwig's on the train, Hawkins thought. *Damn. Got to find him and fast—who knows who's meeting him?*

It slowed. He flung himself down the aisle. The conductor turned. "Hey, will you—" as Hawkins leapt off into the milling, noisy crowd. He quickly bounded down the platform, checking the entrances. It took three sweaty minutes. Then he spotted Ludwig claiming his baggage. He edged up, backward, and gently bumped him.

"Why, Dr. Ludwig! What luck. We can share a cab to the hotel—"

"Ah, Mr. Hawkins, no need. I sent my car and chauffeur ahead last night." Ludwig graciously gestured over his shoulder toward a large black Mercedes. "Do join me, please."

A tall, muscular man in a chauffeur's uniform leaned against the car, arms folded, his leather cap pulled down over his eyes. When he saw them he waited, defiantly tarrying until the last possible second before stiffly hurrying over. A thick, muscular neck pushed a thin roll of youthful fat over the top of his tight collar. Tension seemed to crackle under his smooth, slightly beefy face.

Hawkins uneasily took the stare in. *It keeps getting better and better. A former Hitlerjungen? This one's half a head taller than I am. Probably has fifty pounds on me. Had to give the Hi-Power to Wilkinson, didn't I? And now Ludwig has a car. How jolly.*

"Thank you, Doctor! I'd enjoy a lift in this heat. Where are you staying?"

"The United States Hotel. Couldn't get a reservation anywhere else on short notice."

"Same here."

"Very good, then. Dieter!" Ludwig imperiously snapped his fingers in the air, obviously enjoying the sensation. He headed for the car without a glance. The brim of Dieter's cap lowered over eyes scintillating with a sizzling anger barely held in check, jaw working back and forth, pausing for another long second. Then he began truculently ordering about a pair of hapless red caps. Every word and gesture called up images of blows and kicks. They scooped up the bags and began loading them in the Mercedes' boxy trunk.

Behind them the Laurentian blew a thunderous whistle. It accelerated north out of the station with a powerful low rumble, the last car a blur before it passed the end of the platform.

"Splendid car, Doctor. Why didn't you drive?" Hawkins said.

"Train takes half the time. And you can't get a lobster on the highway."

Dieter quickly steered around the corner and drove down the quarter-mile length of the United States Hotel to Broadway and the entrance. Hawkins watched, curious.

A high mansard roof. Hundreds of cupolas and gables. Twelve hundred rooms adorned by fantastic Victorian curlicues. The States Hotel, as it was known, had a nearby and slightly larger sister, the Grand Union, the largest wood frame building in the world. Together they towered over the town, dwarfing it the way French villages clustered at the feet of medieval cathedrals.

In front a pair of elderly black doormen in worn Victorian jackets and caps emerged and took their bags. They led them up the flowing marble steps, across a porch the width of a basketball court and through a set of double doors high enough for a pair of mounted cavalrymen. The United States Hotel was a stupendous construction, but frayed carpets and worn furnishings showed it had fallen badly behind the times. The new age threatened doom.

"Is the meeting here at the hotel?"

"No, we've rented the Van Schenck estate." Ludwig took one of his business cards and wrote the address on the back for Hawkins. "Ten a.m. tomorrow so everyone can make post time."

"Splendid."

Hawkins held back as Ludwig registered, discreetly listening for the room numbers. Only when the bellhops led his quarry safely out of earshot did Hawkins ease down the ornate marble counter. With a flourish he took out Ludwig's business card, carefully concealing the back.

"I'm with Dr. Ludwig. Is it possible to get an adjoining room?"

"Yes, it's still open." In truth, the old hotel rarely filled up halfway, even at the height of the season.

"Good. Reserve that for ..." Hawkins winked broadly. "Hmmm— let's reserve that for a ... *friend* who's coming. Here's her—er, I mean—his name. And a separate one under my name on another floor."

The clerk broadly winked. "I understand perfectly, sir! That will be Room 307 for *Mr.* Churchill"—he winked again—"and room 455 for you."

-42-

The vast hotel dining room stretched off monotonously. When the hotel was built gluttonous, twelve-course meals taking over two hours were routine. Since multiple seatings were impossible, the era's hoteliers built gigantic noisy dining rooms serving over a thousand patrons. It held only a fraction of that now, all clustered at one end.

Ludwig and his chauffeur sat a dozen tables back. Hawkins carefully watched a moment. *Curious, Ludwig and his chauffeur eating together,* he thought. *What's that about? An ostentatious show of National Socialist solidarity? Probably the only other German around. Given the size of the room, they're in for a long wait.*

Hawkins double-timed it up the stairs to the third floor and circuited the hallway, checking. All clear. He got his thin leather case of locksmith tools from his bag. In seconds he picked the lock on Ludwig's door. In the silence it spun with a thunderous grind. He nervously checked the hall again. Still clear. With one smooth motion he swiftly marched inside and unlocked a connecting door on the side. Peeking out into the hall first, he quickly relocked the main door to Ludwig's room.

Hawkins started entering the room next door that he intended to use as a blind, then paused a moment. Softly calling hello, he knocked on the door of the next room down the hall. No one there. He started picking the lock, then realized it was open. He peeked in. Unoccupied. Relaxing, he unlocked that room's connecting door, too. Then he exited and used his hotel key to enter his "duck blind."

He threw his hat and kit on the bed and looked the room over. A big mess of Victorian gewgaw, slummy and repulsive. Like the once-upon-a-time white marble sink. *Imagine a single cold water tap in this day and age. All the toilets and baths must be down the hall in one of those communal washrooms. And a knotted rope bolted to a hook under the window for a fire escape, there's a nice touch.* The colorful Bakelite radio the only modern, likable thing.

Still—three rooms. He unlocked both connecting doors from inside 307, throwing them wide open—305, 307 and 309, looking back and forth. Not bad at all. Then he relocked the inside door to the empty room, 309, and sauntered into 305, Ludwig's room.

A nondescript collection of German and American toiletries littered the dresser. Nothing interesting there. At that he stopped a moment. *Need to clear the mind,* he thought, *and concentrate.*

Searching a room undetected was one of the most difficult feats to pull off. The real effort was almost all mental. Hawkins had to remember every move he made, everything he touched. That way he could meticulously reverse himself out when finished. It was vital not to disturb too much at a time. He had to be able to get out fast. Too many pieces moved escalated the risk. Much safer to have lookouts, of course.

With great care he opened the drawer and carefully memorized the exact position of everything. Then he slowly began lifting and searching Ludwig's clothes. *Move and replace a small section at a time, exactly like training.* At the end everything was back in exactly the same position. Unfortunately, it could've been a tourist's dresser. Who cared if Ludwig had expensive clothes and cheap underwear?

The initial sense of achievement began slowly fading. It usually did. The idea of getting in was a challenge, almost fun. But actually snooping through another person's laundry? That was another thing altogether, distinctly distasteful, even disturbing.

No matter. Carefully noting their position, he drew the leather bags from under the bed. One and two were empty.

A sharp laugh in the hallway. Tensing, he lifted on his toes. The pair of voices passed down the hallway and disappeared. He pulled out his handkerchief to wipe his hands, ears straining for Ludwig's footsteps while he worked.

Behind the suitcase hid an oblong leather valise, almost like a musical instrument case. The simple locks picked easily. Inside rested a sleek sniper rifle and scope neatly broken down, snug in green plush recesses. A Mauser type bolt action, only devoid of any fancy engraving work or ornamentation. In fact, no maker's marks at all. Probably a custom job, a magnificent piece. Its elegance came from its perfect balance and exquisite fit and finish, equally a precision instrument as the optics on the matching scope. No infantryman ever saw a gun like this.

He held it up and tested the heft. A custom cheekpiece. Made specially to fit one man alone, like a Savile Row suit. He drew a bead on the window. Didn't fit. A bigger man. *Dieter. Must have brought it in through customs in that damn car. Bugger.*

What on earth did Ludwig, or Dieter, plan on doing with this thing? Spies rarely, if ever, actually sought to get involved in killing people. Information and manipulation, that was the real job. And if you had to assassinate an enemy, you did it in controlled circumstances. Gain surreptitious entrance. Or the target's confidence. But do it out of sight, where you couldn't be spotted. Close enough to touch.

A sniper rifle implied shooting a man you couldn't reach any other way. Someone at a distance. Someone protected. Almost a desperation measure. *The big question: on exactly whom do they plan to use this thing?*

This takes everything to a whole new dimension, he thought. *Using American soil to attack Britain, Canada, the Commonwealth, or shipping.* That would be one thing. That's aimed outward, away from the States. Likewise, stealing submarine warfare secrets. That didn't necessarily have to be about America, either. They could be solely interested in getting a hand up on the war already going on.

But a custom sniper rifle? That *wouldn't* be aimed outward. *Couldn't* be. It could only hit something—someone—here. The king and queen already came for hot dogs and picnicking at Hyde Park. The British ambassador or consul general? *Ridiculous*. Nonentities, in the big scheme of things. Accomplish nothing except draw fire on the shooter, enrage the Yanks.

Hawkins uneasily replaced the rifle, drew out the fourth suitcase and got his second big surprise.

-43-

Cased in green plush, the same as the rifle, nestled a complete set of exotic photography equipment.

A kind of microscope? Regular negative film rolled in a slot about two thirds of the way up. A slide at the bottom, where the microscope specimen would normally go, had a space for a very small card. Another small metal plate drew out to expose it. An electric light at the top switched on and off with a timer.

Hawkins plugged it in, flicked it on and off. It produced an extremely small lighted image at the bottom, the size of a pinhead. He shut it off and carefully put it back. Then he examined the rest.

One cubby held a miniature punch. Its rotating head had hollow bits that could cut out round spots as small as the period at the end of a sentence. There was a new packet of small unexposed film cards stuffed in the sides.

Another cubby held a large roll of heavy, opaque airmail stamps along with a jeweler's loupe and tweezers. The usual zippered darkroom bags, tubs, chemicals and stopwatches were there for the development of both regular negatives and prints.

He rechecked the film cans and packages. All the foil wrappers were unbroken. *Dieter probably brought it in with the Mercedes, too. No, probably in the Mercedes, but hidden somewhere.*

Behind the suitcases laid the last treasure, a small briefcase. When probed, the simple latches sprang with hardly a wiggle. Several file folders were inside.

In the first file: Ludwig's speeches. Receipts. Routine business documents. *Boring*, he thought. *Put those back.* The second folder contained a quantity of blank stationery. *Definitely set that aside.* In the third folder, a list of American companies and executives interested in investing in the Reich. *Ludwig's added my name and cover*, he thought. *Now that's amusing. Not exactly hard intelligence. Still, the economic warfare section will be glad to have it.*

In the fourth folder were pages covered by columns of names and numbers. *Ciphers? Maybe. Wait … Orator had been scrawled on one, then Ludwig or someone partially erased it.*

No time to sort through this, he thought. *Let W or General Houghton and his staff puzzle it out. Not enough light for the Minox, not to photograph print. Have to get the Graflex.*

He grabbed his bellows camera from his case in the other room, filling his pockets with the bulky flashbulbs. Laying Ludwig's papers across the floor, Hawkins straddled them with his feet and photographed each side as swiftly as possible. He bounced the hot used flashbulbs on his fingertips, tossing them back into the other room onto the bed.

When he finished photographing every paper, he fetched a small vial of special marking fluid from his kit. Moving smoothly, he drew an invisible line across each side of every one of Ludwig's blank envelopes. He blew on them until they dried without a trace. *Perfect*, he thought. He imagined the little whoops in Bermuda when the streaks fluoresced under the black lights.

Done. Time to report in.

-44-

Tiffany's summer branch stretched across one side of the lobby, the phone booths, the other. *Need three in a row*, Hawkins thought. *Can't have anyone overhear.* He idly browsed along the glittering display cases, trying to act nonchalant, waiting. *Damn this stuff is expensive. Who can afford it?* Every few moments he checked the phone booths across the way. Finally. Three in a row empty.

The office operator answered with a simple yes. Hawkins used his new code number.

"This is 48700. I need to speak to 48100 without delay."

"Hold."

Forty-eight represented the forty-eight states. W's organizational number was 100, the chief. He gave Hawkins the highest field number, 700, ergo, Hawkins was 48700. W immediately came on the line.

"Hello there, 48700, how goes it?"

"Brilliant. And very bad."

"Brilliant first."

"I secured an extra room next to our target where I can eavesdrop."

"Excellent."

"I just searched it, marked his envelopes with fluorescent ink and photoed a large sheaf of papers. Not sure what it all is. No time. I assume it's coded. Saw the word 'orator,' though, written in pencil, then partially erased. I'm sending the film by rail express shortly."

"Good. And the bad?"

"He's got a scoped sniper rifle. Also a suitcase full of the damnedest photo-printing equipment I've ever seen. Apparently unused. Sort of a microscope, only blows the image *down*, mind you. And a roll of airmail stamps. It's pretty clear he's planning to start pasting small pieces of film under the stamps. But I really don't like the looks of that rifle. It's a custom piece, slick. You should see it."

W's voice sounded unusually grave. "A sniper rifle? *A sniper rifle!*" There was a long pause on the phone as it sank in. "Bloody hell—but by Ludwig? He doesn't seem the type—"

"He's got a car, now. A big Mercedes, and a chauffeur, too. Rode from the station with him. Says the chauffeur brought the car out with him from Stockholm."

"Right. Neutral to neutral. All that truck and duffel probably hid in the car. The driver?"

"Young, big bruiser. He's probably the shooter."

"Exactly. Ludwig wouldn't get his hands dirty. Any name?"

"Dieter."

"Last?"

"No."

"Must be figuring to use it. Why bring it otherwise? Merely having it's risky." W paused for a long moment. "We'll get on who this Dieter is. But that photo printer. They must be getting ready to send larger messages out. Under the stamps, you think?"

"Yes. I've never seen anything like that printer. You'll be bowled over when you see the pictures. It can make a print the size of a pencil lead."

"Great God."

"You could lift the stamps and those prints are so small you could still miss them if you weren't careful—might take it for an ink splatter. He's got a set of jeweler's loupes and tweezers to handle them."

"I'll cable Bermuda immediately. Good thing you marked his

envelopes, that'll help. Anything else?"

"I need the Cord, right away."

"I'll have a courier bring the car up by morning. A custom sniper rifle. Son of a bitch! Hardly expected that. You better head for a gun shop, get a piece. Damn good work, Hawkins. That photo printer means they're getting closer to Steel Seine. They'll need it for the blueprints. Stick to him. Tight."

-45-

A long procession of limos rolled up the historic, tree-lined street: Packards, Lincolns, Duesenbergs, Cadillacs, Rolls-Royces. Here and there a wood estate wagon driven by a causal owner playing country squire. The wealthy owners scurried up a brick walkway polished by generations of shoes to a large white Palladian mansion. Hawkins parked the Cord, delivered overnight and freshly washed, and joined them.

A gray-uniformed maid guarded the door. She glanced at Ludwig's card, took Hawkins' hat and gestured to the front parlor. He started in, then paused. There was a small cannon at the bottom of the stairs. A date had been cast in the bronze: 1637. The rest was less military: Chippendale chairs, a Georgian brass chandelier, an unusual diamond-shaped coat of arms, black with age. *Reminds me of … Oh, yes. Boodles. Of course*, he thought. *Same aristocratic milieu. Probably built about the same time by the same sort of people.*

He turned to a framed case on the opposite wall. Inside hung an ancient parchment document festooned with a row of round lead seals hanging from faded scarlet ribbons. Next to it was a framed clipping from a magazine like *Country Life*. It showed the document and a picture of a battle-scarred seventeenth-century man in a lobster-back helmet. Elaborate calligraphy covered the ancient document. *Seems illegible*, he thought. *No—it's Dutch. A really ancient Dutch, not the kind I'm used to.* The caption read,

Van Schenck Patent. In 1644 the Estates General of
the United Provinces of the Netherlands granted a
Patroonship and three million acres in the colony of New
Netherlands to Andreas van Schenck in recognition of his
heroism in battle under Admiral Maarten Tromp.

As he read Hawkins' puzzlement grew. *A manorial estate in America,
before New Netherlands became New York. Who knew? But why are these
people renting their home to Ludwig? Must be Nazi sympathizers. Hard to
believe such people could possibly need the money.* The contents of the place
would fill a good half-dozen museum galleries, a classic country seat of an
old, extremely rich aristocratic family, untouched by a decorator's hand.

A motion in the corner of his eye. Hawkins turned from a Stafford-
shire platter of the house labeled GEN. LIVINGSTON VAN VECHTEN VAN SCHENCK
RECEIVES GEN. LAFAYETTE AT … and found himself eye to eye with a tall girl
leaning on the opposite doorway.

She had one high-heeled foot pressed against the door casing behind
her. Riveting blue eyes. She tipped her head to one side and down and
gazed straight at him with a lightly featured face that would've credited
any *Vogue* cover. Her very straight long blond hair parted to one side
and hung down halfway over one eye. Tall and leggy, maybe a year or
two younger than Hawkins. No tan, almost pale. Surprised, he froze for
a split second.

Very beautiful. Stunning, actually. *Must be one of the family,* he
thought. What was she like? Did she resemble one of those upper-class
youths he'd met on the Continent? Viciously devoid of a sense of noblesse
oblige, they so often found Fascism fashionable and exciting.

"You read Dutch?" she said.

"A little." He glanced back at the patent. "It says the Estates General of
the Netherlands declares Andreas van Schenck Patroon. When they ruled
New York. Three hundred years ago."

"Very good! Most people think it's German."

"Wouldn't want that."

"No?"

"Definitely."

"I see."

She had a low, almost whispery voice and spoke with a clearly enunciated American private school accent, long *A*s and dropped *R*s, but with the slightly hard, almost gravelly edge common among New York Society.

"I'm Roy Hawkins."

"Daisy van Schenck."

"Ah, I rather guessed you were one of the family." He decided to needle her a bit. "You don't look like a hard-charging business lady to me."

She tossed her head back with a small smile. "What does a hard-charging business lady look like?"

"I'm not sure, really."

"What *do* I look like, then?"

"I'm still working on that, but it's pretty good whatever it is."

The smile broadened, and she showed a wide row of perfect white teeth.

"I see. You don't look like a Nazi."

"I'm not. Are you?"

"No."

"That's good."

"It is? Uhmmm. Why are you here then?"

"I'm a businessman. Why are you renting to them?"

Her mouth pulled back a little.

"It was a mix-up. I was going to Newport. So I decided to let out the house. Then I changed my mind. Turned out they only wanted three meetings, and they wanted it in the worst sort of way. So I held out until they made me a great offer. Had no hint who it was."

"I see. It's smart business lady knows how to hold out before letting them in."

"Yes. A real hard-charger doesn't let on he's desperate. He just comes on firm and confident. That's what really impresses a lady."

"That's always been my strategy. You have to know how to do your business—and hers."

"Yes, a woman has to be picky about her business. Are you a hard-charger?"

"I like to think so."

"That's good. You hard-charging businessmen better sit down, you're going to miss your meeting."

Hawkins heard something over his shoulder. Ludwig was getting ready to speak.

"Thanks." He lingered a second. "I *will* see you later."

She flashed him a big smile as he walked into the large parlor.

-46-

A small group of businessmen were clustered in a semicircle on the rented wooden folding chairs. Every little bit they trained one eye over their shoulders lest their official host hear them.

Hawkins picked up a coffee and cruller and edged over. A tall balding man in his fifties was heatedly discussing something, his sunken eyes ringed with creases of worry and anger. An otherwise calm demeanor barely concealed his confusion and anxiety.

"Nick, we're more exposed than you are. If I go out and sign a statement on principles, our facilities over there could be expropriated like that." He softly snapped his fingers.

The man he addressed as Nick sat across from him, face slightly flushed.

"Frank, what are you going to do when they order you to produce military equipment? Don't you see? Eventually you're going to find yourself in a position where—"

"Oh, God … Hypothetical! Hypothetical! You can imagine all kinds of things. The war isn't going to last that long."

"Aw, whose side do you want to be on, anyway, winners or losers?" a third man said. "Would you bet on a slow horse? Of course not. There's always going to be winners and losers in this world. You and I are not gonna change that."

A fourth man jumped in. Hawkins ordinarily would've dismissed him as a ne'er-do-well; there was a dull, pinched look in the eyes that signaled a lack of curiosity. The clothes, too, seemed to say simpleton: a crooked fraternity necktie, soup stained. An expensive Brooks Brothers suit speckled with mud. Manure stained brogans. But a fearless, sinuous line curled his lower lip, creating a cruelly lithe smile, giving the sense of only momentarily holding back a withering cut. The others listened deferentially.

"Oh, balls. Who cares! In the long run it'll probably be easier to run our European affiliates under the Nazis. No strikes, no unrest. I can appreciate that."

Nick gestured at the fourth man, shaking his head slightly in disbelief.

"Chet, what's happening to us? What's this country mean to you?"

"Mean to me? Well …" Chet paused, caught off guard. "It's the land of opportunity, a nation of go-getters. The people that broke the prairies, put the world on wheels," he snickered a little bit, "the land of big gushing oil wells."

"What about life, liberty and the pursuit of happiness?"

That left Chet slightly bewildered. "Happiness? Where does anybody have more?"

"No, for God's sakes, Jefferson wasn't talking about making *money*—"

Ludwig came back in the room. The group instantly broke up and began milling around.

Hawkins eased down on one of the little chairs, mulling at the exchange. *Winners and losers. Did they really believe that? The pursuit of happiness—life itself—nothing but getting and sitting, Scrooge-like, on your big heap of whatever?*

The disgust Hawkins had first felt in Portugal abruptly resumed, invisibly separating him from the rest of the group. *Who are these people? Well, that's easy, actually. More stupid people, that's who. Why am I trying to save stupid people from themselves? Let 'em get what they deserve.*

-47-

Ludwig tapped his papers on a small stand. All eyes were immediately on him.

"Good morning. Germany and I thank you for coming. You are busy men. It's very hot. Let me get to the point. It's clear Britain can't last until winter. Her people, who are reasonable and farsighted, will soon come to their senses and realize they cannot fight a united Europe commanded from Berlin. They will demand peace.

"Therefore, it is appropriate to begin thinking of the postwar economic order. Our leadership is willing to be very generous to those companies that accept the New European Order."

Hawkins noticed the girl's reflection in a gilt rococo mirror. He began idly watching her while Ludwig spoke. The way her hair hung over that eye—

"What does this New Order offer that other systems, including the US, do not? Two things. Labor peace and lower tax costs."

This talk's going to be totally different from the Waldorf, Hawkins thought. *No politics. Totally bottom line. Those blue eyes—*

"First let us consider labor. I am sure there isn't a firm here that hasn't undergone at least one painful and expensive strike in the past. In Europe today, under the Nazi Party, this problem no longer exists.

Unions are under state control. Strikers lose their heads."

Oh, that's funny, Hawkins thought. *I wonder if any of these idiots realize Ludwig means that literally.* When Hitler revised the German criminal code he'd decided Aryans should be beheaded. By the sword. Thought that was appropriate for a "warrior race." Thinking like school boys, the Nazis were. Only the sword proved rather, well, *messy*. Aryans now went to the guillotine. Over a big drain. In the middle of a tile floor. Üntermenschen were hanged.

"Wages are fixed by the state. By setting markets we guarantee your annual profits."

She's still there in the mirror, Hawkins thought. *Is she going to nod in approval?* Instead an uneasy expression crossed her face and passed into a distant frown. She spun on her heel and walked out.

Frank, the anxiety-ridden one, stood up. "There's something here I don't understand. You keep talking about labor as if it were our enemy. It's not that simple. Sure we're adversaries but our employees are also our customers. If you keep wages low, who's going to buy our products?"

Nick bounded up. "You moron! The Wehrmacht, that's who."

"Sir!" Ludwig said. "Please, that's not true."

"The hell it isn't. I'm not listening to any more of this crap. You're looting all of Europe! Offering us the scraps won't make it right. You're nothing but hoodlums with a party and a slick patter."

"Gentlemen, please—my apologies—obviously we have a provocateur—"

Dieter was already slipping around from behind Ludwig. He jumped forward and slapped one hand on Nick's sleeve. "You will leave now!"

Nick snapped his arm away. "Get yer hands off!"

Dieter grabbed his elbow and pulled. "You are going!" They both gripped each other's coat sleeves and began pushing. Dieter spun the smaller man around in a circle. He drove him toward the door. Several of the wooden folding chairs went flying.

Oh, this is rich, Hawkins thought, *like a nightclub floor show. Go to it, boys.* A few of the others began lining up, ready to pick sides. *Even better—a riot.* The two men's wrestling knocked several more chairs flying.

Dieter started trying to reach up into his coat. *No doubt for a gun*, Hawkins thought. But Dieter couldn't quite free his arm from Nick's grasp.

A movement in the mirror. Daisy. Hawkins turned. She was now standing in the doorway, her mouth opened on the edge of a shriek of fright and horror. *Time to do something.* Hawkins jumped over the fallen chairs.

"Okay! Everybody outside! We're going to settle this fair and square," pushing the two struggling men through an open pair of glazed double doors and out onto a brick patio.

Several other men grabbed the brawlers and pulled them apart, shouting, "That's right! Fight fair!" as if it were a sporting match or a schoolyard brawl.

Hawkins pulled Nick away and shoved him, hard. He whispered in his ear, "Gun! Hear me? He's got a gun! Christ's sakes back off!"

Ludwig, horrified, landed on Dieter almost simultaneously, growling at him in German. Nick blanched and dropped back.

"God! Thanks. Bastards."

"I wouldn't go back in there if I were you."

"No," Nick answered quietly, then in a louder voice, "I'm leaving. Who's going with me?"

Perhaps a third of the group followed him off. Hawkins stood on the edge of the patio, watching them stream across the lawn until he heard clicking heels coming behind him.

-48-

Daisy was walking out the double doors, her face as white as her clenched knuckles. The coquettish manner had vanished.

"Mr. Hawkins, I want to thank you for breaking up that fight."

"Don't mention it." He put his hand out to shake. Instead she delicately squeezed the side of his hand with her fingers, holding it for a moment while she spoke, like a swimmer holding onto a dock.

"I had a vision of a riot wrecking the whole house."

"Indeed. It'd be tough getting bloodstains out of those old carpets."

"Blood? Excuse me?"

"Um … yes. Didn't you see it?"

"See what?"

"Ludwig's man. Carrying a gun. 'Bout to shoot that fellow. Probably would've if he'd gotten loose."

"A gun? In my house? Where?"

"Shoulder holster."

"I owe you more than I imagined."

"Quite all right."

She steadied and let go, her face reddening.

"Those brutes! The nerve! I never had any idea anything like this could happen."

"Well, if you don't mind my saying so, you ought to be a little pickier about who you let in your home."

"No, you're quite right."

"You said there were going to be more meetings?"

"Yes." Her face screwed up into a grimace. "They've got a lease for two more. Damn!"

"They pay up?"

"Yes."

"Give 'em the boot."

"But I'd have to refund the money." A little tic. "Not that that's any concern, of course."

"Don't. Kick him out. Claim this fracas was a breach of contract."

"He'll sue."

"No he won't. He won't do anything to draw the wrong kind of attention to himself. Or any bad publicity. He'll go quietly. Trust me."

She started to smile again, an amused, impish grin. "I think you're right. Sticking around?"

"Wouldn't miss it."

Hawkins crept in and sat in the back. Dieter had rearranged the scattered folding chairs in neat rows. Ludwig continued as if nothing had happened. He began handing out references to officials at specific ministries in charge of business and economic affairs in Berlin, Copenhagen, Paris and so on. At the end he also collected the names and addresses of the executives who stayed. Hawkins got on the end of the receiving line. When his turn finally came he piously shook Ludwig's hand.

"That disturbance—that's really embarrassing, Doctor."

"Oh, no, not at all. I should be thanking you." His eyes flicked over at Dieter, then whispered. "You really saved things."

"Aw—only doing what I could."

"I hope my associates in Berlin and I will be hearing from you."

"I'm sure Berlin will be hearing a great deal from us very soon."

Hawkins saw Daisy waiting. He broke off with a final greeting and slipped to a vantage point right outside the patio doors. *Will she do it?* he thought. *Does she have the moxie? Going to be interesting …*

Daisy stamped up to Ludwig. "Dr. Ludwig—"

"Miss Schenck, please let me apologize for the commotion. I assure—"

"That won't do. I'm afraid I must ask you to leave."

"I promise. There will be no more trouble. I understand why you are upset."

"Oh, you do, do you?" She pointed at Dieter. "Does that man have a gun?"

Ludwig's face froze. "That is none of your concern."

"Oh, he does then! How dare you bring a gun into my home! You pick up your folding chairs, your coffee Thermador, your strudel and … and clear out of here!"

"Then I expect our payment back!"

"The hell I will! That fight was a breach of contract—much less a gun. You're not getting a dime."

They both stood nose to nose for about thirty seconds, tense and shaking. Then Ludwig snapped his head at Dieter. "Wir gehen!"

Brilliant, Hawkins thought. *Oh, she sure does have what it takes.*

Daisy silently spun around and stamped back out into the hallway. Hawkins hopped off the patio, took a deep gasp of air. A half-suppressed laugh finally burst out. He slipped around the lawn to the front. Daisy saw him, opened the door and silently motioned him in. He carefully stood out of Ludwig's and Dieter's view. They were loudly and ostentatiously folding and stacking the little chairs.

Hawkins pointed at the old engraving of the captain on the wall. "I can see why the Spaniards were afraid of this old chap."

Daisy folded her arms, plopped back against the cannon and took a deep breath. "Thanks." She broke into a grin. "It worked."

"I'm glad. How much more do you know about those two?"

"A little."

"Could you tell me later?"

"Sure. How about tomorrow morning at the flat track, say about seven. I like to watch the workouts."

"The flat track?"

"Oh. The racecourse. That's what horse people call it. There's only one flat track in the horse world."

"Ah. Tomorrow, then."

-49-

Hawkins carefully spread two washcloths inside the sink basin and poured in the ice. Three bottles of orange soda fit nicely. Gave them a jostle. Not a clink. *There, almost ready*, he thought.

This kind of time-consuming operation always took deliberation and care even if the details seemed mundane. But when you were proposing to surveil a potential enemy for hours, maybe longer, comfort mattered.

Almost ready, he thought. Off with the shirt and tie. Put the old armchair next to the side door. Check Ludwig's room for sound. Nothing yet. Another bite from one of the sandwiches. A bang next door.

Hawkins gently pressed the cup of his stethoscope against the door and fitted the tubes in his ears. Their words penetrated the wood like paper.

A creaking sound. Ludwig's footsteps pacing up and down as he spoke in German.

"The business meetings are ruined! This is a small resort. Everyone in town will hear about the fight by nightfall! It's a damned lucky thing that valve executive stopped it in time."

Me … he's talking about me, Hawkins thought. A guffaw almost burst out.

"And don't forget I've been given the power to immediately send you back home if I have cause, and I do! I don't have to explain what that'd mean."

"Yessir."

Dieter's probably standing at attention in the center of the gaudy but seedy room. No doubt sweating away, Hawkins thought.

"Where did you get that gun?"

"It's standard issue. I thought you knew."

"No. Keep it out of sight."

"Yessir."

"Let me review. You'll never take direct action again without my permission. You'll act in a manner consistent with our covers unless directed otherwise."

"Yessir."

"And what is that?"

"You represent the Reich Ministry of Foreign Trade—" There was a pause.

"And?"

"I am your chauffeur."

"Exactly."

Ludwig's tone softly shifted. "I realize this is a great disappointment for you. I'm sorry. Truly. But the war will be over soon. You'll get your medal and a handshake from the führer, too."

Hawkins thought he almost heard a sob.

"The führer … if it wasn't for him I would've gone to the Olympics last winter. I would be the first combined biathlon and downhill ski champion by now. I could've gone to Hollywood. I could've been the next Sonja Henie, I could've done for skiing what she did for skating. Now here I am spying."

"The war won't last long. You'll get another chance. No one will ever know."

"There won't be a next time. Not for me. It'll be too late. A younger man will take my place." Dieter sounded inconsolable. "He'll be in school all this time, training. I'll never catch up."

Ludwig hesitated, gently searching for the right words. "You're … not alone. Many men are making sacrifices because of the war. The Fatherland needs you. Only you have the right skills for the job. Remember, being a chauffeur isn't your real status in life, any more than an actor in a movie ceases to be an actor. He's still a star, and you are, too."

"I understand."

"Good. That's a real champion. We'll keep this to ourselves."

"Oh! Thank you, sir! It won't happen again."

"That's the spirit. Remember, your superiors as well as mine are extremely enthusiastic about this mission. That's why you're here. Come back down in a few minutes. We'll order dinner in. We don't want to attract any more attention."

Dieter carefully shut the door behind him. Hawkins hovered at the connecting door a moment after Dieter left, listening for anything, straining at the earpieces. Then Ludwig shouted in German, "God dammit! God dammit all to hell!" kicking something in the room. "Idiots! Imbeciles!"

Hawkins reflexively leapt back from the door, ears ringing from the bang in the stethoscope. *The door—damn! He's trying to kick it down. Must've heard me. How? No, impossible.* He waited a minute. Nothing. *No, he's not knocking the door down. It's only the earpieces magnifying everything.*

Hawkins gingerly stepped back and placed the stethoscope on the door. All clear. Ludwig had taken his anger out on the furniture, that was all. He listened to the rhythmic creaking and pounding as Ludwig furiously paced up and down the old floors like a zoo animal. The doctor snapped on the radio and sat down.

Hawkins returned to his sodas and sandwiches, mentally sorting and thinking.

That phrase—"your superiors as well as mine ..." A joint operation, of some sort. In that case, who's Dieter with? Most likely the military. Probably had to join the army to get on the team. War starts, next thing he knows he's here.

An Olympian. *No wonder he looks so powerful,* Hawkins thought. *And no wonder he's so resentful. He knows the truth. He'll never have another chance.* Sad.

Totally misread his anger, Hawkins thought. Yes, probably was a Hitler-jugend. Weren't they all, now? But not the typical brown-shirted bullyboy.

He's angry. Wanted to come to America. Be a star. *Sonja Henie? Key W in on that, with his motion picture industry connections. From Olympian to chauffeur, what a comedown. That's got to be gagging—perhaps he's ripe for being turned?*

-50-

The grandstand's high slate roofs, peaks and gables hovered like a mirage, floating above a morning fog. As Hawkins walked, flowing awnings, red and white flowers and ancient trees slowly emerged from the mist, then white clapboard walls.

No Daisy, yet. He settled at a table under a soaring wooden roof with beams aged dark brown like an ancient country church in Sussex or Kent. The sun slowly peeked above the treetops. Early golden rays chased away little rolling wisps, catching and flashing the dew on the rich emerald lawns. An intense blue sky followed.

Hawkins almost reclined, cradling his tea. The horses whipped along the track, gliding between each bound. Hoofs hit the dirt with distant thuds, sending clods of dirt flying. When the grooms stood and pulled on their mounts steam rose from the horses' glistening flanks, mixing with the mist.

So beautiful, Hawkins thought. *So serene. The war feels so far away. Got to go, get back in. I know. That hasn't changed. But still … here now.*

Daisy was coming. She was wearing a black silk dress and hat tilted at a rakish angle with a net veil that hung halfway down her face. Long hair covered one eye, as usual. She pulled off one long glove as she walked, extending a perfectly manicured hand straight in front of her. Her hair caught the low rays of the sun with a golden flash. Red lips parted. He forgot about the morning. And the war.

"Hawkins, dear, hello. Am I late?" It was seven-thirty. "I'm sorry. You know we girls take so much more time than you boys do."

He took her hand and guided her to a seat. "Nonsense. I've been watching the dawn. It's a gorgeous morning."

She glanced up. "Yes, it is. Generally though, I prefer sunsets. What did Damon Runyon call it, the 'tubercular light of dawn'?"

"I think so. Sunsets are deeper. But mornings are clearer."

"You're in a poetic mood this morning." He smiled and shrugged. "Did you order?"

"Just tea." He motioned for the waiter, inattentively ordering a plate of pancakes. Daisy promptly ordered steak and eggs, coffee and the melon and berries without checking the menu.

She reached up, pulled out a long hat pin and lifted off her elegant chapeau, perching it on the seat next to her. Then she tipped her head forward. She shook her head so her loose hair partially fell down, veiling her face again. Then she swept it up and back with one swift motion. She rested her chin on her fingers. He noticed circles under her eyes.

"You look tired."

"I am, a little."

"Did I get you out of bed early?"

"Oh no, it's the usual summer swirl. Too many parties. It's tiring. Hard to keep up with them all."

"That's a problem?"

"I get invitations for two or three every night. It's impossible to know which one to go to without giving offense. Everyone's exhausted all the time."

"I wish I had problems like that."

"Ohh?—Uhmmm. I'm sorry. Here you have to go to all these dreadful meetings. And I'm babbling about parties!" She tilted her head quizzically. "What business are you in anyway?" He gave her one of his phony cards. She studied it, intrigued, as she sipped her juice.

"Why are you so interested in Dr. Ludwig?"

He grudgingly shifted his attention.

"We want to find out everything we can before we make any … business decisions. What can you remember about them you didn't tell me yesterday?"

"Let's see. Yes. Initially I didn't realize who I was renting to. At first it was a man named Walter Ventnor. You know, on the radio?"

"Really?"

"Yes. Then they told me his office was arranging it for Ludwig as a favor. Ventnor's people were very upset when I wanted to withdraw. They were the ones who offered the deal."

"Which was?"

"A whole month's rent for a mere three meetings. I mean, they were put out and it seemed unduly spendthrift to refuse such a generous offer."

"Of course. If you don't mind my asking, what's a month's rent here worth?"

"In August? Little over four thousand."

He involuntarily gagged. *Incredible. That's … what? Three times the average man's yearly salary? Three new Packards?*

"Just three meetings? Seems a bit steep."

She seemed utterly unimpressed by the number. No big deal at all.

"Oh, not really. Not that many good houses here. Not like the manor, anyway."

"And who paid? Ludwig or Ventnor?"

"Ventnor paid for all of it."

"How?"

"Oh, cash."

"Cash?" She nodded. "How'd they deliver it?"

"Now that part was a bit odd. Bank courier came all the way up from Manhattan. Otherwise it was by phone or through the local agent." He sat silent. "You find that interesting?"

"Throwing money around like that? Absolutely."

"You really don't like them very much do you?"

"No, I don't. I used to work in Europe. Saw them march into Prague.

I couldn't describe what it was like. When people found out I was an American they came up to me in the street offering me bags of cash for my passport or my help. A couple of men even offered me their wives. Can you imagine that? I mean, what kind of fear is it makes a man offer his wife to a total stranger?" He stopped and sighed. Daisy was silent. "The worst thing I saw was this one family. Jews, I presume. They panicked. The mother and father tied themselves and their children together and they all jumped off a roof."

She clearly was taken aback by the intensity of his answer.

"I'm sorry. I've ruined breakfast," he said.

"Not at all. It's just … Why do business with them, then?"

"We can't avoid it." She smiled, lifting her head up, quizzically waiting for him to elaborate. He wasn't about to oblige. "I saw your reflection in the mirror when Ludwig was speaking. You didn't seem to like what he was saying, either."

Caught off guard, she seemed confused by his question and slowly picked at her answer.

"Oh. I don't know. All that stuff about labor peace irritated me. Everybody's got a right to try and make something of themselves. Isn't that why we all came here in the first place? Get away from rotten old Europe, all that trouble, have a better life?"

Daisy's answer instantly switched the train of Hawkins' thoughts to a different track. *Yes, rotten old Europe*, he thought. *Millions had come here to get away from rotten old Europe.* Away from feudal lords and petty feuds. Rotating drafts and ancient hatreds. Escape from everything he'd seen the last few years.

"Everyone … yes. Everyone should have a right to a better life," he said, almost in a whisper. He paused a long moment. "What about the people over there? Don't they have a right to a better life, too?" Only it came out half-hearted. Or felt half-hearted. A question crossed his mind. *Do I feel obliged to say that? Or maybe I expect myself to say that. What about my right to a better life? Maybe that was the real question.*

"Hawkins, you're a very unusual businessman," Daisy said.

"I'm in a very unusual business."

"Now answer my question."

"What?"

"Why are you so concerned with these people? Germany's a long ways away."

"I don't know. I'm not so sure anymore."

-51-

Breakfast arrived. Hawkins buttered his pancakes, curiously watching Daisy dig into her steak and eggs with the vigor of a posh bricklayer. Suddenly she remembered something she wanted to tell him so eagerly she began talking with her mouth half full.

"I just remembered. That man—Ludwig—is going to a party tonight."

"Where?"

"Big annual racing ball—Mrs. Simpson-Saunders. Old friend of the family. I was invited a while back, of course."

"Are you going?"

"I don't know." She glanced up coyly. "I don't have an escort. She's rather old-fashioned. No unattached ladies." They both began probing delicately. "All formal, of course."

"I've always enjoyed formal parties."

"Yes. I do, too."

"Would you like to go with me? If the invitation is still open, of course."

"Oh, yes! I'd enjoy that. I'm sure it's still open. Cassie and I, that's her daughter, we went to Emma Willard together."

"That's great."

"Why, thank you, Hawkins, how kind of you to ask." She spoke as if he'd invited her in the first place, the epitome of genteel grace.

"What kind of music will they have?"

"Oh … probably one of those society sweet bands. Old people's music."

"Ooooh."

She shrugged her arms and shoulders up, snapping her fingers and did a pouting, swaying mimic of a jitterbug sitting in her chair, waving her fork to an imaginary beat.

"It don't mean a thing—"

He instantly jumped in. "If you ain't got that swing—" and they both burst out laughing.

"Just saw Cab Calloway at the Paramount."

"Oh, you are a hep cat! When I'm in the city my friends and I like to go up to the Savoy Ballroom."

"How marvelous." Daisy's smiling eyes and face filled his vision. *Be so easy to slip off, take Kelly's offer, leave it all behind.* They both burst out laughing again as if the song was their own private code word. "In my line of work, I don't get much time for that. You're a city girl then?"

"That's right, never been big on country life. Shoot a little skeet, never real birds. A little boating and sailing, a little riding. Do the August meet, that's it."

"You're here for the parties then, the nightlife."

"That's right. Love parties, night clubbing, smart cafés, music, dancing."

"Where do people go for entertainment around here?"

"You can go over to the colored section around Congress Street— oh, Jack's Harlem Club or the Tally-Ho, they're swell. Or out to—" She seemed to catch herself, as if she lost her train of thought or something, "Oh, I don't know, up and down Broadway."

"I see."

"You know, I don't know much about you, Hawkins. Where do you live?"

"The city."

"Any hobbies?"

"Ah-umm. I guess not. Never had the time or been settled enough. I dabble in antiques a bit. For a time I covered the Continent out of Paris. Amazing flea markets. Les Puces de Saint-Ouen at Porte de Clignancourt. Acres and acres of it. Also at Porte de Vanves."

"Vous parlez français!"

"Bien, naturellement. Et vous?"

"J'ai appris le français à l'école. Ainsi je suis—um, um, rusty."

"Rouillé."

"Oui, rouillé. Never been to Paris is why. I'd love to see those marchés. Go to any galeries?"

"They're all over Paris, especially the Left Bank."

"What's happening in modern art, it's so exciting. You see a little bit, you just know you want to see more."

"New way of seeing the world."

"Exactly! Been to the new Modern in Manhattan?"

"There's a new museum in New York? Where?"

"On Fifty-Third Street. Remarkable Picasso exhibit last winter."

"I was abroad. I'd love that. You winter in the city?"

"Yes. We could go to the Modern!" She smiled brightly, but as she finished her sentence Daisy spotted someone across the tables. She stretched up in her seat and began waving and slowly calling, "Yoo-hoo, Chet! Chet-ly, over here, dear!" She turned to Hawkins. "Old friend of mine."

-52-

The man from the meeting. Only now he'd changed into a loud hound-stooth jacket and lost the tie. He had the same pinched, vacant expression. The moment he arrived at the table Daisy's tone brusquely changed.

"Chet, I'm mad at you. Look what happened!"

Chet acted startled. "It's not my fault!"

"Is so. Ventnor's your friend!"

Chet finally recognized Hawkins' presence, irritably glancing down at him. "Have we met?"

"I was at Daisy's yesterday. Roy Hawkins." Hawkins stood, holding out his hand. Chet mumbled hello, inattentively and weakly shook it, then sat down, still obviously annoyed. "You know Walter Ventnor?" Hawkins said.

"Yes. I'm a big supporter—"

But Daisy wasn't letting up.

"It's still your fault. You shouldn't be recommending someone who'd traffic with a man like that."

"Hey! I was at that meeting, 'trafficking,' as you say."

"Well, a man ought to mind things."

"How would I know what was going to happen?"

A horse raced by. Daisy abruptly changed the subject.

"Ooh, is that Commander York?"

Chet shook his head. "No, that's Commander Penn."

It seemed Chet Branch, of the Branches of Park Avenue, Kentuck and Texas, was very rich, owned a large and successful racing stable and pulled a considerable amount of weight in Thoroughbred circles.

"I thought Commander York was up today," Daisy said. She sounded surprised, intrigued.

Chet's expression wound up in frustration and irritation, as if wires running through his face had been yanked out the top. "Naw—the idiots left a window open in the rail car. He caught a chill coming up."

"Oh, that's too bad! Strange something so big could be so fragile, isn't it?"

Chet sourly looked at Hawkins. "They're fickle, picky creatures."

Daisy determinedly pressed on. "That's too bad. York was heavily favored. Does anybody know?"

"No. We're keeping him out of sight. We've entered Commander Penn in the second."

"But poor Penn, I didn't think he was ready for a stakes race?"

With that Chet's face finally snapped to a real and intense focus, tightly clenching his teeth, curling his lip, his voice a low growl. "He will be."

Daisy lightly inhaled and laughed. "Ooh! Chetly, Chetly! Naughty-naughty."

"I've got this stakes race coming to me. I've had it coming to me for years!"

"So the horseys get their morning glass of juice, too!"

A knowing but somehow jejune smirk lifted Chet's face. "That's a laugh! If I'm not winning, I just change the rules so I do."

"Oh, by the way, Chet, Mr. Hawkins invited me to Millicent's ball."

Chet's face froze, the smirk vanished. He flushed slightly, barely glancing sideways at Hawkins. "Oh. I see."

Obviously, Chet had an interest in Daisy. *And no wonder*, Hawkins thought. As the conversation moved on the splendid morning soured bit by bit. Hawkins mulled the possibilities. *Had Chet failed to ask Daisy to the party? Maybe she wanted to stir him up. Or punish him for the uproar at the house. She really seems interested, though. How can I compete with Chet? His money? His horses? There's no way I can tell Daisy the truth. Don't even know when my next payday will be. Worst of all, I'm lying about almost everything about me.*

What an impossible position. Like to punch the SOB. Then Hawkins got irritated with himself. *What's the point, decking such an insipid creature? It certainly wouldn't take very much. That won't help, either.*

"Will we see you there?" Daisy said.

"Yes, I'm introducing Ventnor around," Chet said.

But you won't be showing Daisy around, Hawkins thought. *Let's rub it in a little.*

"I've heard so much about him. I'd really like to meet him. Would you introduce us?"

Pinned, Chet tightly glanced at Daisy. Then back at Hawkins. His irritated expression restored the morning's glory.

"Why not." With a sharp gesture, he checked his gold watch. "I have to go."

Chet ambled off without another word.

"What was all that—juice talk? What's he mean, change the rules?" Hawkins said.

Daisy giggled slightly. "Oops! Ahem—he's—um—helping the horses out. You know, *chemically*. They call it juicing."

"Is that allowed? It sounds like cheating."

She smiled brightly. "Oh, I'm sure there's a silly little rule against it somewhere. Chet hates to lose. He goes off his hinges when he does."

"I've seen what happens when people decide they don't want to play by the rules. There's no bottom."

"I don't know about you, I know an opportunity when I see one. The betting windows just opened." She gave him a little peck on the cheek. "See you at six!"

Hawkins longingly watched her elegant profile disappear into the clubhouse. Then he poured himself another cup of tea.

That conversation wasn't idle at all, he thought. Not from the moment she heard about Commander York being sick. She knew Chet would be annoyed. Knew he would spill. Yes, played him perfectly.

Don't be a principled idiot, Hawkins thought. He took out his wallet, counted the money he'd made off Madame Delage's vermeil set and headed inside to find a betting window.

-53-

Hawkins kept pacing up and down the newsstand, lying in wait, one eye on the elevator—Ludwig would be coming out any moment. He absent-mindedly bought copies of the *New Yorker* and the *Racing Form* to fend off the impatient concessionaire. But he was thinking about Daisy. The idea he actually had a date with her was still sinking in.

The elevator doors finally opened, exposing Ludwig. Hawkins wheeled around, head down, buried in the *Racing Form*. They nearly collided again. Ludwig seemed delighted to see him.

"Why, Dr. Ludwig! Excuse me! How are you?"

"Myself? Very well. Join me for breakfast."

"Aww, I'm sorry—I already ate. I was out at dawn watching the workouts."

"Dawn? You must be a serious horseman to get up so early. Join me for coffee then."

Inside, the tailcoated maître d' promptly led Hawkins and Ludwig to a table for two. Dieter awkwardly, uncertainly stood by. Once he'd seated the "gentlemen" the maître d', a tall, elderly black man with pure white hair and an aloof, aristocratic manner, beckoned Dieter with a remarkably long curled finger. He led him toward the kitchen to sit with the rest of the servants. It only took a split second for Dieter to fall in and follow. From the back Dieter's neck appeared to flush a deep crimson, almost purple. That the former Hitlerjungen was going to be eating with the "Afrikaner" had to be part of it. Ludwig seemed delighted.

"How are the meetings going, Doctor?"

Ludwig grunted slightly. He deliberately set his menu down and leaned forward to confide in Hawkins.

"I've been forced to cancel them after what happened. I must thank you again. You saved us from a dreadful scene. At least the papers didn't find out. It's nice to know we have friends here."

"I try to make myself useful."

"Did you find the meeting valuable, for your valve business, I mean?"

"The chief's going to be very interested. But enough business. Have you been out to the track?" He detected a twinge of disappointment or irritation or both in Ludwig's manner.

"No, I've been too busy. My work here is too important. I—"

"You ought to take time to relax. Every executive has to take care of himself. Why, I was saying to Chet Branch at breakfast this morning that—"

"I didn't know you knew Mr. Branch."

"Uh—yes—I know him."

"Then you are closer to us than I thought."

"Have you seen him today?" Ludwig shook his head no. "He gave me a tip on the races."

"Is that so?"

"Yes. Now don't tell anyone else." Hawkins peeked over one shoulder, then over the other, eyes rolling from side to side as if eager throngs were listening. "You can keep a secret, can't you?" Ludwig nodded. "If you've a few C's loose, put 'em on Commander York in the first, to win. Here's the scoop. All the insiders in this business know that Commander York's been sick. Although—well, what can I say, that's supposed to be privileged information. You know how that goes—"

"I certainly do."

"They're all buzzing about Commander Penn, instead. Chet entered him at the last minute. However, Penn's only there to deflect attention from York, sort of like a magician's trick—you know, misdirection. Penn's never won anything. What's really happening is Chet's giving York a little help." Hawkins broadly winked. "You know. Chemically."

"I don't know. I'm not much of a gambler."

"I know what you're saying. But listen—chance has nothing to do with this. It's as sure as sure things get. As you said, who's dumb enough to play a game where you don't make the rules. Neither is Chet."

"Aaah—I see. That's quite different. I will! It's kind of you to share this with me."

"It's my pleasure."

"Would you join me?"

"Gee, I'm sorry. I promised to give a ride to a few friends of mine. But I'll watch for you."

Disappointment was written all over Ludwig's face. He obviously would've enjoyed a little friendly company.

"Very well. I'll see you there."

"Good. I have to get going." He bent over and whispered conspiratorially, "I've got an important meeting—with a bookie."

-54-

"You've news—"

W's voice boomed into the booth. Hawkins spotted Ludwig through the glass door, crossing the lobby to his car. He waved. Ludwig smiled, happily waving back.

"Yes. There was a near riot, a real scene, at that house our target rented. He's canceled the rest of his meetings—"

"I know," W said. Ludwig disappeared out the entrance. "Got a telex from Bermuda half an hour ago. Ludwig used that microprinter. Mentions you."

"Really?" Hawkins started to laugh.

"He's furious about his assistant. The man's not Abwehr. He's with the SD."

"Nazi security service? Suspected something like that. I surveilled them all last night from my listening post. Ludwig really chewed him out afterward. Reminded him he had the power to send him back. Promised not to report what happened, incidentally." The sound of W snorting came over the receiver. "How come the SS wants to put its thumb in this pie, though? Shipping times, naval intelligence—that's not their sort of thing."

"Right. The SS isn't interested in helping the navy, dopes like Bailey radioing U-boats. Something else entirely. A whole other operation. Like what are they going to do with that sniper rifle? If there's something major going on, they'll want to be in on it. That tells us something. It's big. Anything else?"

"Yes." Hawkins told him about Dieter's Olympic ambitions.

"Sonja Henie? He's that good? Interesting. Be easy to find. Keep an eye out for any opportunities. It'd be incredible to have him working for us. Put him in a room with a big star, who knows?"

"That'd be his sense of himself. I have the feeling he can't be too far off. He's suffered a terrible comedown. He's a very angry man."

"Who wouldn't be. Anything else?"

"Yes." Hawkins told him about Chet and his connection to Ventnor.

"We'll check them out."

-55-

Hawkins plunged into the dense, surging crowd. Ludwig—and Dieter for that matter—were nowhere to be seen. And Daisy. Was she here? After working and worming his way past the front of the clubhouse he circled into the paddock. No luck, yet.

The August heat at the flat track had risen to tropical proportions, Ascot in an oven. *Damn coat feels like it's shrinking*, Hawkins thought, *shirt must be soaked through already*. A cluster of women drifted by, all flowered hats, print dresses and tanned shoulders. Their faces were pleasantly flushed from the heat and humidity, happily chatting away. No jackets and ties. They won on that one.

Finally, there, Ludwig and Dieter, leaning against a low fence. Dieter was listening to a nearby bandstand filled with musicians stamping out Dixieland, head happily bobbing in time to the music. Ludwig stared down at the ground, arms folded. Is he annoyed at the music? Hard to tell. The bell rang. They both expectantly moved toward the rail.

Hawkins was so preoccupied watching them that he scarcely noticed the race going on, not looking once. The horses burst across the finish line. The crowd roared. At once Ludwig sharply walked away, ripped up and threw his ticket on the ground. Dieter said something. Ludwig angrily glared at him. Dieter stepped back, held his hands up in a gesture of surprise. Ludwig wordlessly turned away. Dieter fell in behind him, then lightly smiled, leaning back.

Only when the meal horns overhead blared out the final results did Hawkins take the ticket from his wallet and, although he knew full well what it was, check it.

Commander Penn had won, exactly like Chet said he would. *Incredible how casually Chet dropped information of such value,* Hawkins thought. *Astounding, actually. That's really the thing, to so casually throw around information—money really—of such enormous value. Have to concentrate a second,* he thought, mentally double-checking the math. A thousand dollars' worth of the two grand from Madame Delage's vermeil set had ballooned to twenty thousand.

Almost in a dream, he found himself moving toward the window, his feet feeling like they were moving on their own. He slapped the ticket on the counter at the hundred-dollar window. The clerk inspected it a moment, put it away, opened the cash drawer and passed out two stiff new wads of hundred-dollar bills. Ten thousand dollars apiece, each with the original green and black Treasury wrappers still sealing them.

Hawkins zipped his nail across the edge of the bound notes. Fresh. Crisp. Even aromatic. *They don't seem real. But they are. More money than my life's savings. A lot more. Actually, more than I've earned in my entire life.* He uneasily glanced over his shoulder, nervously stuffing the bills down into the bottom of his pants pocket. But as he walked away no one seemed to be paying any attention.

In the anonymity of the crowd, he relaxed. The magnitude of his windfall took a few minutes to sink in. *The vermeil set. I could buy it back from Bruno. Give it back to Madame Delage, after the war. That'd be the right thing. Or a car, like the Cord. Easy. The salary, paying my way, not a big thing anymore.* He began drifting across the paddock in a happy daze. A bugle called the next race. *Oh. Damn. Ludwig and Dieter. Yes—still a war going on.*

Fortunately, they weren't far way. Hawkins took off his hat, rolling the brim up, trying as hard as possible to force a downcast expression on his face. It took a considerable effort with twenty thousand dollars in his pants. He slowly, painfully walked up to the pair. Ludwig was not effusive.

"Oh. Mr. Hawkins. Hello."

"Hello, Dr. Ludwig. How about that Commander York. I hope you didn't put too much on him."

"Only a couple of hundred. It's nothing." The nettled tone of his voice contradicted his words. Dieter smirked smugly and made a strangled noise.

Ludwig's eyes snapped sideways at him, sharply. His mouth hovered open a moment but he said nothing. His teeth slowly clicked back together as he carefully exhaled.

"Well, these things happen," Hawkins said. "I've got more tips, if you're interested."

"No. Thank you. I think I'll stick to the two-dollar window."

"Okay. I better go, my friends are waiting. Sorry again."

Hawkins ran off, circled back around where Ludwig and Dieter couldn't see him and let his grin out for a real run. *Score one for the Brits.*

-56-

The porter handed Hawkins his freshly pressed white double-breasted evening jacket. He gave the man a big tip, a whole dollar, not the expected dime or even, generously, a quarter. The porter's face exploded in a smile.

All ready. Then Hawkins checked the time. Instead of looking at the hour he actually looked at his watch. Purchased the old Benrus in school, years ago. The chrome plating was worn right down to the brass. *Certainly doesn't make a very good impression*, he thought. A bubble burst inside his head. *I can afford a hundred watches if I want to and Tiffany's summer branch is right off the lobby.*

A few minutes later a salesman was eagerly following him up and down the beveled glass display cases, certain of a decent commission. The clerk well knew the look of a man in the full possession of a big hit, a man freed from the constraints of expectations, a man who wasn't about to settle for an inexpensive plated case.

Hawkins quickly found his choice, an elegant Curvex shaped like a long, round, sleek crescent. It neatly fitted his wrist, sliding coolly under his shirtsleeve. He paid the previously unthinkable $125 and headed for his room, every few yards popping his wrist from his sleeve, checking the hour.

-57-

The door to the communal washroom slammed shut, the bang a percussive beat to the syncopation of a dozen dripping old faucets. The place had a slightly mildew odor mixed with the sharp sweet smell of disinfectant. Not offensive but not pleasant, either. Hawkins hung his bathrobe on the shower stall's old wooden door. After snapping the latch shut, he carefully took off his new watch and stored it in the pocket. He turned up the shower hard, briskly soaping his sweaty, sticky body. A relief.

Behind came a click or rattle. Something flipped over his face. A hard jerk pulled his head back. He slapped his hands up to his face. A wet towel. It yanked back, hard. His feet slipped, skipping back, almost losing his balance on the slick soapy tiles. Hawkins reached back, trying to grab it. It was wound tightly, twisted into a big rope like a ponytail. He dug into the soaked, smooth cloth, trying to find an edge. It fit over his head like a shroud, nothing to grab.

For a split second Hawkins fumbled, tugging at the towel while his feet skidded on the floor.

"Hey, let go!" as if he were the victim of a schoolboy prank. He inhaled. Only sucked in half a breath, the rest water. It hit him. *Naked. Under attack. Can't breathe.* His heart began racing.

Hawkins swung backward hard with his elbow. Nothing but air. The man with the towel slammed him forward into the shower head. The nozzle crunched into Hawkins' forehead with a shuddering, painful jolt. The shower spray soaked the towel again. Like being underwater.

I'm drowning, Hawkins thought.

The man laughed, a high hysterical giggle. A shiver rippled through Hawkins' skin. His bare feet uselessly spun on the slippery floor. Hawkins swung his fist blindly behind him. Nothing again. *Still drowning—can't breathe.* A tremendous punch hit right in the kidneys. The blow slammed him against the wall. An incandescent cramp of searing pain exploded up his side. Then another, right in the same spot. More water in the mouth. Head starting to buzz.

The pain somehow cleared the frenzy from Hawkins' mind. An image flashed across his vision. *Father. Must be the sensation of water and drowning. We were at the shore, so many years ago. Learning to swim, standing waist deep in the water.*

His smile.

"Remember," Pop said, "if you get out too far or fall out of a boat, don't panic. That's the main thing. If you don't panic you can survive anything." *Don't panic. That's it. Don't, don't, don't panic. Stop trying to get away.*

The man slammed him into the wall again. *The wall. Of course. Stop swinging.* Hawkins slapped his hands flat against the wall, braced the leg on his good side against the tiles. No longer slipping and sliding. The buzzing in his head wailed to a crescendo. He shoved with every remaining ounce of strength.

The push caught the man just as he was reaching back for another blow. He lost his balance. They slammed together and careened backward into the stall door. The frame shattered into a dozen pieces. They tumbled together onto the floor. Hawkins landed on top cushioning his fall. The double impact knocked the air out of the man with a huge grunt.

Hawkins grabbed the bottom of the towel and pulled it forward. Just enough time. A deep breath of air. Head cleared slightly. The man snapped it back.

Hawkins jammed his elbow as hard as he could into the man's stomach, did it again. The man grunted. He tried rolling. The towel loosened a bit. Another breath. Hawkins grabbed the man's arm and held on.

They rolled left, then right. After a minute of struggle the man managed to partly free himself. He pounded his fist into the side of Hawkins' head, the hard bony part behind the cheekbone. This time the towel protected him, the nap blunting the blow. The twisted end the man held with his other hand prevented Hawkins' head from snapping too dangerously to the side.

Every rolling motion momentarily loosened the towel, giving Hawkins a precious chance to breathe. His strength began seeping back. The man dug in his heels, arched his back. A huge groan of effort. He flipped them both over. The man got halfway up on his knees, over Hawkins, on top again.

The man clenched his captive arm up to Hawkins' chest and pulled back on the towel as far as he could. He slammed Hawkins' face into the floor. The shuddering impact momentarily jarred Hawkins. The man yanked his arm free. He pushed down on Hawkins and jumped up. Hawkins struggled to follow. The man swung a vicious, whipping kick, missing his groin, hitting his upper thigh. Hawkins coiled and thrust his arm down, trying to protect his balls. He swung with the other, trying to make contact. Hawkins threw his weight forward against the towel. The man couldn't hold the weight. They lurched forward. A foot grazed Hawkins' ribs, the point of the toe zinging by like a bullet.

Hawkins barely grabbed the ankle on the man's boot. He partly rode it as it tried to crash into him again. His mouth tasted of the pasty, salty, coppery flavor of blood running from his nose and lips.

The man landed one good kick right into his stomach. Hawkins felt for a moment he'd throw up. Probably would have, had he been fuller. The man tried ineffectually to kick him in the groin before landing one last grazing kick on Hawkins' hip that sent him rolling over and over into the stall.

Hawkins barely heard a smashing noise as the man broke past what was left of the door, a few footsteps. Then he passed out.

-58-

Rain. It's raining, Hawkins thought. Then a moment later, *No it's not.* He lay in a fetal position in the center of the shower stall, the towel under his head stained pink with blood and water. His face was vibrating. An incredibly intense burning sensation hovered over the right kidney. He tried to move. The muscles in his stomach and hip ached and twitched. He painfully rolled over on his stomach and achingly rose to his knees. He violently threw up, spraying the floor with vomit.

He lurched over the slime, grabbing hold of the pipes, tortuously pulling himself up to the showerhead. As he stood hanging on, his strength slowly began creeping back with each gasping breath. The hot water gradually relaxed the twitching muscles enough so he could move. He finally stumbled out, holding on to the side of the stall for support, staggering over to the sink. He braced himself on the basin and rested his head against the mirror.

The corner of his mouth and nose were bleeding profusely. He reached up and gingerly felt his nose. It didn't seem to be broken. He pulled a wad of brown paper towels from a dispenser, soaked them and mashed them against his nose and cheek. He licked the inside of his teeth, feeling them out. Still there.

Then, out of nowhere, he started to laugh. Giddily. Hilariously. *Still alive, by God. Still alive and not in too bad a shape. Nothing broken. Still have all my teeth.* Leaning on the sink, he limped to his bathrobe, slowly bending down to pick it up, pulling it on before instinctively reaching in the pocket for his watch. *Gone. No, it can't be,* he thought. *That just can't be, it's here somewhere.* He fell on his knees and started pawing through the pieces of door and stall, throwing them about the washroom. Several minutes later he gave up. Gone. Stolen.

Stolen? The room—half-limping, half-running, he tore back down the hall, hastily racing in and around the bed. It was untouched. Everything in place, clothes, lockpicks, cameras, still there. *Lucky thing the cash is in the hotel safe.*

Then he almost fell down on the bed and began wildly pounding the mattress. *The best watch I ever owned,* he thought. *Stolen after less than fifteen minutes.* Thirty minutes ago it had symbolized good fortune and stepping up in the world. Now someone'd taken it away. Anger flashing to a boil again, he yanked on his pants and shoes and bolted out of the room for the hotel desk. He'd almost reached the elevator before he began thinking and slowed down.

Hotel management will call the police. There'll be questions. He stopped dead in the middle of the hallway. *Actually, don't really know who did this. Or why. Never saw his face. Anyone could've seen me win money at the track. Or seen me buy the watch at Tiffany's. After all, what's gone? Or it could be a stray mugger, passing through the washroom, on the prowl for opportunities.*

And then, it could be Ludwig. He chewed on that a second. No, Ludwig would never do it himself, he'd send Dieter. Hawkins remembered the attacker's chilling, vicious, childish giggle. *Dieter? Maybe.*

And yet if Ludwig did order it, I can't be sure why. Could Ludwig be onto me? No way of knowing. Maybe it's not business—I burned him at the track, after all. What was I thinking, muddying the water like that? Big mistake, too much of a chance, getting in so close. A trick like that—that's personal. And the arrogance—larking about like I'm on holiday, and for small money, too. Wouldn't have done something like this on the Continent. What now?

Daisy … probably late already. Nothing's keeping me from that party.

Back in his room Hawkins dug a styptic pencil out of his shaving kit. Gritting his teeth, he jammed the stick up his nose and ground it around. A remarkably sharp pain, like the pain of a shaving cut, but immeasurably larger, shot across his face up into his eye. Then he ground it into the corner of his mouth. With a convulsive shout he flung it across the room. It worked. The bleeding stopped.

He toweled himself off and quickly dressed, combing his wet hair in the big mirror before he left. On the way out he stopped by room service for an ice pack.

-59-

Daisy flung the door open, a hard expression on her lovely face. It was obvious she was not used to being kept waiting.

"Hawkins, you're—" She caught sight of the ice pack. Her expression instantly changed. Surprise, then horror. "Hurt!" She grabbed his arm, pulling him to a settle. He sat, his side and hip still throbbing.

"Daisy, my apologies. I detest people who are late."

She cringed at the sight of the swollen, gummy cut in the side of his mouth.

"What happened?"

He told her.

"And you fought them off?"

Them, well ...

"Ah—yes."

"Do you still want to go to the party? We don't have to. You can't feel like it."

"Oh, absolutely. This isn't as bad as it looks. Besides, it'll take my mind off it. Let's go!"

Even better than I expected, he thought, *she's more ravishing than before.* A dark strapless gown. Long black satin gloves. Pearls around the neck. He caught a whiff of perfume floating above the whoosh of black tulle peeking from under the skirt.

"You look magnificent." One little twirl. That licking wiped from mind, the throb receding. *On rare occasions I've encountered women like this*, he thought. He'd seen them across a dance floor or in the corner of a busy café and they stood so much above the herd that they ruined the evening, for the very sight of them made it impossible to look at another without a galling sensation of disappointment and regret. *Only tonight, if only tonight, I'll have nothing to regret.*

She hugged a hand around his arm and gathered her rustling skirt with the other. They hurried off.

The immense gray-shingled Victorian mansion flowed down story by story, pressing against the earth, its long porches incongruously lit by strings of gaily colored paper lanterns gently swaying in the breeze. Sprightly music and the happy murmur of a partying crowd echoed from out back. Thankfully, a valet took the Cord. Hawkins and Daisy walked arm in arm across the lawn.

"And you have no clue who did it?"

"I've got a feeling I'll find out."

"Here?"

"Maybe. Oh, it always could be some crook who saw me cashing in. But somebody's probably got a grudge."

"Ooooh, cashed in, did you?" She laughed. "Not too high-minded to take Chet's tip, after all. What did you bet?"

"A thousand. Somebody was going to win on that horse. Might as well be me. I don't think a gentleman boasts about his winnings. That's why I didn't call the police."

"Chet's tip …" She stopped walking, tugging him back by the arm. "Daisy?"

"You bet a thousand? *A thousand dollars!*"

"Well, yes—"

"You trust Chet fifty times as much as I do!"

"You only trust him a twenty's worth?"

"I like hedging my bets. You're curiously willing to take a cheater's word."

"Maybe I've learned to expect the worse."

"Maybe he's shooting his mouth off? He doesn't need the money …"
They started walking again.

"It's got nothing to do with money. It's about power. Rich man like
Chet grows up in a world he owns. If he's not in control, he thinks something's wrong. Chet just thinks he's setting things straight. That's why I
wasn't worried."

They reached the door. Daisy started to knock, then hesitated, intently
gazing at Hawkins, lost in thought, biting her lip.

"Yes … that's our Chet." She started to knock, then paused again,
adding soberly, "By the way, don't let our hostess know we didn't squeal to
the stewards. Her horse came in *second*."

The door opened. Daisy tugged at Hawkins' hand, waving and crying
out, "Hello, Mr. Harris," stretching up on her tiptoes. She gave the butler,
an older black man, a hug and a peck on the crown of his bald head. He
easily grinned.

"There you are—how's our little Daisy!"

Harris ushered them through the darkened mansion. Across the back
threshold came a transcendent, golden light. Overhead, a high yellow
and white circus tent gently floated on a summer breeze. With each puff
hundreds of softly flickering white paper lanterns lofted up and down,
delicately swaying, each one adding its own mellow glow.

Harris led them straight down the rows of tables toward an orchestra
and dance floor. Four hundred guests, at least. It wasn't so much a private
dinner party as a state banquet of the racing world, with the yellow and
white of the hostess' stables as national colors.

Hawkins surveyed the table with a mixture of amusement and wonder.
An orgy of monogrammed yellow and white. On place tags, dishes, swag-
draped tablecloths, napkins and place mats. On the backs of slip covers,
embossed matchbooks and, of course, matching floral centerpieces of
yellow and white roses. Even the waiters rushed about in short yellow
jackets with white piping. The best touch? An artful spray of miniature
yellow and white orchids perched daintily in the center of Daisy's plate.

She shyly waited for him to pin it on. A simple yellow rose boutonniere slipped into his buttonhole. Hawkins carefully hid how he eased down into the chair, bracing his back.

Within seconds waiters set chilled pressed salmon platters before them. *Damn. I am ravenously hungry*, Hawkins realized. *Who would've thought? Getting the shit kicked out of you, an unusual but demanding form of exercise, it seems. Only with a lingering but vibrant afterglow of adrenaline.*

A woman dressed in a severe white Mainbocher gown rushed up to them. The guests at the surrounding tables broke out in animated smiles, softly calling "Millicent! Millicent!" pleading for attention or recognition as their hostess passed.

-60-

Millicent Simpson-Saunders was an attractive, well-kept older woman of uncertain age with graying hair festooned with yellow roses. She began talking to Daisy in an animated matter-of-fact manner, ignoring the low entreaties from the tables around them, which slowly sank in gloom.

"Daisy darling, is this your new gentlemen friend?" She inspected his jaw coolly. "Are you a boxer?"

"Mrs. Simpson-Saunders," Daisy said, "we tried to get here earlier, I'm sorry—"

Hawkins reluctantly and slowly rose, which lent it a stately manner. "No. It's my fault. Strictly amateur, ma'am—Roy Hawkins. And thank you for the invitation."

She placed a finger on her temple, then pointed it at him like a gun.

"You're Anglo American, aren't you?" She commandeered a neighboring chair. He gratefully and slowly sank into his chair.

"Why, yes. That's remarkable. No one ever gets that right. How'd you tell?"

"Process of elimination, my dear. It's not Canadian because that's mainly from Scottish immigrants. It's not American because the vowels are off. Not English because it's not quite plummy enough. So!" She waved her hands out. "Very transatlantic. Ergo, Anglo American."

She balanced on the edge of her chair, reached over and plucked an olive from Daisy's salad. She popped it in her mouth, then reached over and touched a finger to his jaw.

"That must hurt. What happened?"

"Some muggers jumped me in the washroom at the States Hotel while I was taking a shower."

"Oh, that's terrible! I'm not surprised though. There's a lot of riffraff in those old places. Sad to see them run-down, they were so romantic once." She sighed.

Daisy leaned over, resting her hand on Mrs. Simpson-Saunders' arm.

"What's that story? Commodore Vanderbilt's daughter and the telegraph boy?"

"Oh, I remember that, y-e-s! A Western Union clerk met Commodore Vanderbilt's daughter on the porch at the Grand Union. They fell in love. He walked right up to the commodore and asked for her hand. And he agreed. Twombly, I think his name was."

"That is a charming story," Hawkins said.

"Umm, yes. The old hotels were very democratic. That was about ten, maybe fifteen years after the Great Rebellion." She winked at Hawkins. "I always call it that because I like to tweak our Southern brethren. They had rooms in every price range then. Couldn't happen today and it didn't last long then. Times have changed."

"That's right. Millionaires' daughters can't flirt with shopkeepers' sons anymore," Daisy said. "There are so many scamps out there."

"Scamps?" Hawkins said.

"Confidence men and liars! Of every sort," Millicent said, "all on the make, pretending they're something they're not."

"Ah, I—I see," Hawkins said. A wave of unease began rising.

Millicent quickly wagged a finger at Daisy. "You have to be careful," then wagged it at Hawkins. For a split second he felt a chill despite the warmth of summer. "But you got away, Mr. Hawkins? Did they take anything?"

Hawkins took a second to catch up, still stuck on the last distressing exchange. "Uh—yes. They took a brand-new watch."

"That's too bad. That's the kind of thing they like. We had a horrific jewelry robbery three years ago. Took them right out of a safe cemented in the basement floor."

"You can't trust anyone anymore," Daisy said. "I get nervous whenever I take these out," touching the pearls around her neck.

"Well, you have Mr. Hawkins to take care of you. And he seems ve-e-ry capable. Have you seen our guest of honor?"

"Oh! Walter Ventnor? No," Daisy said. "Roy wants to meet him."

"If you don't mind my asking," Hawkins said, "why'd you invite a fellow like that?" It was a blunt, possibly rude question but she didn't seem even slightly ruffled.

"Oh my, you have to have guests who are current. He's a big celebrity! One doesn't have to approve of him."

"You don't agree with him?" he said.

She lifted her shoulders and sneered distastefully. "No," lowering her voice, "he's a low sort of man, a demagogue. No class at all. Everyone knows it!" She waved a disgusted hand. "Oh, well, everyone that reads in the drawing room and not the kitchen."

"Aren't you worried about the war?" Hawkins said.

"The war? Coming here, you mean? Not at all. I can tell you after forty-two years of being affiliated with the oil business via marriage, they need our oil vastly more than we need anything they have. Do you realize how little we trade with Europe? Especially since the Crash. Oil's mainly it. If they tried to attack us, why we'd cut off their oil, that's all. We're the world's biggest producer. Mexico's number two and we ship most of that. They can't replace us."

That totally makes sense, Hawkins realized. The reason he'd gotten the European beat at Bolley was the other, more senior sales reps all took the more lucrative American routes. *Could Hitler fuel an attack on North America?* Maybe not. Of course, Stalin had fueled Hitler's attack on France …

Millicent hugged Daisy. "Get your fellow to enjoy himself, dear. Tell him not to be so serious." She smiled back at him. "Wonderful meeting you, Mr. Hawkins!" She bounced up, grabbed a celery stick from his salad and flew across the tent, munching as she went. She briefly paused at another table, snatching a piece of salmon off a plate, tittering with her guests a moment before spinning on to the next.

"Does she always eat off other people's plates like that?"

"Oh, big parties are sooo much work. She won't sit till midnight. I hate to think about it."

"That's barmy." The orchestra started playing some slow music. "Come on! Let's dance."

-61-

The band was playing a medley of slow waltzes. They gently embraced. The throbbing in his side seemed to subside, then nearly vanish. A cool breeze blew in from the countryside, ruffling the awnings over the violins. In the brush beyond the crickets started their evening symphony. *Everything feels so right*, he thought. *Daisy close in my arms. The pure freshness of her beautiful hair. Her full skirts pressing against my legs.*

That feeling over breakfast at the track. All back. *Was it really this morning? The peace. The tranquility. Seems a long time ago.* Ludwig, Ventnor, all the rest, out of mind, forgotten.

An overwhelming sensation came over him. This was summer, truly summer. Through the chaos and horror of May, June and July somehow it hadn't become summer. It had merely gotten hot. *The change in the season, the return of life. I saw it. Noted it. But I neither sensed nor felt it. Death came instead.* Summer suddenly resonated through him, its specialness. He gave Daisy a little hug against his chest. She lifted her head off his shoulder and smiled. So innocent, so pure.

He bent his head, lightly kissing her neck. She stretched her arms and shoulders, slowly and carefully pressing her lips against his chin. They danced on a minute before he brushed his fingers over her bare back. She lifted her lips, meeting his. They slowly drifted to a stop.

The other dancers burst into applause. They both leaned back with a start. Her face flushed slightly. But the crowd was applauding the band. They both burst out laughing and swung back onto the floor again.

"You know how I told you I recently came back from Europe?" Hawkins said.

"Yes, you saw the war."

"I was thinking nothing felt right afterward, until now. Now that I'm here with you, everything feels right, normal."

She stretched up slightly and kissed him on the lips again.

"I hope summer never ends."

"We'll never let it end."

"No—let's not."

They kissed again and danced in happy silence for several songs.

Hawkins came back again to the single idea that now completely filled his mind.

"Daisy?"

She relaxed back, happily smiling, swinging in his arms. "Yes, Roy?"

"I was thinking about what you were saying."

"About what?"

"People being who they say they are."

"Oh. Yes."

What to say, he wondered. *What to do. But I don't dare risk letting this go a moment longer. Have to say something.*

"I—want you to know I ..." *God, how can I?* he thought. *But I must.* "Daisy, can I trust you to keep a secret? I mean, a very important secret?"

"I know your secret."

"You do?"

"You're a glamorous international jewel thief ... on the run from the law!"

"The law—"

"You're a crack safe-cracker, and—"

The band paused. They stopped. One of those rare moments of genuine clarity and lucidity in life struck Hawkins, an epiphany where a connection suddenly and unexpectedly clicked in. *Of course.*

"Kelly—"

"What, Roy?"

He shook his head. "Man I know—been talking to. It's nothing."

His mental camera iris seemed to be rapidly flicking open and shut. At wide open, he saw new, larger possibilities. *Why not take Kelly's offer? Maybe it is time to say screw all this.* Screw stupidity and stupid people who didn't listen when their lives were at stake. Who gave a damn if the FBI was a big, inefficient, incompetent, overzealous bureaucracy that couldn't get out of its own way? Or that Hawkins probably wouldn't— couldn't—accomplish much of anything? *As long as I get paid well to not accomplish anything, fine. Mrs. Simpson-Saunders is right. The Nazis are not coming here. Time to stop wasting my life on the heedless, the complacent and the selfish. Especially on every type and kind of stupid person in the world. Let them have what they want and get what they deserve.*

It's time to save myself.

Then the iris flicked back in. *Was the offer real?* Kelly himself admitted he, too, had entertained the possibility Hoover merely wanted to break off one of the Service's wheels. *No, it might not be a reliable offer. And how can I not go back? How can I live with leaving that behind, that sense of darkness outside Paris, the faces in the safe house, Mum back in London holding her gas mask in her lap? I must go back. I cannot live with that.* The sense of confusion resumed, the nagging questions. *Don't overpromise. At the very least, check out Kelly's offer back in Manhattan. For now, that offer has one useful purpose.*

"I'm thinking of leaving my firm. I've been asked to take a confidential position in the federal government at a high level. You must understand this is *very* hush-hush. It's been prompted by the situation abroad. National security. The government, because of what I've learned overseas, wants me to come in and organize some things for them."

"With whom?"

"This is serious." She nodded. "I'm going to hold you to your promise—"

"Yes, yes, I won't tell!"

"The Federal Bureau of Investigations. But nothing is final, yet."

Her face went blank for a split second. Then the eyes opened wide as it sank in, an expression that said one thing: *Wow.*

Wow? All Hawkins' anxiety and confusion began slipping away on this powerful undertow, carrying him out into this new sea. Chet? He might have more money. But status, position, it could come. It was possible. Everything could fall into place: Washington. Daisy. Summers in Saratoga. In a flash he saw it all: coming home to her, candlelight dinners, weekend trips to galleries, a night at a club dancing, a good book shared by a fireplace. *Oh, to ride that wave ... ride that wave ...*

"Oh! Roy, that's wonderful. That you'd be doing this. For the country. That'd be a great thing. Really, it's very noble." She gave him a small hug. "So you'll be one of those dollar-a-year men they're bringing in?"

Dollar-a-year? Perhaps there was still room for a bit of disingenuousness.

"Something like that. Oh, I suppose I'll be paid."

"Is that why you're interested in Ludwig?"

"It's all—involved."

"It's safe with me, Roy! If there's anything I can do!"

"I don't think so. As I said, I do have some previous commitments that may make that impossible. But"—that wowed expression again—"I think it's settled."

"Oh! There's the guest of honor over there."

-62-

A knot of listeners surrounded Walter Ventnor, partially hiding him. From a distance his smug, braying tone rode over the crowd, brushing aside other conversations like the cowcatcher on a locomotive. Hawkins and Daisy pushed in. Chet was standing next to Ventnor. He'd replaced his soiled shoes and mixed-bag clothes with an expensive evening jacket in out-of-season black. Ventnor's expression began shifting, along with his hands and shoulders, to one of wounded concern. "… Question is, why? You know what people are saying," his voice ostentatiously quieting to a hush, "the president's losing his mind. The way they so vehemently deny it, you know there has to be something to it, because it makes so much sense with the First Lady spending so much of her time wandering around the dark sections of our nation's capital looking after her pets. You know what *that* means. She's infected the president with syphilis, which you known *they* almost all have, and now it's destroying the president's brain."

What a marvel, in a perverse way, Hawkins thought. The craft, the imagination to create such a slimly loathsome libel. Miscegenation and adultery wrapped up in an accusation of insanity. Then, while the defense of the man and his wife was waged, the primary thrust—obscuring whether the Nazis were dangerous—floated out there undisputed in all its spurious glory. In time it'll settle into everyone's mind, hardening as thoroughly as cement.

Chet impatiently butted into the conversation. "So he's diseased as well as a cripple!"

A flicker of annoyance crossed Ventnor's face at Chet's clanging, artless addition. The crowd murmured slightly. Chet, his head bobbing and laughing, spotted Daisy. Excited for a second, he called out, "Daisy!" then saw Hawkins. His mood promptly compressed into a curt nod.

"What happened to you?"

Hadn't considered Chet, Hawkins thought. *There's a man can afford hired muscle.*

"Some diseased bastard tried turning me into a cripple, too," Hawkins said. "They didn't make it."

But nothing in Chet's relaxed manner indicated recognition, or any cognition at all. "Oh," he said.

Daisy swung in between them. "Chetly! You were going to introduce us."

"So I was. Walter, this is Miss Daisy van Schenck and Mr. Hawkins."

"That cripple stuff, where'd you get that?" Hawkins said.

"Don't you know our glorious leader can't walk?" Chet said. He gestured to Daisy. "Tell him! Your father went to school with him."

Daisy actually sighed out loud, her face crossed by well-worn annoyance. "Oh, Chet! Uncle Franklin walks with braces."

"Right. Braces." He started smirking. "When he inspects the navy they pluck him off the dock with a big electromagnet and dump him on the deck like a pile of junk."

The crowd laughed uneasily and began drifting away.

Hawkins felt something akin to shifting ground—a mental earth tremor—and caught Daisy's hand for a second, whispering in her ear. "Your father knew the president?" She nodded. "*Uncle Franklin?* You've met him?"

"Oh. Sure. And Aunt Eleanor. Well, not lately, obviously. Father and Uncle Franklin were at Groton together. After Uncle Franklin got polio, before he was governor, he used to come up to the mineral baths and stay at the manor. I'll show you the photos sometime."

"Baths—what?"

"Mineral baths. Saratoga *Springs*? For all the racing and gambling and parties that's why the city's here in the first place. They're very good for polios. Mineral water's quite heavy. Heat or cold penetrates. Helps unkink the muscles. Otherwise he couldn't straighten his legs out."

"You mean—what Chet said—*that's true?*"

"Pretty much." She turned back to the circle of people. "Chet's a very bad boy tonight! If you'll excuse me, I'd rather powder my nose." She slipped off, leaving Hawkins frozen in place, mind scrambling to catch up, like he'd fallen into a void, like being back on the Meudon hill outside Paris as the lights went out.

Uncle Franklin. Aunt Eleanor. Can't straighten his legs out. Braces. The man the world's hopes hang on. Can't walk?

-63-

"Chet, that old pile of junk isn't going to be bothering us much longer," Ventnor said.

"No, he won't be …" Chet started to giggle. Ventnor started giggling, too.

"Yessir, we're going to be free of Mr. Franklin Rosenfeld."

Hawkins stared at them, trying to grasp it all, everything he'd just learned—and now this, mind shifting and bounding from one peak to yet a higher summit, accelerating second by second.

What in hell were they referring to? That damn rifle? No. Crazy. But … maybe they were getting overconfident. Shooting people, that's definitely the SS's style. But the president of the United States? They wouldn't dare. Such a crazy risk. Suppose they were caught? There'd be American entry into the war in a heartbeat. The US fleet steaming into Scapa Flow in a week. US fighter squadrons in Kent in a fortnight. Marines in Sussex, maybe a month. The Nazis could hardly want that.

But then think of the things they'd done, large and small, the risks they'd taken: attacking Poland and leaving the Rhine defenseless. The friendship pact with Stalin. Or Göring declaring himself "Grandmaster of the Hunt." Titles worthy of schoolboys in tree houses. All preposterous. Until they happened.

Should've stolen that bloody sniper rifle. But, no, that would've tipped them off. Damn.

"Oh? Really?" Hawkins said. "Going to shoot him down, beat him?"

"By golly, no," Ventnor said, "he's going to beat himself! Americans aren't suckers."

"We're willing to help a little," Chet said. He and Ventnor laughed, a relaxed, easygoing laugh. It simply didn't fit. They had too trifling an air for men in on murder and assassination. *Or the beating I got.*

Chet started moving off. "Right. Main room at Riley's. Later."

The crowd had largely drifted away. One on one, Ventnor's tone was completely different: focused, professional, weighted. None of the onstage bombast.

"You said Hitler wasn't a threat to us," Hawkins said.

"He's not. They're a long ways away."

"Then why bother being friends with him?"

"Because he's a winner."

"That's all?"

"What else is there? Roosevelt only cares about losers."

"Losers?"

"Right. See, the world's divided into winners and losers. Which side do you want to be on?"

"Always?"

"Of course. In every transaction between people there's a winner and a loser—always." As Ventnor began introducing Hawkins to this hitherto unperceived way of the world, he began smirking, that smirk they all seemed to have. Hawkins puzzled over it as he listened.

"Can't people work together, cooperatively, to benefit everybody?" Hawkins said. "Isn't that easier?"

"Naw—never happens. There's always a winner and a loser. Sometimes you simply can't see who it is right away, that's all. But somebody's always getting the best of somebody else, you can bet on it."

"Maybe we just make it that way."

"Nope. Darwin talked about it. Some people are born to lose."

Daisy came up behind Hawkins, listening, too, then curtly turned and walked away.

"Like who?"

"The coloreds. The Jews."

"Born to lose? The Jews, too?"

"Yep. Why do they have to cheat, take advantage so? Because they'd lose otherwise."

"What happens, then?"

"They have to make way. Like the Indians. Survival of the fittest. It's the natural order of things."

"But how did we get where we are—thousands of years of human progress, building aqueducts, curing diseases, didn't that depend on people trusting and working together?"

"Forget that. Some people are destined to be destroyed. There's no point standing in the way."

"The whole world's just a jungle."

"Don't kid yourself about it."

"Then—you're saying—everyone has the right to do whatever they have to do to get ahead. Even cheating, breaking the rules."

"Hey, winning isn't the only thing that matters, it's the only thing that exists. That's what Hitler understands."

Chet had the same smirk when he was talking about cheating, Hawkins thought. It was more than a spoiled rich boy's sense of entitlement. That smirk conveyed a sense he—they—knew something other people didn't, that they were in on the great secret of life and those who didn't were suckers, the butt of the Big Joke.

Hitler was always serious, grim. But the thugs around him, Göring, the SS types in particular, the party elite. They had that smirk, too. The insider's smirk, in on the big joke about winning and losing and power.

The Nazis, people like Ventnor, so many of the things he'd seen happen, all happened because men like Ventnor and Chet believed the world was inherently, inevitably nothing but a big mess of winners and losers. Or men who believed it was and would damn well make it that way.

Winners and losers, that's what I've been missing, Hawkins thought, Ventnor and all the right-wing isolationists. *It's why, if Ventnor's against Social Security, he's also an isolationist, wouldn't help Britain. Selfishness abroad, selfishness at home, it's all the same.*

If life's nothing but winners and losers, you have to watch out for yourself, and the hell with anyone else. Laws, rules, traditions, social customs, all a mirage, illusions that keep suckers from seeing reality. If winning means cheating, breaking the rules like Chet, it's perfectly acceptable, even virtuous.

What's doubly awful, Hawkins thought, *is that if they get in an arrangement, exchange, whatever, a mutually beneficial situation, they'll think there's something wrong. It would have to be wrong, by definition, precisely because there wasn't a loser. A fix like that could only mean one thing to these men: if they weren't the winner, then they had to be the loser. Had to be, since everyone had to be one or the other. And they would probably panic.*

That means you go for the power. You practically worship power, make a cult of it, the way the Nazis and Fascists did, because power is more likely to win. To hell with justice, what's right, helping others. Win at any price. The rest is all illusion.

Naturally, men like Ventnor opposed the League of Nations. They didn't want any international rules. Cooperation? A joke. Or trying to destroy Roosevelt's Social Security. Those people were losers, so let them starve. Or Chet's cheating and breaking the rules at the track. Rules? Merely another hedge on the steeplechase, another obstacle in your way. Underneath, it was all the same, who was going to be the winner and who was going to be the loser.

The idea of sportsmanship, of fair play? That quaint notion was rooted in a humbling recognition life was unfair, and that life could be unfair to you, too. The idea that competition was a dangerous tool, that it could coarsen and reduce everything to the lowest common denominator unless reined in by fair play and sportsmanship? Gone, too. Competition was no longer a mere *means* to make things better. It was now an end in itself, the very nature of human existence, no matter how far it took society back to the cavemen.

What can one possibly say to such twisted logic? Nothing, probably. If you dared reasoning with them, they would merely see a stratagem, a maneuver designed to hoodwink and sucker them, and take advantage. Their belief in winners and losers corroded everything.

Truth requires some sense of cooperation, in that people have to be willing to consider a possible truth as representing something more than a ploy. To Ventnor, Chet, and right wingers like them, there could be no truth, only tactics. Truth had ceased to exist. Winning was the only truth, and a lie that worked was truth, because it worked. Which meant that lies were equal to the facts. When they lied, they probably didn't always even know they were lying.

Why in holy hell am I listening to Ventnor? Hawkins thought. *What a waste of time.* He quickly thanked Ventnor and moved on.

-64-

A quick search. He spotted Daisy. She and Chet were quietly dancing, moving in and out of the crowd. The dancers parted again. The music stopped. Chet led her over to a floral archway with a broad gesture. Hawkins walked through the crowd and across the floor, watching.

Daisy was standing with her back toward him. Chet drew a distinctive blue box from his pocket. The color meant only one thing: Tiffany's. Chet flicked the lid open with his thumb. Inside rested a ring with a diamond the size of an almond. The stone flashed a brilliant bluish white all the way across the dance floor.

Blood surged up behind Hawkins' eyes. He was back in the cemetery, back on the street in front of the Waldorf, all reaction, more feeling than thinking. *Go over there. Grab that bastard by the collar. Drag him out of the pavilion and into the bushes.* It wouldn't take much to break his neck.

No. Wait. Later. There are people here. Maybe daytime. That'd be better. Drive him off in the country. Out in the sun. See the big pink spray of blood and brain and bone fly out the other side of his head. Shove him in a culvert. Let the vermin feed on him for a week or two. Rats, weasels, raccoons, a merry feast. Damn! Why'd I have to give the Hi-Power away?

After all, I've killed people since joining the Secret Service, he thought. *What difference will an obnoxious American millionaire make? If Daisy isn't worth fighting for, what is?* The music picked up again. The crowd started dancing. The dancers pressed around Chet and Daisy. They disappeared. Hawkins caught himself.

No. No. Won't do, he thought. *Get a grip. I'm about to become a G-man. Can't exactly go around ignoring the law.* A passing waiter offered another glass of champagne. He took a deep cold sip. It tasted bitter, hard to swallow. His temper settled slightly. He dumped the glass on a passing tray. After ten minutes of glumly loitering by the side of the dance floor Hawkins' side and thigh began to really hurt again. He went back and sat down.

Winners and losers. Is that what this is all about, too? he thought. *Maybe I'm a sap to think anything else. Does Chet have the power to simply swoop in and take what he wants? Maybe. Maybe my presence pushed him to make his move. No guarantee she'll accept. Could Daisy be using me to push him along? Could I be too late?* He brushed that idea aside with a mental shudder. The connection they'd felt. It was real, it had to be.

Wait—the Bureau. Maybe there's something better than killing, he thought. *How soon could I do something about Chet juicing his horses?* Racing season only lasted a month. But they did move on south. *Any federal laws violated? Fraud perhaps?* They moved the horses across state lines—Chet had mentioned a train. That meant federal jurisdiction. *Get back to Manhattan, call Kelly, first thing. What's a stolen-car case next to rigging a high-stakes horse race? Scandal, money, horses, celebrities. Very much an FBI-Hollywood newsreel kind of story. Think how Kelly's face will light up at this one.*

And what was going on with Chet and Ventnor? "We're helping." What did he mean, *we're helping*—Ludwig? That might be better than rigging horse races.

Humiliation. Disgrace. Ruin. Then jail. A dead man wouldn't know he's been beaten. Give Chet twenty years sleeping on a hard bunk a foot from his toilet to think about it.

That's it, Hawkins thought. *I don't need to kill Chet. I can handle him. This is like the daily double. Send Chet away. Whatever it takes. And put a smile on Kelly's and Director Hoover's faces at the same time. Winners and losers? Fine. We'll see about that.*

Two or three minutes later Daisy spotted him and came running through the crowd. She seemed nervous or distracted.

"Roy, are you having a good time?"

"Yes, I'm having a great time," trying to stay pleasant, relaxed. "How's Chet?"

"Chet? Oh, yes. We were—talking about our investments."

Yes, Hawkins thought, *judging from the size of it, that stone is quite an investment.* "Well, I wouldn't want to interrupt a conversation like that."

"Um, yes." She almost wrung her hands. There was no diamond visible, though. "Roy, I hate to ask this." *Here it comes*, he thought. *Can almost hear the words already.* "I've been having such a wonderful time, too. But could we go back now? I'm getting a headache."

"Of course," he said. Daisy acted correct to form. Always leave with the one who brought you, then dump him privately. She took his arm. They hurried out to the Cord and zoomed back through the already darkened town. When he stopped in front of her house she kissed him on the cheek.

"Please call," squeezing his arm. "Will you?" He nodded. She ran partway up the steps, waved and smiled again, then disappeared into the house. He watched her, feeling very little.

After spinning around in a driveway up the street he eyed her house lights passing by. *Chet'll probably pick her up in a few minutes*, he thought.

"Winners and losers." Then he exploded, slamming his fist on the steering wheel, shouting, "Everything … everything was … Damn! The Hi-Power! Why'd I have to give my gun away! Fuck all!"

-65-

Harris shuffled some receipts and removed a leaf from the back of his thick butler's notebook. He quickly scribbled down directions to Riley's and handed the page to Hawkins, grinning knowingly, slowly wagging a finger.

"You watch out for those wheels, young man, especially those birdcage things. Stick to cards! That's a gentleman's game."

There was gambling, it seemed.

"Thanks, I will."

Moments later Hawkins was accelerating the Cord out of town. The cool, refreshing breeze soothed his mood slightly. Around a corner a chain of taillights wound up a twin driveway to a hill crowned by a necklace of lights. He spun around an illuminated fountain at the top and slammed on the brakes.

A monumental ensemble of stylish structures reminiscent of the Chrysler Building stretched along the rim of a small lake. Nothing even hinted at the shady unease of an illegal gambling operation. The bold entrance surmounting the long main pavilion practically shouted the establishment's grandeur. Four superimposed geometric facades proudly marched forward, each narrower and higher than the other, rising several stories to shape a powerful ziggurat. A pointed alcove in the center framed a vertical neon RILEY's, blinking red.

A group of noisy revelers burst out a side door. With a whoop they threw themselves across an iron footbridge into a long stucco hall on the left. To the right, music poured through the open windows of a tremendous octagonal ballroom.

This isn't the English style of gambling, Hawkins thought, little card games in an upstairs room at one's club, all low-key, clannish and confidential. Amazingly American—bald really. An obviously illegal but protected playhouse the size of a large resort hotel. No doubt run by one organized crime syndicate or another, perched out here on the edge of the piney woods.

At the entrance a short, grumpy doorman in a white evening jacket plumped his hand in the middle of a customer's chest. He wearily pushed the man back, as if he'd done it a hundred times that day already.

"No, you're not properly dressed."

The man had on a regular gray business suit. He angrily waved his hat, sore at being shown up in front of his girl. The face of another man appeared inside the door as he lit a cigarette.

"I came up all the way from Poughkeepsie to this place," the man in the gray suit said, "and I can't get in!"

Two veins popped up on the doorman's face. He clenched his incongruously large fists. "Poughkeepsie! We never let any fucking hicks from Poughkeepsie in here!"

With that the other man cursed and swung. The doorman caught his arm in midflight and yanked him into range, expertly punching one sharp jab in his face. The muffled crunching sound of teeth breaking like pieces of hard candy echoed over the courtyard. Then he pinned the man and ran him across the roadway, throwing him headfirst into the fountain. The woman ran screaming after him, "Billie-e-e-e-e-e-e!"

His head bobbed up in the illuminated cauldron between a pair of spouting dolphins, face streaking blood into the water. The man inside held back, puffing his cigarette, calmly watching.

Hawkins dug for a fiver in his pocket. But no need. The doorman glowered a split second, primed for another fight. His eyes locked on Mrs.

Simpson-Saunders' yellow rose boutonniere still adorning Hawkins' white evening jacket. The scowl and grumpy manner instantly vanished. He actually jumped for the long bronze handle, bowing and swinging the heavy plate-glass door open.

"Good evening, sir! Welcome to Riley's!"

Just as Hawkins entered the ballroom a microphone rolled down to an MC standing to the side of a stage.

"Ladies and gentlemen, Riley's Lake House, the showplace of the Adirondacks, is proud to present Mr. Louis Armstrong and his orchestra!" The microphone reeled up into the ceiling as the stage rotated into view.

Armstrong swung up, pointing his trumpet at the ceiling and rolled an awesome trill up and down. His orchestra sent the chords bounding back.

Louis Armstrong? Actually here. Incredible, Hawkins thought. Another shock. Only a good one. A rather disorienting quality, like a splash of unexpectedly cold surf on a blisteringly hot day, refreshing and enjoyable, but stunning. *Followed Armstrong for years. Never expected to hear him in person, least of all here, now.*

Still—listen but keep looking—Chet said he'd be here. Is he alone?

A silk canopy on a silver frame partly shaded the dance floor and most of the tables. Worse, a set of klieg lamps rotated over the canopy, playing dancing pools of colored light on the walls, camouflaging the revelers walking around the outside. He squinted. Damn hard to make anything out. The crowd was in high spirits, noisy, drinking hard, jumping up from the candlelit tables to dance. The only decent light came from an octagonal bronze chandelier that projected a cone of blue light on the swaying dancers, just hitting the tables near the dance floor.

After a few minutes, his eyes adjusted to the light and shadows. *Look, there, Cary Grant's down on the aisle with a group of people.* A well-known US senator, lesser luminaries, rich debutantes littered the room.

Good—some luck. The dancers momentarily cleared. There he was, Chet with Ventnor, at a table at the far side of the dance floor. *Just in the light, thank God. Sitting silently, listening. But where's Daisy?* Hawkins thought. No third drink. No purse on the table. No chair pulled out.

Chet hadn't picked her up, after all.

Hawkins edged against the side wall, leaned against it, bracing and resting his back as he took an enormous deep breath. *Chet and Daisy aren't together. Not together.* She'd gone home, after all. *Hot damn.* The wave of relief, noticeably physical, pulling up, out, close to the joy of dancing along to Armstrong. His back and side suddenly actually felt, well, almost good.

Another thing was striking. *Chet doesn't seem particularly happy, a man who's just been accepted by a beautiful woman*, Hawkins thought. *That's even better.* After checking the angles to make sure he couldn't be seen, he positioned himself by one of the bundled silver columns and settled in to watch, now slightly bemused, taking in the scene.

All quite enlightening, he thought. Nothing in the papers, no guidebook mentioned this place. Given its scale, the size and character of the crowd, that was extraordinary. And yet these people all knew about it. *Well, naturally. Here, in this room, around tables with little red silk shaded candle lamps, sit the people who own America. Among other things, they don't want an audience.* Merely being here, by virtue of knowing about it and being admitted, meant that you had arrived, you were in the know, an insider, one of the top people, a far more valuable coin than any you could put in your pocket.

Chet and Ventnor—talking a little. But they weren't drinking or relaxing very much either, rather waiting for something or someone.

-66-

A spectacular tall, blond cocktail waitress circled the outside of the dance floor, crossed up the aisle and walked around the outside of the room. A very short black tutu over a froth of white tulle fluffed up and down with every step of her black stockinged legs, barely covering her derriere. Each breath partially squeezed her breasts out of a strapless black bustier. Black evening gloves and a matching rhinestone choker accentuated her bare shoulders.

What an outfit, Hawkins thought. Part haute couture, part Folies Bergère—only not on a distant stage, but close enough to touch. Provocative. Outrageous. Scandalous. Utterly riveting.

Obviously, such a thing could only be worn in an establishment like this, he thought. Every parson and church lady in the state would be demanding a police raid … *if* they knew about it. *Well, naturally.* If this was the zenith of society, not only would one find luxury, mildly safe vices like illegal gambling, but also a large upright finger flipped at bourgeois sensibilities. What did life's big in-the-know winners care about rules or what the little people thought?

Carefully pacing around the mezzanine, Hawkins maneuvered behind the columns. The waitress did a swishing pirouette to another table. Her face was hidden by a large black harlequin mask covered with an effervescent whirl of sequins. Even more outrageous. Too much.

The maître d' seated two more men at Ventnor and Chet's table. Neither one anything out of the ordinary—two middle-aged Caucasian men, one graying, one not, both with thinning hair, spreading middles and rented evening wear. The taller one, with a sharply receding chin and pendulous nose, acted quite nervous, repeatedly leaning forward on his arms, catching himself, then sitting back as if he couldn't get comfortable. The other man, shorter by about eight inches and darker, kept swinging his head around the room, gawking as if he'd never seen a nightclub before.

Neither act like mobsters, Hawkins thought. *Maybe they're involved in juicing the horses.* That might make sense. Fixing horse races was definitely the kind of thing rackets would be interested in.

The cocktail waitress, who'd been steadily circling around the dance floor, stopped at a table and paused, fussing with her tray, her large rhinestone bracelets clinking against the glasses. Ventnor snapped his fingers. She peered over her shoulder at him and froze. He gestured her over. Very stiffly, with a steeliness exaggerated by her long legs, she eased over to their table. Ventnor ordered drinks. She instantly spun on her heel and left. A few minutes later she arrived carrying a silver ice bucket and a bottle of champagne. She started to pop the cork. Ventnor took it from her. She promptly left the room.

They made a toast to something. Smiles all around. More nods. A round of handshakes. Chet and Ventnor stood and rather purposely left. Hawkins followed, holding back just far enough not to be seen. But they weren't leaving. Instead, they passed out of the ballroom, through the marble lobby, another lounge and out a door on the far side of the building.

-67-

The door had a label, VOGUE ROOM. Hawkins pushed it open. No room at all. Instead, an open iron catwalk below. *Ah, of course, a drawbridge,* he thought. When the police throw a raid, the owners can lift the gangplank and cast off. The casino sinks temporarily while the nightclub steams along. No doubt they had quite a bit of experience at this. *Imagine police raids anticipated in a building's very architecture? Remarkable.*

Across, inside a plain door, another brawny bouncer, another inspection. Hawkins paused at the outlet of a long, narrow passageway. To the right a series of balconies rose against the wall. Ahead, a long, high room resembling the lobby at Radio City Music Hall: soaring ceilings, gilded murals, high octagonal bronze chandeliers. The goddess in the black tutu was standing by a gold railing at the far end, as distracting as before. After a second he spotted Chet and Ventnor, together, in the center of the room, in the middle of an intense discussion of some sort. After a few gestures Ventnor sat down at a blackjack table. Chet went to the nearby cashier's cage. For all their motions at playing cards there was more afoot. Their manner was all wrong, too businesslike, perhaps, slightly tense.

The door to the gaming room opened behind. The voice of the bouncer, followed by two women's voices. They were trying to enter the gaming room. No, he said, gentlemen only. Surprise in their voices swiftly shifted through wheedling and indignation to tight resignation. No, came the hushed answer again and again. The ladies weren't about to get the bum's rush the man in the gray suit got out front. *Their husbands are probably inside*, Hawkins thought. Finally the bouncer gently and quietly shut the door in their faces, steadily expressing his regrets, although in no way could it be called polite.

Not that there weren't any women inside. There were several more leggy cocktail waitresses like the blond, only without the mask. Two were operating a birdcage machine and a large vertical wheel game.

Hawkins slipped to the top of the tiered lounge to settle in and watch, resting his steadily recovering back and side again, ordering a gin and tonic. Chet rejoined Ventnor, carrying a tray of chips in each hand. *Not the kind of small round chips you normally see*, Hawkins thought, *five, ten or twenty-five dollar chips*. No, large oblong plaques made of richly colored heavy marbleized Bakelite. For huge sums, the numbers "$500" and "$1000" visible across the room. A few small ones were scattered on top. There was a startling amount of money on the trays.

They started playing the small chips. Ventnor, then Chet, glanced down at the far end of the room. Girl watching? Hawkins bent down, sighting past one of the big octagonal chandeliers. Ludwig was sitting at a table by himself, with a small group of chips arranged in front of him.

The man standing inside the front door earlier, evidently the owner or manager, came in the room. He began moving about, checking with the cashier, the floor manager, passing by the tables, patting the croupiers on the shoulder. At the back of the room, the blond came up behind him, hesitated, then touched him on the arm. He stepped back and beamed at her. She began telling him something. At first he acted disappointed, but at the end he beamed, gave her a hug and a kiss on the cheek and left.

A few more minutes. The two men who'd joined Chet and Ventnor in the ballroom came into the gaming room, one at a time. Each hunted a second, spotted Ventnor and Chet and sat down at the blackjack table. They talked a few minutes. Chet flipped the dealer a big tip. The man took a break.

Time to get out the Minox, Hawkins thought, *take a few pictures, whatever happens, just in case.* Pretending the diminutive camera was a lighter, he snapped a picture, wound it with his thumb while pretending to tamp his pipe, and shot another.

Only seconds later the tall man with the receding chin picked up one of Chet's trays of chips. Seemed nervous, looking around to see if anyone was watching. He stepped over to the roulette table. The man took one of the small chips off the top and put a bet on the black. The croupier spun the wheel. Red. The man visibly flinched, picked up his tray and moved over to the tall wheel. The girl smiled. A second of hesitation—he actually seemed to be thinking about it—then placed a chip on a number. She reached up to the top with a graceful skirt-lifting swing and spun the wheel. Nothing. He visibly winced.

Then the man curtly picked up his tray, walked past Chet and Ventnor, almost imperceptibly nodding, to the cashier's cage. He pushed the tray full of chips in. The teller started counting out hundred dollar bills. The man leaned toward the cage and spoke. The teller stopped, made a gesture in the direction of the bills. The man shook his head. The teller took them back.

Chet and Ventnor—are they watching? Hawkins thought. No. They'd missed that exchange entirely. Too busy talking to the second man, not watching the first at all. A second later the teller reappeared with a checkbook. He made one out to the man's name, slowly following him as he spelled it. When the clerk slid it across, the man carefully folded it twice, placed it in his wallet and unceremoniously left the casino.

The man must have pocketed several thousand dollars, at least, Hawkins thought. And he didn't want the cash, he wanted a check.

Did he drive? That was the next question. Hawkins quickly slipped around the bar, sticking to the side of the tiers. The man reentered the center building. Hawkins jumped down from the drawbridge, waiting for his eyes to adjust to the dark, watching for him to come out the entrance.

Ludwig's Mercedes waited a bit down the driveway. Dieter didn't seem to be in sight. No, there, on the far side of the complex, sitting on the steps of a service building, probably the kitchen, smoking a cigarette. With a bottle of beer. *They must've served him one from the kitchen. The doctor, no doubt, would not approve.*

Dieter was tapping one foot in time to Armstrong and the orchestra, his head bobbing very slightly along, relaxed, smiling. *Naughty, naughty,* Hawkins thought. *The Nazis definitely would not approve of that, either.* Listening to racially impure music could get you arrested back in the Reich.

One of the cocktail waitresses came to the door for a smoke. Dieter eagerly hopped up and offered her a light. Big, eager smile. He made a small motion with his arms and shoulders. *Wants a dance with her,* Hawkins thought. *Well, who could blame him?* The girl was as spectacular as the rest, another blond, no mask. She smiled, obviously intrigued—he was a big handsome guy—had a puff or two, talked a second, animatedly gesturing toward the ballroom with the cigarette, rhinestone bracelets flashing on the dark evening gloves. She did a flirtatious little step, spun around, beaming back, then waved a kiss with her fingers and went inside. *So Dieter likes jazz, swing music. W will be interested in that little scene.*

The tall man came out the front entrance. He curtly nodded at the doorman. No cab. *Perfect,* Hawkins thought. He darted through a wood flanking the road, following the man to a tan Chevy. As he pulled out Hawkins wrote down the license plate. Seconds later he pressed himself straight up on the drawbridge and reentered the gaming hall.

-68-

The second man, the shorter, darker one, shook Ventnor's hand. *Not like the other man*, Hawkins thought. *Very happy they are, laughs all around.* The man impatiently picked up the second tray of chips and made his way straight to the craps table. With a flourish he set it down and began playing with a big smile, throwing out a pair of the plaquettes, breaking them for smaller chips.

Ventnor and Chet traded glances, surprised, more and more obviously checking with Ludwig. *Something's amiss*, Hawkins thought, *but what?* He crouched a bit to see Ludwig. Ventnor raised his hands up and shrugged slightly. Ludwig shrugged back. Not upset, either of them. But clearly, this wasn't the plan, the gambling was merely supposed to be for show.

The man started playing craps—badly. Only took a moment to see he hadn't the slightest idea what he was doing. Throwing chips down mostly on the pass line, idiotically waiting for the charmed seven or eleven to come up. Playing it safe, if such a thing as a safe bet on pieces of tumbling ivory existed. At this level he could roll for hours.

Several other players joined the short man at the table. His bets accelerated. Not making much of a dent in his pile. Instead of standing back from the table after placing his bet he began leaning out over it with each roll of the dice. Unselfconscious excitement began relaxing his flushed face. The blond cocktail waitress steadily circled the table priming him with drinks. The short man shouted at the dealer, "You're not throwing them right!" He'd begun sliding into a serious losing streak. All the dealer's throws landed bad. The man demanded the dice, looked around, then waved at the blond with a frantic gesture.

She delightedly skipped over to his side, eager as a puppy, smilingly standing at attention, obediently waiting with her head cocked at an angle while he readied a throw. Cupping his hands, he'd shake the dice inside, leaving a small hole between his thumbs. Then he'd hold his hands up to her lips. She'd smile, raise her shoulders slightly, pucker up and coyly blow a little lady luck on his bones. Then, *bang!*—he'd hurl them against the far side of the table.

Seven. Then eleven. He began winning again. Every time she blew on his ivories and he won he'd flick a chip on her tray. At five, then ten, then twenty bucks a shot, the little colored discs began rapidly piling up. The short man's gloom abruptly shifted, grinning at the girl with an almost manic giggle. Lady Luck, goddess Fortuna herself, was putting in a personal appearance at his side. Caution flew to the winds. The bets and the tips soared.

Standing almost sideways to the table, the man began calling the bets out. The croupiers rushed to place them as he kept furiously throwing. Two hundred bucks a toss now and rising. An excited crowd huddled around. The blond straddled his left leg, riding it like a saddle, egging him on, one hand rubbing and patting his shoulder and back as he threw with his right. She took his hand and gently drew it around her waist. Then after a few minutes she helped it down into the froth of tulle, placing his hand right on her cheek. She whispered something in his ear. The tongue, the opening jaw, the last syllable, she said … *luck?* Or *fuck?* The short man's face jerked up as he beamed at her. He began enthusiastically, possessively petting her derriere with each throw, then lightly spanking it with each win. With each slap she giggled and went *"Ooh!"* The two of them were moving together like dancers, sinuously swaying back and forth with each throw in a ballet of dice. The chips piled up on her tray.

The blond whispered in the man's ear again. She nodded and smiled, pointing at the roulette wheel. The man shrugged. More whispering in the ear. From the mouth and lips some variation on "fuck" and "luck." Making plans, that was clear. He seemed dubious about something. Probably not the offered sex, though. The man stepped away from the craps table. She led him by the hand over to the roulette wheel. He began betting there. The blond got back in the saddle again, one hand tousling his hair, his hand caressing and petting her cheek at each win. The bets went up. She blew on all the chips now. He was winning big. The manic grin grew. She wiggled forward, squeezing her silken upper thighs around his leg and hip, tightly grasping them, her frothy petticoats suggestively pushing way up his side.

The pile of chips rapidly mounted in front of him. Hawkins glanced down again at Ventnor and Chet. Both men had a worried expression on their faces. What about Ludwig? His hand tensely fidgeted with a chip in his fingers, nervously flipping it over and over.

The short man slipped his arm around the blond's waist. A little hug. He swung around and laid her back in a small tango step and bent forward, waving at Chet and Ventnor. He picked up the tray, held it out and offered it to them. He'd won himself clear. They had a stricken expression for a split second. So did Ludwig. Ventnor then laughed, made a gesture, told him he could hold them. The girl kept cooing encouragements in the man's ear. He laughed and immediately began slapping down new bets on the red and the black, then odds and evens, really big bets. Hit several more times in a row. Ventnor, Chet and Ludwig all appeared to be holding their breath.

Then the winning hits began getting farther and farther apart. The short man's manic mood started melting. The more his high slipped, the more he began to lose. Improbably, his bets jumped again. A few spins later, he was back in the hole to Chet, Ventnor and Ludwig. All three visibly breathed a sigh of relief. Chet ordered fresh drinks. Ludwig deliberately put his chip back on his little pile. The short man jumped to three hundred bucks a spin. Only now the blond wasn't getting any tips for her huffing and puffing. Her hand discreetly slid from his coat. She started slipping away.

-69-

"No!" the man almost cried. He turned to her with a desperate, pleading expression, so easy to read. *Change my luck, masked goddess of destiny! Lady Luck don't go away!* He began throwing chips on her tray even on his losing throws. Radiant smile from her, beaming at him again, puffing on his chips, cheerfully whipping him on more than ever. She began whispering in his ear again. You could guess the words from her lips: *you can do it, you can do it.* As if he were the little engine that could. *Oh yes,* Hawkins thought, *the extra effort, or the exercise of will, or the display of manly élan, or whatever the hell was going through this fool's mind—or pants—will definitely influence the rolling physics of a little chrome ball and a spinning wheel.*

After several more spins the tips stopped. Sweating profusely, hair smeared to his forehead, the dice and chips went down in a frenzy. *Sad. Trying to buy himself out.* The great pile evaporated, gone.

And what about our trio? Another check. Instead of being upset that their gift had been squandered, Ventnor, Chet and Ludwig acted intrigued. They began making little indecipherable finger gestures toward each other.

A loud snapping of fingers cracked down in front. The man who'd been behind the door at the entrance was standing on the edge of the raised lounge. He held one hand up sideways and then passed the palm of his other hand over it. The girl whispered something in the gambler's ear.

The man asked the boss for credit. He shook his head. No credit. The girl slipped away.

Seized by the suggestion, the man darted over to Chet and Ventnor. Obviously, he wanted more money. Chet and Ventnor glanced down the hall at Ludwig. He nodded.

Ventnor patted the man on the shoulder, leaned into Chet's ear and said something. Chet went over and spoke to the croupier. He checked with the casino boss standing on the edge of the lounge. The boss shrugged and made a small gesture with his hand. The croupier hurried to the cashier's cage. The teller came out with papers on a little clipboard. The man hastily signed the credit agreement, in triplicate, without reading it.

At the window the teller gave the man a surprisingly small number of chips. They, too, were gone within moments.

Ventnor came back over and took the short man by the elbow, commiserating with him, patting him on the shoulder. The man had an ashen, clammy pallor. Ventnor was very possessive, happily smiling at Chet and Ludwig behind the man's back. After a few minutes of talking, the man nodded his head. He handed Ventnor the casino's credit contract. Ventnor handed it to Chet. He took the paper over to the cashier and signed for it. Ventnor smiled at the man, gesturing at Chet.

Don't need a script to hear that little comedy, Hawkins thought. *Oh, yes. Everything is fine. A pleasure to do business with you. Of course, you don't have to worry. Welcome to my pocket. Or whatever one says to broke stupid plungers.* The man stumbled out.

And let's go for the daily double again, get two license plates, Hawkins thought. Seconds later he was back on the drawbridge. Dieter was on the steps by the kitchen with another bottle of beer. Probably waiting for that waitress to come back. No fool there.

The man came out and unsteadily stumbled down the driveway. He stopped, moaning loudly, holding his head. Then he headed down the road to his Studebaker. Hawkins followed through the trees. The man viciously kicked the bumper several times, got in, slammed the door and drove away. *Probably thinks he doesn't own it anymore*, Hawkins thought.

Or his house, if he has one. Not going to cover that pile.

Hawkins was back in the casino less than a minute later. Ventnor and Chet had already joined Ludwig at his table. They were highly amused, congratulating themselves over whatever they thought they'd done. Hawkins took out the Minox and snapped the rest of the roll. While he was winding the film the blond cocktail waitress came up to the casino boss. The boss laughed, gestured her over to the side and reached in his pocket for a roll of cash. He discreetly peeled off several C-notes. *Of course*, Hawkins thought. A commission. Good job, girl. Rolled the bastard properly. What the hell, take a picture of them, too. Time to head for the bar or the lobby. Must be a phone booth there somewhere.

-70-

It only took a minute for the office operator to get W on the line. "48700 here—should pass on several things immediately—and I've got something to tell you—"

"Can it wait?"

"Yes—"

"Chet Branch? Be careful, his family owns a bank with connections to several Nazi front companies. And those films of Ludwig's papers. There are things in there we can't figure out. We telephotoed all that back home, had specialists working all last night. We're not sure what it means, but the two left columns turned into lists of names. They cracked that right away. People from all over the country. Several known organized-crime figures. A least two big-city political bosses. Mostly, though, we can't trace them. They think the middle column is a list of numbers. They're still working on the other columns."

"Orator?"

"Right, as far as we can tell this is all part of Orator."

"You said gangsters? They don't have access to secrets. Could they be involved in a plot to assassinate President Roosevelt? Branch and Ventnor were making rather damn strange talk tonight—"

"No. Well, maybe there is a plot, but probably not from this list, that's too many people for an assassination. They'd keep a thing like that very simple, only a few trusted people. And the Mob's too smart to attack the president, or any other top politico. They'd be afraid of the attention it'd bring."

"What about Steel Seine?"

"Same thing. Far too many people involved for there to be a connection. There's most likely one person leaking—probably selling—naval secrets. Whatever Orator is, it's a much more ambitious project. What were you saying, now?"

"I've been following Ventnor, Chet Branch, Ludwig all night. There's a—I don't know how'd you describe it—a sub rosa nightclub up here with an illegal gambling operation. Only nothing shady, posh as posh gets. Must have the biggest gaming floor in the country. You should see it, it's incredible. They passed tray loads of chips to two men here, thousands of dollars. Obviously a payoff. Ludwig sat across the room signaling his approval."

"A casino?"

"Yes. Puts Monte Carlo to shame. Black tie only. Full of millionaires. The whole thing's sheer genius. The casino dead-ends anything—"

"Oh! God! That's brilliant. The perfect cutout."

"Exactly. They can say they got lucky. Well, one of them did, briefly."

"Don't follow."

"Ludwig, Chet Branch, Ventnor, they may have blundered. One of the men took his money and pissed it away at the tables. Chet put up more money so he could gamble some more. The fool lost that. Chet then signed for his credit slip. What's more, when the other man cashed in his chips he refused to take it in cash, he demanded a check. I'm pretty sure they missed that. I got the plate numbers on the two men's cars—"

"Brilliant. Just brilliant. Give them to my secretary in a moment. A casino! How did they ever think of that."

"I got a couple of rolls of pictures with my Minox. Wait until you see them. The light was not great but they should be readable. I'm still tailing them. Send me copies of those lists of names. I may need them."

"I'll call Fleming and send him up. Are they doing anything with the sniper rifle?"

"No. They were bragging about getting rid of Roosevelt, though."

There was a long pause.

"Again, assume nothing."

W transferred him. Hawkins gave the secretary the plate numbers, tossed the receiver down, rushed through the bar, whipped open the casino door and walked onto the drawbridge. He paused in the cool darkness for a moment. *What the hell is going on here? Big lists of people. Chet's family's bank. Wait. Something by Ludwig's car.*

-71-

There it is again—tail on a deer? A dark form moving. No, a glimpse of skin. One of the cocktail waitresses. She was bent over at the waist, leaning through the driver's side window into Ludwig's car. Her tray and a silver champagne bucket sat on the pavement, still chilling. *What in hell is she doing? She must've climbed down off this bloody catwalk and gone to have a peek. Or is she out here … doing … something … with someone?*

There was a clunk. She found the handle, opening the car. A dim light shined from inside. It was the blond. She began searching around the car door, pulling and twisting all the handles, rolling the window up and down, feeling on the end, pressing one spot after another, pulling on the liner, probing. She quietly shut it, then tiptoed around to the other side and reached in to unlatch it, bending way over again.

A shadow burst from the trees, grabbed her by the leg and yanked her out of the window, hard, dropping her a good three feet flat on her face. *It's Dieter,* Hawkins thought, *he must've been watching.* Dieter made a swift motion to his back pocket. Something bright glinted in the moonlight. He grabbed her wrist, snapping a handcuff around it, then the other. With an easy heave he picked her up like a log and hurled her through the window into the front seat.

Hawkins peered out across the yard at the casino entrance. Empty.

Now what? He felt annoyed and disgusted. *Well, fuck all, here we go again. Am I supposed to ride to the rescue? Stick my neck out because some silly bitch of a cocktail waitress gets herself in a pickle? No. I am through saving stupid people from themselves.*

Then a quick second thought. *Wait, there is a point—an opportunity.* It'd make a decent impression on Washington to take Kelly straight to the scene of a crime. *Or … take it to W. We could threaten Dieter with arrest.* Saving him from the Bureau, the local cops, might be the way to turn him.

Hawkins took a flying leap off the drawbridge into the trees. He began quickly walking along the parked cars, watching. Oblivious, Dieter ducked around the car. The sterling champagne bucket flashed in the dark. With a single swift movement Dieter plucked the bottle from the bucket, leapt behind the driver's seat and roared out of the driveway.

Hawkins sprinted for the Cord. Once moving, instincts, reflexes took over: on the chase. The top was down. One step on the rear bumper, one on the tonneau cover. He half fell, half dove for the top of the windscreen, caught it with one hand and swung down into the seat with a crash, his back barely twinging. Hit the ignition. The big Lycoming whirled to life. He backed the car in a hard circle, spraying gravel into the dolphin fountain. The Cord leapt down the road. Two men bounded out the main entrance, pointing down the road after Dieter.

Round the corner onto the highway Hawkins shifted into third and stamped down the supercharger pedal. The port on the blower opened with a low roar. Tires squealed from the surge of extra power.

No lights glimmered down the road. *But no intersections, either,* he thought. *Still have to be ahead.* The speedometer inching toward a hundred. At night the narrow tree-lined road flew by like a spinning tunnel.

Finally, a pair of ruby red cat's eyes gleamed down the road ahead. *Felt like an eternity. Only been a mere minute or two, though. Can't let him know I'm here,* Hawkins thought. He switched off the lights, flipped the crank. The headlights retracted back into the streamlined fenders, the black car nearly invisible in the dark, not even a reflection.

He didn't drive the car as much as aim it at the little red lamps. The cat's eyes grew larger, widening until he had to slam on the brakes.

A door must have been ajar in the Mercedes. The ceiling light was on. A flash of blond hair came up. Dieter waved her back, head darting back and forth, one eye on the road. Another flash of blond, now flying forward. Dieter violently tugged his hand back and forth, the blond hair flying with it. She'd lunged and sunk her teeth into his hand. Dieter yanked it free. He slapped her, then grabbed her by the face and pushed her back. The girl slid over to the far side.

A glimpse of something dark. Dieter jerked his head to the side. Another glimpse of something dark. A foot. Dieter turned, waving his hand protectively. She was trying to kick him in the head. It wasn't working. Dieter kept slapping the foot away. There was a pause. The car suddenly slowed. Dieter hunched over the shift lever. *She must have kicked it out of gear*, Hawkins thought. Another slowing. *There she is, got her back jammed against the door. Knee going up and down. A big grinding of gears. She's pushing on the shift lever.* Dieter took a swing. Then he pushed it back in gear. Another kick, another lurch, then slowing, more grinding, a wailing cat noise. They were having a tug of war over it, he pulling, she pushing on the gearshift with her foot. The big car straightened itself, then began lurching again, rapidly slowing down: sixty ... fifty ... now thirty miles an hour. She wasn't visible now. But the girl had to be putting up a hell of a fight. The car violently careened from one lane to the other as they struggled, the cats screaming when the gears fought. Then Dieter caught her ankle, holding it up—Hawkins could see the outline of a high-heeled shoe. Dieter reached with the other hand and pushed the car back in gear.

Supercharger silent, Hawkins hovered only a car length or two behind them, the white center line barely visible in the Mercedes' taillights. Every few seconds came the intermittent screech of stripping and grinding gears. Each growling catfight of sound marked another lurching bobble, another near stop, another speed-up. Occasionally a flash of tulle petticoat popped up in the rear window.

The twinned cars flew around a bend. Ahead loomed a cast-iron bridge over an inlet of a lake. Its iron members spread like a black spiderweb in the sky, waiting to catch its prey. The Mercedes roared toward it, swaying from side to side. It darted toward the massive steel abutments. Hawkins braked and held his breath. At this speed nobody in the Mercedes would survive. Precisely at the second Hawkins slammed on the Cord's brakes to avoid a pileup Dieter jerked the wheel aside. The Mercedes flew into the opposite lane. Another quick yank brought it lurching across and off the right side of the bridge. Hawkins heaved with relief and crept closer.

After a few miles the Mercedes leveled off at a ludicrous crawl. Dieter finally, slowly drove down a narrow country lane bordered on each side by high fieldstone fences. Hawkins let the ruby cat's eyes recede a bit. Then he followed them. About a quarter of a mile in, Dieter pulled up to an old abandoned farmhouse with a spavined roof caving in.

-72-

Hawkins killed the Cord's motor and silently rolled in a few dozen yards behind them. He quietly slipped out, kicked off his shoes and sprinted up to the edge of a stone fence, crouching down, listening.

Dieter let go of the girl's ankle. He ducked. A lethal high heel sliced by his head again. He ran around the car, yanked open her door, grabbed one arm and pulled her out, twisting and struggling, angrily shouting and shaking her. "How you find out?" Then he reached in and grabbed the champagne bottle by the neck, waving it at her like a club. "How?"

At that Hawkins carefully peered over the top of the stones. *Find out what?* That they were Nazi spies? No, they'd never talk about that there. But—she was obviously searching the car for *something.*

Dieter wasn't getting what he wanted. He shook her again. "How you find out? Tell me! Sprechen! Gottverdammt!"

Dieter threw her forward. She sagged at the knees, pounding both heels into the soft dirt. He pushed her. She jammed them in again, furiously pushing back. Dieter dropped the bottle. He lifted her up like a ballet partner, half-pushing, half-carrying her across the yard. Her legs were furiously flying, trying to get a grip on the ground ahead of her.

The car's headlights projected a spooky shadow of their halting march onto the gray walls of the old farmhouse. Halfway to the barn Dieter stopped and bent over. Her feet touched down. She dug into the ground again, instantly flinging her weight against his one hand, almost breaking free. With an angry lunge he caught her, hurling her back, knocking her to her knees.

Holding the back of her neck with one hand, he reached down in front of her and flipped up several old boards lying flat on the ground, exposing the deep, dark hole of an abandoned well ringed with long, soft, sloping grass.

Hawkins grit his teeth. *A well. Dieter's going to drown her the way a cruel boy drowns a sack of unwanted kittens. Tough break for the girl. Vastly easier to blackmail Dieter, though. No denying what's happened when there's a body. Should impress the hell out of Kelly.*

The girl stared straight down into the dark maw, chest to her knees. A thundering tremor began shaking her, erupting in a deep, sobbing, hoarse, retching, almost wounded cry of terror, screaming, "NO! P-L-E-A-S-E! YOU CAN'T! OH GOD, PLEASE!"

"Dieter hauled her up and around. Her cry rang over and over, through the empty farmyard into the still night.

Hawkins moved along the fence, following them, carefully listening, waiting. *She's going to talk. Any second now, come on, girl, give it a try.* What was it, anyway? Orator? Steel Seine? An assassination?

Dieter roughly shook her again. "How you know? Hey say something—" But there was no reasoning with her. Panic and fear had completely taken over. She probably didn't even hear him at this point. She simply kept crying.

"NO! P-L-E-A-S-E! YOU CAN'T! STOP! DON'T! STOP—"

Dieter screamed at her, his voice rising sharply, the words speeding up and tumbling over each other, shaking her hard, like a bag of rags. "Tell me! Hey say something! Sprechen! Gottverdammt! Hey say something!"

Dieter's overplaying his hand, Hawkins thought. *Pull it back. Give her a chance to think, give her some time.* Instead Dieter kept shaking her, as if the words would fly out of her mouth like a piece of meat stuck in the throat. *Bugger,* Hawkins thought, *he's panicking himself. He's green. He's not used to this, the stress, the anxiety, the fear. Not in control. He's going to blow it. Dammit.*

Dieter kept shouting and shaking, "Tell me! Hey say something!"

How did Dieter know that well was here? They must have scouted out the location in advance, Hawkins thought. Ready to kill and in need of a place to dump the bodies. That is, Dieter was ready to kill, then. That was his job. The man who did the rough stuff.

Rough stuff …

The man in the washroom …

It wasn't someone Chet hired. It wasn't a random mugger. It wasn't someone who saw me cash out at the track. Dieter attacked me. Dieter had to be the one. The man who does the rough stuff.

"Tell me! Hey say something!" Dieter said.

Dieter dragged her to her feet. *Going to pitch her in*, Hawkins thought. *Any second now.* In his mind he could already hear her scream as she went down the well. Imagine what it would feel like going in headfirst. The quickening fall. Hitting the water. Upside down. Drowning. Unable to breathe. The water …

The water. Drowning. Know what that'd feel like. Like being back at the hotel. In the washroom. Going down to the floor of the stall. Unable to breathe. Helpless.

The girl cried, no words, a plaintive moan of fear, despair, helpless, hopeless, mournful. It was too much. Walking through the door of the FBI with a grand trophy. Grooming and recruiting Dieter. Or both. All that flew out of Hawkins' mind. All he saw was rage. He was back in the washroom, back at the Waldorf, back in the cemetery, back in France.

-73-

Hawkins found himself running toward them. In that kind of trance again, a frenzied trance. He halted—*Dieter's so much bigger, an Olympic champion. No match for him. Especially with this back and side. Got to kill him. Want to kill him. Got to get a weapon—damn! Why'd I give the Hi-Power away! Find something.* The road. No stones, no sticks, nothing, only fine gravel.

The car. He sprinted back. The trunk. He tore it open. His hands fell on the cold steel bumperjack. He whipped it out and rushed off as if he'd drawn Excalibur from the stone. Darting in and out of the bushes, he crept up behind them.

Only Dieter wasn't interested in killing her, not yet. Her fighting to free herself had wormed her strapless top down, popping her breasts out, now shimmering and quaking in the car's lights. Dieter froze, staring at her, transfixed. Or paralyzed. From indecision? The enormity of it? Or the horror—had he ever actually killed anyone? Was he having second thoughts? Easy—in theory. Not so easy in cold blood, like this.

Or was rape on his mind? Not clear. She stopped screaming, on her knees, watching him, rapidly panting, out of breath, waiting. Nothing. Still frozen. Just staring at each other.

Hawkins lifted the jack, tensing himself for the effort. *Only one chance.*

Got to make it count. With a terrific burst he leapt toward them. There must have been a noise. The girl's eyes darted to the side, focusing behind Dieter. Instinctively, he started turning. Hawkins swung the unwieldy, flopping jack at the top of his head. Dieter jerked back. It whished by his ear, slamming into his shoulder with a soft, squishing thud, the jangle of metal parts, the cracking of bones. Dieter's knees buckled under the tremendous impact. His shoulder exploded in pain. With a startled gasp he staggered back. His once powerful arm dangled uselessly from its shattered joint.

The girl sprang up and flew into the bushes, crying hysterically. Dieter gasped and heaved again, a harsh, guttural cry of pain. He reached with his good hand for the automatic in his shoulder holster. Hawkins dropped the jack. No time for another swing. He matched him step for step, caught the gun halfway out, his right hand slamming around the barrel. Desperately lunging, Dieter threw his weight against Hawkins, trying to knock him off balance, thrust the pistol under his chin.

Grabbing the barrel with both hands, Hawkins shoved back. He hoisted it straight up in the air over their heads. The two men stood chest to chest, faces only inches apart, wrestling for the weapon. Hawkins twisted first to one side. Then the other. Couldn't break Dieter's grasp.

Dieter strained, too, trying to raise his injured arm. He only managed to lift it a few inches, gritting his teeth, choking a scream, breath shortening to quick pants. He dropped the limb, letting it dangle limp. Tiring, he tried kneeing Hawkins in the groin. Hawkins deftly parried the blow with his thigh.

They twisted sideways into the car's headlights, the pain in Hawkins' side and back steadily mounting, weakening him bit by bit. Hawkins caught the glint of gold at eye level. A fancy watch flicked by—a Curvex. *My Curvex.*

The sight of the watch spilled what little adrenaline Hawkins had untapped. *Yes. Know for sure, now. Dieter. Dieter was the one. The invisible man in the shower.*

He's in pain. Let's give him more. All unthinking instinct. Letting go of the gun with his right hand, Hawkins started punching Dieter's left shoulder like a wild man. Dieter gasped, shuddering, weakening with each blow. With each cry of agony Hawkins felt his exhilaration building. A blind unreasoning joy. Almost an ecstasy, intoxicating, higher and higher. More. More. More. Harder. Harder. Harder. Shifting his pain to Dieter, feeling better with every blow until his own pain seemed to vanish. As Hawkins hit the spot again and again with his fist he could hear and feel the broken bones rattling and grinding against each other inside the muck the man's shoulder had become, the blood flicking back from his fist, speckling his white evening jacket with red.

Each excruciating blow brought a scream from the pit of Dieter's stomach. Still, he kept his iron-tight grip on the precious pistol. Hitting and butting, Hawkins began aiming him toward the dark hole in the earth. Dieter's breath just short gasps now. The sweat of effort and agony poured down his contorted face.

Dieter's feet slipped. Through his frenzied confusion he realized they'd reached the edge of the well. With a shout of panic he scrambled for a footing. With a horrifying inexorability first one foot then the other slowly slid in. Hawkins grabbed his wrist with both hands and held on, holding him up.

Dieter's feet dangled helplessly over the edge. Hawkins took careful aim, kicked him in the groin as hard as he could, twice, swaying back and forth, butting into him from the effort. Dieter screamed again. Finally broke his grasp. He wrenched the pistol free and threw it clear. It landed soundlessly in the grass.

My watch. I want my watch back, Hawkins thought. Grunting, half-screaming from the effort, he held Dieter up with one hand and unstrapped the watchband. He let go.

Dieter landed with a tremendous but distant splash. Hawkins laughed triumphantly. He fell heavily on the grass, panting with exhaustion and exaltation.

-74-

It took a minute or two to sit up again. Hawkins inspected the watch. *Spoils of war indeed,* he thought. It glistened. He rubbed it. Slimy with sweat and coated with blood from the struggle. *Disgusting. Need a new band before wearing that again.*

He felt oddly relaxed, the rage he'd felt a moment earlier, his own pain, gone. *It feels like—well, not only licking Dieter, but Hitler,* he thought. *The soldiers outside the Renault works. The men on the road. Bailey. The whole damn lot.* Adrenaline must've burned off like powder in a skyrocket. He fell back, laughing. *Not like the washroom. Didn't just survive. I won. I beat him.*

He pocketed the watch and climbed up. Something nudged his toe. *A bottle of champagne? Dom Pérignon. Excellent. Just when it's needed. Hope it isn't shaken too badly. The girl. Where is she? Not going anywhere, not like that.*

Won her, too, fair and square. You're mine, darling, the spoils of war, too. Saved you, took you away from Dieter. You're mine. Cheerfully loosening the cork as he walked, he searched around the Mercedes. Nowhere in sight. He finally shouted out, "Hello! Miss? Hello! Hello! Come out come out wherever you are! Would you like a spot of champagne?"

At the sound of his voice the girl flew from the bushes with a joyous shriek. She came leaping up and down on both feet, bounding and bouncing forward, either utterly oblivious or indifferent to her dishabille state, waves of relief washing through her.

"Oh God! It's you! Oh Roy! Oh God! Oh Roy! You saved me! You came and saved me! Thank you God! Oh Roy! You came!"

She slammed into him in a blur, wrists still handcuffed behind her back, knocking him flat on his back again, burying her face between his neck and shoulder, sobbing with joy. They hit the ground. The cork popped from the champagne with a loud POW! spraying them both with white foam.

Hawkins lay back, rolling his head as she buried his face in kisses. *Wonderful. Mine.*

"Oh, Roy! Oh, Roy!"

Something finally clicked. *Roy … Roy? She called me Roy.*

"How'd ja know my name?" He rolled her off, climbed up, pulled her to her feet, grabbed the harlequin mask by the corner and ripped it away, tumbling her blond hair over her face.

Unreal. A scene from a dream, he thought. He blinked hard. *No, not hallucinating. She really is standing there.*

If the Martians from Orson Welles' Mercury Theatre had marched up from Grover's Mill to old Saratoga and melted Riley's into a bubbling hot puddle with a green death ray, Roy Hawkins could not have been more surprised.

"Daisy?"

"Oh, Roy! Yes!" Then she followed his eyes. She stumbled back a bit more. Her eyes followed down, then flicked back up. She sucked a little breath in, cringing, a little manic smile, a slight gasp, twisting her neck and shoulders a bit.

"Roy, it's not—it was a fling! A little summer fun!"

"I'm—um—thinking—what?"

"I know … what am I doing here—there …"

Hawkins had been entirely too dumbfounded to think much of anything, least of all the implications or circumstances of her employment earlier in the evening. But her anxiety primed his mental pump. The energy of his questions now all flowed in that direction.

"Oh—oh—wait." He started laughing. "That was no fling. I watched you hustle that bloke. Oh my God. What a pro! What'd you take off him?" He reached out and roughly grabbed her, pulling her in, wrapping his arms around and swinging her a bit.

"I don't know what you mean—"

"I was in the casino earlier."

That seemed unexpected.

"You—"

"Don't give me this little Miss Muffet sitting on her tuffet—"

"Oh, Roy!"

"Shoot a little skeet in the casino, sail about in this"—he gave her another delighted swing and a little hug—"ride that big horsey?"

"It's not funny!"

"Come on, now—"

"I, um—I already quit! I already quit! It's not what you think. This was my last night."

"How much?" Another swing.

"Maybe four hundred."

"And your commission?"

"Commission?" She started to deny it, "What? Oh, never mind! Three hundred, but that was only for getting him over to the wheel."

"You've an odd idea of summer fun, Daisy. Come now, what were you doing there—"

"When you said you were going to the FBI, and here I was out here—breaking the law, the casino, it's against the law here, you know?"

"Before that. What's the Fourteenth Patroon of the Manor of Beverwyck doing in this rig? Not that I'm complaining. Truly, I *so* hope it catches on."

"Yes—well—you see—" She started sniffling, now on the edge of tears.

"Did your father really go to Groton with the president?"

"Yes. But he lost everything in stocks when the market crashed in '29. It killed him. He died massively in debt. The manor's been in our family three hundred years. I couldn't sell it. I had to get money somehow! Dammit to hell, why didn't I put more on that stupid horse! I—" She started to cry. "I wasn't brought up for a career. Serving drinks is the only thing I know how to do. At least the only thing anyone will pay me for," then a wail, "I can't even type." Almost blubbering now, "All the girls at Emma Willard had money. Everyone always had money. I could lose everything. I could wind up on a cot at the Salvation Army. What am I supposed to do—"

"But why Riley's?"

"I can't make this kind of money anywhere else."

"What about Chet?"

"You don't know what they're like. No man's greedier than a rich one. They *never* have enough. They have so much, they don't feel what it means to other people. It all turns into a game for them, just chips on the table. He'll pay the bills, and he'll save the manor. But it won't be my house anymore. It'll be his. He'll take it. It's been in my family all these years. I can't bear to think I was the one who lost it. It's my house, dammit! I want to keep my house!"

"Daisy, Daisy," he hugged her again, "it's all right, nothing's changed," quietly talking, "everything's all right," patting her on the shoulder with one hand, gently rocking her back and forth as she rested against him, shamelessly crying.

-75-

So, she isn't rich. Who cares? I do not, Hawkins realized, *in the slightest. At the very least she isn't out and about with Chet. No, not off-putting at all, instead, it's all oddly attractive, exciting, more so than I've ever known. Hosting Nazis? Then throwing them out and taking their money? What a laugh. Tickling Chet's ego to get illegal insider tips? Admirable. Rolling suckers in a dress with a skirt the size of a hat brim? A hoot. Burglarizing Ludwig's car? Then trying to kick Dieter's head in, hooking the shifter? Amazing. Didn't whimper and cower in the corner. Kept fighting. Kicking the shift lever. How many women would think of that? Tough. Ruthless. Smart. Simply perfect.*

How could I adore any woman more?

After several minutes of gently holding her, leaning back for an occasional swig of champagne, he softly kissed the top of her hair. She lifted her face and began kissing his chin.

Squeezing her with both arms, he searched out her lips. They deeply kissed. She started moaning lowly, "Oh, Roy, oh, Roy." As she calmed, her emotional high shifted. Unable to caress him with her hands, she wiggled and rubbed up and down against his chest, wrapping a still quivering leg around him, locked in an intense kiss.

His slipped his hands down around her waist. She arched back in his arms. Her bare, luminous breasts throbbed invitingly with each quick, short breath. As he kissed her, she began breathlessly whispering, "Oh, yes, oh, yes, oh, yes," arching her neck and head backward.

Hawkins bent down, kissing her breasts. *Want you more than anything else in the world*, he thought. His hands felt out her zipper, pulling it down through the folds of rumpled satin. So soft, so beautiful silhouetted against the dark night. Her top fell down over her ruffled skirt. He ran his hands up her smooth, naked sides to her armpits before caressing her breasts again. He drew her toward him.

A loud, nearby noise, a startling sound. A cow? A low moan tolled from the bottom of the well. *My God*, Hawkins thought, *Dieter's still alive. The man must be unkillable.* He blinked and scanned the barnyard. They were standing in the headlights of a car in the middle of an open farmyard, who knew where. *What are we doing? Someone might spot us.* He took in her swaying, ready figure. *Wants me, too*, he thought. She stood waiting, leaning back in his arms, shoulders heaving with each deep breath, a completely relaxed, joyous smile on her face. *The hell with it.* He ran his trembling hands up and down her sides again and drew her toward him. A buzzing truck came rolling down a distant road.

Hugging her tightly, he whispered in her ear, "Daisy, we've got to get out of here. Just hold this thought."

She groaned, "No!" shaking her head, straightening up, leaning against him for a minute. Then, slowly, "Ah, right, right," nuzzling his ear. "Gimme some of that bubbly."

She took a couple of deep draughts from the bottle he pressed against her lips, happily spitting a big mouthful out. The cold foam splashed down her chest. She leaned back again, shaking and sighing in relief as it dripped from her nipples.

Oh, God. Maybe—No! Maybe nothing. Then … the hell with it, Hawkins thought. Another groan from the well. *Damn! Why aren't you dead? Damn, damn, damn. We've got to get out of here.* He closed his eyes, took a deep breath and exhaled slowly. *Focus. All right. Let's go.*

With an almost formal gesture he ran his hands along the zippers to the top, pulled her bodice up, straightening it. He held it out like a coat for her even though it was still attached to her waist. She bent way forward in a deep bow, wiggling and giggling, nestling her breasts into it, looking up at him. He slowly laid her back, tugging at the tight, resisting zipper, pulling it all liquid smooth again. When he reached the top she planted a big openmouthed kiss on his lips.

-76-

Splashing noises echoed up from below. Hawkins squatted down and peered in.

"Hello, Dieter! How's the water? Having ourselves a jolly swim?"

"Fick dich!"

"I say. That's quite enough! There's a lady here." Hawkins strode back a few paces to Daisy. With a smooth, grand gesture he bent over, slipped his arm behind her knees and picked her up. Gently swinging her, almost a waltzing dance, he carried her in his arms back to the Cord. Shifting a bit, he opened the door with a pair of fingers. He set her down on the front seat. She rocked back with a childish grin, one foot up on the seat. Another round of champagne. He nestled the bottle between her legs and kissed her again.

"Back in a minute."

First, the gun, Hawkins thought. He walked in circles around the well, sweeping the long grass, feeling for it with his foot. *Found it.* He held it up to the light. A Luger Parabellum. *Not bad. A gun, but a thing of polished beauty, too.* Pulled the toggle back. A shell ejected. *Yep, loaded.* Clicked the bullet back in. Another trophy. *And what else?* He returned to the well, crouching a foot from the edge, gingerly leaning over. The top of Dieter's head was just visible, far enough down, but not too far.

What to do with him? He thought. *Hand him over to Kelly? No. Too soon. Need to crack whatever they're up to first. That's the way to go through the Bureau's door. Or ... could call W, have them send a pair of Mounties down from Montreal to collect him.* But that meant leaving him in the well. Ludwig might know about this place, come get him. Probably cold down there, too, half in the water. He *is* badly hurt. Might not make it until the Mounties arrived. That settled it. *No choice but to get him out. Then take him somewhere, let W work him, like in the cemetery. I need the handcuffs. Even with a busted shoulder he's still big and dangerous. Have to get them off her and on him.*

Too bad. That was rather sporting. Rather? Damn sensational, it is. Ah, well.

"Listen up! You're doing what I say. I have your gun. Throw the keys to those handcuffs up here."

Hawkins could hear grunting and splashing noises. Dieter was diving for something. Or was he trying to climb?

Dieter called up the well shaft, "No. Go away."

"What? Throw up the keys!"

There was a long pause.

"No. You'll shoot me, then."

"I won't hurt you. I'll get you out. Understand? But I want the keys to the handcuffs first."

"Why should I trust you!"

"I won't shoot you."

"No."

Hawkins edged closer to the lip of the well, impatiently waiting for the answer. He heard a faint click. He instantly jerked up and back.

"I'm going to lean down. I want you to throw them up to me. Then I'll drop you a rope." At the edge of a field, a dozen yards away, bobbled a tattered scarecrow. Hawkins ran over, broke it off and carried it back, thrusting it over the well. Looking up, Dieter saw a profile in the dim light. He instantly fired a couple of rounds.

-77-

Several handfuls of straw drifted down. Hawkins threw the scarecrow aside. *So. Tried to kill me again. Thinks he'll wait for Ludwig to come.* He ran back to the Cord.

"Roy, were those shots?" Daisy said.

"Nothing." No kisses this time. Hawkins yanked the spare gas can from the trunk. Carefully edging up to the well, he held the can in front of him and poured some gasoline into the hole.

The first drops hit. Dieter exploded in a string of curses. Hawkins splashed some more gas.

"Mit diesem Mund küsst du deine Mutter?" and laughed. Another burst of curses from below. "Dieter, what time is it? Hey? Welche Zeit haben wir? I know. Time for a spot of petrol," and gave him another splash.

Dieter realized it wasn't pee. He went silent. Hawkins could hear him frantically digging in the side of the well, grunting and gasping from the fumes and the pain, trying to get a foothold with his good hand and two feet. Every time he tried to gouge out a hole to stick a foot in the wall the dirt collapsed with a distant rumble. The more he failed the more he panicked. Finally, even his broken arm flailed uselessly against the side of the well.

"All righty," Hawkins called down. "So! Herr Doctor picked this place, and you think you'd rather take your chances on shooting me and hope he finds you. Planning ahead. Very smart. However, I have a light. Throw up the keys. *Now.*"

Hawkins still had the empty can in his hand. Almost tossed it aside. But no. He started to throw it overhand down the well. Dieter saw a shape, a target the shape of a human head. He fired.

The column of gasoline vapor in the well shaft instantly exploded with a brilliant bluish-white flash. A huge orange and white fireball shot out of the hole, soaring a hundred feet into the air, lighting the countryside like day. The blast knocked Hawkins over, throwing him a dozen feet, flat on his back. A moment later a deep reverberation echoed off the nearby mountains. Then the gas can bounced back into the barnyard with a jouncing *clang*.

Inside the well the explosion hammered Dieter into the burning mud like a spike, right up to his neck. With a crumpling, thudding rumble the walls of the well fell in, leaving nothing behind besides a soft area of loose dirt.

Hawkins slowly rolled over and stiffly pushed himself to his knees and then his feet, fresh pain in his back and side now stabbing him anew, heaving and gasping, trying to get a breath in, the wind knocked out of him, ears ringing. In the distance came the frightened lowing of cattle. He brushed himself off and limped over to where the well once was, tripping over the gas can. He hooked the wire handle with a finger. Flattened. He flicked it aside, gazing at the huge, slightly smoking depression where the well used to be.

It'll take a steam shovel to get the keys. Now what? He knew the instant answer: *find another abandoned farm, that's what. Or maybe the manor. Those handcuffs aren't a problem. Not for me. Probably not for her, either. Not until dawn, maybe later.*

-78-

He stretched across the seat and gave her a kiss. She looked worried.

"What was that!"

"An IQ test. Don't ask whose." He started up the car, patting her on the knee, taking another slug of champagne from the bottle. "Time to get out of here—"

"No."

"No? Why—"

"Ooh—gosh, ooooh!—the money." She bent over, burying her face between her knees, "you've got to get the money."

Hawkins switched the ignition off.

"What money?" He stared at her a second. "My God, you were trying to pinch something out of Ludwig's car in *that*?"

"I overhead Ludwig say all the cash they needed was in the car door."

"Huh—righto!"

The Mercedes was still running. With a handkerchief he pulled open the driver's side door, twisting and fiddling the handles the way she had. There didn't seem anything unusual about it. No storage compartments. No hidden doors. He got in and slid across the seat. His heel touched a square object, a brown leather case.

Anticipation rising, he carried it around front of the headlights, flipping it open. No money. Instead, snug in green felt rested a screw-on buttstock, a few spare clips, ammo, a big snail drum magazine and an empty hollow for the Luger in his pocket. *Exquisite. Never had a chance to find a gun shop. Maybe I should pinch the sniper rifle while I'm at it. Dieter won't be using it now.*

That left the passenger door. He began trying the handles and knobs again. *Nothing.* He knocked all over it with his knuckles. The bottom didn't sound the same. A dead thunk instead of a hollow ring. He searched all around the bottom, pulling on the liner, trying to turn the screws with his fingernails. *Impossible without tools. No time anyway.*

Pushing the door all the way open, he hopped behind the wheel, shifting into gear, angling the big car around the farmyard. Lined the right side up with one of the fieldstone walls. Drove forward, got some running room. Shifted into reverse and stomped on the gas. The car roared back. The door caught on the old stone wall. It neatly sheared off with a grinding bang followed by the tinkling of broken glass.

Hawkins swung the wheel, shining the lights on the door. The liner had been completely shredded away. Reaching inside, he felt a thin metal box. He angled it out past a strut. It was about an inch and a half to two inches thick, maybe fourteen inches long, pearl gray with a folding steel handle. Standard, heavy, fireproof and locked. He switched off the motor, killed the lights and ran across the farmyard. Along the way he grabbed the gun case and tossed it in the Cord's trunk.

"Righto. Back to the manor."

"Roy, my hands are starting to hurt. You've got to get these hand-cuffs off."

Dieter cinched them too tight. Damn. From the expression on her face it was definitely killing the mood. *Got my lockpicks in my pocket,* he thought. *Could open the cuffs easily enough. But how am I going to explain that? Maybe I can fake it.*

"Any tools at your house?"

"No. We've got to go back to the club."

"Ah, I do not want to go back to that place. And I thought you quit."

"But they'll know what to do."

"Why would they know?"

"They're … you know …"

"No—what?"

"Oh, jeesums. They work for Meyer Lansky."

"Oh, splendid. Gangsters?"

"Um, well, it is illegal. But they're really just regular businessmen."

"Who know all about handcuffs."

"Um—ye-ah."

"First Nazis. Now gangsters. And we're going to ask them for a favor."

"Uh-huh."

"Meanwhile, here I am, going to work for the Bureau."

"We won't tell."

"I do hope not." He started the car, pressed the accelerator, then braked to a stop and gave her another kiss. "Don't worry, it'll be all right."

-79-

"I don't think his man was alone in this," Hawkins said. Daisy had just introduced him to her boss, the casino's manager, Jacob Jacobson, the man behind the door who peeled off the C-notes to Daisy earlier. He and Hawkins were standing shoulder to shoulder in a narrow gallery off Jacobson's office. They were peering down through an ornamental grillwork at the casino floor. The back of Ludwig's head was just below. The lookout was obviously well used. Binoculars and empty coffee cups littered a worn shelf. Jacobson's face was partly lit through the grillwork. He eyed Hawkins carefully, suspicious and tense.

"What? You saw him grab Daisy."

"They had that farm picked out in advance. It was a perfect setup. Remote from the road, plenty of trees. Then there's the well. Remember—he tried to shoot me? From the bottom. He knew Ludwig would come and find him. You see? He wasn't worried about getting out."

"But what'd these guys want with a body dump?"

"I can guess. My company sent me to … well… prepare things with them. I've been following him around to his meetings, watching them, trying to find an edge that'd give us a little leverage."

"What kind of meetings?"

"Foreign trade meetings. Don't you know what he is?"

"No."

"He's an official trade delegate to the United States from the Third Reich. He's offering American companies business deals inside the countries the Nazis just conquered."

"What? Here?"

"That's right," Hawkins said. He reached for his wallet, found Ludwig's business card and handed it to Jacobson. His eyes locked on the eagle and swastika. The guarded expression vanished, replaced by genuine shock, confusion and horror.

"But what's Daisy got to do with this?"

"She overheard something. Something dangerous to them. Something illegal."

"What kind of illegal?"

"They're actually spies. They're using your casino as a cutout to bribe people, buy information, probably."

Jacobson acted skeptical, frowning slightly. "But Daisy?"

"She recognized them. She heard Ludwig say the money they needed was in the car, then went to find it."

"How'd she know them?"

"She rented them her house for a business conference. That's how I met her."

"She did? Jesus Christ!" Jacobson bounded out of the closet. Daisy was leaning over a chair with a cushion under her hands while two of Jacobson's men ground away with a file on the handcuffs. "Daisy! You rented your house to those Krauts?" The men stopped filing.

She nodded. "Please don't get mad."

Jacobson's face reddened anyway.

"Daisy? What the hell? How could you! Nazis? I can't believe it! I got people over there."

"I'm sorry! I need the money. You know I do—"

He sighed and shook his head. "I know, but God dammit, Daisy, Nazis? In my club—"

"You have relatives there?" Hawkins said.

"Yeah. In Poland. We haven't heard a thing in months. My father's worried sick, my mother, too. Her sisters and brothers are there now."

"I'm really sorry. That's awful." "We're still hoping for news."

"Of course. Well, anyway. Daisy was eavesdropping on Ludwig. He could still be a threat to her. We can't be sure—"

"I know exactly how to take care of him! Fellas!"

"What? Take care? How—"

"You know what I mean."

"No! Wait—listen."

"Why? We've done it before. Maybe year and a half, two years ago. Meyer, Bugsy, me and a bunch of the guys from the old neighborhood busted up a Bund rally in Yorkville. They had a stage with a swastika flag and photo of Hitler and everything. Threw a couple of Nazis out the windows along with their shit. Mostly they panicked and ran out. One of them broke an ankle trying to get away. We chased them down the block and beat the shit out of 'em. Those fuckers better understand, Jews can fight back."

"How come you weren't at the Waldorf the other day?"

"Aw, well, good God, you can't do that on Park Avenue."

"And you can't do it now, here. We have to find out what he's doing."

Jacobson was back to looking suspicious and tense. "Yeah ..."

"Bring Ludwig under your grate over here. I want to listen. Tell him your boys saw his chauffeur snatch Daisy, followed him and took care of him. Tell him to never come back. Tell him you know he had a disagreement with Miss Schenck and that you'll have him arrested as an accessory to kidnapping if he says a peep to anyone. He won't say a word. He can't stand any official scrutiny at all. Assure him you want everything hushed up, too, he needn't worry about Miss Schenck talking to anyone. Tell him you'll take care of that."

"No way. Why should I do that?"

-80-

"Because they're Nazis. In your club," Hawkins said.

"Yeah, and that's what's pissing me off! Help you with your business? What for? No, we are gonna settle this with him right now."

"My business is your business. I can prove it. Give me the names of those relatives of yours. I have some very influential friends in London. I can't promise anything. Their situation is very bad. But there's a small chance I could arrange a visa for them to get to a neutral country, probably Turkey or across Russia to Shanghai."

Taken aback, he grabbed Hawkins' lapel, let go of it. Then he grabbed it again and started shaking it, uncertain whether to act tough or grateful.

"You could do that?"

"I'm promising nothing. I'll try."

"I dunno—"

"What have you got to lose? Really?"

"How do I know you're not conning me?"

Hawkins thought a second, then remembered something. "Hold on." He took out his wallet and began thumbing through the cards again. It was still there, the Duke of Devonshire's official business card as under-secretary of state for dominion affairs. "I know people." Hawkins handed it to Jacobson. He read it, stared up at Hawkins a second. Then he read it again. "In a couple of days you can call the British consulate in Manhattan and confirm it. Until then, you'll have to trust me." Jacobson was wavering. "You know odds. What are you really risking here? For the stakes?"

"Not much." He quietly handed the card back, tapped out a cigarette, lit it and studied Hawkins for a second. "Okay." Jacobson beckoned to two of his men and went out onto the gaming room floor under the grate. He waited, puffing away, while they brought Ludwig over. Hawkins closed the closet door so his face couldn't be seen through the grill and leaned closer to hear.

Jacobson started talking, lightly punching his finger against Ludwig's chest. Ludwig stayed cool and collected. Then Jacobson told him Dieter was dead. Hawkins watched for the reaction. When it came he uneasily fell back.

Ludwig laughed. He actually broke into a smile, first cracking at the corners before spreading across his face. Then he snickered, goatee vibrating up and down. Ludwig smilingly bobbed his head in agreement to Jacobson's tough points, interrupting partway through to ask about the Mercedes. When Jacobson said he'd have him driven out, Ludwig smiled and heartily shook his hand. In the most sincere tone possible, he thanked him for his discretion in handling the matter, assured him there was no need for the police to be involved or for Miss Schenck to worry about anything.

A minute later Jacobson swung open the door to the gallery.

"Was that easy."

"Was he drunk?"

"No. Perfectly steady."

"He didn't mind at all."

"I'll tell you, I'm glad I don't work for him. He must be the coldest fish in the sea not to give a fig over his own guy getting killed. Actually apologized for the *inconvenience* it might have caused us. Only thing he gave a damn about was his car. No wonder he's a Nazi."

"Perhaps you did him a favor."

"Hang around here awhile, you'll see it all. Our driver's taking him out there now," Jacobson said, "He'll—"

Jacobson was interrupted by a shriek and the thump of a tool.

-81-

"AWW! My arm!"

One of the men threw a file on the floor. "Goddamn freakin' thing! Dull already!" He'd slipped, jabbing Daisy. She was still bent over the back of a big club chair. Two of Jacobson's men had been holding the handcuffs, filing away on the chain links. The cuffs kept slipping back and forth, cutting into her wrists. A miscellany of tools lay scattered about the floor. Gabe, the short, powerful doorman, picked up the file. The other man, Herman, let go of the cuffs.

"Please, can I stand up awhile?" she sobbed, slowly straightening. Hawkins ran over and wiped her face with his handkerchief.

"You mean none of you—considering your business here"—they simply stared at him—"you don't know anyone who can pick locks?" They seemed mystified, except for Gabe, who bristled.

"No. See here, gambling may be illegal but we're only businessmen trying to collect what's owed us." He expectantly looked at the others for confirmation. "Isn't that right?"

"Can't they find a hacksaw?"

"We've already broken two blades. File's the only thing that'll work. Blade rattles right off."

"That'll take hours!"

"Yeah, well—"

Hawkins bent over, examining the cuffs closely. On the underside was a small stamp: swiss. *Damn. Had to be Swiss, didn't they?* The filing had barely scratched it. If his valve company experience held true they were probably nickel-vanadium-chrome-steel something. *Couldn't use plain old carbon steel and plate it like everyone else. Probably take a water cooled, diamond bladed, power bench saw to cut through them.* From the thinness they had to have an easy three-pin mechanism. It'd be ridiculously simple to take them off.

A conference between Jacobson and his men broke up.

"We're gonna go find a pair of bolt cutters." Jacobson said. "Sit down and rest awhile, hon."

She sank into the chair as they trooped out. Alone, Hawkins thought, *Do I dare?* The image of her swaying in his arms at the farm, her bare skin glistening darkly in the moonlight, crept in. One more glance at her strained, tear-streaked face cinched it.

"I've got an idea. Hop up. Let me have a try."

"Do I have to?"

"Yes. Trust me."

She wearily stood and turned around. He had his pick set out and unfolded in a second. *Medium size*, he thought, *up and over: one, two, three.* The cuff clicked and slid open. *Stop it halfway out, move to the other one—need to take them both off at once—*

"I broke it!"

"Oh, thank God!"

Left hand, up and over: one, two, three. She felt the lock spring open and instantly flung her free hands up triumphantly. The hooked pick caught in the opening of the lock, ripping it from his hands. The cuffs flew up, ricocheted off the ceiling and bounced in the middle of the floor. They glimmered on the carpet, picks sticking out of the lock like a floral arrangement. He lunged for them. She tackled him around the neck first.

"Oh, Roy, you did it. You did it again," planting a huge kiss on his cheek, kicking her feet in the air for several long seconds before he broke free.

Jacobson strode through the door the very instant Hawkins' fingers reached the leather case. His eyes locked on the picks. Hawkins palmed them off, casually trying to pocket them. Jacobson flipped out a small nickel-plated automatic with a flick of his wrist. He stood sideways to Hawkins, holding the gun close, gesturing with a pair of bolt cutters in his other hand. His men formed a flying wedge behind him. They began reaching for guns, too.

-82-

"What's a *businessman* like you doing carrying lockpicks around, and don't tell me it's your hobby. You could've had 'em out a lot earlier."

"I can explain—"

"Are you in rackets!"

"No! I—"

Daisy seemed mystified, a confused expression dawning on her face. "You had a set of lockpicks?"

Jacobson cut her off. "Let me guess. You're in town for the annual jewel robbery!"

Hawkins stepped back, shaking his head. "No! Please. Listen to me."

"You're exactly the slick type for a big-time jewelry thief," Jacobson said.

Daisy abruptly shouted them down, "Shut! Up!" A stunned silence filled the room. "You mean you could've got these damn handcuffs"— she grabbed them from the floor and began waving them, increasingly angry—"off in the farmyard?"

"I'm sorry, Daisy. He's been lying to you," Jacobson said.

"You were, weren't you!"

"No—I—" Hawkins started to answer, paused. *No*, he thought. *The coming answer—any excuse—it would be ridiculous.* "Yes—obviously."

"All that stuff about my relatives," Jacobson said, "this business of yours. Why you really following these Krauts?"

"That story about joining the FBI," Daisy said, "that's a lie, too, isn't it!"

The moment they heard "FBI" the gang panicked. They began shouting together, "FBI? He's a cop! Oh my God! He's a cop!"

"Enough!" Jacobson shouted, wagging the automatic at him. "Everyone. If you're a cop, so help me God, you're going into the lake—if Lansky, the others, find out we let the Bureau in here—"

He means it, Hawkins thought. *He's badly frightened. Frightened means dangerous.*

"I have been lying," Hawkins said. "These are professional lockpicks. But I'm not a cop. I work for the British government."

"What?" Daisy said.

"I'm sorry, Daisy. I truly am. I'm an officer of His Majesty's Secret Intelligence Service. My job is hunting Nazi spies all over the world. London sent me to track down Nazi agents here. But the story about the Bureau is true. J. Edgar Hoover wants to hire me away to hunt spies for him. But I'm not about to be a cop."

Jacobson growled, "You work for the British? I'm tempted to turn you in."

"You? Call the Feds here? That'll be interesting. Didn't I hear you say you were dead men if—who was that? Linsky?—knew a G-man was here?" Hawkins waited. Silence. "Obviously, being a British agent, I have contacts in London who might be able to help your family, if we're lucky. Do you want to see the duke's card again? Of course, if you shoot me—" Jacobson slowly lowered the gun. "Thank you. And, Daisy, everything I said about the two of us at Millicent's is true. Please, you have to believe that."

"A spy? You're a British spy?"

"No. I'm an agent, a type of investigator, if you will. I'm not spying on this country. Ludwig is. Actually, I wasn't even supposed to be here more than a few weeks. I'm supposed to go back overseas."

Daisy began unconsciously working her shoulders back and forth. "Roy, why didn't you tell me—"

"Oh, that's the very kind of thing you tell a girl, isn't it? Besides, Your Ladyship, you weren't very forthcoming, yourself—'scamps pretending to be something they're not'?" He grabbed the edge of her tutu and gave it a little tug. She flinched a bit, yanked it away, then glanced off and let out a deep breath.

"Oh. I guess. I wasn't. I … I—" She looked incredibly upset again, on the edge of tears.

"It's all right. Daisy—" He reached out with a hand on her waist.

She threw her arms around his neck. He hugged her tightly. She whispered in his ear, "We're quite the pair, aren't we?"

"Yes. We are."

"How do we know you're not making up another story?" Jacobson said. "Like about my folks?"

"As I said. Call the British consulate in a few days," Hawkins said. "Until then, you'll have to trust me."

"Daisy, do you think it's true those Krauts are Nazi spies?" Jacobson said.

She hesitated, frowning. Then she answered quietly, very carefully, almost a whisper, looking back, leaning away from Hawkins while still holding on to him.

"Yes, I do believe they are. I heard them talking about—things."

"What kind of things?"

"Paying people off."

Jacobson looked like he'd been gut punched. "Goddamn, in my club!" He grabbed a pad from his desk and started rapidly writing.

Daisy tightened her arms around Hawkins. She whispered in his ear, "This, what you told me. It's safe with me. I'll never tell. They won't, either. They can't. You—*we*—can still go to Washington," she squeezed him hard, "it's okay."

Jacobson handed Hawkins the paper.

"Lookit, I don't want to seem ungrateful. I want your help. I don't want to screw that up. But the Bureau! You're making us all nervous as hell. Maybe you oughta clear out of here."

"You want me out of here? I want us out of here."

"Okay, okay, here are the names. Oh, by the way, it's Lansky, Meyer Lansky. And I'd appreciate it if you forgot you heard that."

"I will. I appreciate your help, too. Let's go, Daisy."

-83-

Hawkins got the car door. He opened his arms wide. She stood up. He gently wrapped them around her, cradling her. She stood still for a moment, neither resisting nor relaxing. Then she let go and started shaking, a hard shivering, all over. He gave her a strong hug, pulling her close, holding her tightly.

"It's all over," he said.

She slowly quieted, steadily relaxing and slipping her arms around him. He held her by the waist. They stood embracing for several minutes, then slowly and silently paced to the manor. She locked the old paneled door behind them. With a gesture of ineffable sweetness she wrapped her slim, delicate fingers around his and led him up the great staircase to her bedroom. Every few steps she smiled over her shoulder, tugging him to come.

She dropped her necklace on the dressing table. He embraced her again, sweeping his hands up to the top of her back and down again with the zipper in his fingers. With a single, simple motion he thrust her dress to the floor. As he pulled it down she straightened up slightly, lifting her chin, breathing deeply through her nose, mouth open, smiling slightly, her hand rubbing his arm and shoulder.

It'd been twenty-four hours since he'd had any sleep. But he felt uncommonly lucid. At one with himself. The world. Eternal. He ran his fingers through the back of her perfumed hair. She turned her cheek. He kissed it. She stood waiting and watching in the darkness of the room as he slipped out of his clothes. They stood silently for a moment. Just gazing at each other, openmouthed, breathing deeply. He wrapped his arm under her shoulders and easily swept an arm up under her knees, carrying her to her ancestor's great four-poster, nestling in next to her.

Her soft skin felt so good next to his.

Afterward they fell deep asleep, her head resting gently on his chest, his arms wrapped protectively around her. Birds in the trees outside started stirring in the dawn. Exhausted by days of traveling, missed meals, eccentric sleeping hours and several brutally hard fights, Hawkins slept the dreamless sleep of the truly exhausted.

When he woke, Daisy's sleeping head still rested on his chest. He craned his neck up, checking the angle of the sun on the floor. Had to be close to noon. Daisy wasn't waking. *Should get up*, he thought. But he lay still, holding her. Studying her sleeping face. Her long delicate lashes. The curve at the tip of her nose. The round highlight shining on her shoulder. Her amazing hair.

How indescribably wonderful waking up next to her. So easy to get used to. A real life, home, friends, meals together. A good book shared. No more lonely nights. He ached to think of it. The tip of Daisy's forehead was right under his chin. He could smell her breath. Sweet and rich, an intoxicating liquor, almost.

Being shot at—and missed—that kind of close brush with extinction made you incredibly aware of your own mortality and existence. It provoked a sense of wonder and savoring it. But that was nothing like this. *I've never felt so alive*, he thought. *Not only in touch with my own mere existence, but hers, the world's, all in tune. How could I even think of giving this up?*

She stirred. He gently caressed her silky hair. She woke with a smile, lifted herself up on an elbow and gazed into his face.

"Hello, sleepyhead," he said.

"Hello, Roy. I want to stay here all day."

"Me, too." He yawned and stretched, then laughed. "Oh, damn! I have to get going. What time is it?"

"Time for a kiss."

They rolled back under the sheets again, giggling in the morning light. Forty minutes later Hawkins sat up again.

"I really do have to take care of matters—important matters."

"Hmmm …" She closed her eyes and drifted off to sleep again.

Hawkins watched her for a long moment, totally contented. He idly reached over, mostly not paying attention, fishing for his watch in his pants. He pulled it out by the strap. The blood had dried and flaked off. *What's that on the back?* he thought. *Didn't notice that.* He held it up to the light. There's … an engraving. He rubbed his eyes and checked.

VON MUTTER IN LIEBE

-84-

He lay back for a moment. Then he got up. Walked to the window. Walked back to the bed. Walked back to the window. Held it up and read it again.

VON MUTTER IN LIEBE.

No. Not dreaming.

Not my watch.

His mind began racing, stomach turning over. Dieter didn't steal the watch. That meant it might not have been him in the washroom. *What's happened here?* He began thinking over the chase, the barnyard. Dieter caught her stealing, or trying to steal from the car. He wanted to know how she knew. He was scared. Very scared. He kept saying the same things—*How did you know. Hey say something …*

Why was he so panicked? *Oh God. Was it "I say something"?* His accent—thinking in German, speaking in English. *Sagte ich etwas?* Did he mean, "Did I say something"? Did he think he'd screwed up again? But he hadn't talked to Daisy.

No. The other girl by the kitchen. Talked to her for a good bit. That's it. He got them mixed up. The mask. Thought Daisy was her. He had the wrong girl. Did he say something to her? Or think he said something to her? He'd had a few beers. He thought he'd slipped and screwed up again. Yes. Ich sag etwas … I say something—a question.

Wait. Wait. He did grab Daisy. That was kidnapping. And he really roughed her up. Horrendous. Brutal. Belongs in jail.

But the way he'd stood there, in the barnyard. Dieter froze. He couldn't do it, he couldn't throw her in.

Or ... I stopped him? Okay. Maybe. But what happened then. What did I do? He was in the well. He was helpless. I poured gas all over him. I threatened to burn him alive. Reckless. Dangerous. Got carried away again. And for what?

Hawkins slowly eased down on the bed. His back started throbbing and pounding again. *God. Everything has gone to hell.* He remembered back at the hotel. *"I have lost everything I have worked for because of the führer. I could've gone to Hollywood. I could've been the next Sonja Henie ..."* *He was there on the steps listening to the jazz. Like me.*

What have I done? I killed him for nothing—he wasn't the man in the washroom. I killed a basically innocent man. Well—no—no. Wait. Dieter was an armed Nazi agent. He abducted Daisy. He might have killed her. And he tried to kill me, that set off the explosion. But I am still responsible. He was my prisoner. I should've been more careful.

And that's the smallest part of this. We've lost an incredibly valuable potential asset. We might have turned him.

Great God, this is a disaster. We could've had a double agent traveling around with Ludwig everywhere. Reporting every contact. We could've ripped out the whole network. Or fed them back every cockamamie story we could think of to sabotage their war effort.

Daisy stirred behind him. He gazed over his shoulder at her, studying her sleeping face, so quietly breathing. He came to yet another level of mind.

No. Killing Dieter was not the worst. I almost let her die. I was willing to sit back and watch. That would have made me a murderer. He rolled back and put his arms around her. What if Dieter had shot her in the head? Or broken her neck? Anything but throw her screaming headfirst down that well, into the water to drown. *Water—drowning—that was what hit me, it was me. That set me off. Otherwise I might have held back. I would have let him kill her. I know I would have.*

What would it have been like when she didn't show up the next day?

Would've figured it out soon enough. How could I have lived with that? Not merely that she had died. But that I had stood there watching. Done nothing.

I already wanted her badly enough to kill Chet. Would I have killed that spoiled brat? Yes. I am still that crazy for her. But I almost lost her. I almost let her die. Almost watched her die.

What is the matter with me? What has happened to me?

Daisy rolled over, smiling, saw his face, saw something.

"What's the matter, Roy?" It took a minute to respond. "Roy, you're scaring me—"

Finally, "This isn't my watch."

"Excuse me? What watch?"

"I took this off Dieter in the farmyard. It's identical to the one that was stolen in the States Hotel. Don't you see?"

"Forget the watch." She began kissing his chest.

"I assumed Dieter jumped me there. But he didn't. Someone else did."

At that Daisy scowled slightly. "Oh. Well, he still had it coming."

"No—I mean, okay, but what the hell gives? Who attacked me?"

"Ludwig?"

"No, he was big. I've so fouled up here, I just can't figure exactly how."

Hawkins eased back up with a tight groan, took a deep breath, glanced down and saw the small metal case he'd wrenched from the Mercedes. The case—maybe—something.

-85-

Hawkins fetched his picks from his other pocket and grabbed the case. He rolled back against the headboard and began picking the lock. What was so incredibly important Dieter had panicked like that? The lid flew open with a clang. A pile of dusty old certificates were on top. He tossed them aside.

But Daisy took a deep breath, a gulp, and cried, "Jesus! Roy! Be careful!" and dove over the side of the bed, catching the certificates before they hit the floor. She popped back up with the papers, an awed expression on her face.

He frowned. "'Bout what?"

She began gently flipping through the papers, licking her thumb, eyes darting over them, increasingly excited. "Don't you know what these are?"

He disdainfully glanced over at them, rummaging around in the case. "No. They look like dusty old mortgages."

"Actually, they are, in a way. These are bearer bonds! Denominated in Swiss francs."

"Oh, yes, I think the bear's the symbol of Zurich."

"No! Bear-*er*! Bear-*er*!"

"Well, excuse me for not traveling in your exalted social circle."

"There's millions of francs here!"

At that he really began paying attention. "Swiss franc's worth about fifty cents."

"Forty—fifty—there's eighty of them. Half a million each."

"Forty million dollars? What? You're joking."

"Why, no."

"How can anything possibly be worth that much?"

"Bearer bonds are like cash. You see, there's no bond holder's name on them. Here!" She pointed at the top. It read, in German and French, *payable to bearer on presentation*. "Whoever holds them, has them. Bearer bonds are the most compact form of wealth on earth. Gold, diamonds, they're nothing in comparison. Banks mainly use them to move great sums between themselves. You can walk into any main or central bank office in the world and cash these in a jiff."

She began passing them to Hawkins one at a time. He began studying them. *Horrifying. And a relief at the same time*, he thought. *This is a scary sum of money.* The horror at killing Dieter, the mess, the blown opportunity, began to recede, at least slightly. A scary sum made them scary people again. What men would do for this kind of money. Or worse, what they could do *with* this kind of money. No wonder Dieter was in such a panic.

"What on earth? Ludwig was driving around with forty million dollars in his car? For what? How—where—could they possibly use this kind of money?"

She rolled over on her stomach, still nude, swinging her feet in the air, slyly smiling. "I can see I undercharged him." He lightly slapped her on the bottom with a bond.

"Be serious! This is major, major money. A destroyer, new, costs a million dollars. Churchill's trying to lease a squadron of old destroyers from the US Navy right now. This could buy a whole fleet of them. Forty destroyers. New."

Cooing, she slipped her arms around his neck and began nuzzling his cheek. "I think it's very lucky for us—"

Hawkins gently pushed her off with a finger. "This is very dangerous for us! We don't know why this is here. But it's got to be absolutely massive to require something like this." He bounced from the bed onto both feet. "Time to get to work, report in."

"To who? London? Or Washington?"

"You know who."

"Why not Washington? Shouldn't they be handling it, anyway?"

"Because if I leave the Service I'll be cut off from the sources of information I need to deal with this and keep us both safe. Wherever I'm going or whatever I'm eventually going to do, I have to clean this up first."

"What about the bonds?"

Hawkins already had his pants and shoes on, hurrying. "Chet owns a bank, doesn't he?"

"His family does. Several, actually. It's a bank holding company, branches all over the world."

"Know which ones?"

"Sorry."

"Chet's right in the middle of this, one way or another."

"They were all out there together."

"Righto. So we can't take these to a bank for safekeeping. We might tip off his friends we have them. You better hide them here for now. And don't tell anyone, especially your—what shall we call them—associates, out at Riley's."

"A girl's got a right to a few mysteries!"

"Few!" He laughed. "You've got more than a few!"

He slipped his arm under her, lifted her up and heavily kissed her, gently laid her back down and started leaving. She sprawled out on the bed, relaxing, arms behind her head. He snapped his fingers, stepped back, and plucked the tutu from the floor, lightly tossing it to her.

"Oh! Act natural, like nothing's happened. Go to work."

"What?"

He looked at her in a way and spoke in a tone that meant it. "Like nothing's happened."

"Hmm—you're right." She gently laughed, waving it over her head "Who'd think a girl with forty million bucks under her bed would be carting drinks in this!"

-86-

A piercing whistle from the train yard ripped through the hotel. The noon express chugged north, the low beat of push rods pulsing through the building.

Hawkins lingered with his stethoscope at the side door. Not a whisper emanated from Ludwig's room. *Could he've slept through that blast? No, never. But where is he, then? Could be reading. Got to be sure, before cracking that door.*

His empty stomach grumbled. *Haven't eaten all day. Of course,* he thought. *Food.* He hurried upstairs to his suite, grabbed the phone and asked for room service. In a fake German accent, he ordered a club sandwich, coffee and a fruit bowl delivered to Ludwig's room, then sped downstairs. The waiter promptly arrived, knocking several times without an answer.

Hawkins stuck his head out. "He'll be back in a minute. He said lock it inside."

The waiter opened the door with his service key and deposited the tray on the dresser. Hawkins listened until he was gone, then gleefully opened the connecting door and sauntered in. *Hot, fresh coffee. A tad juvenile, charging breakfast to the enemy,* he thought. *Still, we are supposed to make them pay.*

He checked the rifle first. Too all appearances it hadn't been touched since Hawkins' last inspection: it'd gathered a very slight coating of dust and lint. Most of Ludwig's other things still laid in their places, including his cameras, papers, and the microprinter. But two brown bottles of photographic solution now sat on the old marble sink, along with a small snail-type metal developing can and a familiar black cloth bag with sleeves for opening film and pouring developer in cans.

But where was he? Probably off relaxing in some cool and shady spot. Hawkins relocked the door and leisurely finished his purloined lunch.

Shortly after one o'clock footsteps rang in the hall followed by the grind of Ludwig's key in the lock next door. Almost instantly, Hawkins had his stethoscope pressed to the connecting door, picking up their voices.

"48–9D? Let's see them," Ludwig said.

"Yeah. Here," the man said.

"Good," Ludwig said. "No one saw you take it?"

"No," exasperated. "No one saw me."

Ludwig began noisily moving things off the nearby dresser top. Several minutes of silence passed by. The man began angrily whining.

"Hey—What? You're developing them now?"

"Ja."

"I'm going to miss my train! I have to get those blueprints back!"

"Take the late train."

"Aw hell! Whata'ya need 'em now for?"

"I intend to make sure the negatives are good! Do you want to bring the blueprints back to me yet another time if they're foggy? Eh?"

Hawkins could almost hear the man fretting as Ludwig methodically went about his chore. The sound of running water meant the negatives were still rinsing in the sink. Another high-pitched blast of a locomotive whistle bellowed from the station behind the hotel. The man, whoever he was, had missed his train. The tempo of the man's footsteps increased, pacing up and down, punctuated with little curses. Every little while came the sound of Ludwig's equipment clicking.

"Good," came Ludwig's voice, now relaxed, increasingly jovial. "They're perfect."

"Okay, then, give me the note. I want the note."

"Of course! My pleasure. A moment, please." There was a pause and a rustling of papers. "Here it is. Just think, you saved yourself another trip to Riley's."

"Yeah. Swell."

"Remember, if you have access to anything else, please let us know. We're always interested in what you might have and in helping the friends of peace."

"Like I care. Thanks for nothing." The door slammed shut. For the next hour, the occasional sound of equipment emanated from the room. Then Ludwig left. Hawkins tailed him down to the lobby. Ludwig posted an airmail letter at the desk, then went back to his room.

Hawkins immediately found an empty phone booth and called New York. W was out. He gave the report to his secretary, then followed back up to the room.

Shortly after four o'clock, footsteps resounded up the hall again.

-87-

Ludwig greeted Chet and Ventnor at the door, a trifle short on congeni-
alities. His manner with them had shifted overnight, now careful, wary.
Ventnor spoke first.

"I'm sorry about your man, Doctor. Do you know what happened?"

"No. He simply drove off."

"What about the car?" Ventnor said.

Ludwig was cool. "I'm still trying to find it."

Chet exploded in anxiety, frustration, anger. "The hell with the car,
what about the money!"

"It's missing, too," Ludwig said.

"He stole the money, is that it?" Chet said.

"The case was installed in Germany. He didn't know it was there."

"You expect me to believe that? Isn't it convenient. He's gone, the car's
gone, the money's gone, you don't know where anything is."

"What are you saying?"

"Maybe you've got the money."

That slightly broke Ludwig's controlled calm. "I don't have the money!
Why would I steal it?"

"The fact is, all the people who knew the bonds were in the car are in
this room. For all I know, maybe you stole them, Walter."

"Me?" Ventnor said. "You're the one who's got the connections around here. How would I do that? And I'm not in the hole, you are. Maybe you got them."

"Me? If I had them, would I be here—"

"I dunno, I'm just sayin'—"

"We're all acting crazy," Ludwig said.

"Hey! Crazy nothing!" Chet said. "You've got to find that goddamn money!"

There was a short silence.

"We will. We will pay you back. If I wanted to cheat you, I wouldn't be here, either," Ludwig said.

Chet only barely calmed down. "You damn well better! If the rest of the family finds out I've been rolling all those accounts around to cover—"

"We've come this far," Ludwig said, "we are very close, it will be cleaned up by the end of November no matter what happens."

"You'll do better, so help me God!" Chet said. "Remember, I'm the only one who can set up all those checks and wire transfers so they can't trace it to you! And you!" Listening in the next room, Hawkins figured he must be pointing at Ventnor. "That includes the money to pay for that radio network of yours!"

The list W couldn't figure out. Of course, Hawkins thought. *Checks. Wire transfers. It wasn't code. They were bank numbers. Payments. That's what all that money's for.*

And Ventnor. The Nazis were subsidizing his broadcasts. That's how he came up so fast. But were all those arrangements merely cutouts for Ventnor?

"You won't damage your chances like that," Ludwig said. "Do you want four more years of Mr. Roosevelt? Heh? Haven't we given you the means to take care of the election, pay these men, get rid of him? Ja?"

Right, Hawkins thought, *not just Ventnor's broadcasts—*

Ventnor finally intervened. It sounded like he'd stepped in between them, almost pleading.

"Chet, listen, Chet, calm down, my friend, calm down. Really.

Remember, I've got a lot at stake here, too. You don't see me worrying—"

"Yeah—" Chet's tone was still angry. Ventnor kept mellifluously reassuring him.

"That's 'cause I called Washington first thing this morning. Talked to Hoover himself. The FBI's been alerting every bank in the northeastern states all afternoon. You don't see those things every day! When they walk in with them we'll have 'em. They'll get the bonds back. Don't worry."

"Mr. Ventnor's going to handle it—let him handle it," Ludwig said.

"We've got people on the job—"

"All right, I guess—okay," Chet said.

With that Ludwig acted back in charge again. "We must go, then. There's work to do."

"That's right," Ventnor said. "We can't spend too much time on this ourselves."

"Yes," Ludwig said, "we have to finish setting up the entire project before people start paying attention in the fall."

"What's the hurry?" Chet said irritably.

Ventnor started again, "We've got to lock enough of these guys in now, put the money in their pockets, get them committed—incriminated—so they can't back out. A few are bound to have second thoughts as we get closer to November fifth. A county commissioner called me from the Midwest yesterday. Says he's got to cover five people in his office." There were shuffling noises as they started going out. "We have to plan on that kind of thing happening, allow time to handle it. Some places we're talking to, they're going to create an entire duplicate set of paper ballots. That takes time. A whole bunch are going to send broken voting machines to neighborhoods where Jews, niggers and union members live—you know, keep out people who have no business voting, that's just as good as stuffing ballots in the boxes. They used to do good work with those poll taxes down South, they had the right idea. Wops, Paddys and Polacks, too. Or make 'em stand in line forever so they have to go feed the kids. Others are going to purge the voting rolls in advance. Send the bastards home. Five o'clock at night? What are they going to do? Get a year's worth of power and light bills? Find a judge? Get a court order? At five p.m.? What a laugh. Another has—" The door slammed shut.

-88-

Their muffled voices died out down the hall. The stethoscope slipped from his fingers and he began aimlessly wandering around the room. After a moment or two, Hawkins slowly sank back into the chair feeling slightly buzzy. Everything he'd heard ricocheted in his head without congealing.

Got the Bureau working on it. Wire transfers. Get people incriminated. Find the goddamn money. Means to take care of the election. We've got the Bureau. Do you want four more years of Mr. Roosevelt? County commissioner. Before the fall. An entire set of duplicate ballots. November fifth.

He dug into his wallet for a small pocket calendar. The fifth was circled in red. It was the first Tuesday. Election Day.

That intercept in Bermuda …

It's ballots not bullets.

Images flashed to mind, filling his field of vision, as if he were right there at this very moment. The crowded, crazy streets in Vienna when Hitler drove in. That man in Prague offering up his wife. The half-track clattering around the corner in Paris. The long column of gray troops stretching up the avenue. The tears of the old veteran. The swastika flag unfurling from the tower. Only it wasn't the Eiffel Tower.

It was the Empire State Building.

Coming here. Happening here. Vienna. Paris. New York. All the same. All over again.

I can't go back to Paris. Paris has come to me. To here. Always assumed, took it for granted, this place, America, would always be here, would always be safe, could not, would not change, no matter what happened elsewhere. In what complacency or arrogance or mindlessness did I think that? Not true, at least, not true anymore. What happened there is following me, pursuing me, to here. Like on the road to Cabio Ruvio. Or the U-boat, chasing me to Hawkins Island, right to the shores of the New World.

Paris and New York. France and America. They were the same, now. Could retreat from France. No place to retreat to from here.

He jumped up and stormed down to the lobby. This time he didn't wait for three free booths in a row.

-89-

"Special Agent in Charge Kelly, please. Tell him it's Roy Hawkins."

Kelly came on the line.

"Mike! Figured I'd bring you up to date."

Kelly actually sounded surprised, as if he really didn't expect to hear from him.

"How is it?"

"It's been quiet, been following them around, keeping them under surveillance. I rented a second hotel room right next to Ludwig's—"

"Really? He know?"

"No, he doesn't know—"

Kelly burst out laughing. "That's a gas!"

"Yes, it is pretty funny, now that you mention it."

"It's good you called, I'm coming up."

"You are? When'll you be arriving?"

"I'm driving up in the morning, gonna leave about three a.m., actually. Should get there about ten o'clock."

"You're driving?"

But Kelly seemed enthused. "Yeah, I get to take a car out! Report came down about two hours ago. There's been a big robbery up there."

"That's odd, there's been a rumor here about a robbery."

Kelly's wary tone came back up. "Yeah?"

"People were talking about it all over the lobby. Financial papers, I think."

"Aw shit, locals are probably blabbing all over the place. Right, some asshole stole a load of bonds."

"Bonds? Really?"

"Yep. Dumb bastards, you know? That's the criminal mind for you. Now where are they gonna take a thing like that?"

"Yes, criminal mind, you're right, stupid. Mike, let me know when you're here. I'm buying."

"Where are you?"

"United States Hotel."

"See you soon."

-90-

On Route 9, outside Red Hook, the stainless steel gleam of the Half-Way Diner grew out of the darkness. W was already there, his dark green Cadillac in the parking lot. Hawkins sat at the counter next to him. They expressionlessly eyed each other. The waitress came. Hawkins ordered tea. They silently sat a moment.

"How long have you known the Nazis were trying to rig the election?" Hawkins said.

"June. Only we didn't. Not exactly. It started with the conventions. When they realized Roosevelt might run for reelection the Abwehr started trying to figure out what to do. We got an early intercept saying they paid $160,000 to bribe the Pennsylvania delegation to the Democratic National Convention. Anyone but Roosevelt. It's possible they may have worked their way up to this. I don't know what's a bigger shock, that they're trying to rig the election, or that the bastards actually figured out how to do it."

"And me?"

"BSC and the Secret Service have been strictly forbidden by the Prime Minister to interfere or intervene in American politics in any way. We can talk to the Yanks but that's it. When I realized the Nazis were trying to meddle in the election I sent for you immediately. We can't get anywhere near this, take a chance it looks like *we're* the ones interfering. But you're an American citizen. I can't take your rights here away from you. You can protect the election, stop this. We needed you right away—"

"Couldn't be helped."

"I know. Initially we just wanted to expose their meddling. Maybe it would've brought the US into the war, maybe not. But this is much bigger. It's a new form of conquest, taking a country over through its elections using covert operations. Who needs an army and navy when you can do this? What brought the United States into the last war, the Zimmerman cable, the subs, it's trivial duff compared to this. A child could understand it. Expose this, Roy, and America will get in the war. We won't go down like the French. Maybe we can hold on without the States, but it's iffy. Britain's survival may depend on what you do here. That's the real reason we brought you over."

"And if I'm blown you can deny everything."

"That's always gone with the job."

"I know." The waitress brought his tea. Hawkins stared at it a moment, then aimlessly began swirling his spoon in it, then carefully set the spoon down, studying that, too, lining it up with the rest. "Ah, it's all right, actually." He grunted very slightly, poured some cream in and began vigorously stirring. "Did I tell you I saw them raising the swastika flag over the Eiffel Tower?"

"Christ. That must've been tough."

"It was. Now Paris has come to me. That's what I've been thinking."

"Yes. It has. I gather Chet Branch is laundering the money?"

"Right. Walter Ventnor's working with Ludwig to organize it. He gets the contacts, lines up the people to bribe, or reward, if they're so inclined already. Chet Branch pays for him. All those numbers are accounts, routing numbers to banks across the country."

W brought a folder from his briefcase.

"This was telexed in from London this morning." He spread out a decryption of Ludwig's list between them, poring over it. "All the names are here in this column. According to what you are saying, then, the next must be the sum they received—apparently some get more than others, for whatever reason. Then these columns must be the bank routing numbers, these, the account numbers. A great many are blank, though."

"That's cash, that's why they're up here. That's why they need the casino, for the cutout."

"Right, of course! Probably felt they needed cover, nervous nellies, whatever. London felt the list is incomplete."

"No. They never understand over there. It's not a parliamentary system. Or a direct vote. The president is elected state by state, they only need to turn a few that are close. It's possible to lose the popular vote and still win with enough states. And you don't need to steal millions of votes. Just batches here and there in key places inside those states."

"Ah, makes sense. You were going to tell me something the other day."

"The FBI's offered me a job. Through Kelly. High ranking. Hoover's decided to set up a new intelligence division of his own."

"All by himself? My, my. I'm not surprised. What are you going to do?"

"I don't know. I've met a girl I really like."

"I see. And the operation?"

"I'll stick it through. I think I can shut them down financially. The money is still missing. Chet has to cover his transfers. I think it'll force him out. It'll also shut down Ventnor. Ludwig and the Abwehr are subsidizing his radio network."

"They are? Makes sense, the way Ventnor came out of nowhere. Like mushrooms in the forest overnight. There he was, all over the dial. But the money angle—that won't work. I got a flash from Houghton before I left." W drew another small telex from his vest pocket and handed it to Hawkins. "They've been working on Ludwig's latest airmail. Quite interesting. Ludwig's getting the money replaced. He's blaming it all on Dieter, claims he disappeared with it."

"They'll send more money in? Oh, no—"

"He's suggesting Mexico, this time. Stopping the money is only a temporary solution. The SS can always murder another family of rich refugees and steal more. It's the people who are the problem. They'll keep trying. They won't quit. The only way is to stop the people."

Hawkins thought a second. *Yes. The smirk.*

"Right. They'll never stop."

"Remember the bigger picture."

"How so?"

"We need America in the war."

"This would do it if people knew."

"That's the job. You're going to have to handle it yourself, though, without us involved, do you understand?"

"Of course."

W relaxed slightly, shuffling down to the bottom of the papers.

"I brought this in case you need it—to know what you're looking at, convince Kelly, whatever the case. Be careful it doesn't fall out of your hands. These photos are prints from the first set of micro negatives Ludwig sent out. It's the first half of Steel Seine we intercepted several days ago. No second half. He may not have it yet."

"Half? Why half?"

"The seller doesn't trust Ludwig, or the other way around."

"You never know. I'll take it."

"A couple of things: in the upper right-hand corner. See? There's a note in Ludwig's handwriting explaining this thing. And here's the real kicker." He pointed at the top margin. "The letters are cut off, but you can still make them out." Although the top part had been clipped away, the words clearly read WALDORF ASTORIA.

"Bloody hell, they did this in the hotel."

"Right. That helps us. We can now prove to the Americans we aren't trying to steal it, too. Anything else?"

Do I tell W I have the bonds? Hawkins thought. *No. Not yet. If I tell him about the bonds I'll have to explain how I got them ... where I got them. That Dieter is dead. My prisoner. That I fouled up for nothing. For nothing. I can't tell him that. Not now. Maybe later, when I'm on my way to a fresh start with the FBI.*

"No."

W got up, patting Hawkins on the shoulder. "Eat something. You look thin."

"Here are the names of those people in Warsaw."

"I'll do what I can. Tell your friend he can call the consulate day after tomorrow."

W left. Hawkins picked up the menu, skimmed it, sighed heavily. *Ought to eat. But the idea of food, disgusting somehow.* He cast it aside. He stared for a long time at his teacup, then gulped it, angrily threw the mug down and headed out.

-91-

"What's the son of a bitch doin' out there?" Jacobson whispered. They peered through the grillwork in the observation gallery at Ventnor lounging below.

"Killing time," Daisy said. "He's been here before."

"No," Hawkins said, "they're probably getting ready to start passing more bribes."

Jacobson's face twisted in anguish, or rage, or both.

"God. They're using my club again? Okay, this time—"

"No. You can't—"

"Why the hell not?"

"I've got to link him to Ludwig and Chet," Hawkins said, "wreck this whole thing. Who needs tanks and planes when you can do something like this? What's the difference between attacking a country and hijacking its elections? None. You're being taken over either way. You want that?"

Jacobson was wavering. "Well, no ..."

"You went over to Yorkville and beat up a bunch of Nazi sympathizers? Right? And you don't want to help now? What's that to this?"

"Okay, you win, I'll stick with it for a while. But how are you gonna do this?"

"I have an idea. But I have to get him back to the hotel first. I want to plant him there with some stolen navy papers. That'll tie him to Ludwig. And a well-placed tip should do the rest."

"Oh, that's easy enough," Jacobson said. He glanced at Daisy and gave her a knowing laugh.

Daisy joined in, swinging her hips, swishing her skirt up. "This is a job for a cocktail waitress!"

"What?" Hawkins said.

"We're going to comp him," she said.

"With a Mickey Finn," Jacobson said.

Daisy leaned over and gave Hawkins a peck on the cheek, then rubbed the lipstick off with her glove. "Yep. Send him beddy-bye."

"We do it all the time," Jacobson said.

"You do?"

"Sure! People come in here, get hot, start a streak … like that dope the other day. We're not in the business of givin' money away. See this little pedal on the floor?" Jacobson pointed down at what resembled the clutch pedal on a car. "Watch what happens to the roulette wheel when I step on this thing." He pressed on it with the toe of his shoe. The roulette wheel gently rolled to a stop. "See? When Daisy got him over to the wheel, I was up here working that pedal."

Hawkins glanced at Daisy. "You knew?"

"Why, yes, Roy." She gently laughed. "That's my job. If he didn't move to roulette, I'd have served him a Mickey and made sure he drank it if I had to spit it in his mouth myself."

"Daisy, you're a woman of many talents. Remind me to keep my wallet in my pocket."

"Hey, don't worry," Jacobson said. "We can't do it all the time. The suckers will catch on."

Hawkins took the binoculars and checked Ventnor again. "Daisy, remember what Chet said? At breakfast?"

"Oh, yes. If he wasn't winning, he'd change the rules so he would."

"Let's find out what Ventnor thinks about that."

"Daisy, the drops are in my desk," Jacobson said.

Masked again, Daisy smoothly sashayed over, slinked around Ventnor, picked up his glass and set the new one down. Ventnor barely glanced up, missing her supercilious curtsy and tossed a chip on her tray. He reached for a nice draught. Hawkins sat down next to him.

"Why, Mr. Ventnor, imagine seeing you here."

"Oh, Mr. Hawkins? Hello."

"Winning or losing tonight?"

"Holding my own."

"Maybe you need a little help." Hawkins reached into his pocket and placed a small stack of cards, only part of a deck, on the table. Jacobson came up behind him, gently waved for the dealer to take a break. He spread his arms wide on the table, smiling assuredly at Ventnor. Ventnor blankly stared at Hawkins. "Here." Hawkins reached over, took Ventnor's face card, a six, and replaced it with an ace.

"What are you doing?"

"You want to win, don't you?"

Ventnor gestured to Jacobson. "Get him out of here!"

"Stay or draw?" Jacobson said.

"What the—"

"Stay or draw?"

"Okay, stay!"

Jacobson flipped the cards over. "Eighteen! Dealer folds."

He swiftly scooped up the cards and dealt another round. Hawkins tossed a chip in for Ventnor, then reached over again, plucking up Ventnor's three, replacing it with the ace of clubs.

"Stay or draw?" Jacobson said.

Ventnor started getting angry. "Aw, are you guys nuts? You can't play a game that way!"

"Why not?" Hawkins said. "I mean, if you want to, why not?"

Ventnor's eyes lost their sharp focus. "Because—"

"You said the world's divided into winners and losers. Which one do you want to be?"

"That's not a game—"

"It's not? Isn't this thing with Ludwig a game? You seem to treat every-thing that way, rigging the election—what's in it for you?"

Ventnor giggled, giddy and high. "That's no game—that's real power—we're not taking any chances."

Ventnor began slightly blinking, slowly swaying back and forth.

"What's in it for you?" Hawkins said.

"I'm their guy. I'm no loser! Not me! I'm gonna be top of the pile! Their guy!"

"Why does anyone have to be a loser?"

Ventnor pounded his fist, shaking, slurred voice rising, face flushing. "You! Don't! Understand! You have to have losers! Have to! If there's no losers there's no winners! There's no one for us to kick around! You gotta *make* 'em losers! I want the power to do wha—"

He flopped backward off the stool.

Five minutes later four of Jacobson's men edged out on the open catwalk holding Ventnor by his arms and legs. Two others held the doors to the casino and the club shut. Hawkins backed the Cord underneath. They dumped Ventnor's unconscious body straight down onto the seat. Daisy elbowed Jacobson aside, snatched Ventnor's chip from her tray. She angrily flung it down as hard as she could onto Ventnor.

"I'm no loser! Asshole!"

"I don't like this. You sure you can manage him?" Jacobson said. "I think we should come." *Hard to tell if he was anxious or just didn't like being left out. Maybe both.*

"No—you can't be around, not with the Bureau coming. Got to keep this inconspicuous."

Daisy called after him, "Be careful, Roy!"

-92-

Broadway shone slick and empty at four a.m.

Hawkins bent his knees, muscled Ventnor's thick arm over his shoulder and hoisted him from the car. *Now the worst part*, he thought, sprinting his ass up those big stairs. His legs started burning halfway up. *Damn. Feels like Ventnor's gaining ten pounds every step.* He shifted him at the door and squished his hat over Ventnor's face, comradely embracing his waist. Then he dangled him across the lobby, bouncing him on his feet for effect. The night manager's eyes flicked suspiciously over the top of his paper.

"Big night!" Hawkins said, sheepishly grinning.

The manager sniffed. *More drunks.* His eyes flicked back to his paper. Moments later they stumbled off the old steam-driven elevator. The car huffed and puffed back down to the first floor with a rattle.

Hawkins scanned the empty corridor to his observation room. It looked endless, now. No luggage carts. *Have to gut it.* He threw Ventnor into a fireman's carry, half-stumbling down the hall under the weight, every footstep crashing in the empty corridor. He reeled in, dumped Ventnor on the bed, caught his breath.

Got to tuck him in. Make him look good, Hawkins thought. *A real Rip van Winkle. Too bad, in a way. Love to be a mouse in the corner when he*

*wakes up. With no clothes on. In a strange bed. In a strange hotel room regis-
tered to Mr. Churchill. With a blinding headache. And there'll be the looming
bulk of Special Agent in Charge Mike Kelly hovering over him, pointing that
massive Colt an inch and a half from his nose.*

*It'll be deliciously ironic. Ventnor will tell Kelly God's honest truth—no, I
don't have the slightest idea how I wound up in bed at the States Hotel.* Kelly
will stand there, lips curling, laughing, certain he was in the presence of a
complete fool. It will be hilarious.

He dumped the pants on the floor and reached for Ventnor's shirt
collar. A muffled creak penetrated the silence. Ventnor? No. He hadn't
moved. Hawkins jostled the bed. Wrong kind of sound.

Every muscle instantly tensed still, as if a cottonmouth unexpectedly
slithered over his bare foot in a swamp. A moment later another creak
followed behind the door to Ludwig's suite. His heart began racing.

One creak was meaningless. At this hour two were one too many for a
coincidence. *Someone's outside.* Curtains blew from the open window over
the coiled fire escape rope. Hawkins reached down, slipped off his loafers.
Leaning on his hands, he slowly shifted his weight, one foot down carefully after the other. The layers of carpets muffled any sound. He peeked
over the top of the sill. Down on the street, on the far side, two men were
carefully watching.

I've been spotted, Hawkins thought. *Ludwig must've been tipped off since
this afternoon. Otherwise they wouldn't have held that meeting. Doesn't make
any sense. But there they are.*

A vision of the Luger upstairs flicked to mind. With Dieter gone,
carrying his weapon seemed an unnecessary risk. Hawkins stealthily
retraced his steps next to the bed, moving as carefully as before.

The tiredness he felt a few minutes earlier vanished, every nerve
afire. *The copy of the Steel Seine blueprint on the Waldorf stationery, take
care of that first*, he thought. Carefully lifting Ventnor's coat, Hawkins
inserted it in his jacket, then drew the sheets up under Ventnor's chin.
He clicked out the light. Checked the street again. The two men waved
at the window next door. Hawkins slid under the bed, grasping his nose

and mouth to keep from sneezing in the dust. He slowly began making a snoring noise, softly at first, then louder.

-93-

A freshly oiled and almost silent hiss. The connecting door from Ludwig's side swung open. A dark form briskly stepped in, only a couple of paces. The man fired three shots into the bed. The silenced weapon made a soft popping noise, more like pulling corks from a bottle than the sharp, menacing retort of a lethal weapon. Ventnor's body and the bed rocked slightly as each shot sank home, the bedsprings ominously squeaking, claustrophobically sagging to an inch of Hawkins' nose, stirring up the dust.

The gunman stood waiting. The acrid stench of smokeless powder permeated the room. After a moment the man cautiously reached over and felt Ventnor's throat. He held the vein a second before grunting in satisfaction. The dark figure strode back into Ludwig's room, closing the door. Muffled voices echoed in the distance.

Hawkins instantly slid from under the bed. He tiptoed to the opposite connecting door. He unlocked and opened it, squeezed through and carefully relocked it.

Behind came the slow, shallow breaths of a couple deep asleep. He put his ear on the connecting door, listening.

Footsteps again. Ludwig's voice in a loud whisper, "Thank you, I—" Someone reached up and clicked on the hanging light. Ludwig slowly inhaled, then, "Dummkopf! It's the wrong one! That's Ventnor! We need him! Is he dead? He's dead? Oh my God! This is a disaster. You let Hawkins escape? I cannot believe this! You've got to find him!" There was a door slam. They ran from the room.

Hawkins crept to the outside door. No sounds. Opened it a crack, peeked out. Then carefully angled his head around the frame. No one in the hall yet. The sleeping couple stirred slightly. They were waking. *Have to move.*

He started running down the long hallway. Partway down came the gassy sound of the old steam engine being charged. Then a putt-putt-putt as the elevator started rumbling up again. *Not going to make the corner*, he realized. He began checking doors: one, two, three, all occupied. The elevator cage peeked above the floor. Tried the last one. It opened. He jumped in, pushing it shut fast but silently, bolting it.

The odds were getting a little better. He waited a second, listening for the sound of someone sleeping. Nothing. He quickly flicked his lighter. The bed was empty. He switched the lights on and checked the window. This room was on the inside of the U-shaped hotel building, looking out over a tree-filled courtyard the size of a town square.

The old room service phone rested on the dresser. He grabbed the receiver, clicking until the desk clerk answered.

"Riley's Lake House please."

A voice he didn't recognize answered. He asked for Jacobson. "Emergency." Two or three agonizing minutes later he came on the line. "Jacob? Hawkins. Something's gone wrong. Ludwig was waiting for me with at least three gunmen."

"You okay?"

"Yes, but they killed Ventnor instead."

"You sure?"

"I'm certain. Jacob, Daisy's in a great deal of danger. If they know about me they may know about her. We can't be sure. Maybe you, too."

"We can take care of ourselves. You still at the States Hotel?"

"Yes—"

With a click Jacobson hung up.

"Hey!"

Footsteps raced by outside. *No getting out through there. The window—what's the drop?* He opened it and leaned out. A long way, three stories. His foot hit the knotted fire escape rope. *That's it. Have to risk it.* A soft plop. The rope hit the sidewalk on the piazza. Tightly grasping it with both hands, he uneasily climbed up onto the windowsill in the pitch black, back to the courtyard. The crinkling sisal felt positively ancient.

Okay. Say a little prayer, he thought. *Now. Lay back, swing out, brace the feet against the wall. Walk backward. Past another window.* His sock-clad feet slipped on the smooth painted brick. With a jarring thud his body slammed against the wall. He began climbing down monkey style, hand over hand.

Three-quarters of the way down the rope gave with a loud *thonk*. It whipped out into the air, spinning around. Hawkins fell straight into the darkness, twisting with it, suppressing a yelp. Seven feet down he hit and rolled. He sat up. *Okay*, he thought. *Still in one piece. Just tangled in rope.* He pulled and threw it off. A little jingle. The rope held but the hook and board had ripped from the wall.

He ran to the front of the courtyard, looking through the glass doors into the lobby. Empty. *Good. Get upstairs, get the Luger, go after Ludwig.* He slipped inside. Around the corner he casually stepped into the elevator.

"Four please." With a sigh the operator stood and cranked it into gear. They rose. The putt-putt-putt of the steam engine in the basement echoed up again.

Hawkins plucked up the operator's evening paper, holding it in front of his face. Two men were pacing back and forth on the third floor. The operator called out, "Up?" through the grate. "Down," they hollered impatiently. The car kept rising.

The door opened. Hawkins ran around the corner down the hallway to his own room. The door was open a crack. He pressed himself against the wall, slowly pushed the door, peeked inside. Empty. Clothes and luggage were strewn about. It'd been searched.

He dove under the bed, ripping up the carpet. They hadn't found it.

The cased Luger was still in place. Something'd gone right. He filled his pockets with the flat clips and hefted the snail drum magazine. It clicked in with a satisfying snap. He gratefully pulled the toggle and released it. Loaded.

Hawkins cracked the door slightly open, peering out. A shadow draped across the wall. He slid the door shut. With one swift motion he pulled the heavy marble top off the Victorian dresser and turned it toward the door. He crouched behind it, gun at the ready. Seconds later two men outside kicked the door open with a crash, firing in. The rounds drilled harmlessly into the stone, spending their strength, cracking and smashing the marble in Hawkins' hands.

The Luger flipped four rounds up and out in a steady arc. A man staggered back. Heavily crashed against the opposite wall. He made a strange wheezing sound—air hissing out the holes in his chest. Footsteps echoed in the distance, running hard down the hall. Hawkins threw the marble pieces aside, jumped to the near wall and peered around the door.

The gunman sat upright against the corridor wall, feet sprawled out in front of him, chin slumping on his chest. A bright red stain ran down his shirtfront into his pants. The second man had vanished. The man's chest heaved. Little fizzing bubbles of blood sprayed out around the edges of the bullet holes, crackling and spattering. Hawkins checked his pulse. It stopped. The blood had already begun running close to the carpet. Grabbing him by one hand, Hawkins dragged the body into his room. He flipped open the window, lifted him up and dumped him into the bushes four floors below.

He ran up the hallway, carefully checking at the corners for the dead man's partner, racing down to the elevator. The foyer was empty. The operator was sitting inside the cage, reading the paper. Hawkins backed into the car.

"Down!"

-94-

"Put it down."

The elevator started descending. Hawkins spun around, back to the open car door, holding the Luger out. He and Ludwig were standing nose to nose, pistols pointed at each other's heads.

"No, put your hands up!" Hawkins said.

"No. My men are coming and I know you're alone."

"I'm not alone."

Ludwig jerked the handle. The car stopped.

"No, you're all alone. Britain is finished. You're all finished."

Hawkins backed into the corridor, gun out. Ludwig followed.

"Doctor! Stop and think. Ventnor's dead. You can't hide that. He's Hoover's friend. The federal police, the cops, this town will be teeming with them by nightfall. You can't get away. They'll put out a nationwide manhunt for you. Your only chance is to come over, work for us. We'll take care of you, protect you—versteht? You are very valuable to us. If the Yanks catch you, you'll fry! If you kill me, there's no escaping that."

Ludwig stared, his gun hand minutely trembling. Jacobson and his men rounded a distant corner at the far end of the corridor. They spotted Ludwig and Hawkins' reflection at an angle in a gigantic tall pier mirror. Ludwig saw them. He gasped in utter astonishment, "*Nein!*"

Jacobson and the gang let loose with a set of pump shotguns, sending a volley down the long hall like a shooting gallery. The shots smashed into the mirror. It shattered in a rolling tidal wave of flying broken glass and gilt wood. Hawkins threw himself to the floor. Ludwig ducked into the elevator. More shots ripped the door. Then he leapt back out and ran down the hall to his room.

Jacobson and his partners were carefully working their way up the hall, checking doors. Hawkins pointed where Ludwig disappeared. A nod from both. Hawkins stepped to one side, ready to try the knob. Herman misunderstood. He squeezed off a pair of rounds, blowing out a jagged, manhole-sized opening through the center of the door. Hawkins winced at the gaping splintered mess.

"No wonder you got bagged on breakin' and entering!" Jacobson hissed. Hawkins carefully bent down and peeked through. Empty. He motioned for them to stake out the adjoining rooms and climbed through.

Ludwig and whoever he brought had run. He checked the next room. The sheets were pulled off Ventnor. Hawkins carefully poked at the jacket. The papers were still there, partly soaking in blood. Back in Ludwig's room, Jacobson pointed at the window. The fire escape rope hung out. It'd broke about halfway down. A black form lay below.

"Going down," Hawkins said. Jacobson nodded and followed him back to the other room. Hawkins flipped the ancient rope down. *This time no climbing. Slide down fast, before it breaks.* He hit the pavement, hands burning.

Hawkins flicked his lighter over the body. Not Ludwig. A man dressed all in black, including a black stocking cap. His leg was twisted under in a gruesome position, obviously broken. Bloody footsteps darted away toward the center of the courtyard. Hawkins rolled the man's head over. There was one bullet hole in the jaw and several in the chest. The man fell, broke his leg. Ludwig shot him, used him as a cushion to break his fall and stepped in the blood.

Hawkins groped next to a column, his eyes adjusting to the dark. Ludwig probably went out the open back. Probing his way with the

Luger's barrel, Hawkins began running from column to column under the covered piazza. In the distance Ludwig ducked behind a bush.

A shot rang out. A bullet struck the column in front of him, tearing off a long splinter. Hawkins jumped behind the pillar. The other gunman, the one running down the hallway. From the loudness and the echo he was firing a rifle from above, across the courtyard. Hundreds of windows lined the side of the hotel wall. *Impossible to see*, Hawkins thought. Overhead Jacobson and his men began taking blind shots at Ludwig slowly crawling along the perimeter of the bushes, working his way toward the back entrance.

Hawkins shouted up, "There's a sniper on the other side!" The gunman fired again.

They caught the muzzle flash. Jacobson's voice floated down, "He's on the inside porch roof!"

They began blindly firing, missing wildly. The sniper started running around the sloping inside porch roof, trying to get to cover over them.

-95-

Twenty feet ahead hung a steel fire escape ladder. With a quick rolling motion Hawkins ran, leapt up and grabbed the bottom rung. He furiously climbed up past the lower three floors to the porch roof.

The peaks and gables of the old hotel were silhouetted against the stars. A motion. The sniper had climbed to the edge of main roof, another two stories up, crouching behind an ornate cast-iron filigree roof ornament. The sniper fired. A bullet zinged overhead.

Hawkins reached up over the roof, angling the gun in the right direction. The Luger spat out the shots, nearly emptying the snail drum magazine.

The sniper threw himself flat behind the ironwork. Hawkins straightened up and glanced over the top. The second he stopped firing the man dashed up a ladder to the top of the high metal-covered mansard roof and leapt over to the other side.

Hawkins climbed up over the ladder and began running. Halfway up the sloping porch roof his sock feet, shoeless all this time, started slipping on the slick metal. His knees cracked down. He shot toward the edge in a terrifying slide, fingernails uselessly scraping on the green copper sheeting. He looked back. More than four stories down. With a quick lunge he threw himself on his belly, spreading his legs wide. The friction of his entire body and hands broke his slide. His feet stopped inches from the edge of the roof.

Craning one knee up, he carefully reached down and pulled off his socks. Bare feet gave traction on the cool smooth metal. Now he sprang up to the top of the roof. He found the ladder and rocketed up over the mansard. Another shot rang out. Hawkins fired back, missing, finishing off the big clip. He hastily slapped in the small one. The man ran toward the front side and began climbing down the fire escape.

The Luger clicked uselessly. Hawkins pulled back the toggle. Jammed. He frantically picked at the stuck cartridge. Two dust-blue Lincoln Zephyrs from the casino were parked near the front. Daisy had come with them. When she heard the firing she ran up the street, shotgun in hand, watching the sniper climb down the ladder.

Hawkins shouted, "Daisy! Shoot!" She hesitantly pointed the shotgun. "Shoot!" The barrel agonizingly wavered in the air. "Shoot!" Shooting a man on a ladder, she couldn't bring herself to do it. The gunman would kill her the instant he got down. "SHOOT!" She closed her eyes and squeezed the trigger. The shot missed by a dozen yards, sending tinkling window glass falling to the sidewalk. Hawkins remembered.

He drew in a deep breath and calmly called, "Daisy! Pull!"

She stood frozen in the middle of the sidewalk, shaking, face angled down, shotgun muzzle pointing at the curb. The instant he shouted "pull" her reflexes took over. She flipped her head up. The shotgun deftly snapped around. The shot rang out. The sniper fell several stories and vanished into a large hedge.

Hawkins waved. She looked up at Hawkins and uneasily smiled. He pointed across the roof. She nodded and ran to the car.

Hawkins ran back down to the far end of the roof, watching for Ludwig. Jacobson and his men had split up. Some took a chance on the escape ropes. The rest hit the stairs to the lobby. Now they were fanning out across the small park in the interior of the hotel courtyard, slowly stalking Ludwig through the bushes.

Hawkins watched, his eyes straining in the darkness. They almost had

Ludwig trapped. He found another fire ladder and swiftly scooted down, jumping to the bottom, his bare feet padding silently on the cold paving stones to the back of the piazza.

Ludwig had managed to make it to the far side of a bandstand three-quarters of the way down the courtyard. A locomotive in the yard blew its whistle, steam up. Just as the drive wheels surged around with a heavy, momentous chug, Ludwig drew out a pair of small round objects he'd taken from his dead assistant. Pulling a pin, he paused a second and chucked the grenades. One hit the fence, another landed at the end of the piazza. Hawkins heard the clank of iron on the stone tiles, recognized the sound and threw himself behind a small fountain.

The grenade exploded with a cracking roar. The shrapnel screamed overhead, chopping the arms off a zinc statue guarding the fountain. Ludwig instantly burst for the hole in the fence, running madly for the train tracks on the opposite side of the street. The grenade's brilliant flash blinded his pursuers. None fired in time. In a split second Ludwig broke away.

Hawkins dashed through the hole after him. But Ludwig timed it faultlessly. He held a moment, like a runner on the blocks, then dove in front of the train a second before it passed. He landed safely on the other side as the freight glided by.

Hawkins skidded to a stop inches in front of the big wheels. He nearly threw the Luger down. Then—*wait. It's a slow freight*, he thought, *isn't moving that fast. I can catch the ladder on the side of the boxcar. Only a few hard yards.* He began sprinting. The ladder approached. He threw himself against the side of the car, catching it with one hand.

The freight started slowly picking up speed, rolling faster and faster, dragging Hawkins down the tracks. He scrambled for a footing, pulling up straight, grabbing higher with the other hand, lifting himself up and got a foot on the bottom rung. He climbed up and over the top of the car and found the ladder on the other side. He half fell down. The momentum of the train carried him along with a few huge lurching, tumbling steps. He fell on his hands and knees, throat raw and burning, heart ricocheting from side to side from the effort.

In the distance, the sound of tires screeching. A car was speeding down a side street into the dark countryside. He caught his breath, got up and staggered back down to the point where Ludwig leapt across. The yards and streets were empty.

-96-

The train thundered into the distance leaving a shocking silence behind. Hawkins collapsed in the middle of the street, hands flat on the pavement, shivering as if chilled. He began shaking his head slightly, his breath pulsing in his ears the way the locomotives roared in the train yard.

Behind him came the sound of running heels rapidly clicking toward him. Daisy cantered through the courtyard entrance. She flicked her hair back to see and frantically ran toward him. She skidded to a dead stop at his back and flopped over him, wrapping her arms around his chin and neck, legs pressed against his back, squeezing his shoulders, her hair cascading down into his face. She started crying.

"Oh, Roy, I was so scared something would happen to you." She stood for two or three minutes hugging him upside down, rocking back and forth, her face pressed next to his.

"It's all right, I'm quite all right, quite all right," Hawkins said. He tried rising. *So desperately want to stand*, he thought. Legs were rubber. No time to indulge in any false chivalry. "Come on, help me up. We've got to go." She tugged him to his feet and steered him, swaying, back into the hotel courtyard, legs wobbling.

Jacobson and two of his men were standing with their hands in their pockets curiously studying the body he'd pitched from the window, the way a commuter might stand and wait for a trolley.

"You okay?" Jacobson said. Hawkins nodded. "We better not push this too long." Pointing at the body, "Get him, and the ones outside." They all planted a hand on the corpse, yanked him up in the air and began wordlessly carrying him through the deserted hotel lobby back toward the street. Jacobson heavily huffed alongside with his share of the burden. He seemed unconcerned.

"Aren't the police coming?" Hawkins said.

"Naw. I told them to scram."

"Excuse me? How'd you do that?"

"They're all on our payroll." A contemptuous edge slid into his voice. "They do what they're told. For a while."

Hawkins stumbled down the front stairs hanging on to the dead man's shirt collar, clutching Daisy's waist with the other. The corpse's arms bounced aimlessly off each riser, forcing them into a chaotic high-stepping strut, almost jumping to avoid tripping. They reached the car. Hawkins pulled at Daisy, blindly kissing her, his lips banging onto her cheekbone.

"Go home. I'm not finished yet."

"Come up later," she said. He banged another kiss on her cheek. She climbed into the back of the second car. It sped off. The rest of the gang ran up with the other two bodies and unceremoniously lobbed them on the Lincoln's wide rear floor, piling them like cordwood. Jacobson, Gabe and Hawkins awkwardly clambered in on top of them. Herman spun the car around and raced back through the dark empty streets. Hawkins was about to direct their way to the abandoned farm when Jacobson gently tapped Herman on the shoulder.

"Blocks."

Herman nodded as if he knew exactly what to do. In seconds they were cruising the back streets on the outskirts of town. He slowed a couple of minutes later, creeping to a stop in front of a dark construction site. Gabe hopped out and ran in, dashing back a second later balancing three hollow concrete blocks. Herman sent the car rolling into the night again, swaying down the backcountry roads.

They rolled the bodies over faceup. The first man, the man Hawkins shot in the hallway, had a large, ruddy, blocky face with a crew cut heavily tinged with white. *Probably about fifty*, Hawkins thought. He had yellow, rotting teeth, shabby, worn clothes, thick, orangey-yellow calluses on his hands. A muscular man who'd obviously spent a lifetime working hard.

Practically no money in the wallet, a few small bills and change. His ID gave an address in a prosperous New Jersey suburb. *That has to be fake*, Hawkins thought. *The man's hardly an executive type.* He began shuffling the man's billfold back together. His finger felt a small bulge wedged in a side pocket. The leather easily ripped apart. A small flat saint's medal fell out. At the top protruded a loop for a neck chain. *Why hide it so?* It hadn't served its owner very well. He started to slip the medal back in its hiding place, then stopped and pressed it into the dead man's hand, sadly squeezing his lifeless fingers around it.

Hawkins angled over, studying the mute, enigmatic face again. The man simply didn't have the cast of a professional agent. Spies were mainly educated, middle-class, civil servant types, not proletarians. *The man can't be in Ventnor's employ, either*, he thought. *Simply too working class. And what about the saint's medal? None of it fits the mold. But someone, somewhere had decided Hans Ludwig's freedom and safety were worth this man's life.*

They switched places and pulled up the gunman who so conveniently if unwillingly offered up his body to break Ludwig's fall. With a finger, Hawkins rolled the man's head over by the chin. The blood had already begun congealing into a hard crust over the single bullet hole. *A young face,* Hawkins thought, *no more than thirty. Has a hardened cast to it, though. This man does look the professional assassin, right down to the black clothes and crepe-soled shoes.* His pockets were completely empty. Exactly as one would expect. The man's smooth hands were devoid of identifying jewelry. *We'll get nothing off this one.*

It took all three of them, grunting and heaving, to pull the third man, the sniper, up from the bottom. A middle-aged man in casual street clothes. Hawkins checked his hands for calluses. They were red and chapped, with angry cracks around the knuckles, like he'd spent years washing dishes. His shotgun wounds didn't appear very serious. Hawkins lifted his head and rolled it. Broken neck. The fall killed him. He'd probably flinched and slipped.

Jacobson took over. He rolled each body on its back, knotting the big man's necktie through the block. Then he hooked the other blocks through the two men's belts. When he finished and sat back, Hawkins noted a glint. He reached down, pulled up the black-clad assassin's wrist and rolled the man's sleeve back. A watch. A gold Curvex.

Hawkins hastily peeled it off. New. No engraving. *My God, my watch,* he thought, *the man in the shower.* He pocketed it.

"You shouldn't keep that." Jacobson said.

"It's mine. I have the receipt for it."

"This guy robbed you?"

"Yes. Attacked me in the washroom at the States Hotel."

Jacobson looked down at the man's face, shaking his head quietly. "Damn."

"At least I know Ludwig sent him."

"Why didn't he kill you the first time?"

"That was personal. This was business."

That Ludwig summoned this man, this time, made sense, Hawkins thought. *Dieter was dead. But why hadn't Ludwig sent Dieter earlier? Dieter—*

"Ludwig's car. Who took him out there? What happened?"

"Herman," Jacobson said. "When you drove that German guy out to his car, what'd he do?"

"He was really upset about his car getting wrecked. I was waitin' for him to faint for a second. So I took him back to the hotel."

"Is the car still there?" Hawkins said.

"Believe me, it's not going anywhere, the shape it's in," Herman said.

"Jacob, you've connections to the local police," Hawkins said.

"You could call it that."

"Tell them to go out there."

"First thing in the morning." He looked out the window. "Not long now."

The three of them sat abreast in the back seat, silently and tensely waiting, feet resting on the bodies covering the floor in front of them, their knees chin-high in the air. After several minutes the road narrowed. The spidery framework of an old iron bridge loomed out of the darkness, the one Dieter had almost collided with. Herman slowed at the top of the curving deck, searching the road ahead and behind. The highway was empty. He jammed his foot on the brake.

Gabe flipped the right-side door open. With one motion the three men bent over and picked up the first body. They clumsily shuffled sideways two steps, stumbling over the other bodies, struggling to keep their balance. They flung the corpse over the rusting iron rail. The dead man sailed out into the dark. A distant splash followed. Seconds later the others followed, arms eerily flapping at their sides, flying to their watery grave. Hawkins, Jacobson and Gabe piled back in on top of each other. The car sped off the bridge before the third splash echoed across the inlet of the lake.

The bubbles subsided in a matter of seconds. The thick, deep weeds wove a clutching nest around them, holding them to the lake bottom, even without the drag of the blocks. The three men in the car straightened themselves out.

"Any chance they'll float up?" Hawkins said.

"No. Gas can't get trapped inside with those holes in 'em."

Jacobson's matter-of-fact tidbit sank them all in deep silence for several minutes. Finally Herman craned his neck back, squinting.

"You know, if we keep throwing any more of them stiffs offa' dere—some boat's gonna run aground someday." A collective guffaw broke out. In a split second, it pitched up into screaming shrieks of laughter. Distorted by speed into the howl of a banshee, it poured out the open windows, sweeping the little clapboard cottages lining the lakeside road. A few restless vacationers fitfully rolled in their sleep.

-98-

The lights of town finally winked invitingly ahead. After plunging through the tree-lined tunnels of streets they dropped Hawkins at his car by the hotel. They leaned out the windows, childishly waving goodbye like a cheerful ball team back from a weekend match—just another sporting night at the Spa. Hawkins managed a terse smile and a little wave.

Only a couple of minutes back to Daisy's. She dashed out the door in the gray dawn light before he had the motor shut off, awkwardly running across the soft lawn in her heels. An overjoyed expression of relief was written across her face. But she stopped a foot short of him, hesitating.

"I was afraid you weren't coming back."

"No. I wouldn't do that. I couldn't do that. Here I am."

She reached out. He embraced and hugged her and smelled again the perfume of her hair and the intoxicating liquor of her breath. She pulled him toward the house. He kissed her again.

"Ludwig is gone," she said.

"Yes. He's out there, God only knows where."

"What about Ventnor?"

"Dead."

"Then it's all over—"

"What's over?"

"This crazy chase. What more can you do? What more can they expect of you? It's not fair."

"I'm not sure. I have to sort this all out. What happened here tonight, the craziness. None of it makes any sense."

"Roy, why even think of sticking with this? Washington, the FBI … Now is the right time. Why leave, why go back to Europe? It doesn't make any sense. Don't you want to catch Ludwig? Do it there. At the Bureau."

"I don't know. Maybe. Let's go in. I need to make a phone call."

"Roy, I need you. Please. Think what could be—"

"I know. I think about that all the time, too."

-99-

Kelly drew up alongside. An air of tight officiousness barely masked a small, eager smile.

"Morning, Mr. Hawkins."

Let's see how he reacts, Hawkins thought. *Just drop the news like a stone in a pond.*

"I'm afraid you're too late, Kelly."

"What?" A wave crossed the happy expression on Kelly's face. Then a ripple of confusion spread. That and the smile disappeared. He tapped the steering wheel a few times, staring down at the dash, palpable disappointment written in deep furrows across his face. "Get in." Hawkins got out and climbed in Kelly's car. "Let's have it."

"Ventnor's dead. Ludwig shot him. He may have had help. I can't tell you much more, the locals are crawling all over the site."

Kelly instantly drove up the street. He nonchalantly double parked in front of the hotel, blocking in a police black-and-white. Every few seconds he'd glance sideways at Hawkins. Deeply suspicious. The opaque expression he'd had when they first met back in place on his face.

Inside the lobby doors a buzzing mob of people in bathrobes were fervidly exchanging wild stories about … rubouts … an army of midget mobsters with machine guns … a whole chorus line of showgirls …

shooting that went on for hours. Several unshaven men began pressing their versions on Kelly. He grimly elbowed his way through, ignoring them, and marched up the stairs. Hawkins directed the way with a few curt gestures. Several blue-uniformed city policemen and a gray-clad state trooper with his peaked Mountie hat filled the corridor. Kelly sighed.

"Do you know if he had anything on him?"

"I saw Ludwig hand him papers in the dining room. Try his breast pocket."

"Okay."

Hawkins caught his sleeve.

"But the jackpot's next door, in Ludwig's room."

"Jackpot?"

"The latest secret Nazi microphotography equipment. Creates a negative the size of a match head. You're going to be impressed, I promise you."

Kelly's tense posture eased slightly, his expression still opaque.

"Okay. That's what I need." He started to move, looking back, pointing at the local police, "These guys? You talk to them?"

"Mike, I gave you my word. Anything that came to my attention, you get it first." Hawkins gestured at the door. Kelly's blank expression lifted a bit. He smiled slightly.

"Yeah," almost whispering, then, "Follow me." He flipped out a gold FBI badge, marched in and curtly snapped, "Step aside." The patrolmen instantly jumped back against the wall. Kelly sauntered into the room like he owned the entire hotel. He introduced himself in a staccato declamatory manner, "FBI Special Agent in Charge Kelly, New York region."

All the officers inside either jumped to semiattention, too, or swung around at Kelly's declaration, staring at him. Their faces lit up with slack expressions of surprise and almost adolescent awe at being in the presence of a real live G-man.

The chief of police jumped up, tumbling his notebook to the floor in haste, offering his hand. Kelly studiously ignored it. The chief twitched his hands back to his sides, nervously wiping his trousers.

"Pleased to meet you, Agent Kelly. We'd certainly appreciate any professional assistance from your level." The tone was distinctly deferential. "May I ask, what's the FBI's interest in this case? This little killing of ours is hardly a federal matter."

Kelly poked a thumb at the gory mess on the bed. "Find any papers?"

"No, we haven't examined the victim's effects."

Kelly pulled the sheet down, delicately lifted the jacket up, reached in and whipped out the partially bloodstained photos. He studied them for a second. Hawkins leaned over his back, playing it up.

"That must be it. See, he wrote on it in German."

"Hey!" Kelly angrily jerked it away, glowering. "What's in here?" He walked into Ludwig's room, put on a pair of thin white cotton gloves and began pulling the cases out, dumping them on the bed. The open bottles of solution were still standing on the dresser. Ludwig couldn't have had much warning. Kelly cracked open the big case holding the microprinter and began examining it. His face lit up, whispering to himself, then glancing with a barely suppressed, grateful smile at Hawkins. "Now this is a career maker—"

Hawkins and the chief followed him in. Inspecting the room, too, the chief picked up one of the bottles on the sink by the cap. Kelly cursed under his breath and snatched it back, frowning inquisitorially, holding up the blueprint.

"Have any of your men seen this paper?"

The chief hesitantly put his hand forward. "No, I don't think so. I know I haven't."

Kelly snatched the paper away, folding it up. "This paper contains highly classified military material."

"Classified?" The chief squinted in confusion. He evidently hadn't heard the term before.

"Top secret!" darkly scowling, "US Navy! I'm afraid I'm going to have to ask you to leave. This is a national security case. We're taking over jurisdiction. I am sealing this site for our forensics."

The chief stood in the center of the room and stared at Kelly for a long moment, dumbstruck. He wavered, frowning. Then his face began winding up in irritated disbelief.

"Wait a minute. We have it on an excellent source," he drew out the word "e-x-c-e-l-l-e-n-t" for emphasis, "this is a routine syndicate shootout over some rackets operation. Word on the street is," he visually swept the others for confirmation, "some boys from Chicago were trying to muscle in. I know there aren't any military aspects to this case."

"Word on the street? Oh, really?" Kelly mockingly repeated it again, "Word on the street." He stepped right into the chief's face, inches apart. "I know exactly what that particular chestnut means." Kelly's face darkened. He tapped the chief's chest with his finger, then his own. "Now get this straight. *I'm* the Federal Bureau of Investigations. *You're* a local flatfoot. Under the US code these classified papers give me unconditional jurisdiction. I'll have your cooperation or I'll have you up on charges for obstructing a federal espionage investigation." He started shouting. "You better think twice. I'd like nothing better than charging you 'cause then I can stick my big federal snout into all the dirty shit goin' on around here. How will your crooked mayor and your crooked commissioners and your crooked Republican county chairman like that? What, you think we don't know who they are? What they're taking in? What's going on here? We know about that thing you call *The List*. We know who's on it. We know what they get, including you, right down to last fucking dime!" The chief looked as stunned as a dynamited fish, his mouth motionlessly hanging open. "Well? You happen to know who that is?" The chief shook his head. "Walter Ventnor! The radio celeb! You still want to stick your dick in this?"

The chief stepped back, bleakly opening his hands out, barely nodding in assent. Kelly's mood abruptly changed. Smiling, he patronizingly put his arm around the chief's shoulder.

"Now I realize you have to go along with what goes on here. I know you didn't start it. That's why I'd personally consider it a favor if you would take charge of outside security." The hapless chief agreed with all the dignity he could muster and left. His patrolmen followed him, excitedly looking back, still carrying the same starstruck "gee-whiz" expressions on their faces, apparently unconcerned about any threat to their monthly "tips" from the casino owners.

Kelly took the blueprint photos back out, unfolding and shuffling them, reading.

"You said this is German?"

-100-

Kelly pointed to a note Ludwig placed next to the blueprint when he photographed it.

"Yes. I saw it said 'first.' Didn't get the rest," Hawkins said.

"You can read German?"

"Yes, I used to work on the continent as a salesman."

"Swell, here." Kelly folded the top photo so Hawkins couldn't see the rest, held it up for him.

"This is the first section of Steel Seine submarine sonic detection project. Second half to arrive in a few days." Hawkins pointed. "Did you see the top margin on the note?"

"No. What?" He pulled it back, squinting.

"Printed letters across the top, clipped off in the margin."

Kelly puzzled at it a second.

"Christ. Waldorf Astoria. He took this upstairs when we were there. The asshole who had this thing was probably hiding in that big crowd."

"That would make sense."

Kelly dove into Ludwig's briefcase, pulling out several handwritten notes.

"Yep. Can't miss that European handwriting. Perfect match. By the way, you're officially not a suspect anymore."

"So pleased to hear that." Kelly refolded the blueprint photos and whirled back into the other room. He flipped over the sheets on the bed and yanked up Ventnor's undershirt, quickly examining the three small holes. "I suspect you'll find those bullets are custom loads fired at close range."

"Ummm … small! Maybe .25-caliber."

"Probably."

Kelly threw the sheets back down.

"Okay, what really happened here?"

-101-

"You tell me."

"What'ya mean?"

"Did you pass the word up I had this room for surveillance?"

This is the question, Hawkins thought. *Where do we go from here?*

Kelly paused for a moment and frowned, "Yep."

And his life ahead passed in front of Hawkins' eyes. Not the life he had lived, the way your life supposedly flashed in front of your eyes when you died. No. The life he might have lived. *Home, friends, meals together. Dancing into the night. Trips to galleries. A good book shared by the fireplace. No more lonely nights.* He saw it all in a flash and in a flash it was all gone. *Too late now,* he thought.

"I was coming back to check up on them when they ambushed me. I barely got away."

Kelly's eyes and mouth opened a millimeter or two.

"Oh, no, no don't tell me this—"

"You were the only one I told."

"You sure?"

"Yes."

"Here at the hotel? This room?"

"Yes."

"Absolutely sure?"

"Yes."

"Whose phone you use?"

"Pay phone in the lobby. Nobody listened. There's probably a dozen in a row down there."

"And you didn't tell anyone else?"

"No."

Kelly's face went limp as the implications sank in. His voice dropped to a whisper. "Aw shit, that's really bad." Then he bent over as if he'd been punched in the gut. "Oh shit," he shouted in anguished anger. "Oh shit! Shit! Shit! We got a guy upstairs working for the Germans? Oh God—*oh my God*, and Ventnor—he's a pal of the director—he was involved?"

"Maybe not. I don't know how deeply Ventnor was involved in that part of it. I do know where those navy blueprints came from. Ventnor helped organize the payment but he might have believed he was doing it for another reason."

"Who got the money?"

"A man by the name of Howard Layton." He took out a copy of Jacobson's credit agreement. "2913 Bethesda Boulevard, Newark, New Jersey. I believe he works for the contractor. He has access to the blueprints."

Hawkins handed the contract to Kelly. *Now for the only good part of the whole thing*, Hawkins thought.

"There is someone who knows, a horseman here by the name of Chet Branch. He passed six thousand dollars' worth of chips to Layton at a local card game. Ventnor was there with them, helped with the whole thing. Layton's name on this credit agreement. But Branch signed for it. See?" He pointed to Chet's signature. "I witnessed the entire handoff. Branch is in this thing up to his neck. Ludwig photoed those blueprints with that gear in there. There should be a negative around. But be careful, it might be extremely small."

"What? Ventnor thought he was doing—what? What were they doing? Why did Ludwig kill him? Why dump him here?"

"They were probably planning to have my body and his in here. Maybe set me up. There's another conspiracy here, a much larger one. They were trying to rig the presidential election. That's what the money, the bonds were for, millions of dollars' worth of payoffs."

Kelly actually gasped. "And Ventnor?"

"He was organizing it with Ludwig. Ludwig brought in the money. Branch was supposed to cash the bonds and handle the payments. His family's in the banking business. Some of them were bank transfers, some of them were paid in cash."

"Were they out at those damn casinos? Is that why they were up here?" Hawkins hesitated, unsure what to say. "Yeah, yeah, I know all about them. Hey, there's nothing I can do about it."

"You can't?"

"No jurisdiction. Not a federal crime."

"Oh," relieved, "I was wondering about that a minute ago when you were talking to the chief."

"Don't think we're happy with it."

"Yes, anyway, they pass chips to a contact at a casino. Then the contact cashes the chips in. There's a sheaf of papers in Ludwig's room. It's all encoded." He took out the copies W had given him. "We intercepted this overseas. This is a key our crypto staff did back in England, and a complete decryption. It's a very simple code, the kind of thing you could keep in your head, that's all he could use. He couldn't bring code books or cypher machines with him. If you sit down with it, it all checks through. Names, amounts, banks, transfers."

"And someone upstairs knew."

"There's no other conclusion."

"If I hear any more I'm gonna get sick."

"I know the feeling."

Kelly got up, slowly moving, feeling along like a blind man in a corridor. "But why'd Ludwig murder Ventnor?"

"I don't know. Maybe they had a disagreement. Maybe he found out about the naval secrets and confronted him, or they had a falling-out for some reason and Ludwig needed to silence him. Why are those papers in his pocket? If you could find Chet Branch—"

"Right, okay, that would make sense. One thing at a time, though. We want Ludwig for espionage and murder. We've got probable cause on that." Kelly jumped to the door, opened it, and barked at the chief, "We have a murder suspect. Also an espionage count. German national by the name of Hans Ludwig. Put an all-points bulletin on the wire. Consider him armed and dangerous. Walter Ventnor's the victim."

"Yessir!"

Kelly closed the door. Back in Ludwig's room he began sorting through the papers, checking for several minutes between the key and Ludwig's original. He slowly abandoned it, reading from Hawkins' copy alone.

Hawkins sat on the open windowsill in the bright sunshine watching Kelly read.

My mouth. So terribly dry, he thought. *Such a still feeling. Can almost watch that sunbeam flow across the floor. Not warm and sunny, though. Bleak and cold. Like the day Pop died.* It had been such a long time watching him die. When it finally happened, it was like this. A quiet emptiness. A total silence in the mind. *Didn't feel anything. Like falling in a void. Odd thoughts. A guy upstairs. Kelly's conclusion, too. Unknown, of course. What will Daisy think? How will she react? No use thinking what might have been.*

Kelly'd read enough.

"Yep. Yep. You're right. Payoffs. But who's got the bonds?"

-102-

A knock at the door. Kelly shouted. The chief slipped his head through.

"Your suspect—Ludwig? His car's been found outside of town."

"I rode in that car," Hawkins said.

"When was that?" Kelly said.

"Ludwig and I took the same train up here. He'd sent his chauffeur up ahead with—"

"He's got a chauffeur? Where the hell is he? Anybody see him?"

"No. I haven't seen him in a couple of days, now that you mention it."

"We've got to find him. Come on, Hawkins, you're going with me! You!" Kelly pointed at the chief. "Seal this place till I get back."

A convoy of black-and-white squad cars sped out, a tow truck in the rear. The abandoned farm gave a completely different mood in the daytime. Green and pleasant, the decaying house and barn were mercifully smothered in lush, thick vines. The Mercedes sat off to one side, canted at an angle by a flat tire and bent rim, pointing at its own door like an Irish setter.

"That it?"

"Yes, that's the car," Hawkins said. "Mercedes-Benz, four-door, hardtop."

Kelly walked around and around, inspecting everything. He squatted down at the ripped-open door silently snapping his fingers. Hawkins wordlessly came up behind him. Kelly stepped back, motioned to the police photographer, pointing in circles around the door and the car.

"Get pics of this … this … all of that." Hawkins followed him across the yard. "Blood all along here."

Hawkins bent down, peering at it. "Quite a bit."

"If the chauffeur found out about the bonds, this mess would make sense, except for the blood all over."

"You're thinking he stole it."

"He's one possibility."

Hawkins slowly paced over toward the collapsed well, stopped, then motioned toward it.

"See this soft dirt here."

Kelly promptly walked into it, kicking it with his shoe, making little noises with his tongue. "Real soft. Captain?"

The captain came over with his officers, looking down, too. "I'm going back to town. Get your men together and dig this thing out, find out what's down there. Hire a steam shovel if you need to, we'll vouch for it. And tow that thing in, impound it and check it for prints." Kelly and Hawkins got back in the car. Kelly started silently driving back to town.

"By the way," Kelly said, "you got an alibi for last night?"

"Yes, I do. Several people saw me at a party with a girl."

"Good. I figured as much or you wouldn't be here. You better not come back to the scene. I'll drop you off downtown. If you get anything else, come around to the station later."

"I will."

"I'm going to be counting on you now, you know that. With this whole business upstairs, you getting jumped, it's gotten a lot more serious."

"I know."

-103-

Kelly slumped over a sprawling pile of papers at a table in the police station. His head jerked up with a tired, stagy grin.

"Hey, you were right about that load," Kelly said.

"I thought so. Probably a custom job for a silencer," Hawkins said.

"Yep! No doubt! Dug 'um out of the mattress myself. Not much deformation. Low pressure. Smoothbore. Very unusual caliber."

"Metric, probably."

"Yeah, foreign job. Found something else from overseas in that room, too."

"Yes?"

"I found two pairs of shoes in there. One ordinary pair of Florsheim's belonging to the victim, Mr. Ventnor." Kelly paused, reaching under the table. "And one pair of expensive loafers made in faraway London," sarcastically pronouncing "faraway" as if were from a fairy tale. Hawkins' loafers landed on the tabletop. Kelly relaxed, hooked his thumbs in his pants. He grinned knowingly, watching for Hawkins' reaction.

Hawkins smiled easily, nonchalantly fingering the local and federal evidence tags on the shoes.

"Previous guest must have forgotten them. Pity."

"That's my official opinion, too." A small smile, perhaps a little too bright. Kelly picked up the shoes and heaved them in the basket with a rattling bang. "I've learned the key to making a criminal case is knowing what's evidence and what's useless trash you throw away. Previous guest must've left them."

Bugger, Hawkins thought. *Those were expensive, hand lasted. Oh well. Too bad the local cops saw them, he has to dance the dance, too. And how could Kelly not feel some resentment? Not a good situation from his point of view.*

Kelly pushed himself up from his chair and ambled over to a coffee urn at the side of the squad room. He searched all around the counter, then reached up and took down not one, but two cups. After plunking one down next to the urn, he dug in his pocket and dropped a nickel in the empty cup.

Hawkins leaned out, scanning the squad room, alternately fascinated and saddened. *No one's watching. It's not for show, a lesson for the locals. A nickel?* Kelly wouldn't even take a cup of coffee? No one would know if he did. Not one police station in the land would begrudge a federal officer a cup of coffee nor would any likely care very much if he took one out of bounds. *What an extraordinarily impressive gesture, not priggish at all*, Hawkins thought. *Kelly's nickel is his personal badge of honor. He isn't in it for himself. Not even a nickel's worth. He alone knows, and that's all he cares about.*

Kelly slumped back down, slurping the coffee. The pretense of the big dance dropped.

"By the way, Hawkins, as a matter of curiosity, what kind of piece were you carrying out there last night when they jumped you?"

Hawkins dumped the Luger on the table. Kelly swung forward, picking it up with keen professional interest. "Uhmm. Nine millimeter. Very nice. Murder weapon was a smallbore." He smiled at Hawkins, flicking the toggle breach back and forth, smelling the firing chamber. "Been used." He drew a bead on the clock, smiling appreciatively. "Ah— feel that. Perfect balance! Must have been expensive. Figures the British Secret Service would have the best."

"I'd rather have a Browning Hi-Power, actually. Left one in Europe recently."

"Really? Never heard of that. We don't see that many automatics here, other than the Colt Army."

"Bigger magazine, more reliable. That damn thing jams."

"Ugh. Right." He scowled. "You can't carry this inside the five boroughs of the City of New York, you know."

"Oh, yes."

"Good." He flipped it over by the barrel and handed it back. "What's in the folder?"

Hawkins threw a manila envelope on the desk. Less than an hour earlier one of W's clerks had brought it up in her purse on the Laurentian. Hawkins drew out the photos. "They're rather grainy, it's a small negative. The light was poor, too, but they are readable."

Kelly reached over, intently and possessively taking hold of one corner. Hawkins took his Minox from his jacket pocket and set it on the table. Kelly let go of the prints and picked it up, rolling it over and over in hand.

"That's a camera?"

Hawkins nodded.

"Holy shit." He handed it back and reached for the prints again. "Go on."

Hawkins started fanning them out.

"This is the ballroom. Here's Ventnor and Branch. Here they are with their two accomplices. This is the gaming room. Here you see Branch bring two big trays of chips. Notice the size of those buggers. You ever see chips like that?" Kelly shook his head. "Sits with Ventnor. Accomplice number one takes his, cashes them in. Gets a check. Accomplice number two takes his, goes to craps table, gets rolled. Signs credit agreement, blows that. This is Ludwig. Ludwig again. The three of them sitting together. Let's see. Oh, yes." Hawkins pulled a note from his pocket. "The license plate numbers on the cars of the two accomplices. No idea who the first man is, the second is Layton, of course."

"Newark office is already out picking him up."

"As you can see, Branch spent a considerable amount of time with Ventnor."

"Sure did. And Layton. And you don't know who this other guy is?"

"No. Oh—wait, I do have that." Hawkins dug out the name Jacobson had given him and handed it to Kelly. "Do you have any leads on Ludwig?"

"Not one."

Hawkins tapped Chet's picture. "He's the only way to get at him. He's not buying all those chips out of his own pocket and giving them to these two. The money's coming from Ludwig, part of it for that stolen blueprint, of course. Branch has got to know where Ludwig is."

"Yep. This is what I need to question him. I'll have the men here bring him in, call in this other tag." He strode out of the office, leaned back in the door and excitedly motioned for Hawkins. "Hey! Come on, they found a body at that farmyard."

-105-

This time they rode out to the farm behind a squad car with the siren running. Six Saratoga city police officers, two deputy sheriffs and four state troopers triumphantly stood around the well, arms folded, stripped to their undershirts, smeared with sweat and mud, identifiable only by their uniformed pants: blue for the police, plain clothes for the deputies and gray with blue stripes for the troopers. Buckets, ladders, and shovels were strewn around. A body lie under a gray canvas.

"Any ID?" Kelly said. They shook their heads. "Hawkins!" Kelly lifted the sheet, exposing Dieter's face. The body was already crawling with insects. His face looked badly sunburned. "Recognize him?"

"That is—was Ludwig's chauffeur. His name's Dieter."

"Any last name?"

"Never heard it."

"Well, we know one thing."

"Yes?"

"He hasn't got the bonds."

The captain pointed under the sheet. "We found a .30-caliber automatic marked 'Made in Spain.'" Kelly threw the rest of the sheet back and kneeled down to look at it.

"Any spent cartridges?"

"Three," the captain said, "down at the bottom."

"How'd they fill this thing in?" They all shook their heads. "See if you can find any evidence of a charge, dynamite wrapper, cap, spent fuse. He looks burned."

Kelly then went around and thanked the officers and deputies at length, asking them their names. He carefully wrote them down in his notebook before a second round of handshakes. They hurried back to the office. This time the siren was off.

"And you last saw the chauffeur two days ago?" Kelly said.

"That's right."

"That's consistent. He's been down there a couple of days, you can tell from all the bugs."

"Ah. I wouldn't have thought of that. Chet and his transfers, that's the key, you can't clear it up otherwise."

"They should have him there when we get back."

-106-

"Go in there." Kelly gestured toward an open jail cell. In front of them, sitting at an old oak table, was Chet, in his usual houndstooth jacket and mismatched pants, and two very well-dressed men with briefcases. A city patrolman watched from the side. Hawkins charily slipped into the fetid cell, his shoes sticking to the floor. He carefully sat on the tattered, dirty mattress, out of sight.

Kelly hung up his hat and went around the front of the table. "I'm Special Agent in Charge Kelly, New York region. Which of you is Mr. Branch?" Chet answered yes. Kelly stuck out his hand. "And you, gentlemen?"

One half-stood. "I'm Gordon Russert, attorney-at-law, and this is my associate, Milton Gericke. We represent Mr. Branch."

A bemused expression on his face, Kelly sat down, hooking his thumbs in his suspenders. "I see. You brought your attorneys, Mr. Branch. You gentlemen certainly are speedy. Is it those ambulances we have these days? Like the Indy 500."

"We're on retainer to Mr. Branch and his companies," Russert said.

"I'm glad he's getting his money's worth." There was a long silence as Kelly waited for a response, then picked up his folders. "Mr. Branch, do you know why you're here today?"

Russert started to speak, "He's—"

"I asked Mr. Branch the question. If you wish to give him legal advice you are free to do so. However, I am conducting a criminal investigation here and he must answer his own questions."

"No," Chet said, "I can't imagine what this is about."

"Are you familiar with a man by the name of Walter Ventnor?"

"Yes."

"Are you familiar with a business establishment called Riley's Lake House?" There a pause. Chet nervously eyed Russert. He silently mouthed "*yes.*"

"Yes."

"Were you there two nights ago?" Another pause and nod from the lawyers.

"Yes."

Kelly took out the photos and began setting them in front of Chet. His head snapped at the two attorneys. They glanced at each other. Chet's head swung back. Hawkins caught a glimpse of Chet's face. *Chet's expression*, Hawkins thought, *there's real fear there.*

"You are sitting at a table here with three men. Could you help me identify them?"

Chet glanced at Russert. He leaned behind Chet's back to confer in whispers with Gericke. Then he whispered in Chet's ear. Chet sat up a bit straighter. "That's Walter Ventnor." Kelly nodded. "That is, I believe, Howard Layton," Kelly nodded again, "and his name is Patrick."

"First or last?"

"I don't know."

Kelly pulled another picture out. "And who is this man?"

"Hans Ludwig."

Kelly swept the photos away.

"First thing yesterday morning, Mr. Ventnor filed a criminal complaint with us concerning a large number of financial instruments called bearer bonds. They were allegedly stolen. Are you aware that he filed that complaint?"

Another round of whispers.

"Yes."

"Who owned those bonds?"

"Dr. Ludwig and Ventnor."

Kelly rummaged through another manila folder. He spread out a series of police photos of the farmyard, Ludwig's car and the door.

"Have you ever seen this automobile before?"

"Yes. That's Lud—Dr. Ludwig's car."

"The police found the car in this condition this morning. When was the last time you saw his chauffeur?"

"I don't know. A few days."

Kelly wordlessly and expressionlessly got up and left the room. Chet glanced back and forth at his lawyers. They shrugged slightly. The three men waited in complete silence, almost motionless. Kelly returned about fifteen minutes later lightly waving dry a photographic print fresh from the developing tray. He sat down, still waving it for another thirty seconds before placing the print on the table in front of Chet.

-107-

"The police found this body buried near the car this morning. Could you please identify this man for me?" Kelly was very carefully watching Chet's expression.

"That's the chauffeur."

"What's his name?"

"Don't know."

Another folder, another set of papers, this time, the photos of the blueprint. Kelly spread them out. The block letters US NAVY CLASSIFIED: TOP SECRET were visible all the way across the room in the cell. The two lawyers carefully eyed each other, obviously startled. "While inspecting Mr. Ventnor's remains I discovered this in his pocket. Have you ever seen this document before?"

Chet glanced at his lawyers. Russert shook his head.

"No."

Gericke slid to the edge of his seat. "May I ask what that is?"

"No you may not," Kelly said. Gericke slid back in his chair. "Is this your handwriting?" Kelly pointed to the note in the upper corner. The attorney's faces didn't so much freeze as harden. Their eyes flicked sideways at each other, waiting for Chet's answer as much as Kelly.

"No, I think it's Ludwig's."

Kelly filed the photos away, poked back into his file again. He drew out Layton's credit agreement.

"Have you ever seen this document before?"

There was a slight warble in Chet's voice. "I'm—not sure."

"Is that a credit agreement?" Russert asked. "Mr. Branch is a very affluent individual. He wouldn't need to ask for credit."

Kelly leaned forward, ignoring Russert, thumping his finger down on the bottom.

"Whose signature is that?"

The attorneys stared for perhaps a half second. Then they jumped like their chairs were wired, talking at once.

"Mr. Branch is exercising his right to immunity from self-incrimination," shoving their chairs out, grabbing Chet by the arms, partially pulling him to his feet.

Kelly snapped his fingers twice, then angrily pointed at the two of them. "Hey! HEY! I am not through here. If you two want to go, you may go. Mr. Branch, you haven't answered the question." The lawyers hovered a second, then sank down. "From you. Not your lawyers."

"No."

"No what?"

"I," Gericke prompted him in his ear, "I exercise my Fifth Amendment rights."

"Do you."

Russert stood up. "Agent Kelly, I strenuously object to what you have done today to our client. Mr. Branch is a pillar of the business community in his industry, this state and this country."

"Sit down, counselor." He sat down. Kelly drew out the lists, including the decrypt. "Mr. Branch. Have you ever seen these papers before?" Chet shook his head no. "I need you to say yes or no."

"No."

"These are papers from Mr. Ludwig's room at the hotel. They have a large number of names, amounts and bank account numbers on them. Do you know of any financial transfers for Mr. Ludwig or Mr. Ventnor?"

"I exercise my right—"

"Yeah, fine."

Kelly said nothing. A minute or two passed. His head nodded occasionally, fingers lightly tapping on the tabletop. Kelly finally broke the silence.

"Counselors, tell your client that he is a material witness and possible suspect. Until this investigation is completed he is not to leave the confines of this county. Is that clear?"

The lawyers pulled an almost limp and expressionless Chet from his chair. They rushed from the police station.

-108-

Kelly sat at the table, watching them go. After a moment Hawkins slowly ambled over. Kelly shook his head, twirling a pencil in his fingers.

"Son of a bitch. Son of a bitch! You know in all these years on this job that has never happened to me."

"What's that?"

"Have a dope sit there"—he gestured at the empty chair—"and say he was taking the Fifth."

"How many had lawyers in silk suits?"

"Ha! That's a good point. Two, no less. Son of a bitch! They got here before we did. Can you believe that? Why not put a fuckin' sign on yer ass that says, 'Kick me, I'm guilty'? Son of a bitch. Knew when I walked in the door."

"I couldn't see his face. Did he know about the car, the chauffeur?"

"No. That caught him cold. I thought he'd swallow his tongue. Then he got pissed. Face got red, started breathing hard. Got the same expression when I asked about the checks. Ludwig took the bonds, stuck him."

"Why didn't you ask him where Ludwig is?"

"Oh, he wasn't going to tell. See the big problem for him is a bank fraud charge. There's nothing those lawyers can do for him on that. Either the money's there or it's not. He's running like crazy now to see if he can get those bonds back."

"Suppose he does? He'll be able to cover—"

"Naw, naw, I called the bank examiners hours ago. He's too late. If he shows up with the bonds now it's actually worse for him because it's proof he can find Ludwig and get them. Either that or he stole them himself. Remember—the bonds belong to Ventnor and Ludwig. He's digging himself in deeper, right now, that's all. He didn't tell those lawyers or they wouldn't have taken him out of here."

"What about the espionage case?"

"The blueprint? That's another matter. It's a real weak case."

"Why? He paid Layton."

"Yep. And he paid for the classified information. But Chet never had possession of the blueprint. He can make all kinds of claims. That he didn't know what it was for. He was duped. It was a donation to the bastard's church. Anything those two sharpies can think up. Bank fraud is the real one. He can't wiggle off that. There's a grand jury sitting in Albany. We'll indict him tomorrow. If he cooperates—and he will 'cause his lawyers will be back in the know—he'll plead to fraud. Trust me, little Lord Fauntleroy with shit on his shoes? Overgrown spoiled brat like that'll do anything to stay out of jail. You think that type knows what loyalty is? He'll give us Ludwig in a heartbeat. US attorney will be happy to drop the espionage charge 'cause it's not much anyway."

Not what I want to hear, Hawkins thought. *Especially Kelly getting Ludwig. Kelly's spot-on about Chet, though. Spoiled brat loyal to no one but his own narcissistic sense of privilege. He'll move heaven and earth to hand over Ludwig, save his own sorry hide.*

"What about rigging the election?" Hawkins asked. "That's what brought him into this, along with Ludwig and Ventnor. They were trying to steal something a lot more valuable than bonds."

"I know. I agree, actually." Kelly stopped. He leaned forward, still twirling the pencil, obviously thinking hard, an inward expression in his eyes, a hurt look. "I've been at the Bureau fourteen years. This is by far the worst thing I've seen. Who could even imagine it. Bootleggers, kidnappers, murderers, embezzlers, it's always like they're over *there*," snapping the pencil at the empty chair. "This is scary, it's like they're *here*." He flipped the pencil back at his heart. "I've never felt that before, not this way. But we don't know who's involved. That's the big part of the scary. It's not only goin' on down here, on our level. It goes upstairs or they wouldn't have tried to kill you here at the hotel. How did they know you had that room? You told me and I passed it up. Well, you knew that right away. Here's the real problem, Hawkins. We don't dare pick a fight when we don't know who we're picking a fight with. We gotta find out first, if we ever can. You almost got it. That could happen again. Bullet in the back of head, never see it coming. You and I are the only people we can trust. With Ventnor dead, this one indicted and Ludwig wanted, they'll all scatter. You see? When we keep it on our level—*down here*—we keep the election safe." Kelly stood up, furiously shifting through the papers. He pulled out Ludwig's original encrypted list, the key and the decrypted version from London. "As a matter of fact, gonna get rid of this shit right now—" He pulled a lighter from his pants, flicked it on and lit the corner, holding them over the basket. "We don't need it anymore."

"My God! Mike! What're you doing? No!" Hawkins leapt up, reaching and grabbing after the burning papers. Kelly waved them away, blocking him with an elbow. "You can't! Mike! They attacked the US! This is an act of war!" Ashes began floating down.

"Don't you think I know that? Listen to me, Hawkins, listen hard. Keeping this shit is fuckin' dangerous. If we save this stuff, it has to go upstairs. *Has to*. I don't even dare bring it back to the office. We'll! Never! See! It! Again! Get it? Hawkins! Think! How far up does this go? Who upstairs tipped off Ludwig? For all we know it could be Director Hoover himself. Have you forgotten he was a pal of Ventnor's? He loved the bum. Sent out memos quoting him. Hoover's already made himself the second most powerful man in Washington. He's doing a good job, but I'm not kidding myself about him. It's going to his head, it's human nature. This isn't evidence. It's a goddamn do-it-yourself manual. People may have fantasized about doing something like this. But these assholes actually figured out how to do it! That's the thing here. The really incredible part, every little detail. Having people not knowing who was really behind it. Moving the money. The cutouts. Using the casinos. How much you need, on and on. That it's equally important to keep some people from voting—you wouldn't think of that, but it makes sense, it's just simple arithmetic. We can't turn this knowledge loose. Bust 'em on the election? No way, Hawkins. We gotta get rid of this shit to make sure no one can try this again. When we keep it between you and I, we keep the election safe. Ventnor's dead. They'll never reassemble it."

"But people have a right to know!"

Kelly knowingly smiled, as if to say, *You know better than that.*

"Oh, that's exactly what we need. Hey, I read the papers. Sure. It'd give your Limey bosses what they want—us in the fight. I get that. But I'm tellin' you—it ain't worth the risk!"

Hawkins watched the last of the papers drop into the basket in little flaming shards. *Another numb, empty feeling. But the camera iris isn't closing down*, Hawkins realized, *not this time. Instead, a widening sense of clarity.*

The black embers winked out and began to cool. *Kelly's right*, he thought. *Can I promise my country—my countries, both of them—that Orator will not be restarted? No. And then there were people like Chet.* "When I'm not winning I change the rules," he'd said. No reason that couldn't include elections. Men like him had the money to do it by themselves, if they wanted to. They didn't need foreign help, certainly not once they got the idea. *Rig it like a horse race because they think they're entitled to win. Merely setting things right, that's how they'd see it. Yes. Safer by far to end it down here.*

W's disappointment will be terrible. Can Britain hold on? It'll have to, now. But if the isolationists, men like Ventnor and Chet triumph, Britain's doomed anyway. Kelly's right. If we keep the election safe, we not only keep Roosevelt safe, but Britain. The world will just have to wait for its savior.

Hawkins nodded and sat down, fiddling with the brim of his hat. "Chet Branch is probably trying to phone Ludwig."

"Wish I had time, I'd love to put a tap on that."

-109-

"Why don't you go to the exchange and listen in?" Hawkins said.

"No, everyone thinks we can do that but we can't. The exchanges here aren't like the European ones. There never was a security or law enforcement angle in mind when they were built."

"Probably just as well, make it too easy."

"Yeah, maybe, I dunno." Kelly mulled a second. "Jesus ... right. The director'd build bunks in the goddamn places." A long pause. "But it is a pain in the ass. We have to hook into the line on a pole before it goes into a main trunk. I've run wires by hand for five or six blocks, along the utility poles, over rooftops, down into sewers, you name it, until we could end it up where we could listen in private. No use running a wire down a pole into a car where the whole world sees you sitting there."

"There must be a better way."

"Not unless you know somebody in the neighborhood."

"How so?"

"The easiest thing is to take a neighborhood phone and convert it into a tied-in line. The problem is you've got to find somebody you can trust. That's not so easy."

"Get your gear, Kelly, I've got the place."

"You do?" He quickly dialed his office and told whoever answered to get a warrant for Chet Branch's phone. "Tell them to date it today."

-110-

"Nope." Kelly tapped the gas pedal. "Nope. Not that one." He tapped the pedal again. They rolled up the alleyway behind North Broadway. He craned his neck out, checking the next pole, looking up for the junction box. Fences, bushes and trees hid them. The big mansions behind them were invisible, too.

"There!" He stomped on the brakes. There was a pole half-hidden in the leaves. He darted around back, rummaging through a collection of junk in his trunk, knocking boxes this way and that. He emerged with a set of long cleats and a wire with a pair of alligator clips on both ends.

Hawkins climbed up on the running board, intently watching.

First Kelly meticulously rolled his pants past his bony knees. Then he vigorously strapped the cleats to his fish-belly-white legs. Noticed Hawkins watching. Slowed. Deliberately cinched the last two buckles. His eyes flicked sideways, lips tightly pressed. He straightened up, trying to stare Hawkins down. Then he shrugged.

"Ah, hell." He clambered up the pole with practiced ease, the jumpers dangling in his mouth. Hawkins stepped off the running board. Kelly flipped the long, narrow gray door open with one hand and scanned down the rows of penciled-in numbers next to the screw posts. Glanced uncomfortably down. Scowled. He shifted in front of the box, trying to hide what he was doing. Hawkins dodged around on the ground, covering Kelly like a basketball star, angling for a better view.

Within seconds Kelly found the two correct addresses. He snatched the wires from his mouth and snapped the alligator clips onto the two sets of posts. Checked Hawkins again. Right underneath him.

In a semishouting whisper he called down. "All right, ya prick, it's the green wire ya cut, okay?" Hawkins smiled and nodded. With a flick of his jackknife, Kelly severed the wire connecting the second line to the trunk, freeing it from the system. Now it was an extension to Chet Branch's phone. He slapped the door shut and crashed down the pole like a fireman. Kelly started laughing. "Never had a freakin' audience before!"

Less than a minute passed before they reached Daisy's. She was waiting by the door.

-111-

"Daisy, this is ..." Kelly rushed right by her.

"No time! Where's the phone?" Puzzled, she pointed to the left parlor. Within seconds he whizzed the cover off the black baseboard unit with a worn Yankee screwdriver and plugged another box on with a set of clips. After vigorously flicking several toggles, he satisfied himself it worked. He finally stood and turned to Daisy.

Hawkins introduced him again. "Daisy van Schenck, meet FBI Special Agent in Charge Mike Kelly." She leaned back slightly, bending a bit at the knees before extending her arm and gently curled fingers straight out in front of her.

"OH! Of the FBI!" Her head swung back to Hawkins, a delighted expression undulating up her face. "Well!" all breathy at the cheery news, "the FBI! Welcome to the manor!"

Kelly's eyes followed her gesture around the foyer, then snapped back to her, rather dazzled, his mouth relaxing in wonder.

"Very pleased to meet you. Is it *Miss* Schenck?" gently taking and shaking her fingers.

"Yes. Still 'miss.'" She shyly looked at Hawkins. Back at Kelly. Then she turned the raptured look full power back on Hawkins. "I just got up. I'll make some coffee. Roy, darling," she gave him a little kiss on the cheek, "show Agent Kelly in," and left for the kitchen.

Three little letters. Such a reaction to three little letters, Hawkins thought, his stomach, or something, dropping to his ankles. A long moment passed. Hawkins turned back to Kelly. He was intently gazing back.

"Why don't you come in here and take those things off," Hawkins said.

Kelly whispered, "You told her about the job." Hawkins nodded. Kelly's face sagged, followed by his shoulders. "Aw, balls. Not again. Hawkins, I— fuck all—I'm so sorry. Honestly, I am. What are you going to do?"

"I wish I knew."

"We've got to work opposite sides of the street on this thing. You know that."

"That was my first thought. Knew it the instant you said you passed it upstairs." Kelly grimly nodded. He held out his hand. Hawkins shook it. They went in the parlor. Kelly began unbuckling the cleats, glancing around.

"Who owns this place?"

"She does."

Kelly sank back, slightly nonplussed. In his imagination terrific blond bombshells had always gone with the money and the houses, not the other way around. It forced a certain mental adjustment.

"It just gets worse."

"Yeah."

"Where'd you meet her?"

"Oh, this is where Ludwig held his meeting. She works out at Riley's."

"I've set a tapline in mob moll's house?"

At that moment Daisy walked in with a tray, humming a little ditty under her breath, happily pouring their coffee into a pair of small, cylindrical white porcelain cups. The same diamond-shaped coat of arms with the three beavers that hung in the hallway graced the side of each bowl. She smiled brightly.

"Since we're having a visit from the federal government, I thought I'd use our patriotic set. We ordered these from Canton in 1787. They were first used for General Washington's visit."

Kelly had barely started taking a sip. He swallowed hard. "The one on the front of the buck?"

"Yes." She giggled, thinking it a joke. "That one."

"I suppose he slept here, too?" Kelly said.

"As a matter of fact, he did," Daisy said. "I'll show you the bed, later, if you like."

Have to give Kelly credit, Hawkins thought, *he's good for the game.* Kelly uneasily put the cup down, picked it up again, carefully cradling it with both hands. He slowly lifted it to his lips. Hawkins nudged him, silently mouthing "*mob moll.*" Kelly glanced down at his cup. Up at Hawkins. A sharp snicker, more like a hiccup, burped out.

A bit later Daisy brought a very old bottle of wine from the cellar, an excellent Petrus covered with dust that'd been down there forty years. They hovered over the phone most of the night, waiting like anglers for fish to bite, killing time with a board game of Daisy's. After three hours the green light blinked on Kelly's box.

-112-

The other phone'd been lifted from the receiver. Kelly carefully followed suit with a handset attached to the box. Hawkins lifted Daisy's phone. Five rings. A man answered. A flash of concern instantly crossed Kelly's face. Not Ludwig's voice. An American. He looked at Hawkins, silently mouthing "*Who is it?*" Hawkins shrugged. Kelly began frantically scribbling notes.

The first voice sharply cut off Chet's greeting. It sounded angry, tense and thoroughly put out. "What're you doing? You're never supposed to call here!" Chet ignored him. "I want to speak to Dr. Ludwig. Is he there?"

Daisy was sitting on the sofa next to Hawkins. She stiffened very slightly at the sound of Chet's voice, bending closer to the phone, listening intently, too.

"No," the man said.

"Where the fuck is he, then?"

"Not here," the man said.

"You tell him I know he's got the bonds!"

"I don't know what you're talking about," the voice said.

"You tell him I want the bonds. I've got to cover the transfers."

"I haven't heard anything about any bonds."

By now Daisy was sitting with her hands clasped in a prayer-like gesture over her lips, eyes tightly shut, gently shaking her head.

Chet started shouting, an edge of panic in his tone. "Listen, asshole! You get this straight! The bank examiners are after me. I want those goddamn bonds! I got hauled in for questioning by the FBI. They had a secret navy blueprint with Ludwig's handwriting on it. You tell him he gets me those bonds or I tell them whatever they want. You tell him I'm not going to jail alone! If I go, he goes! You understand that! You tell him that! I! Am! Not! Going! Alone! He has—a day! A day to get me those bonds! Have you got all that straight?"

Nothing in Chet's voice reveals any sense of the danger in which he has fecklessly placed himself, Hawkins thought. A mere tinge of confusion as to who might have the bonds was collateral for his life. A blast of anger, fear and entitlement just burned that fog away.

There was a long pause on the other end of the line.

"I'll get ahold of him. I'll call right back."

"You better." They hung up. Hawkins and Kelly waited in silence. Daisy got up and left the room. A few minutes passed. She came back in and lightly put her hand over Hawkins', tensely waiting with them. Five minutes later the phone rang. The green light went on. They picked up the handsets and listened.

The same man spoke. "He'll bring the bonds up tomorrow."

Daisy slowly squeezed Hawkins' hand.

"Good," Chet said. He hung up.

Kelly began crowing the instant he set down the handset. "Ludwig! He's got the bonds! I knew it. Dammit, Hawkins, we're gonna get them!"

"Chet Branch," Daisy said. A simple statement. Not a question. There was something eerily quiet about her tone.

Hawkins started to answer, searching for something to say. Kelly firmly headed him off.

"Yes. He's the subject of a major investigation. You'll be reading about it in papers very shortly. Until then I have to ask you to keep this to yourself."

"Of course. I guessed as much when Roy called."

"You should know that Hawkins has been absolutely indispensable to this investigation. This never would have been possible without his assistance. I'd appreciate it if you could keep that confidential, as well."

Hawkins very deliberately held out his hand. "Congratulations, Mike. You want to stake 'em out tomorrow? I'd like to be there for the arrest, if that's okay with you."

"You betcha."

With a curt nod and a quick, "Thanks," to Daisy, Kelly rushed out of the manor, leaving his equipment hooked to Daisy's phone.

Hawkins went back into the parlor. He expectantly eased down on the sofa, eyes locked on the box. Daisy slipped in beside him.

"Something's going to happen?"

"Ludwig is still in the area. He'll be calling."

"What will he do?"

"I don't know." If Daisy knew that was a lie, she chose not to confront it. She clicked on the radio. A slow instrumental tune was playing. She pulled him to his feet. They began a slow dance in front of the box.

"Roy, how do you know all these things?"

"I'd rather not say. I just do."

"You said it was our special summer. Is it still our special summer?"

"I feel it more than ever."

A half hour passed. The light blinked on.

-113-

No streetlights in the alleyway behind Chet's mansion. *How will he do it?* Hawkins wondered. *Has to be quiet. Otherwise every dog in the neighborhood will be howling in seconds. Going to be interesting, from a professional point of view.*

A dim light went on in the garage. Probably only a forty-watt bulb, followed by a crack in a door. The owner of the garage across the street had fortuitously left his garage door open and the top down on his Cadillac convertible. Hawkins waited in the dark, comfortably stretched out in the back seat. A large black silk scarf of Daisy's was wrapped around his face and head, obscuring all but a single eye.

"Got to be quick," Ludwig had said on the phone. Car lights shined up the street. A new black Ford V8 glided to a stop in front. Ludwig, now clean shaven with a fresh crew cut. He got out. Chet emerged from his garage, silhouetted in the door. *Going to be quick, indeed,* Hawkins thought. Ludwig offered Chet his hand. Chet ignored it.

"Where are they?"

"They're in the trunk." Ludwig opened the trunk lid and gestured. Chet bent over, looking inside. The trunk light lit his face. Ludwig stepped slightly back. He reached into his pocket and drew out a small fine loop of piano wire attached to a short wood handle. With a simple, relaxed gesture he flipped it over Chet's head. He snapped it back hard, drawing it tight around Chet's neck. The wire slid through a tiny ratchet with a soft, high-pitched shriek.

Chet reflexively grabbed his neck, lunging forward, trying to escape. His forward motion and weight cinched it tight. The fine shiny wire instantly cut in. Only a low, rasping hiss managed to escape Chet's throat as Ludwig slowly pulled on the stick, Chet's every move tightening the shiny wire. He tried to scream, "No! Please!" His cry was almost inaudible from where Hawkins was sitting—the short, quick sound of cricket chirping "No! Please! Don't! Oh God! Help! Don't! Please! God! No!"

It was a warm night. But at the horrible cricket sound Hawkins felt the chill one hears about but never really feels. His stomach uneasily tightened.

Chet's face darkened in seconds, purplish veins rising to bursting from the pressure as his heart started racing out of control. A heavy torrent of sweat instantaneously flooded from every pore, drenching him. Panicking, he tried to free himself. Digging his fingers deep into his throat. Getting his nails under the wire to lift it up. Get one more breath in. But the wire had already sliced beneath his skin. A fine line of blood now marked the cut. His fingers hysterically rubbed up and down in a violent caressing motion, trying to find the wire. In seconds Chet's nails tore the skin on his own throat to shreds.

The cricket chirping quickened, incredibly short. Only one word now, over and over, "Help! Help! Help!"

Ludwig threw his weight forward, knocking Chet to his knees. He rode the garrote back and forth like a cowboy holding on to the reins of a bucking bronco. Quickly stepping with him. Skillfully staying out of Chet's grasp. Squeezing his sides with his legs, pushing on his spine with his free hand.

While he had been waiting, Hawkins had wondered how he was going to react to Chet's murder. Detached professional interest, he'd assumed. Maybe the post-Paris pointlessness and futility: yet another fool getting what he asked for. And what of it? Or maybe a sense that justice had been done.

But he also wondered, would there be a sense of pleasure at seeing a man die who had tried to tempt away the woman he loved with a diamond the size of small bird's egg?

But no. His reaction surprised him. Broke into a sweat, too, a cold sweat. Arms and legs tensing, the muscles itching and crawling. Two more cricket chirps, he wanted to leap and move, do something, stop Ludwig.

Chet's suffering. Unbearable. Can't watch. Have to stop him, he thought. He started rising. Then pushed himself back down, against his instincts. *No. I cannot. I know I cannot. If I save Chet, Kelly catches Ludwig. That's inevitable. Ludwig knows it. I know it. The price is too high. The elections. Subs off the coast. Blueprints. The identity of the informant who tried to have me killed. All wrapped up together.* But it still took every bit of discipline, every ounce self-control to stay in the car.

Chet's dying panic gave him an unimaginable strength, a power he'd never known. His entire body began to snap back and forth, racked by the frantic effort to force one breath in and out of the pinhole-sized throat. Finally the larynx completely collapsed, sealing the last burning breath in his lungs. Chet's lungs heaved against the impenetrable barrier that was now his throat, feeling as if they would tear his ribs out. With one last, wrenching, fibrillating spasm, his heart exploded. He fell forward on his face, dead.

Legs are shaking, Hawkins realized. He pressed his hands down on them, trying to keep them still.

Ludwig dragged the body by the handle back into the garage, trailing a stream of pee. He punched the lightbulb out, closed the door and drove away.

Hawkins unraveled the scarf. He slipped back up the alleyway. Halfway up the block nausea overtook him. He threw up all over the alleyway. Back in Daisy's house he poured a bath, pulled off his sticky clothes and climbed in, head reeling.

He sat there for a long time, slowly unwinding. Finally, calm returned. *What the hell was that?* he thought. *Going soft? A few days ago I poured petrol all over Dieter. Felt like a big joke. Why give a damn about Chet now?*

A few minutes later he slid in bed next to Daisy. She sleepily rolled over and kissed him, then fell asleep with his arm around her. *And there it is*, he thought. *Everything felt so pointless before. Now it doesn't. Life makes sense now. At least a little, or enough, for me, right here, right now. That pane of glass between me and other people. It's gone. They're no longer distant, unknowable. Foolish, perhaps, but human, too. If they don't understand, they will. Only a little bit ahead of them, that's all I am. Have been ever since the tour of that poison gas plant in East Prussia three years ago. Daisy's the biggest part of that, too. How can I not care about the world, and love it, too, when she's in it?*

He waited for the dawn, thinking about how much he loved her.

-114-

Hawkins came out of the police station. Daisy was waiting in his car across the street. The breeze picked up. She got out as he approached, grasping the edge of her large straw hat. Ludwig's thin metal case with the bearer bonds was in the other. They embraced and kissed in the middle of the sidewalk, oblivious to the pedestrians slipping around them, the case lightly dangling from Daisy's hand. When they broke she gently reached up and straightened Hawkins' hat.

"What's going on in there?"

All day long there'd been a tumult of people: policemen, state troopers, investigators, district attorneys, federal assistant attorney generals, lawyers and several leading local politicians. Now a host of reporters and photographers loitered around the entrance, talking shop. Hawkins rubbed her arm. He gently broke the news.

"It's Chet. His driver found him dead when he came to work early this morning."

She acted slightly detached. Definitely not amused, more like lightly intrigued. "Chet's dead? Really!"

"He was strangled. By a professional."

"That's awful. His poor mother."

"You're not upset? I'm so relieved."

"I guess not. Was it Ludwig?"

"I'm rather sure of it."

She studied his face for a long moment in a very measured way.

"You knew—"

His answer was firm, without hesitation. "Yes."

She seemed lost in thought for a second. "You're all done here."

"Yes. Kelly wants me out of town for a while. I have to get back to Manhattan, anyway."

Her expression began settling, resigned. "The FBI …"

"Not possible. Not anymore. I'm so sorry, Daisy. It's all changed."

She sighed, grimly looking down. "Oh, I guess I knew. Saw it coming when you two were listening in on Chet. Are you going back to Europe?"

"No. I've got a big job to do here. It doesn't matter who signs my paycheck."

"I'm glad."

"Me, too."

"You know I'll be here," she said.

"I do."

There are miracles in life, Hawkins thought. *Yes, she will be here.*

She held the case out flat in front of her, pensively caressing it with her thumbs. "Here are the bonds."

He gently reached up and gripped it, too, as if they were holding hands together. They stood there for a long moment, their eyes soberly locked on it.

"Wouldn't it be nice to keep just one," she said.

"Yes. Wouldn't it be nice."

She sighed and dropped her hands, leaving Hawkins with the case.

"Better go buy Mr. Churchill some destroyers." She kissed him on the cheek again.

Hawkins nodded. "They're expecting me at headquarters. This should take the curse off some."

"I don't understand. I thought they'd be happy."

"Oh, they will be. But I didn't blow the lid off the plot to steal the election. The US won't be getting in the war. They're going to take that very hard."

Daisy nodded, took a long, slow, deep breath and squared her shoulders. They started walking back to the car. "Well! I have to get to work, too. Pulling a double shift tonight. Big stakes race today. There'll be a helluva crowd."

Kelly pulled up in his car, peered over and waved at Hawkins.

"Come on, come on, gotta go!"

Hawkins threw both arms around Daisy, lifted her up a bit, gave her a big kiss, then handed her a plain brown envelope.

"I'll be back when things quiet down." He hopped in the Cord, revved it and pulled next to Kelly in the slow summer traffic. Daisy opened the envelope. It was full of cash. She ran out into the street and alongside the Cord.

"What?"

"It's from Chet's tip. Pay off the mortgage."

The light changed. The two cars accelerated down Broadway side by side. Daisy reached up on her toes, waving to Hawkins. At the last moment he turned back and smiled.

She watched the traffic for a moment, opened her purse, put the envelope in, then saw a small blue ring box. She took it out and flipped it open with her thumb. Chet's huge diamond glittered. She smiled, snapped it shut, tossed it up in the air, caught it and rushed through traffic to the United States Hotel and Tiffany's.

-EPILOGUE-

Hans Ludwig shut the door of a phone booth on Broadway in Yonkers. He dropped in a nickel. The phone rang three times.

"Spring came late," he said.

The call was answered at a booth in the rear of a Slavic delicatessen near Avenue A on the Lower East Side of Manhattan. A hand not so much large as meaty tightly gripped the handset in anger, as if it would twist it like putty, if it could.

"The supervisory committee is extremely upset."

"I'm sorry about the three men. I realize their loss was costly but it was their inexperience that was at fault."

"We'll be the judge of that," the man said.

"I will make it worth your while. I promise. Everything will be easier now that I don't have to worry about my assistant filing reports behind my back."

"Nonetheless, I intend to penalize you for your handling of this affair."

"I assure you, the next payment will not be necessary."

"Very well. It's a shame the Nazi effort to manipulate the election has failed. A neutralist pro-business regime would've hastened the onset of the proletarian revolution. We may have to endure a longer phase of bourgeois democracy than originally anticipated."

"I'm sorry, I know that."

Colonel Gabentin Krylenko paused, thinking, his watery blue eyes darting from side to side across his wide, sunburned face. *Ludwig's been getting complacent, slacking off,* he thought. *I can sense it. It's difficult in a country like the United States. So many decadent temptations, like trips to Coney Island.* He leaned forward in the booth, easing his sunburned back away from the hard corner. *Damn.*

Need to prod Ludwig into tightening up. Have to be careful, though. Ludwig's a proud, arrogant man, sure of himself and his judgment, competent acting alone. He'd had that quality years earlier in that Volga German community in the Ukraine. A dangerous quality on a collective farm. An indispensable one in a spy. *Can't afford to antagonize him.*

Suppose he "went private" or defected to the other side? Ludwig had acquired degrees—some fake, but all credible—position, a little wealth. A few of the attitudes of the elite surrounding the Nazis had obviously rubbed off on him.

Penetrating not only the Abwehr but also tapping into the American defense establishment was extraordinary, perhaps unique. The copies of his reports to the Abwehr arriving regularly at the NKVD's mail drops in Lisbon were outstanding.

"Despite this unpleasantness, which I trust will never be repeated—"

"Oh no, of course not."

"I have been authorized to tell you that your promotion to major will be approved shortly. This affair should not affect your rating. We have great respect and confidence in your abilities."

"Oh, good! Thank you, Colonel. Give my sincerest thanks to Moscow Center."

"Of course. Congratulations."

Ludwig hung up and quickly left the neighborhood.

Colonel Krylenko wiped his hands on his white apron, jammed his white paper cap back on his head and returned to the counter. A customer stood impatiently waiting for half a pound of sliced Lebanon bologna.

Ludwig's lucky, the colonel thought. *Got that call from the NKVD resident at the consulate with only hours to spare. What's next on the agenda? A recommendation to SMERSH about this man named Hawkins, clearly. Three good Party comrades were dead, like a horrid cowboy movie. That could not pass.*

"Can't you hurry up?" The women's pinched, irritated face poked out from underneath a worn old scarf. He waved the meat on the wax paper over the counter.

"Hey, we're three men short. I'm doing the best I can."

THE END

AUTHOR'S NOTE

This novel is based on real events.

In September 1940, at the Battle of Britain's climax, shortly after the events of this story, Prime Minister Winston Churchill uttered one of his most famous quotes—"Never in the field of human conflict was so much owed by so many to so few."

In today's media-saturated age Churchill's ringing words probably strike most as a politician's empty, hyperbolic rhetoric. Nothing could be further from the truth. They were, and are, a very sober statement of the facts. He was speaking of the RAF, but he could've equally honored the men and women of British Intelligence.

In the summer of 1940 the civilization democracy represents hung by the thinnest of threads. Only a handful of democracies remained. If Britain had fallen to a Nazi invasion humanity wouldn't have regressed to the relatively benign despotism that prevailed before the American and French Revolutions, but would've instead leapt forward into a new Dark Age of incomparable savagery and duration, abetted by modern science and technology, the full realization of George Orwell's *1984*.

We now seem to believe the survival of democracy was somehow inevitable. Fifty years of hagiographic popular entertainment, indifferent public education, and, paradoxically, the legacy of wartime propaganda itself has blinded us to how narrowly the kind of society we cherish escaped complete extinction. Our very survival itself—to say nothing of victory—wasn't at all certain until after the successive victories of Midway, El Alamein, and by far and most paradoxically the most important, the immense *Soviet* triumph at Stalingrad in February 1943.

When France fell in June 1940, Britain faced a terrible prospect. On the other side of Europe, Stalin was locked in a de facto alliance with Hitler. Across the Atlantic FDR was committed to aiding Britain and resisting Nazism. But a popular isolationist movement led by a powerful right wing sympathetic to Nazi Germany was rising, spreading hate and fear, cynically preying on public anxiety, paralyzing the US and locking it into isolationism and neutrality, menacing democracy in the land of its modern rebirth.

That threat to America was greater and more complex than we realized.

Historians have learned that in the spring and summer of 1940, over a year and a half before Pearl Harbor, the Nazi German intelligence service, the Abwehr, attempted to rig the 1940 presidential election. Hitler—and Nazi Germany—feared President Roosevelt so much they sent five million dollars to the US to block his renomination and reelection. This was an enormous sum coming out of the Great Depression, the cost then of one hundred Spitfire fighter planes or five naval destroyers. At one point it's known that 160 thousand dollars was spent just to bribe the thirty-nine members of the Pennsylvania delegation to the Democratic National Convention *not* to vote for Roosevelt—that four thousand per delegate would've bought a large mansion in a prestigious suburban neighborhood. It was the most expensive espionage project in history until that time. By comparison the entire British Secret Intelligence Service in 1939 was only budgeted a mere seven hundred thousand pounds.

Britain, struggling to survive after the fall of France, created a covert organization based in Rockefeller Center called British Security Coordination, staffed mainly by Canadians and headed by one of Britain's top industrialists, another Canadian, Winnipeg-born and -raised William Stephenson. If Britain fell to the Nazis as France had, Stephenson and BSC was to direct resistance inside Occupied Britain from the neutral

US (a government in exile, what was left of the fleet and the royal family were to go to Canada). In the event Britain won the Battle of Britain and survived, at least for a while, BSC was to fight Nazi espionage in the US, the Western Hemisphere, and elsewhere in the world. Although the FBI did try to catch Nazi spies, the US was comparatively wide open, with no true intelligence or counterintelligence service. In 1940 Britain and BSC would provide much of that cover.

Stephenson and BSC later organized the US's new spy agency, the OSS. BSC eventually occupied several floors of the International Building in Rockefeller Center with over a thousand employees.

Per its longstanding policy of never revealing intelligence operations, Britain still refuses to discuss BSC, other than to deny almost everything about it, but Stephenson has been described as the effective Supreme Allied Commander for Intelligence. Not well known in the US, he is one of Canada's greatest national heroes. At his funeral in Bermuda in 1989 the USAF honored Stephenson—a Canadian citizen who had never been an employee of the US government—with a "missing man" flyover, not of the usual fighter jets, but U-2 spy planes, an unprecedented action in USAF history, and never repeated.

We will never know the full story of what happened or what was done. At the end of the war, Stephenson ordered BSC's records destroyed while many of the records of the German Abwehr were lost in a bombing raid. But we do know that in the summer of 1940 British Intelligence was opening and scanning all the mail between the Western Hemisphere and Europe, as well as intercepting radio and cable traffic.

Is it credible that Britain didn't know of the Nazi effort to intervene in the US election? The reader can judge for him or herself. It's the author's opinion that it is close to axiomatic they had to know, given the sheer scale of theirs and the Nazis' operations. Equally, if they did know, is it credible Britain and British Intelligence would have sat passively by and just watched?

Attacks on democracy and, most important of all, our elections—which is what democracy is all about—were and probably will remain under threat as long as nations and democracy itself exists. There was *nothing* new about the Russian attack on the 2016 US election, and as James Comey said, they will be back.

We need to be equally aware of the real issue, the mentality, the *motivation* behind these kinds of attacks. This danger will continue as long as people believe in winning at all cost, that the world is inevitably divided into winners and losers, that we aren't all in this together, and the kind of values and politics that thinking leads to. We must never again take democracy, and the willingness to play by its rules, for granted.

A final note: the venues and scenes in Saratoga Springs may seem exaggerated but they are (or were) all real. The United States Hotel and its slightly larger sister, the Grand Union—to this day the largest wood-frame building ever constructed—were astonishing, elaborate, and stupendous creations. But they were doomed in the new automotive age and were deteriorating as described. The States Hotel closed during the war and was demolished in 1946, the Grand Union in 1954. Riley's Lake House was one of largest nightclubs in the nation. It was one of a tiny number that could be compared to the ultra-posh Rainbow Room in Rockefeller Center, the only such clubs that actually matched the glamorized thirties and forties Hollywood movie image of nightclub life. (Most in fact were quite small. I was once in El Morocco, the favorite hangout of New York high society and movie stars like Errol Flynn, Marilyn Monroe, and Clark Gable. I was shocked at how small it was—a large row house or two, nowhere near the size of Riley's Lake House. I looked around in wonder thinking, *This is it?*) The Saratoga Racecourse is a legend, of course, and banquets like Millicent Simpson-Saunders' lavish dinner-dance were and still sometimes are for real. British Security Coordination really did set up shop in plain sight in Rockefeller Center. Ian Fleming was assigned to it for a time. The mail cover operation in Bermuda, again, mainly staffed by Canadians, was real as well. Finally, virtually all of Walter Ventnor's attacks on the Roosevelts are either direct quotes from the time or minimal paraphrasings.